A Jaggedy New World

A Novel History of the Conquest

S. L. Gilman

iUniverse, Inc.
Bloomington

A Jaggedy New World
A Novel History of the Conquest

iUniverse books may be ordered through booksellers or by contacting:

iUniverse
1663 Liberty Drive
Bloomington, IN 47403
www.iuniverse.com
1-800-Authors (1-800-288-4677)

ISBN: 978-1-4502-6999-5 (sc)
ISBN: 978-1-4502-7001-4 (dj)
ISBN: 978-1-4502-7000-7 (e)

Printed in the United States of America

iUniverse rev. date: 6/21/2011

For Charlotte Gilman, who performed the most creative job of proofreading in the history of literature; for George Ireland, without whose intelligent suggestions this work would be incomprehensible; and Betsy Valbracht, who read the book and didn't quite get it—so she actually read it again.

"O how slippery is this earth we walk upon.
On such a jagged edge we go."

From a Nahuatl poem

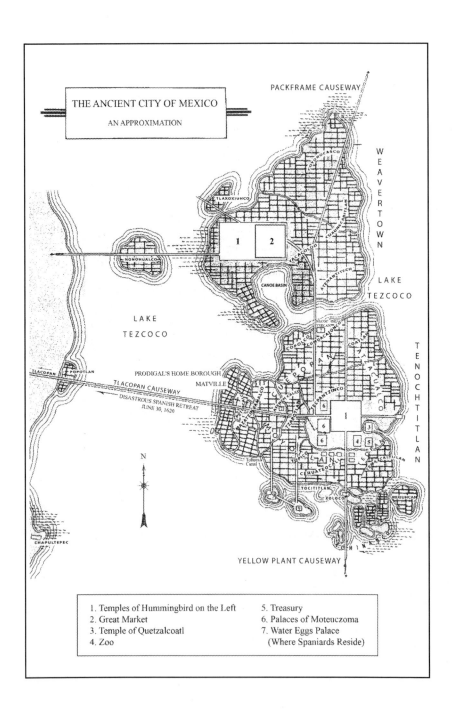

THE ANCIENT CITY OF MEXICO

AN APPROXIMATION

PACKFRAME CAUSEWAY

W
E
A
V
E
R
T
O
W
N

T
E
N
O
C
H
T
I
T
L
A
N

LAKE
TEZCOCO

LAKE
TEZCOCO

CANOE BASIN

TLAXOXIUHCO

NONOHUALCO

PRODIGAL'S HOME BOROUGH
MATVILLE

TLACOPAN CAUSEWAY
DISASTROUS SPANISH RETREAT
JUNE 30, 1620

TLACOPAN

POPOTLAN

N

CHAPULTEPEC

YELLOW PLANT CAUSEWAY

1. Temples of Hummingbird on the Left   5. Treasury
2. Great Market   6. Palaces of Moteuczoma
3. Temple of Quetzalcoatl   7. Water Eggs Palace
4. Zoo   (Where Spaniards Reside)

Contents

Some Principal Characters in the Tale

Conquistadors

Hernando Cortés–Captain general of the expedition. Born into the lower nobility at Medellin, Estremadura, Spain. Some education at the law school, University of Salamanca. (In fact, the captain toted his law books all over the New World.)

Pedro (Pepe} de Alvarado–Second-in-command, from Badajoz, Spain. Known for his blond good looks and deadly temper.

Andres de Tapía–Calvary officer. Probably Cortés' best friend in the expedition.

Francisco de Lugo–From Medina del Campos, Spain. Infantry commander.

Father Bartolomeo Olmedo–Head chaplain for the expedition. His patient wisdom kept Cortés out of trouble more than once.

Juan Diaz–A lay priest and assistant to Father Olmedo.

Bernal Diaz del Castillo–Foot soldier, swordsman. Disgusted with Cortés' version of the Conquest, decided to write his own—at age eighty-four.

Nuzi Duka–Cortés' secretary. Highly literate young man of Romani descent.

C. Cruz and A. Cruz–Two foot soldiers in the ranks. They were not related.

Juan Ortega (or Orteguilla, little Ortega)–Youngest member of the expedition.

Father John Aragon–Franciscan priest and renowned scholar. Arrived in New Spain with the first boatload of missionaries.

Panfilo Narvaez –sent by the Cuban government to take Mexico away from Cortés.

<u>**New World Natives**</u>

(NOTE: Nahuatl names have been translated into English when possible. Reader must beware, therefore, of Nahuatl and English words popping up in the same tribe.)

Malinalli Zazil Ha (or Marina)–Mayan from He-Who-Hasteneth, town in southwest Yucatan. Presented to Cortés as a slave after the battle of Potonchan.

John Prodigal–Ex-Mexica company commander from borough of Matville, Tenochtitlan.

Lord Tribune of Tenochtitlan–Mexican–Chief ambassador to Cortés when the fleet landed at Hummingbird Beach.

Lords Holynose, Drygod, and Noble Manner – Mexicans -Assistant ambassadors.

Moteuczoma Xoyocatl (Montezuma)–The Cadet, the Kid, first speaker of Mexico-Tenochtitlan.

Lord Good Shopper–High priest and secretary of state at Tenochtitlan. Served under the ancient title of "Snake Woman."

General Bumblebee–Head of army of Tlaxcala.

Little Corn–Young heir to the throne of Texcoco across the lake.

Vanilla Orchid–Little Corn's older brother. Definitely in rebellion against Moteuczoma.

Smoking Tree–General in charge of Mexica troops that besieged the Spanish garrison in Nauhtla on the Gulf Coast.

Captain Bellringer–Mighty warrior of Tenochtitlan and one of the last to fall fighting in the streets around the temple.

Eagle Swoops –of Weavertown. The last ruler fighting in ancient Mexico. Surrendered on Lake Texcoco on August 13, 1521.

At the Coahuila Mission

Nacho Bé–From Dzibichaltun, Yucatan. Librarian and scribe.

Ambrosio of the Well–From Barcelona, Spain. Blacksmith and ironworker.

Bumblebee the Elder and his son–Master carpenters from Tlaxcala.

Gosata, Ouchcala, and Ocoya–Titkanwatits visitors to mission

Some Places and Peoples`

Mexico–a nation of people living on the adjacent islands of Tenochtitlan and Tlatilulco (Weavertown) Their language is Nahuatl.

Mexica–a term invented by scholars. Equals Mexican in English, Mexique in French, Mexicano in Spanish.

Cempoal–A town on the Gulf Coast about twenty-five miles north of Veracruz. Capitol of the **Totonac**–nation, a people who were recently conquered by the Mexica and very friendly to Cortés.

Tlaxcala–A Nahuatl-speaking city about fifty miles to the east of Tenochtitlan. The Mexica tried for many years, without success, to conquer it. Cortés' first major battles were with the Tlaxcalans.

Chalco, Texcoco, Skinny Coyote (Coyoacan)–Towns around the edge of Lake Texcoco. Along with many others, they have long since been subsumed by Mexico City.

Mexico-Tenochtitlan–The center of Aztec power consisting of two islands on the west side of the lake. The southerly one is Tenochtitlan. Just to the north and separated only by a narrow channel is the island of Weavertown.

Anáhuac–Nahuatl word meaning "The One World." The Nahuatl-speaking area of today's Central Mexico.

Coahuila–A large state in today's northern Mexico. It borders on Texas.

Titskanwatits–A Coahuilan-speaking tribe of hunter-gatherers wandering around in Texas for about ten thousand years, since the end of the ice age.

Known today as the Tonkawa, a Waco word meaning "the ones who stick together." Remnants of the tribe still live in Oklahoma and Coahuila.

Great North River–Known today as the Rio Grande.

Preface

The following pages are replete with Nahuatl-to-English translations, and I think they require a word of explanation. To the English speaker, some of the phraseology may seem dramaturgic and a little overblown. Formal Nahuatl can be very complex. It depends heavily on elegant metaphor, subtle wordplay, and delicately designed repetition. For example, when a concept calls for a strong modifier, the sentence may be repeated several times, each with a different version of a key word or phrase. It is as if we should write in English: *He left in dreadful weather. He left in horrible weather. He left in weather unfit for travel. In the midst of a deluge, he was gone.* This is effective perhaps in poetry, but not easily shaped to the confines of English prose.

Nahuatl proper names also present special problems for the translator. They all relate to things, places, actions, or events embedded in the culture, but no one thinks of them like that. The English name "Spencer," for example, means "butler," yet when it is pronounced we don't visualize a fellow in a cutaway holding a tray of hors d'oeuvres. I have chosen to render the Nahuatl names in English for a very simple reason. The original names are, at least for most of us, unreadable and unpronounceable. When a reasonable English translation is not available, they will be spelled out according to the sixteenth century Franciscan orthography. The juxtaposition of English and Nahuatl names—sometimes in the same sentence—may lead to some confusion, but it can't be helped.

What's more, it must be admitted that the structure we know as "history" is actually missing a few planks. On the advance into Tenochtitlan, Cortés often warned his officers: "If you don't fill in the gaps in the canals, you'll have no clear line of retreat, and that's a deadly mistake." Well, we too have the problem of filling in gaps—five hundred-year-old gaps. How did Moteuczoma really die? Was he actually able, from captivity, to order the massacre of Spaniards down at Nauhtla on the Gulf Coast?

For answers to these questions, I have dug deeply into the writings of those early historians and brilliant proto-anthropologists of the sixteenth century. Here they have been quoted, paraphrased, and, in general, greedily sucked dry of their nectar, a mixture of mood, eloquence and elegance—an elixir for the resuscitation of long dead worlds.

Part I

Approaching the Edge

Chapter 1

Young Hernando—Winter 1503-04

"Castilians always corrode their great institutions
with the acid of their individual personalities."
Madriaga

When first we meet Hernando, he is a mere eighteen years of age and lies half buried beneath a great pile of rocks, broken masonry, broken glass, roof tiles, and the pieces of a smashed window frame. This enormous mess he has brought down on himself while trying to clamber up to the bedroom window of a young lady friend living in the suburb of Caldo de Moro. Hernando had been preparing to climb out onto a tree limb leading to the girl's room when the wall on which he was crouched began to crumble. Our young adventurer took off with a mighty leap but, unfortunately, not toward the limb directly overhead.

It should be noted that Hernando's career, though fraught with crises, will be marred by surprisingly few serious errors in judgment. This, however, was without doubt, one of his worst. Apparently he tried to enter the house by flying across the intervening alley.

The lad actually managed to reach the window with a pretty good grip, and might have been able to boost himself through, except the frame tore loose from its stone mooring. Hernando, wooden sill in hand, went crashing to the ground in time to get himself thoroughly battered by chunks of the old wall, which was just finishing its job of collapsing.

The unlucky event described here took place on a moon-soaked night in 1503, just outside the Andalusian city of Seville, shortly before he was to embark for the West Indies. The season would have been spring. Then again, maybe it was autumn, for these are the two seasons in which ships departed for the New World. It really behooves us to find out. The fits and starts, obstructions, and sudden clear channels that characterize

3

Hernando's life, even through the years of great accomplishment, will sometimes result from weather conditions.

Hernán lies stunned. (We'll shorten his name now; everyone else does.) A sclerotic old man, the young lady's father, points a sword to his throat. *Oh my,* he thinks, *what a joy 'twould be to push the thing through and ask questions later.*

On such a course sets forth the true Spaniard, seeking not only honor but also personal satisfaction. So! "Spaniards always corrode the foundations of their great institutions with the acid of their individual personalities," do they? (The notion, recently read, still rankles.) Well, we'll just see about that.

Suddenly a stoutish woman comes leaping out of the shadows. That's right. A stout lady. She actually leaps out of a shadow.

"Wait, wait. Hold up. *Yesu akhbar.* God pity us," she cries in a harsh whisper, the sort of voice one uses merely to pretend consideration for others—a kind of polite acknowledgment that, for anyone nearby, the cause of sleep is a lost one. And indeed, neighbors have poked heads out of every door and window facing the little courtyard.

"We'll all end up in chains! Holy Mother! That could be the archbishop under there!"

The old man starts to turn around, but the movement proves too much for his sense of balance. Stumbling sideways, he lets the sword slide off Hernán's neck. Its steel point, though slightly rusty, punches a nice hole through the shirt collar and doublet. Then it jams into the rubble with a little twang.

Oh, Dios mio, thinks Hernán, but keeps the thought to himself.

"Archbishop? Archbishop? This is a bum. This is a loser. This is a *chambón.* He's taking a trip to hell—leaving on the instant."

"That piece of tin is making me nervous." She gives the old fellow a mighty shove.

From the top of the junk pile emerges a voice. It seems to be clearing its throat. Hernán attempts to address his hosts as if all were ensconced in a velvet-draped reception room.

"Gentle folk, I say gentle folk … if I may be permitted to introduce myself. I will gladly compensate … or that is to say, I can easily provide remuneration for any little damage this inadvertent fall may have inadvertently caused. You see, the wall … well, it broke, and then, of course, it fell, such activity representing the expression of God's eternal will." *Pese. I can't move a finger. Forgive me, Holy Mother. You know I'm not a blasphemer, but when did you last come across so ridiculous a situation?* "I am Hernando Cortés of Medellín on the Guadiana, always at your service."

"Now isn't that good luck for us." The woman casts a deadpan around the yard. "What do you think, Flaco, is he a heretic? We could wake up Tommy the Torch. He won't mind."

"He's out of town."

"Oh."

The couple refers, of course, to Tomás de Torquemada, inquisitor general and chief administrator to the holy office since 1483.

Hernán ignores this sally and without so much as a glance at the blade sticking up past his nose, he continues: "Presently I am enrolled in the School of Laws at the University of Salamanca in the city of that name. Soon I will be permitted the presentation of pleas before any court in the land, including the Valladolid chancellery and the *permanent audiencia* of Castile. Laws relating to the regional governments of Asturias and Galicia, along with the *fueros* of Aragon and Sardinia, are well within the purvey of said flexibilities, as are those rather tricky and overly clever regulations of the Organization of Cantabrian Seafaring Towns."

Such speech from the buried youth must seem stunningly out of place, for the old gent's lower jaw begins to drop, sword hand soon to follow. The woman sends her eyebrows to the stars, perhaps to ask for directions. She leans in closer for a better look.

Hmm, muses Hernán, *doesn't smell so bad for an older lady, and not really fat either, just rounded. And no mustache. Above all no mustache.* He has spotted the little silver sheep pinned to her dress. *Not from Andalusia, that's certain. Maybe Aragon. Can't go wrong with Aragon. Easy enough to deal with that gaggle of bleeding hearts.*

> "Though thy presence thrill,
> contented still
> Such rosy flesh to bless,
> I'll don cold mail,
> And hit the trail,
> For my duty lies to the west."

"Ausias March [pronounced 'Mark,' by the way], the great bard of Teruel. How often have I lazed beneath the willows with a copy of … ah …", mumbles Cortéz.

"March was Catalan, kiddo, from Barcelona. You didn't know that? How barbarous." The woman stands arms akimbo.

Hernán is hardly nonplused. "Then let me propose a cheer for the great court of Aragon. The Courts General. The Justiciar's Court of Aragon. Guardian of the people's rights. Protector of liberties. Oh, that golden time in Aragon, a time of justice: the humble poor weighed along with the gentry and were given a fair shake." Hernán's voice has taken on a sort of sing-song quality, and were there more light in the courtyard, we would note his glazed eye and unfocused stare.

The rounded lady takes a step toward the rubble pile and the bruised youth within and then raises a hand to the heavens, to the spirits of the medieval liberties of Aragon, to the neighbors.

"All Isabel ever wanted was justice for Aragon—but that Fernando, well, he's another story. Oh my," she simpers, "'Love holds their wills together when necessity separates their persons.' Folderol! Whoever wrote that *ca ca* just wasn't in the know. It's the king's floozies what separates their persons. Oh, what our saintly queen puts up with."

A low note of disapproval, a somber rumble like the first gust of a tempest rolls around the courtyard. "Ooh, aah," breathes the crowd.

At this point, an ironic inconsistency in our rounded lady's political outlook should be noted. Isabel is Castilian to the core. She has always been very much opposed to the special liberties of Aragon and was once heard to remark, "the place ought to be re-conquered." Our backyard commentator's ignorance of that royal attitude seems out of place. We can suppose, however, that gender loyalty calls forth greater passion than does ordinary fact or realpolitik.

With a little extra effort, the old sword wielder extracts his weapon from the rocks. This process doesn't seem to disturb Hernán. He is probably not exactly conscious.

"Oh, certainly, certainly." The elderly man's eyes roll heavenward. "And I guess the old girl is as chaste as a Sister of Mercy. How about that Columbus fellow, eh, my love?"

"That's a filthy lie." The words rumble forth like ice blocks sliding down a mountain side, a tone frigid enough for a grand inquisitor. "There is no basis for those repulsive accusations."

No one pays the slightest attention to the weak mumble once more emerging from the rock pile. "The *Servicio and Montezgo*, more commonly known as the sheep tax, can certainly be regarded as one of the most regressive governmental interventions since … oh, where are you now, my Cid!"

The elderly chap leans on his sword. For an ancient in a nightcap, he looks somewhat dashing—at least in the moonlight.

"Right. Colón hangs around the court six, seven years 'cause he likes smelling her ... well, let's say her handkerchiefs. Come on. Everybody fools around once in a while, but with an Italian? That's going too far. The queen of Castile, León, Aragon, and Sardinia playing house with an Italian wool peddler? Oh, a sailor. Pardon me. So, he's still a *pastolo*."

"Hey, hey, hey. Not nice. Not nice at all. You should be ashamed to speak thus." It is Mr. Agugliaro, the Latin teacher, who lives in the little basement apartment behind what used to be a garden wall. His students call him "Googs" and not always behind his back.

"Italy is Rome, idiot. It is the language of Rome upon which our religion and our Christian state are founded." Googs is almost foaming at the mouth now, " Why the queen herself is studying Latin, though not making a great deal of headway, I'll admit. Also the duke of Villahermosa, the duke of Cardona, don Juan Carillo ... all that crowd. They're all working on their Horace and Juvinal. And about time, too. This country's a cultural wasteland. Always has been."

The heavyish woman turns to her husband with that harsh whisper of hers. "Now see what you've done?"

"Listen, Mr. Agugliaro. My old man has a big mouth. You know he thinks the world of you."

Ignoring this, Mr. A. rants on, "Why, even your artists only steal from Italian masters. That Blanco Vago, what's-his-name ..."

"Vélez Blanco," someone in the crowd calls out. "You're the *vago* [tramp] and a barbarous one at that."

"Yes? Well, his very best work is only copied from Italian prints."

"What? What? You're comparing a few scraps of paper with a fifty-meter frieze cut from solid oak?"

"Yeah, yeah. I've seen that thing: *"Hercules Rescuing Hippodamia from the Centaurs."* Some rescue. Looks more like he's trying to stick his tongue down her throat. Oh nuts, what's the use," says Mr. Agugliaro and slams the door to his rooms.

In perfect synchronization, husband and wife send a "universal salute" in the direction of the teacher's door. For those unfamiliar with the salute, it is executed as follows: the right hand, held stiffly, descends in a chopping motion into the crotch formed at the elbow between the left forearm and upper arm. The left fist remains tightly closed. At the same time, the lower lip is gripped between the teeth. Air is then sucked through the teeth in short bursts, producing a squeaking sound somewhat like a frightened rodent.

The yard now buzzes with inter-window and door-to-door debate, but it is difficult to make out more than a few scattered words and phrases.

"… no seat, they just squat over a hole …"

"Not even a handle to hold on to …"

"So, I imagine knee arthritis is big trouble down there …"

"… smokes tobacco and talks Arabic? … eat out his throat …"

"… you call that hot sauce …?"

"… lousy voice, anyway …"

"Thus paving the way," Hernán carries on, though with little awareness of his surroundings, "toward unification of the regions and the formation of this sovereign kingdom and great empire we know as *Spain*."

A great ruckus of cheers, catcalls, and shouts breaks out across the court. The nightcapped gent, sword at shoulder arms, marches up and back. "Hup, hup, hup, hup," he sings out sharply.

"Spain? Spain? What's that? Never heard of it," someone exclaims.

"Spain is Isabel. Spain is the queen. She gets her authority from God."

"The hell she does. She gets it from towns around the land."

"Spain is God; God is Spain. And I'm the pope. Oh, dear God in heaven! Such a thorny thing it is, this business of being Spanish."

Strong voiced and wild of eye, Hernán goes on preaching to the assembly. "And from what quarter descended that unholy holdup of God's will? And where would'st we now be had not the king reminded all Catalonia that it was Castilian blood that paid for the re-conquest?"

"Hupah, aha," the crowd grows tense.

"And it was Castilian blood that bought land in Italy for Catalan money grubbers."

"Talk to me, baby," screams Mrs. Riuz from her rooftop. Cous Cous, the Pekinese, joins in loudly. "Ralph, Ralph!" he shouts.

"And Castilian blood it was that soaked into the ground at the fall of Granada."

"Ole, ole," roars the little group.

"Oh, come on, come on. Nobody got a scratch at Granada. Boabdill surrendered without a fight." It is "Googs," the Latin teacher, coming back out of his little apartment. "He was surrounded and didn't stand a chance. I know. I was there."

"Oh, for heaven's sake. The boy just fell on his head. He can't be expected to get everything right. But in general, he's perfectly correct."

"No, he's not. In general, he's perfectly wrong, and so is Fernando. What kind of king is it who shuts down the courts for … what? Twelve, thirteen years?

"Come on, come on. There was a war on."

"Exactly. Now you've got it by the little finger. There was a war on. Ferdi needed troops, and when the eastern realms refused, he went up to Zaragosa and strangled the entire city council with his own hands."

"Sir, you exaggerate. It was one member, and I doubt Fernando did the job himself."

"What's the difference?" sounds a deep voice from an upper window. "We all know what that business was about."

It is Eliazar Záquis, the ceramist, who speaks. Those giant hands of his can paint on bowl or plate the most delicate little scenes from history: Ruy Diaz, called *el Cid*, strapped upright on his horse for the attack on King Bucar, features serene in death. Or Prince Ródrigo of Ceuta, prowling the women's quarters in search of the attractive and exceedingly well-brought-up doña Cava, daughter of Count don Julián. Well, she was ready enough—at the drop of a hat.

"It had nothing to do with the army or the war or the Moors," says Eliazar. "Fernando and Torquemada tried to start up the Inquisition in Aragon again. No one up there would sit still for that."

Silence reigns in the courtyard. What means this sudden cessation of gossip and opinion? Does Eliazar impugn the Andalusian character by means of pointed comparison with Aragon? "No one up there would sit still for that," he says, and all grows quiet, as when a black cover is slipped over a cage full of canaries—even quieter.

In the mid 1480s, it's true, Inquisition in Aragon and Catalonia was unthinkable, but now they have permitted entry to the investigators. Now Spaniards begin to grow a bit uneasy and perhaps ashamed of themselves. In the mid-1480s, the city of Teruel locked its gates and refused admission to the Inquisition priests. Fernando called up the Third and threatened to occupy the city. Citizen's resistance groups formed, and all Aragon stood at arms.

Then occurred one of those little "incidents," the kind that often show up in troubled times. A complex and delicate problem is simply nudged off the edge of a cliff. After hitting bottom, its parts are well homogenized, and the thing no longer looks so complicated. On a September day in 1486, the fresh young inquisitor Pedro de Arbués fell dead on the tiles in Zaragosa cathedral—run through the habit from two directions. This convenient murder was blamed on *conversos*, converted Jews already under suspicion for lack of sincerity, and the populace believed it was so. Obviously, an organization dedicated to the investigation of heresy was a must for Aragon and all Iberia.

True, for many years the vast majority of citizens had favored some sort of purge of Semitic elements. Yet they were of two minds, storing a love for traditional civil rights locked up alongside their prejudices—treasures of the same heart, so to speak. This small split in the soul of Spain will widen and fissure and crack off in all sorts of conflicting directions. It is a serious birth defect that afflicts this infant nation, boding ill for full development and long life.

While Hernán lies semi-conscious beneath the Andalusian moon, the new anti-Muslim administration in newly conquered Granada is barely getting underway. Like most youths of eighteen, Hernán shows little interest in national affairs. Yet the facts and figures he reels off the top of his head are only slightly inaccurate. Such improvisational abilities, when polished and refined, often characterize the expert confidence man. Hopefully, Hernán will find a way to practice this natural talent in a nobler cause.

At this moment, however, it's not doing him much good. A rather severe pain in his left leg is rapidly clearing out the mental cobwebs. Now Hernán wants only to get himself extricated from this mess.

The nightcapped sword wielder looks around the empty courtyard. Nothing but fastened shutters and closed doors in sight. *What a bunch of old hens,* he thinks.

A low moan emerges from the shadowy pile. The chubbyish wife leans over the rubble.

"Just a minute, young fool," she stares into the dimly lit face. "Cortés. Ay. Cortés of Medellín. Oh, sure. On the Guadiana already. Whose leg do you think you're pulling around here? School of Laws, eh? School of Laws, my left—. I know who you are. Oh, heavens. Oh, God, save us! Your poor father. Such a fine officer. Caught a bolt in the chest at Naples and nearly died. No, wait, that's Olid. Your daddy is Martín. Infantry, right? Well, he must be terribly disappointed anyway. And your mother. Ay, ay, ay, so sad. She's what? A *Pizarro*? Right. A Pizzaro. Well, somebody like that."

Our up-to-date lady jabs the swordsman a good one in the ribs with an elbow, but that worthy doesn't move very much.

"And now he's on Ovando's list. I saw it myself at the shop. He's on the boot list. The governor pulls out when? When?" Another poke in the ribs produces little sign of life and certainly no response to questions. *Where are they going? Cuba? No, they'll have to take on the Indians in Hispaniola first.*

"Two weeks. Two weeks at the outside. Wretch." This last to the dark lump groaning slightly at her feet. "And don Nicolás was going to buy you new boots. An excellent pair of boots to tromp around the islands in. Well, there's a few *maravedi* saved. That leg looks broken to me."

Dear God, my leg is broken. Now what? Up spirits, then. I say, spirits up.*

The elderly warrior is reviving. His head seems somehow connected with his sword point. As the former lowers, the latter begins to rise in the direction of Hernán's face.

Dear Mother of Our Lord, forgive me for what I am about to do. I'll make it up to you somehow, I swear I will. "Ah, *ahem* ... I should add ..." Hernán tries hard not to bleat. "I should say that this very night I was planning to pop the question, and hopefully doña ... ah, doña ... oh, the fall has addled my wits ... the lady will consent to be my wife. Considering the trouble you've been put to, there need be little or no discussion of dowry." *Hernán, old boy, sometimes you go too far. That last part might just as well have been left out.*

"What? Do you take me for a chiseler?" screams the old man.

That bit of iron is from where? Toledo? No, even in this light, clearly it's an inexpensive item. Hernán knows his arms and armor. It's a hobby, more like an obsession, really. The thing, however, waves perilously close to his nose.

"You marry my daughter, you get ... well, something, and that's guaranteed."

"Now we're talking sense, and it's about time," the round woman chimes in. "Española can do without you for a while. They'll manage to limp along. Hah, hah, that's a joke, my son."

While carefully removing rubble from around Hernán's bruised and tender body, the lady introduces herself. "I'm doña Benani de la Ay, your future mother-in-law. And this gentleman, don Lorenzo de la Ay, has the honor of being the bride's papa. By the way, your new wife is called Isabel. That's right, just like the queen."

---

* In fact, doña Benani de la Ay was wrong; Hernán sailed as planned. He lived and prospered in Cuba until 1519 when he was elected to lead the third expedition to the mainland.

Chapter 2

Young Moteuczoma—Winter 1492
Pedagogy in Mexico

And where there has been eating, let him
quickly clean up after the eating, and let him
brush his teeth again after each meal.
And he must see immediately to the sweeping.
Rules at Star Skirt Academy

"Lip clacking and other disorderly states of behavior will be castigated forthwith. Silence in the presence of authority is an attribute beloved of the gods and a quality of virtue respected at heaven's every level. Cannot reticence thus be seen as the key to learning's sacred gate? Will not the student who remains mute, mum, dumb, muzzled, and hushed, even as to equal the silence of a post, always gather, take in, absorb, assimilate, and suck up more than his wooden-lipped neighbors?"

The professor of art comprehension walks up to face the class. He passes a narrow window or opening in the stone wall. Visible at some distance are fields of tall maize, and in the foreground, a thin strip of lake glows blue. Just there, for a second or two, sunlight falls between shadows cast by great masses of summer clouds. Green, cobalt, and a series of grays, some rich and heavy as gold, form an image in blocks of color. In four centuries, painters will believe such visions of earth and light hold all the purposes of art, but our teacher walks past without a glance.

He holds up before the class a rectangle of coarse *amatl* paper. Eyebrows raised toward the ceiling, he moves the piece from side to side so all can see. Then the maestro bends his neck around and takes a look himself.

"Well, it's a drawing all right. Not much doubt there. Still, the thing is a problem to behold. Is it perhaps merely silly? Is it perchance both silly and pathetic?"

"Or doeth the silly shape,
Well steeped in pathos,
Some hint of the tragic,
Reflect to boot."

"Hmm ... maybe we ought to skip philosophy for just a minute and try to identify the subject matter. So what is this drawing meant to represent? Any ideas, my brilliant pupils?"

This class has suffered splintered pride before, so there is no great rush to respond. Whoever volunteers an answer will be made to feel foolish. That much is certain. No one feels this more keenly than Moteuczoma Xoyocotl (also known as the Cadet or the Kid). Young Moteuczoma has slid around behind his half brother, Five Twister. He should have known better. Trying to hide from this magician is the surest way to be noticed. The professor of art casts a piercing eye about the room. Had he been a wearer of spectacles like certain eighth-grade teachers in years to come, he might have surveyed the class without facing it, that is, via the reflective technique.

"Lord Moteuczoma the Cadet. Your opinion on this matter, please."

"Ah ... Reverend Little Prof, to me, it looks like a tree. O most certainly and assuredly, a tree." *Babbler! Useless lump of flesh. What need to be so certain?*

"A tree, you say?" the teacher's eyes widen in mock surprise. His eyebrows again reach for the ceiling, neck twisting from student to drawing and back again in the most dramatic fashion.

I knew it, Moteuczoma moans to himself, *I knew it.*

Moteuczoma the Cadet, prince of Mexico, blood descendant of Toltec kings and likely heir to the "Seat of Tenochtitlan," is certainly the school's most gifted pupil. Yet, for reasons unknown, even to himself, he submerges all those contemplative yearnings, that deep-seated attraction for the joys of academia. Philosophy, art, poetry, liturgical study—to Moteuczoma these things seem unmanly, effeminate, and unproductive. Such notions originate ... well, who knows where?

Perhaps it's the company he keeps—Uncle Irrigator, Uncle Whitewash. Among the older relatives, he hears nothing but talk of battle tactics: how to get under a lance thrust, how to execute the crotch feint—a move guaranteed to startle an opponent into lowering his shield. Oddly enough, Uncle Irrigator is a great patron of the arts, but as with his skimpily clad dancing girls and tattoo artists, such inclinations he keeps to himself.

Moteuczoma's school friends, Slaveboss and Five Twister, are dedicated athletes quite determined to achieve Eagle status. To Moteuczoma, however, little of life's meaning seems very clear. He suffers from a case of cloudy destiny. Nevertheless, the boy sweats and bleeds alongside his friends on the drill field.

"A tree, a tree … hmm … to me it looks like a pole sticking out of the ground wearing a fuzzy hat of some sort."

Titters rise from the back of the room. The professor of art looks at each face before him. Nodding slowly and rather sadly, he speaks gently, as one who carries bad news to a friend.

"Let us look more closely. If young Moteuczoma is right, then these things at the top would be its leaves. And indeed, they make admirable leaves. See how delicately each vein is rendered. Look at the little acorns. How gracefully they hang. Ah, such perfection of form. Truly, the hand of a master portrayer of acorns has been at work here. And the bark. How real it seems, each node and crack so clearly visible. Yes, a master of bark was here. No doubt about it."

The teacher looks toward the window. A thin column of black smoke rises from the temple compound not quite visible across the rooftops. Face as hard and blank as any jaguar mask, he turns back to the class.

"Yet, I say to you that something in this so-called tree is seriously awry, askew in spirit, damaged at the heart. What can it be?" The teacher looks down at the paper, but one eye is out there, perusing the faces of his pupils.

"Well, a hint then. Something is missing. Yes? Ah, now you see it. Now you see it clearly."

"No roots! No roots!" the class sounds off in unison.

"Excellent. Perhaps we haven't been wasting our time here. Not entirely, anyway. A paucity of roots, a scarcity of roots, in actual fact, no roots at all. And what is a tree without roots? Nothing. Nothing whatsoever. It is the root that connects us to Our Mother Who Art in Earth. How can there be a tree without a root? It is an absurdity. Remember this: it is not the job of the artist to show us some image of nature as it appears here in the world. Every one already knows this. Rulers and slaves, wise men and fools—all know what a tree looks like."

"No, it is the artist's work to plant in our hearts the godly essence of that creation we call 'tree.' It is a serpent's jaw. It is a strong beak anchoring the trunk to earth. Like the tree of life, so also is a virtuous person anchored in sacred ground."

The art teacher walks to the window and stands facing out toward the lake. He seems to speak to the scene before him, but the class can hear him all right.

"True knowledge is never visible to the naked eye," he says, "Always it lies buried, awaiting revelation at the artist's hand."

He plants his hands firmly on either side of the window-opening. The blue *tilmatli* he wears spreads out and the room darkens a bit. That pillar of smoke has widened at the top, and a black cloud now floats over the city. The wind catches it and scatters the smoke for a while, but it soon forms again.

"I know nothing of these scratchers of false trees. They walk about pretending Our Mother Who Art in Earth does not exist. They fear her sacred womb, and their hearts are not edible. Here I see only filth and disorder. They shall drink the water of shame. Perhaps they will perish from fear, having seen that which does not exist. On the other hand, mayhap they will fail to note the real thing and thus step off a great precipice."

"Just as our sins will one day lay us low," whispers the art professor to the gray haze above.

Now the walls of the academy begin to tremble a bit as at the start of an earthquake. They are pounding away on the big drum over at the temple. The sound, something like thunder but more felt than heard, carries a great many miles throughout the length and breadth of the valley—especially to the north where the slopes are gentler and there are no great ranges to stop the vibrations.

"Now, now, young sirs. No need for frenzy or any other discommoding frame of mind. That is not a call to arms, it's a call to council. No doubt something to do with the Toluca treaty. About time, the fools. Air's too thin up there to think straight. Nevertheless, you'd all better report to the company commanders as soon as possible. Best to get a jump on things. Makes us all look good."

"Monteuczoma Xoyocotl, at the first opportunity report to the temple of Our Mother and toss a little blood on the image of the goddess. This will serve to remind you that daydreaming, flights of fancy, and poor concentration in class are offensive to those beings who fought their way out of the womb in order to give us life. For this purpose, the ear lobes will not suffice. You are hereby advanced to the penis. Stop by my office. I'll see you get a good sharp spine."

Now the afternoon glows away. On the other side of earth, each star dons thick cotton armor and picks up sword and shield. The sun also arms himself and gets ready to fight those twinkling warriors of the night sky. He understands the situation well enough. Defeat is inevitable, and then time will come to a stop. He is the fifth and last sun. There will never be another.

Chapter 3

The Prodigal Monster

The Nahuatl name *Xolotl* (Sholotl) is of considerable historic import for the area we know today as Central Mexico. In English, the name is best rendered as "Prodigal Monster" or just plain "Prodigal." Sometime in the last quarter of the twelfth century AD, a leader of desert barbarians calling himself by that name was able to subdue a few towns belonging to the more or less defunct Toltec empire. With his son, Sir Prickly Pear, Prodigal then gathered a great horde of wild archers and flung them against the city of Culhuacan on the south shore of Lake Texcoco.

Soon after the victory at Culhuacan, Prodigal began marrying his relatives off to local nobility. Through these alliances, he managed to gain recognition as the rightful heir to Toltec legitimacy. Deep awe and envy in the presence of civilized life was always the fuel by which Mexico's ambition was driven. Its people also expended considerable nervous energy worrying about losing the luxuries of that life. Yet the Mexicans, in their richest of chocolate-pudding days, never ceased paying lip service to the old stoic virtues required for survival in the hard northern world.

"Know that when our ancestors lived in the wilds, in the thorny deserts, they lived by the bow and arrow—if they were not assiduous, they did not eat—and that was in the days of those godlike wild men, our ancestors."

The John Prodigal we meet here is in no sense barbaric. After the Spanish occupation, he became literate in the new Nahuatl script and in Latin and Spanish as well. (It should be remembered that the Franciscans taught Latin first. Spanish came later.) These skills Prodigal learned under the tutelage of his good friend, the Franciscan scholar Father John Aragon of the University of Salamanca.

Prodigal was born in 1487 or 1488 to a family of lower-middle nobility living in the borough of Matville, Tenochtitlan. He was most likely baptized on the feast of St. John the Baptist, June 24, 1522, in a mass ceremony among a number of other would-be Johns. Observers have joked about the Johns and Marys of early New Spain. "There are more of them in this land," it has been said, "than in Spain, Portugal, France, and Italy put together."

Prodigal speaks but little of his military career. We know he rose to command a four hundred-man company based in his home borough of Matville. He began active service about 1505. This means he campaigned during a long decade's worth of the worst defeats in the empire's history:

> Battle of the Lands Beyond: 70 percent of officer corps killed.
> Ambush and disaster inflicted by Tlaxcala at Eagle Mountain.
> Revolt at Willowtree: twelve hundred dead in garrison massacre.
> Revolt of the Mixtec at Tlatchquiahco.
> Revolt of Texcocan forces under Vanilla Orchid.
> Fall of Mexico to Spaniards-Tenochtitlan, August 13, 1521.

On August 14, 1521, Prodigal emerged from the drowned wreckage of Weavertown—sister city to Tenochtitlan—wearing a ragged and bloody woman's *huipil*, his broken sword held chest high. A great many pounds underweight, Prodigal still moved under his own power. The survival of several family members was due to a fortunate encounter with some healthy rats.

At Salamanca, Xolotl's friend, Father J. Aragon, had been fairly well known, spending much of his youth carving out a reputation as the university's top-notch scholastic and qualifying as general academic superstar. Aragon's longish pamphlet, *Cost of the Lutheran Rebellion to the Populations of Europe, Sworn and Attested to as Accurate Within Plus or Minus One Hundred Seventeen Thousand Souls,* even the university janitors devoured.

Unfortunately, fame and recognition in Europe did not serve well in Coahuila. That environment was quite unresponsive to European honors, degrees, and scholarly medals. There exists a suggestion that Father John Aragon was not at all satisfied or happy with the results of his mission in the northern deserts of New Spain.

Most importantly for modern scholars, Prodigal presents a new slant on certain aspects of the conquest. The voice of this Mexican officer throws some light on the last days of Moteuczoma's life and the plight of the

Spaniards trapped in the palace of Water Eggs. The official Spanish version of the death of Moteuczoma is most certainly untrue. Cortés claimed the *Tlatoani (long translated as King or Emperor; the correct meaning is 'He Who Speaks' or' First Speaker')* was struck by a sling-stone while up on the roof trying to calm a rebellious crowd. Scholars no longer believe this tale, and Mexicans crowded along the canal bank that June day scoffed at it. There is an irrepressible suggestion that the man we know as John Prodigal participated in a plot to murder Cortés. The conspirators may have, wittingly or unwittingly, involved the speaker himself.

Prodigal opens an enigmatic little can of worms. He seems to imply that some bit of treachery, perhaps mutiny, took place in the palace before the retreat of June 30—some deceit that cut Cortés to the heart. For once, the silver-tongued confidence man from Estremadura was shocked to silence. The officers present must have believed, as well, in a compelling reason for the cover-up. Its consequences were not noted for years. More immediate concerns claimed attention that last desperate night. Priorities were simple: find a way to get across the Watertown causeway and through the rain-drenched fields to the Anáhuac border.

Chapter 4

Prodigal Speaks—Spring 1524

"So we'll go no more aroving,
So late into the night.
Though the heart be still as loving,
And the moon be still as bright."
Byron

Unlike the occasional detours that lead off our fine public roads, those encountered along life's strange and twisted path are not laid out to serve some nice practical purpose. O quite the opposite. The avoidance of hard pain, wrecked dreams, and those flash floods that drown hope and wash it along to find rest in some fetid pool—that is *their* wont. It would appear life's chief surveyor conceived his map with many a cutoff and many a scenic loop but no real choices—for at the end of every path, one of hell's infinite portals stands ajar and waiting. Is not even the smallest human trial approached along a skillfully leveled and finely plastered avenue often displaying misleading signposts?

Great ghosts of literary kings, I Prodigal beg pardon, and of you, too, friend reader. Having managed to plow through the above scarlet-limned lines, you are owed an apology or at least an explanation. You see, in my youth, that is, before the Fall of our great City, most of the knights of our borough were taken with versifying—the making of poetry. I'm afraid this habit influenced our means of expression so that we often sounded a bit, well, affected. Our sister city, on the east bank, was always the real fountain from which flowed the empire's most sophisticated arts and mores, and I believe we felt ourselves a mite inferior. How we longed to emulate the simple grace and easy wit of Texcoco's nobility.

Still, lords of the night, you watched over us. Bright Mamalhuaztli (Pleides), you witnessed our joy. O those long winter nights in the stalls along the boat basin. Poetry, pulque, juice of the tree of life (not strictly legal for us—training rules, you know). On the fifth day of the week, market crowds filled the streets, and, midst the confusion, no one bothered to ration the foaming cups. Then our verses soared. They rose like snow geese spinning out of the sun. Then down and down they swooped, through changing colors toward the darkened ranges of the east. Torches were lit along the boat basin and mirrored in a harbor so calm and quiet that one could hardly distinguish reflection from reality. Yes, those were indeed the nights of our lives.

> O we'll drift no more so sweetly,
> Through the darkened halls of night,
> Though we haven't changed a bit, you see,
> And the moon? Still up there, all right.

I've no idea whose verse that is. The thing just popped into my head. Admittedly, none of my own poems were prizewinners. There's a very good reason for this: stiff-necked, low-brow, reactionary critics—including that little weasel of a Tlatoani, who later turned traitor. Anyway, they are all of one skin, those critics. Present something the slightest bit unconventional and it's "armpits up" around the room. All the talent in the world goes unnoticed if it's not in style. For "in style" read: trite, insipid, and common. Furthermore, and perhaps of utmost importance, I never took the trouble to stage fancy dinner parties for the neighborhood nobility. I never "ate earth" before the tigers of the art world as did the other officers of the Matville borough.

But all this is beside the point. I only meant to apologize for those meandering lines on an earlier page of this manuscript. My extensive experience in literary composition makes it difficult to resist the dramatic phrase and sonorous word combination. And that's true whatever the language. So, with a firm vow to eschew all bathos and reject the jejune, I'll begin again. The part about life seen as a twisting path, however, should not be discarded. Now there's a metaphor that really catches the *tlacahuachitl (Dideiphus virginiana-opossum)* by the tail, don't you think?

All right, then. This wandering trail of dreams called life leads through many a misfortune, plenty of discomfort, and even comes across a few simple pleasures. Yet rarely, very rarely, does it open out into the broad country of the "big laugh." I do not speak of those ridiculous and clownish sight gags (slipping on papaya rinds, guacamole shoved up the nostrils, etc.), nor do I refer to cleverly told jests like the one about Maxtla's unfaithful wife in which the offended husband skins his wife, drapes himself in her pelt, and dances at the paramour's dinner party. Frankly, that story's not so funny anymore—too much repetition. Every generation since founding has told one version or another. You're supposed to picture the lover's expression when he gets a look at that most definitely uncured and still-bloody skin of his fair lady.

No, friends, the sort of laughter I speak of builds very slowly. First, it catches the heart unaware. Then slowly, oh so slowly, it begins to fill those rimes and fissures where dwell illusions, deformed ghosts, and absurd idols. Finally, superstition's lease is canceled, and when it departs, the spirit of the laugher is changed forever.

By our calendar, it was on the day One Serpent in the Year Three House that my turn to sneer at the gods arrived.. On this day, information was divulged regarding a possible move of everyone—every last man, woman, and child, from the old Matville neighborhood up to the northern wilderness—to build new towns and new lives. We were all gathered at the old center for Divine Liquid and Ashes (then a parking lot for supply wagons) where one of the hoods of St. Francis rolled out a notice and began reading.

The short speech was delivered with a pretty fair command of our Nahuatl (or Mexican) language; I'll give the little fellow that much. Who would have dreamed that one day we would live closer than comfort allows—our lives tangled like an ill-woven *tilmatli*. It's been my experience that these lads of St. Francis pick up languages as fast as ladies learn new dance steps. They're better than we are, and language acquisition has always been one of our people's most developed skills. Administration of an empire reaching from Huasteca to the foothills of Guatemala made such abilities imperative.

The brown hood rolled up his paper in the midst of a silence so profound it was as if the packed square held only ghosts. How quiet was it? Really want to know, dear friend? Well, it was so quiet that had hay bales then existed on our agricultural horizons, you could have heard a duck feather hit one. It was so quiet that you could have heard an ant backstroke across a bowl of chili. You could have heard Pope Adrian VI whisper sweet nothings in Luther's ear.

After about fifty heartbeats, a great cry of pain went up from that crowd. Everyone had been eating pretty regularly for a while, so plenty of energy went into that shout. All the winds of creation racing through mountain pines couldn't have outrun it. They tore the clothes off their backs. They pulled out hair by the handful. They ripped flesh till the blood ran. As the saying goes, "they were mad enough to claw the feathers off a turkey," only there wasn't a turkey to be had in the valley just then.

So how do we find humor in such a spectacle? Only attend, dear friends, and perhaps the matter will become clear. Hypocrisy exposed invariably carries some touch of grim humor. You see, in the old days we were forced to suffer quite a bit of sanctimonious propaganda, delivered, for the most part, by incompetent public speakers. We took it all on our feet, in full uniform, and usually during the day's hottest hours.

Now, most of the speechifying shoveled into our ears over the generations had been religious in nature, but some of it was plain political propaganda, patriotic ranting pure and simple. At almost every public occasion, prayers said over one of those muddy irrigation ditches, or the dedication of a new popcorn stand at the city market, some shining bejeweled prince wrapped in the skins of half the birds of Guatemala, would get up and make a speech. What Lord What's-His-Name told the people never varied.

"Your unshakable faith in God, my people; your strength like that of a tiger, O citizens; your unfailing courage and stamina in the face of overwhelming odds have made of you a great nation. And all of these splendid qualities, I say, all of them, I mean every last one, is owed to your soul's formation up there in that place we know as Godland." Then Lord Whoever would climb back into his palanquin to be toted back to a villa in the suburbs and a bowl of chocolate.

Begin to catch the point, O readers? When it came time to take a proper stroll up among those blessed and O-so-holy Godlands of the North, of a sudden we begin raving about some cursed desolation, a place of misery, pain, suffering, fatigue, poverty, torment, failure, dry rocks, death, thirst, a place of starvation. It is to the north. O, O it is to the north!

Each morning, on that endless trip up through the cactus, I awoke laughing a little louder, and by the time we camped in this place, the old life seemed quite unreal. A chain had bound my soul, but now there was not a solid link along its length, and god was as dead—as dead as those dirty little flags some ex-priests had planted along the way. I suppose the fools were trying to recapture the lost glory of that ancient migration out of Aztlan. Somebody should have told the old boys they were heading in the wrong direction. Even so, one of those primitive lumps walked about toting "the bundle," a few rags twisted in shape as though to hold a baby; that baby, we all knew, was us, the infant Mexico, first child of our mother

Weary Snake. When the swaddling wraps were opened, no human child appeared—only a long, finely worked obsidian knife. Such was the birth we had endured. Such was the Mexico we had made for ourselves.

Nor were we prepared for the coming of the Catholics. The matter of the flag, for example. A beautiful woman and a cute baby! Who would believe such a thing? What kind of banner is that to carry before fighting men? *Only cowards hide behind women and babes,* we thought.

Of course, the imprisoned Tlatoani made effective resistance impossible. In arrogance, we forgot where power lay. It never rested on the shoulders of our fair city alone, but on the three legs of the League of Cities—as a pot sits on a tripod. When one leg broke, the whole business came tumbling down. Those of sense tried to mend the broken pot. "Come," they said, "let us have an understanding with these invaders, and then bide our time." Too late. That glue could not hold. With the Tlatoani dead, Tenochtitlan was forced to bow to Eagle Swoops. Thus, rule was handed to the fanatic and irresponsible knights of Weavertown, and that was the real end of our Mexico. The plagues were but a footnote* writ on air, on the breath of destiny. Read it if you would, but precious little understanding is to be gained thereby.

Actually, we haven't done badly up here, though it was touch and go for a while. The local inhabitants objected to our presence. To be frank, it was Father Aragon who got on their nerves.

Now, reader, I beg you, let there be no misunderstanding with regard to this matter. Our padre was, without doubt, the most talented man in all the "New World" (as he persisted in naming these lands, although there was, we told him, nothing new about the place). Along with his native tongue, Father spoke two others of that European land, Coahuilan, my own elegant Nahuatl, and all three of those ancient languages in which his theology was written. The oldest of these, Father was convinced, formed the root of all languages in these lands. So certain of this was the padre that he used to sit me down and read long hours from The Book, all the while asking in anxious tones if any of the words sounded familiar. No luck there. It was all *Tzotzichel* to me.

Father Aragon made himself into an architect and also a painter of little flying babies and sad angels with eyes rolled up in their heads. If anybody deserved the old title *Toltecatl*, "Master of Ancient Arts and Crafts," he was the one. Unfortunately, the padre's character was flawed in

---

* Some footnote! Nearly 40 percent of the population of Anáhuac perished in the smallpox epidemics of the 1520s

one minor respect. Like priests everywhere, he was not merely hardheaded, but possessed of an inappropriate sense of timing. That is to say, he didn't know when to keep his tongue still. After a while, the locals grew tired of being told what to think, when to sing, and when to spit. What's more, they were soon convinced it was the holy water of baptism carried the plague—and that's when the trouble began in earnest.

But wait ... perchance the pen doth move too fast. Perhaps it doeth outrace the mind. I am yet Mexican enough to despise disorder, loath disorganization, condemn anarchy, regret confusion, deplore chaos, and confront irresponsibility whatever the cost. I began this work with the avowed purpose of reviewing, from the beginning, those peculiar circumstances that led to our time of trouble. So now, gracious reader, perhaps it would be best to gaze squarely upon and with all courage, the weird and evil scenes that shook our Mexican souls and also our bodies, and to carefully consider under the aegis of that virtue we call honesty, the character of our Mexican leaders and our Mexican people and the consequences thereof.

Part II

Walking the Edge

Chapter 5

Moon over
Hummingbird Beach—Good Friday, 1519

"Caballero, eh? Thanks for the title, but
I didn't come all this way to shovel manure.
Word has it there's some real action out here."
Cortés to the governor's secretary
Santo Domingo, 1504

Lately Cortés is coming apart at the seams and is all too aware of it. His brain pecks away uncontrollably at various sorts of trivia and then turns it all over and starts nibbling away again. Such fits of misplaced energy are particularly uncomfortable since they attack a body pinned to a patio chair in near helpless lethargy. He drinks too much these days, and he perspires too much—even for this tropical clime. That cane out there will do very well on its own. It doesn't need inspiration from the gaze of Sr. Cortés half a day at a time.

But of course we'll squeeze it, and then we'll grind it, and we'll wash out the brown bodies who die in the grinders, who die in the vats, who die in the field twice topped by leafy stalk. At the rate we're going, brown bodies are a crop we'll soon be running out of. So where's Las Casas and his Africans? Such a critical kid, but never around when you need him. Indians are people, he says. Real folks. Unenslavable. So, what do we do? What do we do? Why, go get some Africans, bobo! When it comes to Africans, Church got no opinion, Church is ruleless, Church is policyless, philosophically disengaged, theologically disinterested, spiritually out of it. Bless me, Father, for I have sinned. It's been thirty-five minutes since my last confession. You see, Father, I used up three blackies and a bunch of bananas while trying to declare bankruptcy. Wait a minute. What's the date? Auguary? That's not right. They're overdue, they're overdue, they're over—!

Ugh … Jesus, Mary, and the saints, you'd better wake up, son. That's the salt sea beneath your nose and Hummingbird Beach in spitting range. No cane around here. Shouldn't nap in this damned lawn chair. Should have left the cursed thing in the backyard where it belongs. Four hours to dawn.

I'll have to start getting the horses off before light. That'll be a real picnic. Is this thing possible? Can this be done? Most of us are full of holes already. At Pontonchon alone … maybe, what? Ten thousand strong? And disciplined? Not a rear end in sight. They quit the field moving backward, for God's sake. No, this thing is not possible.

But such uncertainties will be kept private. Any display of weakness, be it before friend or foe, sets one on the road to certain defeat.

What is it now? Ten years on this blessed island? Oh, Cuba, my Cuba, go on forever always lovely, always green. Land of breezes fresh as new-cut flowers. Land of eternal paradise. Oh, Cuba, my Cuba, land of everlasting boredom. Another year and I'd have turned into one of those mindless planters—like my neighbors, the fellows over carousing every Sunday. Now there's a notion fit to make a skunk sweat. All that retching behind the garden wall. My poor flowerbeds. Those stupid chicken fights. Deadly long nights on the dance floor, doing the courtesy hoof with nameless pairs of blotchy chests.

Perhaps Judge Cortés should have hung around the Santiago office a little more, closer to those events that shake our times. By heavens, he used to believe that. Now he knows what the main event is likely to be—another rehash of the Anacaona war with old Velazquez. My, but the governor gets a wallop out of that. Throwing his arms around, forward, and then sideways like cannon shots, the old man bounces around in that chair till finally it's impossible to follow a word he says. One only waits in high suspense for a leg to crack and that great body to go sprawling across the tiles.

"Hernán, Hernán, damn your eyes. No one knew where the devil you'd got to. I didn't have a clue. Pepe couldn't find you. Then here you come out of the trees, exactly behind the huts. It was brilliant, brilliant."

Yes, indeed, very brilliant. Oh, what a great fight. Oh, such a war of significance. Holy Mother of Our Savior, those children weren't even armed. Pointed sticks they carried.

It would be nice to forget that little chief what's-his-name. "If I go to heaven, will I have to live with Spaniards?" He shakes his head and steps right up to the stake. Calm he was, with a little smile—not exactly contemptuous, not precisely superior, that little curl of lip. No, forgiving— that's it—like a martyr. St. Sebastion perhaps, or perhaps—. Oh no, oh no, Hernán, old boy. Keep clear of that. Stay away from such notions. It's absurd. It's … it's lunacy.

"Enough already!"

"Ya basta," says Cortés. The words are only whispered harshly, yet they seem to flow along the ship like a great shout. Down along the rails, they set the lamps to flickering. Every head on deck pops up in alarm and turns to stare at the beach. All but the women, that is. They stay buried under the capes of their men. Not very romantic cuddling up to cold metal or those thick, cotton-wadding coats removed from enemy dead. Most of the boys are too nervous to take off their armor. Del Castillo doesn't move either. The man sleeps like a hog. Oh, to be nerveless thus, Cortés, deep in a brown study on the nature of man, has often pondered. No one on deck thinks to check on the captain.

The next thing Cortés sees clearly is a hairy black clump slowly resolving itself into the eyebrows of young Nuzi Duka. It costs Cortés no effort at all to put back into place his usual bland and pleasant gaze. Nuzi bends and picks up the copy of the *Poem of El Cid,* which has slid from the captain's lap.

"Ah, Duka, dear fellow. No, no, all is well, really. But I wonder, my friend, if you would mind doing me a little favor. I know it's a bit of an imposition …"

Strictly speaking, Duka should be someplace else. He belongs to the Cortés household all right, but his highly intelligent and skilled person should not be gracing any one of these New World Indies. It is quite illegal. The Dukas are an "Egyptian" family (Gypsies in today's politically incorrect terminology), recently converted to Catholicism from Judaism via Islam, with a half-generation hitch in the Greek church. No matter. Throughout sixteenth century, all "new" Christians are ineligible for residence in America. Everyone in the islands is aware of Nuzi's status. They also know those expulsion decrees published by the "Catholic kings" went too far. They would never have been signed had not Torquemada frightened Isabel out of her wits with threats of eternal hellfire.

At any rate, the subject is rarely discussed. Cortés' brother-in-law, Juan Xuarez, brought it up once—ensconced in this very patio chair. "You know Hernán," he said quietly, "this could mean trouble down the line. Especially if they know you knew. And if they know you knew they knew ... well you're a lawyer. You can see what that would mean."

"No, I never got my license. Not a born scholar, they said. Hmm ... Juanillo, my dear friend and brother, as surely as you sit there before me, I can swear we are simply not turning out the same quality of cigar as in years past."

Cortés held his cigar out at arm's length and drilled it with a piercing stare for a few seconds as if all his daily little annoyances were wrapped up in that chubby brown tube. Then he flicked the ash and returned the thing to his mouth.

"Find me a good writer who is also a real Christian, and I'll sack Nuzi on the spot."

Xuarez only scratched his beard.

"Exactly. No such animal. Tell you what, *cuño*. When he gets too old to work, I'll burn him myself."

Cortés held his liquor glass to the light. "And another thing, dear brother. This is not the best barrel of cane we've made out here. Not by a long shot."

Cortés is definitely himself now. "Nuzi, mi hijo. It will save getting someone up from much needed rest. Would you mind corking this up and putting it away?"

Duka appears genuinely shocked. "Why, General, you know it's always a great pleasure for me whenever I can do you some service. Anything at all."

"Thanks a thousand, Nuzi."

Long ago, Cortés formed a strict code for dealing with servants and others under his authority. He treats those subject to command with unfailing courtesy of tone and expression. When punishment is necessary, the miscreant is always delivered a full and concise explanation of the sentence meted out and its relation to the sin committed. True, sometimes these explanations are a bit self-serving and don't always fit the facts as others see them, but they are indeed thorough. Cortés simply refuses to lose temper with those who work under him. Later, in the field, he will slip up on this more than once, but mostly with his highest-ranking officers.

Duka gets to the bottom of the ladder before curiosity overcomes him. He opens the book of El Cid to the marker, holds it to an overhead lamp, and frowns deeply. Well enough he knows this passage:

"They would have asked him in gladly, but did not dare,
for King Alfonso cherished such anger.
His letter had come to Burgos the night before
with all formality and sealed with a great seal:
that to Mio Cid Ruy Diaz no one must give shelter,
that who should do so, let him learn the truth of the matter,
he would lose all that he had and the eyes out of his face
and, what is more, they would lose their bodies and their souls."

Quite annoying, thinks Duka. *Is it prophecy?* His eyes shift around every nook in the little passage. Suddenly this intelligent secretary feels a bit claustrophobic. *And Burgos? Is there anyone who hates the captain more than Bishop Burgos? Now they have him at Seville and in charge of supplies for all the Indies. We could find ourselves stuck out here without so much as a fresh bottle of mass juice.* Duka raises his face. He wants to see the stars up there in the open hatch, but the lamp has blinded him.

Nuzi lifts a hand to cover his eyes and in so doing seems to drag upward, as though from the hold of the ship, a heavy cloud of ambrosial incense—certainly nothing produced in the bowels of this smelly tub. A burst of fresh essence something like … what? Flowers? Yes. Only heavier. A surge of sweetness totally out of place in these fetid cubbies. Nuzi can't identify the odor because he has never smelled vanilla before. He doesn't know that girls on the prowl in these parts use some form of vanilla extract as a sensory trap for the man of choice. Perfume, to put it simply.

Now he sees, as though mirrored in a shadow, the calm, mahogany visage of his boss's new interpreter. *Marina,* the Spaniards have baptized her. The girl's eyes reflect the lamps. Two tiny spots of light shine in her pupils.

"Marina? Marina! What are you doing sneaking around down here? You should be up on deck." He points to the overhead. *"Arriba. Arriba."*

Marina giggles sharply. "Aggiba, aggiba, aggi-. O, O." Again she laughs. "That's not easy to say. O what a word is that."

Suddenly the sound strikes her as quite familiar. It's like the noise made by a little *chiqujmoli* (ladderback) pounding away in search of a meal. Only lower. Lower in pitch." Ah ha," she expostulates. "Arrriba! O my. Arrr, arrr, arrriba." She points to the planks above.

"That's right. You're improving. Later, I'll teach you a little writing. Of course, you'll need to know the alphabet first, such information being basic, that is to say, essential for complete …"

Duka is beginning to ramble. Those tiny double lamps burn in another universe, some out-of-the-way galaxy, a medium quite disconnected from the here and now. Duka switches the book to the hand holding the bottle and then reaches out and touches her arm just above the elbow.

"Go on now. Get on up." He delicately nudges her toward the ladder.

Perhaps Marina turns her head a fraction, for quite suddenly the little lights are gone, leaving only a couple of black holes. She speaks in her precise and delicate Nahuatl, and the words seem to come at Nuzi from every direction—like a big cat humming in the night, confusing the prey, directing it straight into waiting jaws. Nuzi gasps and freezes against the bulkhead.

"O Sir Duka. How well I know you. Dukatzin the wanderer. Descendant of dried-up, puny twigs unable to send roots into the earth. Little offspring of a lineage consisting of worn-out raggedy pieces of feces. Always living in the ditches along the roadsides of earth. How is it you dare address me in this manner? Mayhap you find yourself under some delusion. Could be you think yourself the master and I, therefore, the servant."

Marina reaches out and takes the book from Duka's slack hand.

"Mio Cid, O si. El Campeador," she says, switching to broken Spanish. "Mio Cid. Ruy Diaz. Very great man. Has many, many fine friends. To el Cid it not pleasing insult friends. To el Cid makes angry insult friends and compadres. O Señor Duka. Careful, careful. You not in your house now. You far, far away from your house. Maybe you get help, more eyes to watch back of head."

Marina nods pleasantly and heads up the ladder.

Nuzi comprehends not a word of Marina's Nahuatl and misses most of the Spanish. The tone, however, is shockingly familiar. Nuzi is a Rom, and though no longer in "the trade," he can spot a hustle when he hears one. The way that voice bounces around the little cabin—like his grandfather's act in the fancy parlors at Florence or Vienna, playing mind tricks on the good city burghers while Pardo steals the silver. Now that's entertainment.

Wait, wait, he stifles himself. *What has all this to do with you? You're not a boy anymore. Those days are long gone.* Duka shakes his head. *Anyway, I could never come near old granddad Duka's flawless execution. What a player he was! As for me? Just an assistant. A cute little helper and that's all.*

Oh, come, come. You're not exactly standing still. Things are going quite smoothly, as a matter of fact. Why this job catches the ear of the king, for Christ's sake. Just get out of this alive, come up with a decent manuscript for

"Iberia," and you'll find yourself on the tenure track at U. of S. Nifty little town, Salamanca. Lots of big time collars come through there.

He opens Cortés' cabin, walks over to the wardrobe chest, and tucks the bottle under some linen. He sits on the old box for a while, head in hands. The landward port is wide open. It serves to provide free passage for clouds of tiny stinging gnatlike creatures known as *sancudo*. Now everyone refers to the little monsters as mosquitoes, and among the men they contribute liberally to some very creative and original groupings of ancient vocabulary sets.

Actually, when it comes to mischief making, the mosquito can't hold a candle to this nearly invisible manifestation of the Maker's creative imagination. The nip of this little beast (Sarcopsylla penetrans) burns and itches. Vigorous scratching can lead to skin damage: irritation, swelling, suppuration, and infection.

Marina stands under the awning by the lawn chair, book in hand. The captain seems to have drifted off again. The moon is much lower now but still too bright to allow a clear view of morning stars. In fact, a rising mist obscures most of the sky along the horizon.

Still time for an hour's oblivion, thinks Marina, and so she stretches out on the deck planks next to her captain, the story of el Cid tucked into the bosom of her *huipil* to keep it dry. Rest, however, seems a long way off, replaced by some annoying questions and irritating self-doubts. Nor are the chilly boards beneath her back of much aid to relaxation. She grunts and twists over to the left side.

Portocallero-Portochinguauhpero-what's-his-name. Snoring every night as if he'd torn his nose off. Now why, O why, did Cortés turn me over to that ancient and broken-down hulk? Then he walks up bold as you please and says, "Give her back to me. I need her." For what? What did he fear in the first place? Dumb. Dumb as a Huastec! Who can comprehend such absurd inconsistency? O how slippery is this earth we walk upon. On such a jagged edge we go.

Most brilliant lord of courage who never skips a beat, who never misses a chance, he knew I commanded perfectly the two tongues, and yet I was almost abandoned, almost left on that stinking beach. Perhaps because I was sold to slavers he thinks me tlatlacolli—damaged goods, rotted trash. Yes, of course. That's why his tongue jams in his teeth when he tries to address me. That's why his glance strays all over the horizon when we must speak. Dear lord of ways, where is the water clean enough to purify the likes of me?

Cortés lies motionless in his lawn chair, but he remains very much awake, no less so than the crickets sounding off in the brush along the beach.

The captain general's reputation for rapid and accurate decision making, especially with regard to critical policy considerations, has already been discussed. At that time, it was also necessary to point out the embarrassing consequences of a few overly hasty and poorly considered actions of a personal nature—dealing mostly with the subject of romance. And now, on the poop deck of the little fleet's flagship, sometime during the predawn moments of Good Friday, April 21, 1519, Cortés is once more deeply confused regarding this touchy subject.

Later in the century, a trusted noncom will attempt a description of the captain's appearance. Says the sergeant: "He would have looked better were his head a little larger." To the casual observer, Cortés' head appears acceptable enough. True, it looks a bit baggy-eyed and distracted, and quite clearly, Cortés had not taken the trouble to have his hair dressed before the sitting. But in no way does this likeness of the Marquis del Valle de Oaxaca merit the sobriquet "pinhead." No, there is nothing wrong with the head of Cortés—at least in outward appearance. The captain's mind, however, is once more in a jumble, scrambled by an eggbeater in the hands of a woman (a crude metaphor, escape from which requires too much effort).

Cortés' trouble only appears simple. Actually, it is immensely complex. There at his side lies an extraordinarily attractive girl, one who is, to some extent, his responsibility. Her hip rounds against the sky, an Olympus where desire reigns. Her skirt is pulled up to reveal a length of smooth thigh. Cortés sees all this from the corner of an eye, and he is also very much aware of the chill mist enveloping this delightful figure. Here, then, is his problem. Laugh if you will, but remember, you are not the captain general of an important expeditionary force dependent on complete respect for the maintenance of morale and discipline. Should he remove his cape and cover the girl in order to protect her from the night air? What will the commanders think of such an action? Consideration for native girls? Does this appear as weakness? The common soldiers, well, they can be a little more understanding, with a tendency to mind their own business.

To cover or not to cover. For Hernando Cortés, conquistador, the question reaches critical proportions. It casts something of the aura of an uncomfortable and stilted love scene, something from ... who? Poliziano? No, more like Pygmalion. Quickly he gets to his feet, and in the same motion tosses his cape over the girl. Then he looks up at the sky. Time to get the horses off. We'll let the cavalry handle it. No sailors, no scholars ... no mistakes. Can't afford them.

Down on the foredeck, the eyes of A. Cruz pop open. Hardly anyone is getting any sleep this night. A. Cruz hoists himself onto an elbow and leans across the girl at his side.

"I say, Charley. You get a good look at the boss' new chick?"

"Yes, and indeed, I must say, I was kind of taken aback. Not exactly a great beauty, is she?"

"No? I thought she was kinda … gorgeous, really," whispers Orozca, the Greek-trained gunner.

"Right. Listen, Charley." A. Cruz shifts to the other elbow. "Of course she's beautiful. She has to be beautiful. You know our captain. He wouldn't be caught dead with an ugly broad."

This confusion over Marina's looks has its roots in some rather complex matters, yet it is explained easily enough. Marina's portrait is never easy to paint. She is one of those girls found often enough in all times, who can flick on beauty with some internal circuit. Then she glows transcendent, calm, lovely, a libidinous angel of mercy. But when the current is off, Marina sometimes takes on a positively homely appearance. Something like a fried egg wreathed in black beans.

"Andy, Andy. Three weeks at sea, remember? Anything with long hair and a chest would look good to that guy. She's a dog, Andy. A real dog."

The slight disturbance there at the bow causes not so much as a stir among the reclining bodies on deck. After all, it's not time for reveille just yet. No need to stir the sprained limbs and clotted punctures for an hour or so.

Chapter 6

Morning at Hummingbird Beach

"We Spaniards have a disease of the heart."
H. Cortés

Good Friday, 1519—Hummingbird Beach and lagoon have taken on the appearance of market day in the grand bazaar at Basra. Canoes are all over the harbor, loaded near to flooding with gaping families, local troops in battle dress (but unarmed), and some groups of fishermen who, had they understood the importance of this holy day, would find themselves a little underdressed, even raggedy. A large crowd from two nearby villages is swarming up and down the beach. Some want only to eyeball these black-bearded, strange-looking foreigners. How absurd they appear. Each wears a full black cape held up behind by the point of a sword. From the side they look exactly like barnyard roosters strutting their stuff.

Some individuals, more enterprising than curious, have set up market stalls selling gold jewelry, arts and crafts, bread, baked fish, and other dishes cooked with plenty of chili. As a medium of exchange, the Spaniards present pins, glass beads, looking glasses, scissors, and sewing needles. The locals consider themselves well paid. When it comes to the execution of fine embroidery, a real needle must beat a cactus spine every time.

Cortés, seeing the amount of gold flying around, issues orders carrying a heavy penalty. No one in camp is to accept another grain of the yellow metal. He wants to avoid the appearance of avarice on the part of his little army and dispel any notion that only greed drives them up onto these sands. Cortés feels certain the low exchange rate is some kind of test or trial of Spanish intentions. Quite clearly, the captain's thinking on this matter is not perfectly rational. It's his first tinge of culture shock, and it happens to all leaders under pressure in foreign parts.

On the deck of the flagship, beneath a wide awning gently flapping in the gulf-shore sunshine, Cortés struggles to keep his temper, to hold onto his composure. His request for a visa to pay a visit to Moteuczoma at Tenochtitlan has just been rejected, and rather rudely so, thinks the captain. Lord Tribune, governor of the province, finds Cortés' request extremely importunate.

"What? What?" he stutters, "You've been here less than a day and already you ... you *demand* an interview with the holy speaker?"

Cortés gazes at the governor with studied calm. In his right hand he holds the bundle of straws Tribune had presented during the introductions, the upper few inches of which are colored a dark, reddish brown. Tribune has dipped the end of the little bouquet in his own blood (according to Marina—but who knows, could be merely chicken blood). Such visitation offerings are the custom of the land. Some say they represent a giving of an intimate part of oneself in appreciation for the invite. Others compare it with the Christo-Semitic custom of bringing a coffee cake from a local bakery when visiting friends or relatives. Marina takes the straw bundle from Cortés' hand and, using an empty blue wine bottle as a vase, places the little display on the table.

"Perhaps I can further enlighten Your Excellency as to the purpose of our visit," Cortés explains patiently, "We have heard many fine things regarding your ruler, and we are certainly going to visit the great Moteuczoma in his capitol. You can talk about obstacles till the moon turns blue. The fact is, we are quite accustomed to overcoming all sorts of problems: diplomatic, military, religious, social, and financial." Clearly Cortés is beginning to ramble, but it hardly matters. Only a few of the Spaniards catch on, and they have every confidence in the commander's gift of gab. "I come as the official representative of Charles V, emperor and supreme ruler of all Europe, the world's most powerful king. Submission to his love and protection will bring countless benefits, both material and spiritual, to your people. Permit me to inquire. Are you yourselves not subjects of the Lord Moteuczoma?"

"Good gods," replies Tribune, "What a question! I must admit this is all something of a surprise. I was unaware there existed anyone on earth who is not a vassal of Moteuczoma. How can this be? At any rate, you may rest assured, noble sirs, Lord Moteuczoma is perfectly aware of your presence in his land. We here are in continual contact with Mexico. We can expect another communication in ... O seven days at the most. Rest assured, the great Moteuczoma will be happy to meet with you. He certainly wishes to learn more of your … ah, King Carols, is it? It's just not convenient for the ruler to travel down to the sea at the present time. In the first place, he hasn't been feeling well lately, and his wife is also a bit under a cloud. Furthermore, he's got a couple of big religious holidays coming up requiring a great deal of meticulous preparation. Then, of course, there's the organization of weaponry manufacture for—"

Aya! Tribune's spirit shivers as security breach alarms begin clanging in heart and mind. He hopes he has stopped himself in time. Not much point in revealing divisions in the land—not to these clever foreigners.

The blood-soaked straws are beginning to give off a slightly unpleasant odor, a little too strong for the gulf breeze to dissipate. Under the pretext of clearing the table, Marina removes the vase. No complaints are forthcoming.

There is probably some curiosity on the part of the reader as to the manner in which all this fairly complex communication is being managed. Here's the way it works. Marina translates from Nahuatl to Yucatek. Lay brother Jerónimo de Aguilar (a long-time captive of the Maya near present-day Akumal) puts the Mayan into Spanish for Cortés and any other Spaniard listening in. Sounds like a hotbed of confusion and misunderstanding, does it not? By the time the army starts its long march, however, Marina's Spanish is greatly improved and communication facilitated.

"Ah, listen here," Tribune continues, "why don't you just accept these fine gifts the speaker bids us present to you, and we'll let the future take care of itself. Time enough to talk about visits. Ah, who's got that cursed list? There it is. Just look at this."

1. Ten loads fine cotton mantles—plain.
2. Ten loads fine cotton mantles—embroidered.
3. Five loads fine cotton mantles—plumage embellished.
4. One chest gold articles cast in various plant and animal forms—lizards, frogs, fish, scorpions, corncobs, pine cones, lilies, etc.
5. Three sets gilded armor—leg and arm covers, shields, helmets with plumes.

At this time, the presents, including the gold-laden chest, are brought aboard. The Spaniards begin oohing and ahing over the delicately wrought pieces, though it must be admitted, they are not much impressed by the aesthetics of the work. They have a tendency to visualize all that gold melted down into nice heavy ingots.

Cortés, barely able to keep from leaping with glee, still manages to assume the heaviest, deadpan expression in his repertoire. "Oh, noble chief," he sighs, he lowers his eyes, he chokes back tears. "For us there can be no finer gift item. It's a lifesaver." Cortés extends an arm toward the golden articles. "You see, we Spaniards suffer from a terrible disease of the heart, and gold is its only cure. The next time you communicate with Moteuczoma, please inform him of our great need."

The translation of these remarks brings on a spate of hemming, hawing, and throat-clearing among the governors. Tustepeque actually falls victim to a rather violent coughing fit. Cortés himself fetches a glass of water for the chief.

Marina, having disappeared some moments previously, now shows up again in the company of three private soldiers. The men are staggering under the weight of some large, canvas-wrapped object that appears to be shaped like a giant wedge of cheese—beveled at one end, square at the other.

"And this, noble sirs, is a little gift your master Lord Moteuczoma should find acceptable." Cortés bows deeply.

"Who?" whispers one of the privates, "He means Montezuma, doesn't he?"

"No, I don't think that's the right way to say it."

"Oh, come on. We've got enough tongue twisters as is. Try saying *Popocatepetl* three times fast. As far as I'm concerned, it's Montezuma from now on."

The ropes are untied. Cortés whips off the canvas cover disclosing a large, ornate oaken armchair. "Charles V himself, ruler of the Holy Roman Empire, king of Castile, Aragon and Sardinia," Cortés announces grandly, "presents this fine article of Spanish craftsmanship to His Most Exalted Majesty, Moteuczoma, in the profound hope that it will suit his taste and prove a valuable addition to the decor of his palatial residence, the grandeur of which we've all heard quite a bit."

Of course, Charles V knows nought regarding this hunk of furniture, much less has he laid eyes on it. Actually, the chair belongs to D. Velazquez, governor of Cuba. Cortés borrowed the elaborately carved item one evening to sit in while presiding over a meeting at the Palacio Municipal (town hall). This is not to imply the captain is accustomed to an ostentatious lifestyle. *Au contraire.* He even dresses quite simply in a plain, well-made, black cloak, a heavy golden chain his only ornament. Those who know the man will tell us the expensive chain serves more as a hedge against sudden financial setback than as decoration or symbol of wealth. Yet Cortés understands very well that when a show of power is necessary, the accouterments are an absolute must. Hence the fancy seat. Later, when he was rounding up gift articles for distribution among native rulers and other mainland bigwigs, he remembered the decorative chair and had it toted off to the harbor. Well, why not? He and Velazquez were on the outs again. (Diego, in a fit of paranoia, deeply regretted appointing Cortés as head of the expedition.) And besides, the old boy would probably never miss it.

How nice it would be to forget about this article, to drop it for all time (maybe over the stern rail). However, the chair carries a potential for causing somebody big trouble later on, and so perhaps a closer examination is needed. We find ourselves confronting an excellent example of fifteenth century Spanish furniture design. It combines elements so disparate as to verge on lunacy. The back is tall, plain, and straight as a North Gothic church tower. The arms and legs though are covered in blindingly intricate carved designs: grape leaves, fruit salads, pinecones, swirls, and curlicues. The form might have lived on a while longer had not a dullish museum curator come up with the cliché: "Moorish Rococo," thereby cramping its style. Disguised among these twists and turns, and visible only to the trained eye, are some Arabic letters. Charles V, His Most Catholic Majesty, were he to read the phrase they spell, would fall over with a coronary. Charles V, our most Holy Roman emperor and defender of the faith now presents great Moteuczoma with an article bearing the delicately designed inscription: "There is no God but God, and Mohammed is his messenger!"

Reflect on the sacrilege. Only recall that the event here described takes place on a Good Friday—the anniversary of the very day that saw the Spanish God entombed in preparation for his Ascension. Oh, scandal! Oh, corruption! Should word of it be leaked to the public, riots would engulf the world from La Habana to the Pyrenees and perhaps beyond.

Tribune nods blankly. *How in the name of the nine levels of death are we supposed to pack that thing through the mountains,* he thinks. *Not really my concern, though. Mexican tamemes can handle anything.*

And so they did. When the Spaniards finally achieved guest status at Moteuczoma's, they found the item sitting against a wall in perfect condition.

By midnight, the entire company, including the watch, have left the ships to join the beach party. A great crowd of mixed race gathers on the sands, S. *penetrans* not withstanding. And the singing! European harmony is a new and moving sound for New World ears, and most of the locals are crying in their pulque.

> "Tengo un hermano en el Tercio, oh … oh oh oh … oh oh oh
> Oh oh oh … oh oh oh … oh oh … oh oh.
> Otro tengo en regulareh … eh eh eh … ehs
> Y el hermano mas pequeño oh … oh oh oh … oh oh oh … oh oh oh
> Oh oh oh … oh oh … oh oh.
> Esta en carcel en Buceh … eh … eh … eh … ehrros.

> *("Got a brother in the Third*
> *Another in the regular*
> *And the youngest brother of all*
> *Is a prisoner down in Bucerros.")*

This well-known Spanish tearjerker is a *jota* and is clearly ancestral to contemporary styles of Mexico. These tunes, without exception, reach a climax of a very special kind. At a particular note (and everyone knows exactly which note), it becomes necessary to howl at the moon or at the liquor bottles lined up behind the bar. Here the word "Tercio" serves as the trigger and slides into a nasal, quavering descent—Moorish in mode and guaranteed to make the constellations gasp.

Cortés' tent has been set up on the highest dune among the reeds and sea grapes. The night breeze is very light. Giant fireflies flash bright enough to compete with the stars but are too unstable to bear on human destiny. They weave and dodge around the dunes and through the reeds like crazy candlelight processions. Inside the tent, a single oil lamp burns. Cortés writes at his little camp desk.

"One very horrible and abominable custom they have, which should certainly be punished, and which we have seen in no other part, and that is whenever they wish to beg anything of their idols, in order that their petition may find more acceptance, they take large numbers of boys and girls, and even of grown men and women, and tear out their hearts and bowels while still alive, burning them in the presence of those idols, and offering the smoke of such burning as a pleasant sacrifice. Some of us have actually seen this done, and they say it is the most terrible and frightful thing that they have ever seen."

Ordinarily Cortés dictates correspondence to Nuzi. This particular letter, though, is heading straight for the throne and may require a few bits of historical revision. The captain wants to be dead certain all America doesn't know about it.

Cortés' concentration is suddenly disrupted by a violent itch in the region beneath his codpiece—a sensation common enough among the members of an army, large or small, camped in open country. The captain feels certain that Marina, seated cross-legged on a mat in the darkest corner of the tent, must be staring at his crotch—again. Remember, this is an era in men's fashion renowned for the stuffed codpiece. Handkerchiefs are used, pieces of rag, anything to present that smoothly rounded, evenly bulged, modestly exaggerated effect the style masters have decreed. First developed to serve an eminently practical purpose, a matter of life and death, to be sure, the codpiece was a heavy, rounded steel hemisphere bolted to the *cuisses* or armored thigh protectors. This was the hardest metal in a suit of armor and worked admirably as a groin protector. Its transition to civilian styles, however, is a confused tale. It features certain clothiers involved in the development of "alternative lifestyles" and "New Age" (Renaissance) design concepts—so we won't go into it at this time.

Again, Cortés picks up the quill. What is it about this young woman that so inhibits his natural inclinations? Why can't he simply reach down and give himself a good scratch like any soldier in the field. 'Tis not that she resembles some great and high-tone beauty lounging about the court of Castile. Saints above! She is only a slave. Nor is she among the most gorgeous he has met of that class. But still, there is about the girl: a delicate femininity, a proud glance, strong yet tender—oh yes, quite tender, and even a bit sardonic. It pulls at him like the moon at a high tide.

With a sigh, Cortés drops the weight of his head onto the heels of his hands, digging them into the eye sockets. Soon he begins to see great jagged flashes of blue, lightning-like flame, and on the far horizon, a million leagues away, an endless line of pointed and barren peaks. With a start, he raises his head, blinks a few times, and glances over at Marina. She sits with legs folded sideways, leaning on one arm. The other rests in her lap.

Today Marina has dressed for the beach party in her best outfit. She wears a shift covered with embroidered dahlias and gathered at the waist. The skirt, in contrast, is quite simple: white cotton with thin black vertical lines and a narrow border the same color as the dahlias. Her hair is twisted with yellow ribbon and wound about the head. The overall effect, you may be certain, is quite stunning. It is probably responsible for Cortés' unease. The vanilla perfume the lady wears only adds to his confusion.

Marina's fine skirt and blouse were made by her mother, lovingly packed and presented to the twelve-year-old girl on the day the slavers came to pick her up. That's right. Marina was sold into service by her own mother, a woman of noble lineage and high standing in the province of Proper Snake. Hopefully, we will find space for an explanation of this seemingly barbarous action. For now, let the reader be assured, the sale was not an ordinary one. It involved a contract fraught with caveats for the buyer and special considerations for the "merchandise." This female child was not to be used in the usual manner.

And so, Marina has been spared the common slave's fate: ritual sacrifice at the yearly fete of one guild or another. After the Spanish victory at Potonchan, local officials along the coast rounded up twenty of the best-looking girls they could find and presented them to Cortés.

"You gentlemen will need some women to do the cooking," said the chief with a discrete cough.

Thus, Malinal Zazil Ha found herself among the first women of New Spain to be baptized into the Christian faith. Father Olmedo named her Marina. Now she sits in Cortés' tent, attempting to attract his attention in order to ask a favor.

"O my lord and master," she says softly. Cortés waves a hand irritably. He is in no mood for formality, and the *lord and master* business gets on his nerves.

"Listen," he says, "forget that lord and master nonsense, will you? Just call me "Captain" like everybody else."

Marina shifts her mat a little closer. "Captain, will you read me?"

Cortés is startled. "My copy of Cid! Where did you get this? What—?"

Marina's expression grows animated. "O I know much, much of this thing." She taps the book with the back of one hand in a manner that strikes Cortés as professorial. "It is a great story of your land. It is …" Marina looks up at the tent ceiling, obviously trying hard to recall some exact wording. "Spain's great epic of sword and … O, O, O … *teolitia*, teolitia!"

The exhausted captain is startled into a harsh laugh. "Spain's great epic of sword and … What? Teolitia?"

Marina presses both hands against her breast. Cortés notices, perhaps for the first time, the give of soft flesh.

"Oh, heart," he says.

"O no, no. Heart—*yollotli.*" She pushes harder against her chest. Now the captain sees her breast bulge out beside the pressing hand. Marina stretches her head back. With eyes closed, she pokes a finger into her ribs as if pointing to something further within.

"Soul. You mean soul. 'Spain's great epic of sword and soul.' Oh, good grief! From whence cometh such phraseology pointed and poetic both. Sounds like Nuzi Duka to me. Who else in this bug-ridden hell can throw words around like that?"

Marina only stares at her feet.

"So, Marina," the captain begins again in gentler tones, "you've been talking to Nuzi, have you?"

The young lady raises her head and looks Cortés in the eye.

"Tell me something, child. What do you think of Nuzi? Do you like him? Is he a good man?"

Marina is about to shrug her shoulders in a deprecating manner but catches herself in time. Her chin comes up a couple of centimeters. "He very cute man," she says, using a slang word meaning monkeylike, but it can also mean destructive.

Cortés wonders at the acuteness of her observation. He reaches out for the *Poem of el Cid* and opens it randomly. "You're a fast learner, Marina," he says with no trace of expression. Silence falls between them. Captain Cortés gets up and places the lamp on the tent floor. The girl stretches out flat, and Cortés lies down beside her. Really, all he has in mind is some comfort for aching muscles. He knows it would be best to sleep for a while. Marina stiffens out like a board and stares fixedly at the ceiling.

Cortés holds the book up a little, the better to catch the light. "Ah. Here we have the sad part. Doña Jimena waits in the castle at Valencia. Ruy Diaz is not due home till sundown, but at noon already she grows impatient."

Marina frowns deeply. "But why did he not go to her quickly, quickly? Why did he not fly to her side very fast—faster than the wind?"

"Oh, Marina. A man on a horse can cover only so much ground, no matter how much in love he is. All right, then. Ruy Diaz de Bivar has refused to execute his Moorish prisoners, and so King Alfonso brands him a traitor and sends him into exile. But really, he does this only out of fear and jealousy. Like King Saul and David. Ruy Diaz is given but a few days to get out of Valencia, so it's good-bye wife and kids."

"'Grace. Campeador of the excellent beard
Here before you are your daughters and I.'
His two daughters in his arms he took,
Drew them to his heart for he loved them dear
He weeps from his eyes and sighs deeply
'Ah, doña Jimena, my perfect wife,
I love you as I do my own soul.
You know well we must part in this life;
I shall go from here and you will stay behind.
May it please God and Santa María ...'"

Cortés' eyes seem fixed on the distant stars as if the tent cloth were transparent.

"Why did he not dispatch the traitorous Musselmen according to custom and king's orders? Oh, well. So the man was misunderstood. Binding together all of Spain—that was the true purpose. Christian, Moor, it mattered not—one people, one Spanish land." Now the captain heaves a sigh. "Well, he failed, but he got plenty rich in the process. Hmm, yes indeed."

Cortés glances over at Marina. Eyes open, she stares at the ceiling, tears pouring down her face. Cortés bends over to kiss her lips, but they seem cold and lifeless. He looks at her for a moment, unties the sash at her waist, and raises the dahlias as far as they will go—but it's not far enough. Now she must cooperate, if only a few centimeter's worth, raising her back so the cloth can be lifted higher. Cortés bends and kisses the nipple of her right breast. Marina screams and flings her arms backward over her head. The oil lamp goes flying across the tent. Quickly the captain twists around and sets it right. By the time he turns back, she is sitting up, tugging at his shirt with both hands—hard enough to tear the cloth.

"*Quita, quita,*" she rasps, "off, off." When both are stripped from the waist up, she pulls him down so that they lie naked, breast to breast. The warmth of contact makes Cortés groan with relief. The power in this woman's skin is like a dose of laudanum, unwinding every wracked nerve and muscle in his body. Cortés, today rated first among the great Latin lovers, is hardly a stranger to the touch of female flesh. But some, he now sees clearly, is nicer than others.

"Oooh," gasps Marina as the current of pleasure coils around her being. "But what can this mean?" Loosening the grip of her arms a bit only refines and spreads the sensation. "Ahhh," breathes Marina.

Suddenly the voice of old granny sounds in her ear. *"I'll tell you what this means, my girl. Drunkenness. Gluttony. Too much pleasure and the spirit abandons the body. There you'll be: just a useless two-eyed lump of flesh."*

O Granny, shut up please. I'll just have a little talk with Tlazolteotl. She's the one who stirs us poor girls up, and now she can finish the job. I will confess, and she will eat my filth. "I hope," she giggles softly.

"What?" says Cortés, moving aside a little. Marina rises, and with her back to the captain, she carefully folds and puts away the dahlia shift. Then she picks up a white cotton mantle and, holding it in front of her, lies down again. She spreads the cloth over them both. They lie there, touching only from shoulder to hand.

Cortés begins drifting off, thinking about his plans for the next day. He must make a good speech discouraging any behavior that might seem insulting to the natives. These rough-hewn soldiers—should they turn the population against them, all would be lost. Only one guiding principle, really: respect for the savages. Keep the brutes happy, friendly, and helpful all along the sixty leagues to Mexico. Ordinarily such a train of thought would clench the captain's jaw and tie knots in his stomach making sleep impossible. But not tonight. Tonight, uncertainty holds no power to torment him. He can't remember feeling so … what? Free.

Soon Cortés becomes aware of some pain reminiscent of teenage years, but he is far too sleepy to do anything about that. Turning his head to look at Marina, he finds her wide awake, bright-eyed, and staring back.

"Listen, Marina. This is important. The people here—who do they say I am?"

She smiles slowly and looks away. "Common people. Simple people. They say you Quetzalcoatl Topiltzin, come to take back your country."

"And you. Who do you say I am?"

She turns and whispers into his neck, "I say you Mio Cid el Campeador. Mio Cid, he of the splendid beard."

Chapter 7

Marina's Former Life—Early Spring 1519

"The Mexican is an inhuman person, supremely wicked.
When it comes to evil, no one can surpass the Mexican."
Non-Mexican informant

The town of "He Who Hasteneth" (Painalla, in the language of its Mexica harassers) lies under a chilly rain, product of an early spring norther. Clouds the color of dirty cotton scud down the beaches in long dark rolls. In low places, the cold deluge forms puddles as big as lakes. "O chronic arthritis, now bestir thyself," the grim sky demands. Mud is everywhere. Mud is ubiquitous. Mud is very depressing. The youth called Malinal (from Ce Malinalli: One Grass of Penance) stands in a window at the back of town hall. She stares out into the dreary morning, frustration and anger evident in her pose. And that face? What an expression. Just now, she looks something like an irritable nymph cast in plaster. That curled upper lip might crack, but it certainly won't bend.

"Will someone be good enough to close the shutters?" comes an authoritative voice from the platform. "We are not trying to recreate here, sacred as our purpose is, the trials of Lord One-Hunapu and Lord Seven-Hunapu in the famous and proverbial House of Great Cold."

No, thinks Mali. *More like the house lined with sharpened knives.* She refers, of course, to the cutting contest about to take place in the hall: Nahua interlopers versus native Yucateks.

"Grrr," Mali softly imitates, at least in her mind's ear, the sound made by an angry jaguar. *So what to do? Not much point in going home. Place is empty. Old Master is around here someplace. In the hall. Old Master. What a clown. What a turkey. Turkey? No, that's Mexican. Aya! Can't even remember my own language. Actually, he's pretty good company is Old Master. As long as he keeps his hands off me. Yagh. Well, maybe not all that bad. He treats me well enough. Perhaps I don't deserve it. Perhaps I'm not exactly a nice girl, a useful girl.*

"No, no," he says. "You have a very edible heart. If I'd wanted somebody who could weave and sew and bake those little fruit cakes with the seeds that stick in your teeth—nuhtoni? No, that's not Yucatek. What do we call them? Anyway, I'd have bought a girl like that. That's not what I was after."

O gods! You weren't? What a revelation.

Painalla's original name, though not quite forgotten, is rarely used these days. Really, it is an ordinary sort of town and yet held apart in its own imagination and in that of the neighbors. It occupies the sort of space Hispanic poets, in the mood for a bit of existential hyperbole, might refer to as *el medio 'e la nada*—the middle of nowhere. Yet the place is not choked off from the rest of the world by some great stretch of desert sand, nor is it one of those far-off and lonely sea islands where the dreams of artists and children are often stillborn. Nor is Painalla enclosed by impenetrable jungle, though there is a swamp that makes access to the open gulf a matter of clever engineering and endless maintenance.

No, this business of *el medio 'e la nada* is not to be taken literally. It is only a metaphysical notion or maybe some sort of metaphor. In reality, Painalla is completely surrounded—beset about by awe, admiration, envy, and technical spies. In other words, the town's isolation is strictly spiritual in nature.

Of course, Painalla participates in the regional economy (sea foods, boat building, rare bird skins, jade, stone cutting), but Painalla's true manufactory (to the which no other can hold a candle), is the refinement of a different sort of raw material: its careful preparation, development, and finally, public display of the finished product—top-notch athletes, really fine and talented ballplayers.

Here is the subject that occupies the hearts and minds, not to mention the conversations, of each and every citizen. Only two topics compete at discussion time: the incompetence of Mexican officers and the standings of regional teams. Painalla's coaches, those "little professors" of tactic and strategy, can name their price anywhere in the known world, including Cholula and other centers of religious fundamentalism and game-worship-by-the-book. The Painalla clan chiefs, acting as the player's legal representatives, have negotiated a new multi-ethnic league in consultation with Tenochca and other Mexica officers stationed at Proper Snake barracks. All members of the aristocracy, along with talented commoners, are invited to join. Regardless of rank and ethnicity, however, they had all better show up for practice on time.

That the early meetings proved fairly successful was due to the application of some quiet pressure quietly applied by certain marketing concerns (the Pochteca, or Mexican Merchant's League) heavily invested in the gambling concession. The inclusion of Mexica "occupation" troops had seemed a necessary sop to their o'er weaning arrogance and snobbery but has carried a price: endless pressure for a change in the rules of the game. Mexica officials are still insisting on a legalistic interpretation of the sport as sacrificial ritual.*

"O gods," grouches Painalla. "As if we didn't know all about it. It's our darn game to begin with."

The whole sacred sport business got underway just after the beginning of time. A couple of young heroes (in the mythic, not the filmic sense) annoyed some underworld gods by playing ball on their roof.

"Respect? We just don't get any," the gods complained, and the boys were soon beheaded.

And now comes the part the little kids really get a kick out of.

"All right," the old storyteller croaks harshly, "who's the head monster of the Underworld?"

"The great Lord Pus himself," the children answer joyously.

"And what does the great Lord Pus have for dinner?"

"Fumes! Fumes!"

"Fumes? Fumes? Dolts! Dolts! What type of fumes?"

"Miasmic fumes."

"And what else?"

"Underground gaseous anomalies."

"That's better. Then Lord Pus spoke up in that voice like a crocodile with tonsillitis: 'Take the head of One-Hunapu and hang it from a tree in the forest,' he said, 'and no nibbling along the way. Especially the eyes. Stay away from the eyes.'"

"Meanwhile, an aggressive young lady of the land (her name was Blood Moon) decided to go looking for Hunapu's tree. Blood was determined to

---

* This violates tradition. Mexican hegemony, like that of ancient Rome, grants no say in local custom. Only two controls are established: collection of yearly tribute and "capture" of the local god. Mexican engineers blanched at the thought of toting Painalla's giant effigy of K'uk'ulkan two hundred miles uphill. They scratched their heads a while and then ordered up a miniature version. At the time of our tale, the mini K'uk'ulkan sits in storage in the basement of the temple of Coacalco, Tenochtitlan.

51

grab a piece of that power the gods had turned loose in the jungle. When she located the head, it spoke to her in a voice hoarse and creaky from lack of use."

"'Just stick your hand up here,' the thing ordered, and then it spat in her palm. The lady soon found herself pregnant and in big trouble at home. 'Why, you little slut,' the father shrieked. 'Leave this house immediately. Just hit the road. I'm sending some owls to cut your heart out.'"

"In time, she gave birth to twin boys. The lads grew up to be great artists and musicians—a lot smarter than their dad or uncle. Why sometimes they did nothing but sit around and write all day! Imagine that! Finally, the boys got hold of a rat and tormented the poor creature till it showed them where the family athletic equipment was hidden—ball, hip yoke, arm guards, you know. To their credit, the boys eventually fed the dazed animal. Yes, yes. Virtue is its own reward. O absolutely."

Well, perhaps that's enough of ancient storytelling. Let us introduce brevity into a longish tale. The boys took their newfound gear and faced off against the Underworld dream team. They managed to defeat those loathsome and disgusting lords of misery by following a game plan combining an odd mix of elements: athletic prowess, voluntary self sacrifice, and bodily resurrection. Does the strategy seem a bit bizarre? In the light of our churchly theology, it is at least vaguely comprehensible.

Later, the young chaps dug up their father's body and tried to re-attach his head. Too late. Some sort of brain damage had occurred. He could only stand there gazing around. What's more, even under close questioning, Hunapu couldn't recall the names of his body parts. So the boys left him stationed on the center marker where he remains as chief caretaker and guardian against any who would defile the place by urinating on the grounds.

The lesson here is straightforward: A society whose spiritual underpinning is formed in a ballpark is bound to imbue sporting events with a plethora of sacred meaning. So it doesn't appear unseemly that lots of blood should be spilled in commemoration of that first gory contest with the gods. But this rarely happens in Painalla. As has been indicated, Painalla does things a little differently.

An odd multicolored pattern of footprints decorates the covered path up to the meeting hall, a design in red, black, and white: red earth of the hillsides, black milpa soil, and the white tracks picked up from Painalla's caliche paths. At the door, footgear is removed, of course, and placed neatly along the wall.

A Jaggedy New World

Mali slumps to the floor just below the windowsill. *Well, no practice today*, she broods. *The boys will have excuses at the ready. Girls are not supposed to play. We could all get ourselves executed. O ridiculous. Please. This is Painalla, not Hummingbird City.*

The truth is no one wants to risk a broken leg slipping around in all that greasy mud. When the ball comes across low, it's necessary to slide under it, to make solid contact with hip or butt before the rubber touches ground. No hands allowed. It's that slide that causes most injuries. Mali's thighs are already bruised and tender, and so it is with all the players.

Prayers having been said, officials are milling about and preparing to take their seats on the platform. The town speaker converses quietly with a slightly cross-eyed merchant nobleman bending over him, tablet and marker in hand. This gentleman is bundled to the ears in cloaks and sashes. He also wears a hat made of palm fronds. Obviously, the fellow's been walking around in the rain this morning.

The speaker doesn't look up. "Give me one extra left and, O ... seven service or plus," he says softly. "Lone quill," he adds, referring to a quantity of gold dust.

Playing it safe today, aren't we, thinks the Mexica merchant. "O quite," he answers. "Got it. And for the day of Tlacaxipeualiztli (Progenitor)."

Speaker Stonewall the Younger looks up sharply and does a sort of double take.

"That would be inappropriate," he says, once more lowering his gaze. The Mexica, though most certainly shocked by what he perceives as peremptory dismissal, shows no reaction. He manages to hold his ground long enough to get in some reasonable argument.

"Well, the question of duration remains open, you understand. That's a wager in anybody's book. Prisoners often do well, even on an empty stomach." The merchant noble devotes a couple of seconds to the study of his fingernails.

"Listen," he says, bending closer to the speaker. "I have it on authority that the team will be unbound and fed at least once before the whistle."

Not much point in offending the business community, thinks the speaker. Though seething within, he couches his reply in the blandest of tones. "Many thanks, dear sir, but of course you understand, ah, the Flayed God celebration, or Progenitor as you name it, has never been one of our holidays. And, er, uh ... you must be familiar with our simple Yucatek aphorism: 'What God doeth fix, no man should risk.'"

Not the slightest tinge of sarcasm mars Stonewall's speech, as he declines to hazard the upcoming ecclesiastical match. The Pochteca heaves a great sigh reeking of smoked jalapeño and disappointment. Then he turns away.

"But it's the only game in town," he whines.

Ah, yes, Stonewall groans inwardly. *Such rigged matches are our custom, too, though more honored in the breech. Those prisoners should be interviewed. By what authority do the Mexica hold them?*

The speaker faces the hall now, but he appears unfocused and unaware of his surroundings. There comes a harsh grating sound from behind the platform. It is the emcee reminding Sir Stonewall he'd better speak up. "The graffiti, sir! The graffiti!" he says.

Speaker Stonewall is very much awake now and cool enough to use that long, inadvertent pause to advantage. Slowly, very slowly, the left side of his mustache curls upward. The crowd gets the hint and the hall quiets down. Only a few Tenochca and a Weavertownie or two are still throat-clearing and harrumphing in the front row.

"Seven Akbal, eight Cumku this year," the Speaker intones. "O surely you remember: Pearl Divers Association versus Painalla. Last phase. Mayhap you don't recall? Our Packstrap leaps halfway up the end zone stands. Diver fans try to block him, try to grab the ball. Children in the top row throw turkey legs at his head. Some lunatic flings a bowl of pulque in his direction. A full bowl. Hoo! Now there's a fanatic for you.

"But Packstrap is unstoppable. With one grand sweep of his arm, he clears the bench. Popcorn flies in every direction. Then he drops to one side and butts that ball the length of the court, clear past the Diver line. A record distance. O surely you remember." Stonewall glowers fiercely and slams a fist on the podium.

> "And then in the night what unscrupulous sot
> Crept into court with some paint in a pot?
> Such finely made stroke, what brush work divine,
> Recreated the scene, O evil design, besmirching
> The wall near the center line. 'Tis a crime,
> 'Tis a sin, such a terrible shame.
> Already us gods got a bad enough name.
> Off with his head. Let's finish that job,'
> All Underworld cries—"

The speaker is interrupted by a violent pounding of boards in the front row. They are quickly followed by some equally loud knocks made by the staff that the emcee always carries. Then the announcement:

"Captain Sir Skinned One, Division Commandant, Army of the Three City League, wishes to be heard. The floor, sir, belongs to you. It is yours, all yours."

Skinned One is outraged. He launches into a tirade and then stops abruptly with a shake of his scepter. The entire council nods vigorously as though in perfect comprehension, but actually, they all look a bit blank. Finally, Sir Begetter leans over to Stonewall.

"Whatsaid'e ? Whatsaid'e ? I didn't get one word in ten."

"Don't know. Too fast for me. We better get Mali up here." And then to the emcee "Call for Mali, will you?"

Thump, thump. "The slave girl Malinal must report to the speaker instantaneously. Delay will not be countenanced."

Mali steps up to the platform with a deep bow, but before she can straighten up, Stonewall whispers impatiently.

"Whatsaid'e? Whatsaid'e?"

"In brief, Reverend Little Speaker, the official, demands you take back the dreadful accusation that one of his people perpetrated the desecration in the sacred ball court."

"What? What? Are you certain you understood correctly? That's ridiculous. Ridiculous."

"The gentleman also mentions some unusual circumstances regarding your conception. Er, ah, ahem … an alleged liaison 'twixt your mama and a warty toad—or a garden slug. That wasn't clear."

"Very original," mumbles the speaker. "One of their people, eh? O my grandma's broken pot! O slap me with a rabbit! As if ever there breathed a Mexican with artistic talent. It's a contradiction."

"Listen, Mali, apologize for me, will you? And make it abject. Very abject."

If the truth be known, Speaker Stonewall and the council are perfectly aware who the culprit is: none other than that accomplished artist-athlete Packstrap himself. A public relations discussion has already taken place at Stonewall's little villa in the avocado grove. Speaking first, Sir Egret had blandly mentioned that the offense called for execution, followed by expulsion from the league.

"Well, he was drunk. Extenuating circumstances. How about suspension for a couple of games?" suggested Begetter.

"Which ones? Bring forth the schedule. Four Ahau, eight Cumku, it's the Divers again. Then Tuxtla Toucans, nine Kayab, and Proper Snake barracks finishes the season. That's not an easy lineup. Without Packstrap, we can't count on a single one of those meets. You understand, there may not be much time left. Mayhap the Beards will put their sail-houses to land at our port. On the other hand, perhaps not. Personally, I'm betting against it. I'm betting they'll hasten straight up to Hummingbird Beach and the old Culhua road."

For a few beats, no one spoke. Frog and cricket sounds flowed in through the open window till they filled the room, loud as battle din.

"Permitting us to finish up here on the earth with a championship season," Sir Begetter nodded thoughtfully and then turned and stared into the dark.

"What can be more important?" asked Stonewall. "This much do we owe the spirits of the unborn. The sacrifice of our ancestors shall not have been in vain. Can we strive for greater glory? No, I think not."

"Ah," breathed Egret with a sigh. "Then I suppose the graffiti affair will have to stay buried till the end of time."

"Indeed, 'twould seem so. The day after tomorrow, I'll make a simple but thunderous speech decrying desecration and sacrilege, and then we'll just 'keep our eyes crossed' as the saying has it. After all, isn't a truly great athlete entitled to some ... well, special consideration?"

Back in the hall, Captain Sir Skinned One holds forth on his favorite topic—techniques for dispatching sacrificial victims. It must be understood that Skinned One is no trained priest, merely one of those soldier-wizards the army likes to have around as insurance. Not one of his spells has ever stopped a lance thrust nor stopped the razor sharp maquíhuitl from slicing through somebody's flesh, gristle, and bone. And yet, Skinned One, so they say, can frighten the Tlatoani himself, even as His Majesty sits bethroned in the capital—and this with only an angled glance from those opaque eyes. The man needs no dowsing rod to find the springs of fear. He's a natural terrorist.

"The thing to remember, fellow citizens," he practically burbles, "is that the process is virtually painless. As I am sure you will recall, there can be a second or two of discomfort, but it has nothing to do with the blade. When an offering is stretched out across the receptor stone, the edge of the block catches him just at the fifth bone o' the neck." Now Skinned One points thoughtfully, yea, even feelingly, to the upper part of his neck, and then reaches around to the small of his back, delicately searching out the coccyx.

"And here, at the backbone's end. The sudden application of pressure at these points causes immediate paralysis of the spirit, and nothing more is felt—except perhaps, ecstasy," he ends in a whisper.

Skinned One glances at Mali, and so she stands and begins to translate. She seems a half foot taller. Eyes alight, neck gently arched, she carefully points out the upper vertebrae. Now she sways to the right in a sort of ballet movement, her left hand indicating the position of the coccyx. All attention is glued to the young lady's movements. Skinned One himself seems more than a little wide-eyed.

"The, ah, next step requires some practice. The blade point must be brought down on the center bone o' the chest accurately and yet with enough force to shatter it. This enables the rib cage to be easily spread, allowing fast access to the heart. In order to perfect the skill necessary for faultless execution, our novice priests are given only children for offering. Softer bones, you understand."

Mali translates, and it seems all air is sucked from the room. Silence reigns as in a vacuum. Faces in the crowd blank out in absolute stillness. How perfectly they command that empty gaze, that mahogany stare, those of the nation tribes of the double continent. When the tension breaks, Stonewall's lungs draw breath again. Everyone in the room begins gabbling at once and so it is difficult to make out more than a few scattered words and phrases.

"… blood on the feathers …"

"… those things aren't cheap …"

"… tied in a circle and rolled down the temple steps …"

"… a whole lot cleaner …"

"Iguana? Not without hot sauce."

"… break every bone in the spine."

"You mean like one at a time?"

"Hush, child. All right, so thin it, thin it …"

"But not with guanabana, never with guanabana …"

"… used to do it that way …"

"What, with fruit juice?"

"No, bounce 'em down the temple steps."

"O gods, we're getting nowhere. I'm calling a pause for refreshments," Stonewall announces to no one in particular.

S. L. Gilman

First speaker Sir Stonewall the Younger, chief magistrate of the district of He Who Hasteneth and knight of the Order of the White Bone Serpent stands abruptly, faces the window, and motions for the shutters to be opened. He claps his hands loudly three times and begins shouting out some orders.

"Now we will take refreshments. Bring food for ... hmm ... twenty-one officials. The rest can go home for lunch or visit the market concessions. We'll take fish, fresh if you please, and chicken or turkey as the case may be. And some nice cool branch water to wash it all down. And tortillas, of course. I refer to the thin variety presently in vogue."

The caterer rushes off to fill Stonewall's order, but the young translator who bears responsibility for presenting a proper Nahua version of the menu is still in a trance. Mali rises from her humble crouch with oddly stiffened limbs and a peculiar fixed expression. The Mexica spot this right away, and it makes them nervous. Remember, the holy mother of their nation walks around with a flint knife in her womb and her children dream of giant toads sprouting teeth at every joint. They are bound to grow up somewhat neurasthenic in temperament, and a bit jumpy as well.

Perhaps the necessity of playing a role in the feeding of so many enemies is a shock to Mali's system. They were Mexica slavers, after all, who put an end to her childhood play around the backyard well. First, she pivots and faces the window just as the speaker did. Then, as though spellbound in some copycat enchantment, Mali claps sharply three times. In that flawless Mexican of hers, she begins a translation, but the meaning is not Stonewall's. Far from it. In her rendition, there is no mention of chicken tacos. Once more, the local crowd freezes in their seats. Only with difficulty do they comprehend her language, but that hand-clapping imitation clutches within and shakes the spirit.

"*Tlacatle, totacoe, tloquee, titlacavane auh eoatzine,*" Mali drones on. Her clear brown eyes are almost invisible. They seem bruised and sunk in her skull. "*In axcan ocujmontocac inocujmomma* ... for the lords find no relief on earth. They do not settle in that restful land with no fleas or chiggers. Already they are punctured in the body and have not repose. Already they scratch all day and also in the night. Great Smoking Mirror shall not avail them, and so suffering overtakes those measly sprouts, those unimportant little twigs."

Mexica eyes stretch wide, lids propped by fear. Maya eyes are unreadable as usual. Forefingers clenched between teeth, however, indicate a degree of worried nervousness.

"In the name of the split turtle, he whose rotting intestines feed the mighty tree of the Milky Way, may they fall through its branches, through the stars, through the hole in the universe, straight through to the Place of Emptiness."

Captain Sir Skinned One of the army of the Three City League leaps to his feet. His fancy staff drops from nerveless hands and rolls under a bench. The Mexica delegates make a break for the exit (there's really no other way to put it). Oh, their efforts toward affecting a dignified exit are valiant enough, but there's a crack in the facade. It is clearly visible as that group of very dignified officers trip austerely over each other's heels as they push out the door.

"Ah, well," says Stonewall, staring at the receding backs of that bunch of snooty fanatics, those promoters of boozed-up, regimental-size jaguar hunts. "So what can it matter now here on the earth," he sighs.

Nowadays, down in the lands where our old-fashioned tale unrolls, sport is every bit as important as in times long past. In every village and hamlet in today's greater Mexico, in every town and barrio, can be found the soccer players—tangled, shouting gangs of boys (girls rarely play) charging remorselessly around the yards of rural schoolhouses, to and fro between urban manhole covers, and even along the shady side of an occasional sixteenth century cathedral. *Futból*, it can be noted with certainty, occupies an important position at the heart of the nation. In his tragic ballad about the murder of a priest and his soccer-playing altar boy, Rubén Blades finds a couple of lines pointing like a beacon at the game's exalted place.

"Antonio fell, the host in his hand, and he never knew why.
Andrés died, there by his side, and he never met Péle."

Rules for soccer (officially *association football*—somehow the abbreviation "assoc." got twisted around to sound like "soccer") were formalized in Britain in 1863. Thus, the sport is about 150 years old. Some years before Christ made that long, last trip up to Jerusalem, the *teotlachtli* teams in Mali's home area were already executing their high holy leaps and spiritual rebounds. Sacred the game is, re-enacting nothing less than that ancient play off against the gods. Yet its attending bureaucracy is shot through with strongly secular management notions. Teotlachtli, like soccer, requires some thoroughly unholy training methods. For example: in the 16th century a Castilian eyewitness reported a practice session in which just two players managed to keep the ball airborne for over an hour—using hips and elbows alone. Such skills cannot be picked up through a study of theology. They must be practiced daily from an early age. Training is best accomplished by means of a widespread system of amateur teams and neighborhood pickup teams—and the younger they start, the better. In the times of which we speak, these youthful groups are closely watched and encouraged. Painalla offers no official little league organization, but everyone keeps an eye on the "sandlot" players.

Mali's group, though, must practice away from prying eyes. Their field is not really a great distance from town, yet far enough to the north of the winding sea inlet and heavily trafficked port road.

Just beyond the last ridge separating Painalla's croplands from salt marsh, down among the strangler fig, gumbo-limbo, and giant ficus trees, the remains of an ancient prayer center lie hidden in shadow. Only a few howler monkeys visit the place, and sometimes a flock of scarlet macaws screech over the old ball court at sunset. The beautifully carved dates and legends, executed lovingly in limestone and plaster (by state-endowed artists) have long since worn away. The slanted walls of the court still stand, though somewhat cracked and sprouting weeds here and there. The breaks often cause highly erratic rebounds and irritating interruptions of play. Most sandlot athletes, however, are used to less-than-perfect field conditions and take them in stride.

At the north end of each wall are the remains of a pair of stairways leading up to the seats. Mali stands by the west balustrade bouncing the ball, concentrating, getting in the mood. In front of her, where the center line hits the west wall, the worn out head of old Pitzal stares across the court. His nose forms a circle just big enough for the ball to pass through. This is the "winner-take-all" goal, a difficult shot, rarely executed. Pitzal, or what's left of him, is a great bald fellow with huge ears, a heavy mouth, and what appears to be two, long curly hairs sprouting from a bare and unwrinkled forehead. As with any good referee, those stern eyes betray no trace of emotion. His thickish lips are open. "Pitzal! Pitzal!" he cries. "Play ball! Play ball!"

"Let's go, Let's go," yells the South protector. Mali initiates from the Twins marker. The return is short and much too high. Mali's forward easily slithers past the South guard, gets under the vertical drop, and whacks the thing into the end zone. Mali is furious. The point belongs to North, but she doesn't care about the score. Who wants to watch the antics of an incompetent guard? Is he planted like some old willow? In a flash, she sees right to the heart of the problem. It is indeed, his feet. Both are locked solidly to the ground, weight divided evenly between them. Such positioning makes the fast pivot impossible. Well, no great problem of the soul here, only a technical glitch.

"Hey, Packstrap II," comes a jeering cry from the end zone.

"O really? Was it me butted that thing halfway to Venus?"

Mali walks to the center line. "Toss it here," she yells to the goal protector. When the ball arrives, she lowers her voice. These remarks are for young Screaming Bird only.

Birdie hangs his head to one side. It is beginning to drizzle again. The boy can feel the light drops on the back of his neck, but at least it is not cold anymore. At least the air is quite warm and still in the forest clearing. Mali bounces the ball a few times and then holds it waist high. Birdie looks up at last. There are tears in his eyes.

Mali takes his face in her hands. "O Screaming Bird. O great bird of the field of play. There you can be seen taking in all the field of play with but a single glance—all fakery foreseen, all trickery noted, strategy, both offensive and defensive an open book. In other words, nothing happening holds any mystery, observing as you do, all the field as a oneness, a unified singularity."

Mali has moved closer and is stroking Bird's arms from shoulder to wrist. "Listen Bird. This is a rare talent, but not one you can brag about. Don't worry, they'll find out soon enough."

"This business? That which only just occurred? Forget it. One day's practice will straighten you out. You see, it is necessary for the guard always to keep his weight on just one foot for the fast pivot. With such agility, no one, but no one, will ever get past you again. To this I will swear."

"Screaming Bird, my young friend. It is certain this game is the most incredible thing there is, but to do it well is very difficult. It is necessary to do it, to learn the skill very well, to have strict self-discipline, and above all to have love, to feel a great love for the game. You understand me? Yes, I'm certain you do." She kisses him and shoves him gently toward center field.

The other players are crouched around the court sitting quietly on their heels. "Your serve," Mali yells, but when the ball rolls out nobody can move.

"Whew," says the protector Spoonbill to young Egret. "Maybe we should start making a few mistakes ourselves. You know, just once in a while."

Chapter 8

Some Ordinary History—April 29, 1519

"Has not the epoch proved profitably instructive?
Friend, be not disconcerted. Neither the events, nor
any part of the spirit of that time, can ever repeat
themselves. There is, simply put, nothing to be learned
through its contemplation and study."
Pardo Duka II conversation at Riki el Sucio's

About a week after landing, Cortés' entire "army" moved up the coast a few leagues in order to get away from the bugs and to find something to eat. It was here the trouble started.

"Over the gold! Over the gold!" we hear the reader cry. Well, naturally over the gold, but the usual motivations, greed, envy, jealousy, were, oddly enough, but a minor part of the mix. The partisans of Velazquez, led by De Leon, Diego de Ordaz, and Montejo began complaining loudly and openly that it was time to head home.

"You have no authority to establish a colony here," yelled Montejo, "and besides, our little army wouldn't stand a chance. We'll all be sacrificed, and our arms and legs thrown into the stew pot."

"Oh well," sighed Cortés. "Death is the fate of war, as we all know, and it's nobody's fault but our own if we can't get along swimmingly in this very plentiful land. On the other hand, far be it from me to stand in the way of a majority vote."

"Looked at in another light," Cortés added mildly, "perhaps I am indeed duty bound to return." On hearing this, his supporters staged a tantrum equal to that of the Velazquez bunch. Crowding around, they demanded he accept command of all those who wished to serve God and Majesty here in the new land.

"Well, all right, all right, if that's what you really want," answered Cortés with a shrug.

Plans to lay out a town square were soon under discussion. "We're going to need at least two gallows," announced the captain. "One at the center of the plaza, another some little distance out of town."

At this, the faction of Velazquez turned ugly, enraged beyond all measure.

"Well," said Cortés, sitting calmly on an upturned box eating a chicken leg and a day-old tortilla, "nothing is further from my desire than to exceed instructions. So if the army wants to go, let's go. Start getting it together and we'll leave—tomorrow if you want."

Cortés glanced down at the old tortilla. *These things wouldn't be so bad if made daily and served hot,* he thought.*

As the captain stood to speak, his tortilla abandoned itself to the sands of the New World, but the chicken leg he shook and waved in order to emphasize important points.

"Oh my dear friends and brothers," he began, the hunk of poultry extended so as to include all present. "I hereby resign my position as captain general of this expedition. I'm just a civilian now. Anybody wants to go home, just take a ship or two and head out. Anybody wants to form a colony here, you've got my blessing. Puertocarrero and Montejo should take on the job of alcaldes (mayors)." The former you will recall, was Cortés' fast friend and *paisano*. The latter, a tried and true Velazquez loyalist, was recommended for that very reason, as smart a stroke of policy as any Fernando II ever came up with. The *regidores, alguacil,* treasurer, and other officials were appointed, and before a single wall was erected, that finest of port cities here on the east coast of North America was named Villa Rica de la Vera Cruz.

This speech, delivered in the very mildest of tones, was terminated with an action we can interpret as a touch of temper. Cortés reared back and flung the half-eaten chicken leg over the heads of the crowd. Every dog in camp immediately made a rush toward the bushes, and for a couple of minutes the ensuing growls, yips, and snarls served to drown out all human conversation.

The next day, Cortés presented himself, cap in hand, to the new council. "Look here," they told him. "There really isn't anybody else qualified to

---

* A culinary notion still apt from Comitan to Truth or Consequences to Round Rock—outside of which triangular boundary no one really cares.

run this outfit, so we hereby appoint you captain general and chief justice of this colony. Put your hat back on."

Years later, when Narváez sued Cortés for usurpation of authority, assault and battery, and the loss of an eyeball, he swore in deposition that Cortés was possessed by the devil. By no other means could he have persuaded a Velazquez loyalist like Montejo to switch sides. The events described above occurred with a kind of staggering rapidity, taking everybody by surprise, especially the Velazquez party. They broke into the wildest shouts and invectives, denouncing the proceedings as a planned conspiracy against the governor. Both sides grabbed pieces of the driftwood scattered along the beach (no one really wanted to draw a sword) and charged each other across the sands. The wood, however, was so old and rotted that most of it broke just from the force of the backswing, chunks flying in every direction. When somebody actually connected, the piece merely shattered into powder, doing little damage.

"Wish I hadn't ditched that chicken leg," said Cortés to himself, once more seated on the upturned box.

Just as the melée reached its peak, Alvarado's foraging party emerged.

"Now," said an American historian, "the cravings of the stomach, that great laboratory of disaffection, were about to be appeased."

The rival factions dropped their weapons, embraced, and cried in each other's beards. Peace was restored, and all felt themselves to be brothers-in-arms once more. Nuzi Duka, who had been standing behind the captain, smiled with the sort of cold-eyed look ha'pence writers are fond of describing (he smiled with his lips only). Then he retired to the tent. Marina's eyes, equally blank, followed him every step of the way.

Next, the army occupied itself in cutting building materials and mapping out the site where one day would stand the busy New World port of Veracruz—that glistening tropical metropolis; home of the orchid and the prawn prepared to perfection's peak; and the land of matchless chipotle, coconut ice cream, harpists, and guitarists strolling beneath white-washed arcades while senior citizens vigorously cumbia away across a spotless concrete plaza.

Chapter 9

The Ambassadors

"Thereupon, before them the captives were slain; they cut open the captive's breasts; with their blood they sprinkled the messengers. For this reason did they do so, that they had gone to very perilous places."
Mexica historian

On the morning of May 7, 1519, Moteuczoma's ambassadors leave Cortés' ships and head back across those mountains looming to the west. In the grip of a mild panic, they move rapidly along the road to Tenochtitlan. The Tlatoani's parting warnings still ring in Noble Manner's ears. "Nothing but fearful news on both ends," he shivers.

"And if they eat this food," said the Tlatoani, "truly, he will be the one we are waiting for, Feathered Serpent. And should he wish to eat human flesh and eat you, so much the better. Don't worry about a thing. I personally will take charge of your house, wife, and sons—never doubt it. And should they eat Dung Hauler, well, that is what we bought him for, as the slave he is." And, as an afterthought, "Better take a couple of extra slaves along in case they should ask for blood to drink. Remember, a Mexican is always prepared." Such pleasant words to ponder along the road home.

At Xicalanco, the messengers are greeted by an obsequious official.

"Gentlemen, gentlemen," that worthy says. "You look exhausted, worn out, even a bit weary. Wouldn't it be best if you rested here awhile before continuing your journey?"

The ambassadors nervously decline the offered hospitality and stay only long enough for a cool drink. At Tecpantlayacac, the posthouse director addresses them with a deep bow. "O noble lords. You are tired from your journey. You have suffered fatigue. You have endured weariness. Rest here for the night, and tomorrow you can travel on much refreshed."

"No time," Lord Holynose answers. "But we could use a bite to eat."

Only sardines are available that particular day—a great load of crispy sardines, grilled whole, guts and all, and tortillas, of course.

Not very appetizing, you pronounce in righteous tones, tinged with disgust. Wrong, reader. The crunchy little tidbits are not only delicious but loaded with life-giving minerals and a benevolent variety of fatty substance.

Now it is close to sundown, and the convoy has halted in the tall prairie grass just below the range we know as East Mother Mountains. Mosquitoes rise in great clouds on the lookout for an evening meal. The chief bearer slaps at his neck and gazes longingly toward the blue hills looming in front. Up there lies Xalapa—cool refreshing breezes, some real food, and a good night's sleep beneath a roof. "What in Cihuacoatl's creation is holding things up now?" he mumbles.

The chief bearer and guide, up at the head of the line, is unable to see that which is occurring behind him. Here's what's going on, and it's not a pretty sight.

Lord Drygod of Tepoztlan squats on the path, his robes trailing in the dust. "Now we shall surely die," he vociferously wails. "Lord Moteuczoma will chop off our arms and use them to beat us about the head and shoulders. He will skewer our eyeballs and grill them with the evening hors d'oeuvres. Of our skins he will make a drum for the whores to beat up and down the avenue."

Drygod, still loudly crying to the heavens, grabs huge fistfuls of dust to heap on his head. Or anyway, so it appears. Actually his hands are quite empty. Anxious not to soil his clothing, Drygod only goes through those motions indicating self-deprecation.

Lord Noble Manner is incensed. In tones haughty enough to freeze the fiddles of hell, he addresses, he berates, his colleague whining there on the dusty path. It should be noted that for all Mexica nobility, snobbery is second nature. It's part of their training. "This unseemly, pitiful, and piquish display can no longer be endured. Such a frenzied and disorderly state of emotion! Unconscionable! It must be controlled instantaneously. It is wicked, wicked."

"And that's the least of it," pipes up Lord Holynose, "How dare you clothe the Cortés in Smoking Mirror's garb, that dissolute sorcerer, that half-naked trickster with his overpriced chilies, forever challenging Quetzalcoatl, I mean the Priestly Lord of Ways."

"No, wait! Wait!" cries Drygod. "The dress lay in four piles upon the deck. Is that not right? Is that not perfectly correct? I selected the feathered headpiece with stars of gold, the golden earplugs, the necklace of seashells, the breast ornament decorated with small seashells, with a fringe sewn on them—"

"Not correct. Not correct. Absolutely wrong! What about the mask of turquoise mosaic, the quetzal feather headfan, the neckband of green? I mean the plaited green stone neckband in the midst of which is the golden disk."

Still whining, Drygod continues, "and a sleeveless jacket all painted with a design, with eyelets on its border, and a feathered fringe, and still another thing—."

"Tlaviscalpan in muchioaz," interrupts Lord Noble Manner. "Let us no longer contend one against another," he announces, sounding slightly confused and a little less haughty. "That which lies hidden from the Tlatoani's understanding can do him no damage, nor ourselves, nor our descendants. Let's move this spectacle up the trail before someone starts spreading rumors. May the Lord of Ways forbid they reach the city ahead of us."

While this is going on, Moteuczoma enjoys no food. He also endures a bad case of insomnia, being unable to stop thinking about something his spies have told him. It was mentioned only in passing, but the Tlatoani can't get it out of his mind: the dogs—giant Spanish dogs with fiery yellow eyes and great dragging jowls—and how they went around panting nervously with tongues hanging out.

"What will now befall us?" groans Moteuczoma. " Who will lead the nation? Up to now, it was me, but lately my heart suffers greatly, as if it were washed in chili water, it burns, it smarts."

"Now, listen carefully. No matter what hour the ambassadors arrive, even if I sleepeth, which is unlikely, give me a call. But I won't see them here. This place is a wreck—and illegal for human sacrifice. Pull a couple of those thieving stewards out of the cages, chalk 'em up, and take them over to the Coacalli. First, we'll have a little ceremony, and then I'll interview the ambassadors over there."

The convoy arrives at the east shore of Lake Texcoco about three hours before dawn. Noble Manner dismisses the bearers and sends them around the long way to the western causeway, the Watertown bridges. Then he wakes up a Texcocan boat crew for the thirteen-mile paddle across to the capitol.

As fate would have it, the Tepetzinco dike entry is locked tight, the keeper being off on a toot at Watertown pierhead. (As a disabled veteran, he is entitled to all the pulque he can hold.) Of course, the dogs on the wall around the gate are easily audible, but this night they have all gone hunting down at Iztahuacan Island. So there sit the downcast passengers and crew in the city boat, within spitting distance of the basin, cursing the Port Authority and all its ancestors. Well, clearly, when it comes to journeys via water, the last mile will always be most difficult, hard of heart, vindictive, and relentlessly sans mercy. "So it befalls us here on the earth," as the Nahua has it.

With much cursing and moaning, the ten exhausted men manage to haul the large canoe over the dike and into the basin for the last mile home. Mexica nobility, unlike their European counterparts, are not adverse to a bit of physical labor. In fact, they take pride in it. "Learn a trade, young man," instruct the fathers. Plumbing is popular, metalwork or stone carving for those who show a little talent. "You never know when it'll be necessary to go back to the old life," say the fathers.

While scurrying around the southeast corner of the temple of Quetzalcoatl, our travel-weary nobles collide smartly with a squad of Shorn Guard led by Sir Yellow Sweet Potato. As the Tlatoani had ordered, Sir YSP is escorting a couple of heavily chalked prisoners over to the Coacalli for the brief ceremony. Both victims have been carefully sedated and appear completely undismayed. (No indications of anxiety, sweaty brow, nervous tremor, etc. are visible. Now perhaps we can finally put to rest those ugly rumors about the sadistic glee with which the executive technicians are wont to approach their work.)

Lord Noble Manner, Moteuczoma's chief ambassador to the Spaniards and highest-ranking officer present, extracts himself from the chalk cloud and staggers over to take a seat on the bridge rail leading to the zoo.

Sir YSP bows, touches his fingers to the ground and to his mouth in the traditional earth-eating gesture and then snaps to attention. "O Lord Noble Manner, he of excellent repute and faultless ancestry. The perception of your countenance, the safe return of your face, now gladdens the city and brings happiness to all citizens. From our lord the Tlatoani Moteuczoma, joyous greetings and a special message—or maybe instruction puts it more neatly."

"O yes. I've no doubt," Noble Manner manages to choke out.

"Well, to start with, you seem to be heading in the wrong direction," continues YSP. "'I shall not hear it here,' meaning the palace, says the Tlatoani, 'but over at the Coacalli. For there is a place designated as Temalacatl, appropriate for sacrificial ceremony. There let them go. I will join them there.'" Sir YSP takes the two grinning and white-faced offerings by a sort of bridle attached to their wrists and heads the group back around the corner of the temple. "As we all know," adds Yellow Sweet Potato, "implementation of Holy Death on palace grounds is most definitely illegal."

The ambassadors seem quite subdued. Drygod especially appears downcast and jittery. Three times he tries to speak up but is hushed repeatedly by Noble Manner. Finally, he manages to register his complaint.

"Yes, yes," answers Noble Manner, "this is not something a man worries about. My sister worked for a long time in the royal laundry and understands perfectly the methods utilized for removing bloodstains from fine cotton. She knows all the tricks. Now drop the subject, for heaven's sake."

"I hope so," answers Drygod. "Because it's obvious to me we're going to get quite a liberal splattering. Road dust is one thing, but blood? And, of course, I wore my best mantle to greet the Castilian gods."

Gods? Gods? thinks the chief ambassador. *Some gods. If Great Lord of Ways Quetzalcoatl carried an odor anything like those Castilians, it's no wonder he got himself booted out of Tollan.*

After the ceremony, the hearts removed, the bodies dragged out for dismemberment, Moteuczoma, to the surprise of everyone present, gets up from his throne and begins pacing the floor. All the while, he moans softly, "They're gods, they're not gods, they're dark haired, they're blond, they're white, they're black, they're—"

"The black, kinky-haired ones, the people call 'dirty gods,' dear little ruler."

Moteuczoma stands up straight like the warrior he once was. "Don't 'dear little ruler' me, you useless, two-eyed chunk of excrement." The ambassadors, servants, and attendants are wide-eyed with shock. The very hall itself, walls and plaster, ceiling beams and all, seem to slip into a profound coma. Never in memory has our dignified and trimly goateed little Tlatoani expressed himself in such thoroughly common terms. Understandably, the cosmos is temporarily silenced.

Noble Manner attempts to calm the frightened ruler with some soothing half truths. "It is indeed correct to say that the Castilians are good fighters, and yet they are also cowardly. How they cringe at the sight of human blood. To a Spaniard, the smell of blood is intolerable. It makes him sick. It causes him to empty the contents of his stomach all over the place. He understands nothing of the holy meaning of that sacred liquor. Thus, we see those Castilians are only barbarians, inferior in every way." Lord Noble Manner holds up a hand and counts off his fingers, "Paucity of character, lack of honor, theological ignorance—together these traits present an open portal by which ..." The ambassador stops short and then hangs his head with a sigh. Quite obviously, Moteuczoma's attention is elsewhere. In fact, he hears nothing. Nothing at all. Noble Manner's words are wasted.

Now the Tlatoani's face takes on a sly expression, a grinning, crafty look. "Wait a minute, wait a minute," he says. "Didn't your mother used to work in the laundry? Right over there. At the palace!"

The chief executive of all Anáhuac winces noticeably, suddenly aware of his own faux pas. He clutches his head and looks out at the stars. He begins to spout a few tears. *This may be the night,* he thinks. *If ever Our Father the Sun is to be beaten by those flashy warriors of the darkened sky— this may very well be the night.* "Oh, who can save me now?" he mutters. "Where, oh, where can I hide myself now?"

"Noble, Noble. Listen, my sweet little brother, please forgive me. By what right do I address thee in such lowbrow terms, in such crude tones? Absolve me! Absolve me for the sake of ... why some of my best friends have worked in service here. Minister Tlacotzin himself loves to dig in the garden, doesn't he? And his hands get plenty dirty, too. Certainly we've all seen that. Nor is he always so quick to cleanse them, often sitting down to dinner unwashed. And I—do I not keep a zoo and feed the animals myself? And, O yes, only last month I moved the bees over into a shady spot near the avocado grove. By myself. No help whatsoever. Those hives, are they so very light? Are they perchance weightless?"

Noble Manner bows deeply, hands upraised, as if to say, "It is forgotten my ruler. 'Tis of no import."

Moteuczoma, eyes tightly closed, plops back down in his chair but quickly straightens up. The Tlatoani does *not* slouch on the throne. "Noble, Noble. We go back a long way, you and I," he announces abruptly. "So your ancestral home lies on the wrong side of the canal. O well, so what. How do they call that place? Weavertown? Yes? Am I right?"

These nervous, heavy-handed, and grossly sarcastic remarks he wants to pass off as humor, though gods and mortals alike know broad comedy is not the ruler's strong suit. This is not to say the Tlatoani is a humorless man. He often gets off a good one—though his gags are usually a bit too subtle for general comprehension. In fact, Moteuczoma Xocoyotl is the most intelligent speaker ever to grace the Seat of Tenochtitlan. He is, unfortunately, a rather poor leader of men. Trapped in the stickiest web of all—superstition—he passes his time with the temple priests in the study of "magic." A good course in realpolitik, perhaps under the supervision of Coyote Fasting at Texcoco, would have proven more useful. Moteuczoma's obsession with the supernatural, say our 21st century psychologists, will lead to the breakdown of his personality and the fall of Mexico.

Noble Manner has a really special souvenir for the Tlatoani, presented by an interesting young lady onboard the sail-house down at Hummingbird Beach. Noble snaps his fingers, and a servant hands him a dark wooden box bound with metal braces. In the flickering light of oil lamps, the brass gleams golden. Moteuczoma frowns deeply, his irises widen and shimmer in black shadow. His teeth also glow blackly, though perhaps it's only the remains of a chocolate pudding snack eaten just before leaving the palace.

"Ah … dear ruler, it is a thing used by the brown-robed priests. An ordinary enough rite," explains Noble, "yet never failing in its power of transubstantiation."

The box rests lightly on the ruler's knees. He makes no move to open it.

"Transubstantiation? Ah, shape-shifting," breathes the wide-eyed Tlatoani. Then smoothly, evenly, like sand flowing past the crimp in an hourglass, his expression slides from awe to deep puzzlement. "And this … transubstantiation unto …?"

"Well, my Lord, when the priest eats one of the little cakes within the box …"

The Tlatoani's eyes roll in his head. "There are little cakes inside this box? Are they any good?"

"Er, uh, I have no idea sir—never having had the honor of consuming or even nibbling at one," he adds with some irony.

"O of course not. Very wise, Noble. Most perspicacious, circumspect, and discrete on your part. After all, why take unnecessary risks? But … how, who, or what is transfigured?"

"I was getting to that, most reverend speaker. When the Castilian priest takes a bite of the little cake, he is changed, he is transformed, verily he becomes the Mother of God herself and appears thus before the worshippers."

The speaker smiles gently and then heaves a sigh. "O these false priests. I suppose such types are to be found in every part of creation. They should be reminded that in me they deal with a scholar and theologian of some renown. Our beloved Ciahuacoatl is she who gives birth to the gods, to the holy blade, to Mexico itself. No doubt these Castilians descend from our Lord of Ways, yet their beliefs are much perverted." *On the other hand, they've been away so long ... perhaps we're the ones who got it twisted somewhere along the way. Such a horrible thought.* "Well, go on, Noble. Surely they do not call her name in that ceremony."

"O no, my lord," Noble Manner forces the words past an incipient yawn. "Her name bears no relation to our own dear mother. They call her Mari, and she occupies a position somewhat inferior to her son."

"What? Eh! Feh!" barks the Tlatoani.

"The child of Mari is the true God ... or so they all claim." Noble is tired enough to weep. "What more can I say? Ah, yes. Immediately upon appearing before the worshippers, she removes her robe to the waist and shows her breasts to the son. Once he has seen her bosom, the god can deny her nothing. All the people then beg Mari to intercede and ask God to forgive their sins and, having seen her breasts, he cannot deny the request. The whole business is, indeed, a little strange."

"The whole business is evil and perverse," exclaims the Tlatoani, his little goatee nearly standing on end. Moteuczoma can't take his eyes off the little box. Noble's story is incomprehensible. It passes all understanding. Notions so outrageous in nature, by their very existence, must contain more than a grain of power.

Chapter 10

An Education in Cempoal—May 20, 1519

In a flood
of family's living blood
"Black havoc wading
to the chilly reckoning at last
of that gory dishful of children."
The Agamemnon

Duka spends some time writing out Cortés' new orders. They have been issued in the most adamant terms. While on the march, no officer or enlisted man is to indulge in any sort of behavior that the locals might consider hostile or even mildly impolite. Still, the move up into Cempoal does not go smoothly. The troops are feeling isolated and edgy. Morale is not so good.

There is, for example, Sgt. Villanueva's dangerous little tiff with his superior officer, Capt. Pedro de Alvarado. Its cause remains a bit hazy, but, as in any army, rumor is a chief source of entertainment, and here we have a really lively one. Supposedly old daddy Alvarado had once graciously offered to pay the Villanueva family sheep tax—only to learn the government's bill covered some of his own animals as well. Apparently, the Villanuevas, don A.'s share-tenants, had been engaged in a bit of rustling in the master's pastures. All this, it is said, took place a few generations back. Of course, we are dealing here with Spaniards of the rural persuasion, among whom such insults (whether actually delivered or not) are never forgotten.

Unfortunately, there exists but a single document referring to the altercation occurring there on the trail to Cempoal, but the thing is quoted by scholars everywhere, so who are we to question its authenticity? An anonymous ranker reports tuning in on the conflict at its height:

"My father? My father?" rages Villanueva. "Your mother! Listen blondie, throw that damn badge away and we'll get to it. Just climb off that nag. *Merde!* What is it the locals call you around here? Tonatiuh? The sun. Son of a bitch is more appropriate."

In a motion almost too fast for the eye to follow, Alvarado lifts his lance and lets fly at Villanuevas's chest. Fortunately, the blade slides off a shoulder strap of the heavy leather cuirass the sergeant wears. Its edge barely slices the upper part of an arm. At first glance, the wound seems superficial, but later it grows infected and never heals properly.

Captain Don Pedro de Alvarado: golden-haired good looks, guile, charm, ruthlessness. He serves beneath the motto, "When in doubt run it through." Cortés chooses Captain Pepe as the army's second-in-command, but that officer's strategic abilities play no part in the decision. They are practically nonexistent. He is singled out for pretty much the same reason G. A. Custer was put in charge of the Seventh: thoughtless, reckless disregard in the face of danger. Alvarado seems to care little for his own life and still less for that of his soldiers. As a front line officer, he is perhaps a little demented, but Cortés believes he will need such fanatics in the coming struggle.

More trouble on the trail. A trooper called de Mora returns with a couple of chickens he has "liberated" from the backyard of a small homestead. Cortés, on hearing of it, grows thoroughly incensed at this impolitic outrage committed in a peaceable country. Wild-eyed, he stares around the fields in search of a tree from which to hang de Mora. Quickly the soldier is strung up from the main branch of a large ceiba. When Cortés turns away, Captain de Alvarado straight away draws his sword and cuts the poor fellow down—in time to save his life. It can't be doubted that Cortés never really intended this trooper's execution. He can hardly afford to lose competent cavalrymen. According to the latest estimates, Moteuczoma and his allies command odds at about fifty to one. (Sad to say, de Mora was later killed in action—fighting for possession of a rock in Guatemala.)

Cortés steps out of a rock-walled nightmare in Quiahuastlan. He emerges with a hand covering mouth and nose. The nerves of his back and shoulders, once irritated by a severe attack of Estremaduran prickly heat, begin to burn and itch as though reliving that summer afternoon so many years past. No one can make out his expression. "Get Father Olmedo over here," Cortés shouts in a choked voice.

Somebody hands Olmedo a torch, and he steps in.

Cortés stands next to the door. "It ... it was too dark. I couldn't really—"

"Seventeen, Captain; I make it seventeen."

"You're a truly brave man, Father," says Cortés.

Inside that stone-lined room, the corpses (really just the trunks) of seventeen little bodies are laid out along a wall. All are torn from sternum to naval and the limbs cut off. Hearts and intestines have been pulled out and piled in a concave stone basin that sits atop a large altar carved from a single rock. The childish corpses have been stashed behind the long altar and so are not immediately in view when the door is opened.

"No doubt we'll find those arms and legs hanging in the city meat market." Cortés, who rarely shows emotion when the troops are around, now buries his face in his hands.

Nuzi Duka sits apart on the low stone wall across the courtyard. He is both puzzled and disturbed. *Nothing really new here,* he thinks. *Perhaps this business represents the degradation of a noble idea. No, it seems to me our problem with these murders is aesthetic, not moral. Not at all moral.*

The army is too depressed to eat its dinner. Cortés walks around trying to cheer everybody up. "Hey, Fonseca," he yells. "Hey, supply! Break out a couple of kegs, will you? There's too much drinking of water going on over here. Somebody's liable to get sick." *Morale is getting to be a big problem,* thinks Cortés, looking about for his supply sergeant. *Up spirits then. Spirits up, I say. Maybe I'll borrow a leaf from Caesar's book. Work out a couple of routines like the radish bit—the one where he makes that speech all the while gesticulating obscenely with a radish. What that man could do with a radish would make the dead laugh ... or anyway, so says what's-his-name.*

On the trail the next morning, a bleary-eyed Cortés is barely aware of his surroundings. *This place,* he thinks, *these people, are making of me something I never was—an alcoholic.* A facetious thought, the Captain knows. The fact is, this place and these people are making of him a believer—truly something he never was.

Around a turn, cut by a boulder-lined brook, the army is met by a large group of warriors in full regalia. So full, indeed, they seem overdressed. The gold pendant each wears attached beneath the lower lip certainly goes a touch too far.

In the midst of the company, draped in an extravagantly feathered cloak and embroidered sashes, a fat man in an open palanquin nearly

bends double the carrying poles of his conveyance. The chief of Cempoal
rarely ventures far from town. He is too much weight for the servants—or
his own legs.

Cortés calls for Marina, and fortunately the "Fat Chief" (as the
Spaniards dub him) is facile in Nahuatl, perhaps overly so. Marina and
the captain can barely get a word in edgewise. The chief is anxious to begin
his tirade of well-catalogued complaints, so introductions have been greatly
abridged. The big man rattles on and on, all the way into Cempoal City.
The litter bearers suffer most of all, tripping and stumbling over roots and
rocks as their enormous boss bounces around, gesticulating expressively
on his precarious seat.

"O that Moteuczoma," he moans, "O those Mexicans. They are born
rotten, I tell you. From the moment they slice their way out of their
mother's womb, they are destined to be evil. I mean really, really bad. Did
you know they dice up somebody's penis and eat it wrapped in a tortilla?
Just as though it were normal food like … like dog's head. Did you know
that Moteuczoma himself skewers someone's eyeballs and serves them up
as hors d'oeuvres at state banquets? Raw! Quite raw! This dish is placed
uncooked upon the table!"

Marina has been doing her best to get all this across. Now a grim smile
distorts the lips of Cortés. Yes, his hunch is right. This land is more deeply
divided than he had imagined.

Fat Chief continues his harangue. "All right, then. Down to business.
As descendants of the original caretakers of this place, surely you have
been, more or less, keeping up with current events around here. You know
that Moteuczoma's armies have only recently conquered us here in the
Totonac region and that their tribute requirements surpass all reasonable
demands."

Now the chief's voice begins to crack, and tears pour down his cheeks.
"Children," he cries, "They want our little children, our innocent babes.
They want to carry the kids up to Tenochtitlan for sacrifice. It's unbearable,
unbearable. And … and did you know that up there," he sobs wrenchingly,
"in the month of Teotl Eco, they throw people in a fire and pull 'em out
with hooks while still alive. Only then do they permit the blessed honor
of holy sacrifice … gahh, wahh."

Cortés remains silent. He understands perfectly the uses of hypocrisy
and knows better than to rail against it.

Comfortably ensconced in the cool gloom of Fat Chief's front parlor,
Cortés makes a short speech. "My friend," he says, "we can only repay your

gracious hospitality with good works. Soon we will take such measures that will relieve you of the terrible tyranny of which you speak and of which you now endure."

Soon a couple of the chief's servants bring in the chocolate. The bowls are exceptionally large, but Totonaca is the very heart of cacao bean country, so there is no need to stint. Later, in the highlands, portions will be smaller, niggardly, in fact. Cortés has become a connoisseur of the whipped refreshment and digs in with a will. Before he can get it to his mouth, a tremendous racket breaks out in the front yard, and a servant comes bursting through the door.

Marina can't follow the Totonac. Cortés, swallowed in a wave of helplessness, sees the chief try to rise only to fall over backward, his pudding splashing across the stucco floor.

"It's Mexicans," Marina groans, the harsh sound squeezed out of some deep pocket of fear. But then she holds up a hand, her features startled into sudden relaxation. "Ah, ah," Marina breathes, "so what's to worry about? There are but a very few of them." Now she turns to Cortés. She holds his gaze, eyes aglow with relief.

"Tribute collectors, I think."

Outside a line of five gentlemen pass through the courtyard in great state, looking neither right or left, nor deigning to cast a glance at the Spanish troopers hanging about. Each holds a bouquet of flowers, which he delicately sniffs from time to time. Mexica lords always seem to carry flowers or perfume in the presence of Spaniards, a strong yet subtle comment regarding the personal hygiene of conquistadors. Each lord is attended by a servant with a fan and some sort of hooked stick with attached cord. The purpose of the latter instrument has never been determined. Maybe a backscratcher?

Slowly Cortés comes to life once more. The elixir, which sets his pulse to pounding again, sends his heart rate soaring and wears away every trace of depression. It's better than any pharmacist has in stock. Inspiration is its name—and its essence can't be found on any drugstore shelf.

The roots of inspiration rather, are slippery, eel-like, hard to grab hold of. It requires the impulse to some creative action, and here in Cempoal, the first steps are taken. Here begins the fall of Mexico-Tenochtitlan. For Cortés, the pieces come together and, in Nahuatl style, now the plan is formed. Now it comes to life.

"Twenty men, women, and children," demand the Mexicans. "Twenty hearts. That's the price for entertaining Spaniards without permission. Of course, there are a number of far more severe punishments that might be inflicted under the ruler's authority, but the sacrifices ordered will suffice for now. Clear enough?"

"Oh yes, very clear. When it comes to issuing orders, couldn't have done a better job myself," says Cortés to Marina, who is doing the translating as usual. The captain picks up one foot and stamps firmly, trying to shake off a blob of chocolate stuck to his instep. Chocolate. Diaz and Alvarado wonder what he sees in that stuff. "Listen, gents," Cortés draws close. "We've got to put those Mexicans under wraps, and quickly."

"Oho, nothing to it, Captain," whispers Alvarado. "You want 'em dead? Or only in irons?" Diaz feels his stomach turn. He's never yet shrunk from a brawl, but is this the place for it?

"No, no. Listen. You've got to get fatty there to make the arrest himself. This is of extreme importance. As for me, I'll be stationed right here just inside the door. Go, go. Leave me out of it for now. Explanations later."

Alvarado outlines the plan to Fat Cacique. Pedro announces with his usual cheerful firmness, a tone that is never mistaken for less than deadly serious. "We deem it proper that you and your warriors seize these Mexican officers and hold them until Lord M. can be informed of the terrible tyrannies they commit on his subjects."

The chief and his lieutenants receive the order with some trepidation. In fact, the proposal terrifies them out of their wits. They back up a few feet, eyes popping, with complexions paler than most Totonacs ever achieve. Alvarado, however, is not to be deterred. He insists the Mexicans be seized and fastened in the usual manner: wooden yokes or collars tied together so that the prisoners can't twitch a limb. In a jiffy, the job is done, and they are led away.

Diaz looks around with some trepidation. He thinks these officers are slightly over the top, tactically incorrect and dangerously so. The crowd in the courtyard is going crazy. The chiefs who, a couple of minutes ago, couldn't look those Mexicans in the eye, are now wild to sacrifice them.

"Right on the money," says Cortés. He comes rushing out from the chief's house joined by Montejo, Ávila, and old Herredia, a Biscayan musketeer with a fearfully scarred face and one glaring eye. Herredia squeezes off, the musket crashes, and the crowd in the plaza grows as quiet as a pole-axed donkey.

"These Mexicans are my responsibility," announces Captain Cortés into the silence pervading the plaza. "They'll be put under a guard of our soldiers and well protected until we can get to the bottom of the whole business."

Fat Chief glances around, a wonderfully puzzled expression decorating his features. "We were not hatched yesterday, you know. It was you who encouraged us to take these officers into custody."

"Not me," answers Cortés. "I was nowhere in the vicinity. The whole thing was accomplished without my authority. I can tell you this. Here in the presence of the royal notary, Diego de Godoy, it is declared that Totonac and Spaniard are brothers and allies. What's more, you are all free of the vexatious demands of Moteuczoma and his agents from this time forward and forever, by order of His Most Royal Majesty King Charles of Castile and Aragon." Marina finishes her translation and the crowd roars, or anyway, the Nahuatl speakers heartily approve.

At midnight that same day, Cortés, wearing a look of angelic innocence, questions the Mexican prisoners as to their land of origin, their leader's name, and why they are kept prisoner.

"I can't tell you how sorry I am about all this. Now you will be released to return home. Here's some refreshment for the road. Please tell your king how much we all wish to be his friend and servant. Better get going now as fast as possible."

The Mexicans are reasonably suspicious. "Impossible. It will mean certain death to try to pass through this country without escort."

Not so dumb as they look, thinks Cortés. *They got down here all right.* "Marina, tell these gents I'll be glad to provide transportation south as far as Villa Rica. That'll shorten the journey considerably. We'll put them aboard before dawn."

More than a little annoyed at the escape of the prisoners, the fat chief makes a rather strong speech. "Now that you are our everlasting friends and brothers," he tells the Spaniards, "you must remain among us, for we are still in dread of Moteuczoma's vengeance. Here you see some really good-looking girls. You must marry them in order to cement relations, legally and officially. You could do worse," he says, leering at the girls. Then he stomps upon an old pot and swears he will never abandon his gods.

Next morning, Cortés wakes up early and wishes he hadn't. Many of us know that feeling: nothing in the new day holds the smallest value, nothing to pin a hope on. A simple "howdy do" seems more than soul can bear or tongue wrap around. And so, Cortés reaches into his kit, extracts a tiny piece of opium and washes it down with a gargle of sour red wine. In the absence of inspiration, opium must suffice. The product of the poppy, he knows, is a reliable mood changer, and there is no time now for disabling depression. The use of opium Cortés reserves for the gravest of emotional emergencies, and this time the drug's effect is quite unexpected. Slowly his mental state slides out of lethargy and into intense, teeth-grinding irritability. Mood changer, indeed!

He spills himself out of the hammock and onto his feet as though that net of twisted cord were a bed of springs. A good thing he went to sleep fully shod, for no soldier breathes who is capable of fitting on a pair of army boots while seated in a hammock.

Eyes wide, Nuzi sits at his little table, pen in hand. "Oh, good morning, sir."

And now, the spurs. Will he need them? Hardly important, but the image of proud Spanish soldiery must be complete. Cortés looks about impassively. "Pass the word, and quietly mind you, that all are to arm themselves immediately. Then bring me the nearest commander you can locate and my bugler. Now."

Cortés steps across to the door, but Marina stands there before him, holding out a turkey-filled tortilla. Cortés stops dead in his tracks and looks at the girl. His lip curves in some sort of expression, maybe a smile, maybe not. He turns away and heads out into the square. Staring pensively after him, Marina takes a bite out of the taco. "Never eat standing up." Her mother's rule comes back with shocking clarity. "It means you will marry far from home." Gagging a little on the morsel, she looks over and catches Nuzi's eye. He hasn't budged. He sits there holding up that pen as though turned to wood. Carefully, one might say delicately, the girl puts aside her breakfast and follows Cortés out. Obviously, she will be needed at his side.

Chapter 11

The New Wife and the Thorn—May 30, 1519

"Montejo, our agent, was secured to Cortés'
interests by a gift of two thousand crowns."
Army Historian

Come to think of it, the quotation above requires clearer identification, that is to say, a better signature. The term "army historian" is a misnomer. "Expedition historian" would be more accurate, for really, there is no "army" on the mainland of North America. Nor are there more than a very few professional soldiers among the conquistadors. The first thing we note is that the conquerors never call themselves soldiers. In that century, the term is insulting. It implies rootlessness, irresponsibility, greed, and quick poverty. "Footmen" and "horsemen" are often used by the old chroniclers; only much later are these divisions turned into "infantry" and "cavalry." A term from Anglo-American experience seems generally applicable. The men of the conquest are surely "frontiersman." Anyone hanging around in the Indies in early days becomes an "Indian fighter" and a landholder—in the same sense as the men and women who will penetrate our own eastern woods a century later. The reader is therefore forewarned: political terms encountered here may be taken literally, but the military ones need a little salt.

Very well, then. Before the Spaniards leave Cempoal, some of the marriages suggested by the chief actually take place. Fat Chief's niece is baptized *Catalina*. A woman as homely as possible, she is nevertheless received by Cortés in a courteous and affectionate manner. And this is ironic, for his wife in Cuba is also Catalina. Is someone displaying a slightly twisted sense of humor? Can it be Father Olmedo? Or one of the lay brothers in charge of baptism? Remember, the men of this tough little expeditionary force have always felt free to kid the leader along a bit, to play harmless jokes at his expense.

Students may speculate about the naming of Cortés' latest wife, but we … I believe we have the facts.

On the eve of the wedding ceremony, a "civilized" name is not yet chosen for the chief's niece. The ancient Hispano-Christian appellation "Catalina," with its connotations of ladylike behavior, high-class demeanor, and noble blood, will be the one used to complete the sacrament of baptism—but not, as has been hinted, in the style of some absurd and ham-handed army gag. It will be a thoroughly pragmatic choice, inspired by security concerns. Hardly a laugh anywhere in the concept.

Just now wedding plans are the last thing on Cortés' mind. He is thoroughly preoccupied with the problem of getting some letters through to Charles at Valladolid. And it must be done without alerting Velazquez in Cuba. This means navigating up through the Bahama Channel, a feat never yet accomplished, and he is not certain Alaminos is up to the job.

Cortés and Montejo stroll into the courtyard of Cortés' assigned house. They are deep in conversation.

"Listen, Montejo. The letter composed by the men is not to be delivered. It would be a mistake of the gravest sort."

"I see," responds Montejo, "Of course, the men have unanimously agreed that His Majesty must have the truth and all the truth. To deceive them in such a manner …"

Inside the door, the two men walk into a wall of flowers: bougainvillea, lilies, hibiscus, all the tropical blooms. Marina sits in a corner tying them in bundles. She does not raise her eyes. Cortés only glances once in her direction. Possibly Montejo doesn't even spot her, camouflaged back there in her flowered huipil.

"I have written a letter of my own." Cortés goes on, "It covers pretty much the same ground. Of course, it leaves out the matter of the two thousand crowns, but it clearly emphasizes the men's fears of mischief and treachery on the part of Velazquez and his pip-squeak partner in crime, Bishop Burgos."

"Captain, the fact is, Diego Velazquez is officially responsible for this expedition. He is, as you know, tax assessor and collector for the western Indies, and that authority may very well extend to the mainland. Nobody knows exactly what orders Valladolid has charged him with. We're taking a big chance here."

"Maybe you're right. Very well, let's do it this way. Stay clear of the court. Charles may very well be in Flanders anyway, and who knows what kind of characters are hanging around the throne. Look you. Go straight to my father Martín and licenciado Nuñez. Nuñez is also a relative of mine. Both are part of a powerful group of nobles, all of whom despise Burgos. They'll get my letter through if His Majesty is in the heart of China."

When Montejo takes his leave, Cortés falls into deep study. "But can I trust him?" The words are thoughtlessly spoken aloud. "O Captain, that's a good question," says Marina, believing she has been addressed—or anyway, pretending so.

That's the extent of her remark, but it's the first time she addresses Cortés with regard to policy, foreign or domestic. The captain is so surprised he doesn't think to tell her to stick to the flower arrangements, but instead answers instinctively.

"Not important. Puertocarrero will be in charge, and he understands the situation perfectly." Coming to himself, Cortés gives the flowers a little kick. "What's all this?" he growls.

"O it's for the wedding. Father Olmedo asked me to help. He knows you want to leave this … *basurero* [garbage pit] as soon as possible." Still holding his eyes, she speaks of the baptism and the wedding. "Father Olmedo has decided that both ceremonies will be short and sweet. So there will not be the usual overly elaborate … O what's the word … yes … protocols … aha, yes, pro-to-cols. You must, however, choose a Christian name for your Totonac wife."

Cortés, somewhat dumbfounded at this new control of Spanish, only grumbles, "*Merde*, let the Father take care of all that. I've other things to think about. I want no part of any of it."

"Yes, O yes, and so I told him. But then he suggested a name of which I was certain you would not approve and so … let me now be so bold as to recommend the good Spanish lady's name "Catalina." Truly, it is not an affair of mine, but knowing of your great anxiety to leave this place, I take the liberty …"

Cortés turns whiter than the calla lilies piled at his feet. He has probably never been so shocked in his life. "Quite right," he says calmly—but what a sound, colder than Dantes' deepest layer. Marina's face says nothing, but she is more than a little frightened. Have I lost him? She spreads her fingers and looks down at her hands.

"Indeed, it is none of your affair," adds the Captain.

Now he turns toward the open door, and his face, the color of bleached cotton, slowly takes on the shade of morning roses. With a roar like a wounded jaguar, he scoops up a huge armful of flowers and heaves them through the opening into the dust of the courtyard.

"Gah," he screams, still louder, and whirls about clutching his hand. Apparently he has driven a thorn deep into the flesh of his right palm.

Marina rushes over and grabs the hand before Cortés can pull it away. "O goodness, that is deep. Maybe *huisache*, I think, though I picked none of those. It must come out. Quite poisonous, you see. O deep, very deep."

"Leave it be. I'll poke it out with a needle. It's not the first little splinter that's ever stuck me."

"O yes? O yes? and if it breaks? Then you will lose the use of that hand for a long time. At the tip is a little black sack loaded with much poison. If the spine does not come out whole … O how you will suffer. Lie down in hammock please." This time she slips off his boots as he stretches out.

She kneels by the hammock takes his hand in both of hers. "Loosen the hand—must be very loose," Marina whispers softly. "First we clean." She begins to lick his palm very slowly, very gently. First, her tongue slides along the length of the thorn. After a while, she begins a kind of sucking motion with both the tongue and inside of the lower lip, near the opening where the thing entered the flesh.

Cortés no longer feels the hammock beneath him.

"Ah, there we have it." She bites into the palm of his hand and with a quick jerk of the head extracts the spine. Marina holds it up to the light. "Look, look," she cries joyfully. "Such a monster. See the black tip? Not huisache. Really, I don't know what."

Lying there, totally relaxed and somewhat dazed, there comes to Cortés' mind a bright picture of his front yard, lawn chair and all. Overhead, the palmero rustles and clacks like maracas while a couple of guitars slowly weep through the forest. Later, much later, Princess Charlotte Hapsburg will hear the tune at a party and burst into tears. She will know it as "La Habañera," but for now, it is nameless.

"Catalina," says Cortés out loud. Marina, on her stool among the flowers, does not look up.

It's not really a bad idea, thinks the Captain. *Confusing. Nicely confusing. This way, if anyone speaks of my wife Catalina, nobody will know which one they mean. What's more, if I should talk in my sleep, Catalina will be flattered. After all, she's bound to show up here someday—if I live, that is.*

"Listen, Marina. What are these things? They look like calla lilies. Get rid of them, will you? In Spain, we use calla lilies only for funerals."

Chapter 12

Prodigal Speaks Low
When He Speaks of "History"—Coahuila, Fall 1540

First, let me, Prodigal, explain something about my position in the military hierarchy at the city of Tenochtitlan. At the time of the Spanish invasion, I had been recently honored with the captaincy of a four hundred-man Heel and Toe company based in my home borough of Matville. Technically, we were part of Sir Fertilizer's eight thousand, but we often operated on TDY (U.S. military term for temporary duty provides the best translation) wherever our particular skills were most required.

The Heel and Toe company is perhaps the oldest military unit in all Anáhuac. It was formed hundreds of years ago when we were desert barbarians fighting as mercenaries for any city requiring our services. At the height of battle, our job was to drop facedown to earth as if stricken, all the while praying that everyone was too busy to notice our very much alive and highly unprotected buttocks. We'd lie there for a while with an eye cocked and then begin squirming and swimming on our bellies through the dust of the melée. The idea was to find one of our boys and improve his chances by slicing into the opponent's heel tendon. If it proved impossible to get around behind, well, there's nothing like a good whack on the toes for throwing a fellow's timing off.

> "First the swordsman lost a stroke,
> Then understanding dawned,
> The light of glory was lost from his eye,
> While his brains were lost from his head.
> With a ya ya xplut,
> And a ya ya xplut,
> His brains were lost from his head."

Sweet bit of doggerel, no? O we thought it the finest of marching ditties. It was our theme song, after all.

Old men sometimes regarded us with disapproving brow. "In our time," they said, "there was not so much death on the field. In our time, it was no disgrace to be taken alive and presented for dedication. Without our living blood, the universe would decay into dust and be blown away and scattered forever. This business of splitting heads to left and right," we were assured, "was highly immoral—begun by greedy rulers more concerned with the acquisition of corn lands than the glory of the gods. It would lead to our downfall and also our despair."

I have, it can be plainly noted, come to understand something of that method of organizing past events which is called "history." Such skills were learned under the gentle and patient tutelage of Father Aragon. It is a wonderful thing, this history, like standing atop the world's highest tower and viewing all the flow of human affairs with a single glance. It is a godlike power, no doubt, but very difficult, requiring hours of study and much conversation with people with whom one would rather not associate.

Here, for example, is a tale I plucked from the lips of a most unpleasant person—no less an individual than the chief assistant to Lord Good Shopper, the Snake Woman and head priest of all Mexico. Of course, the language has been adjusted a bit and all crudities and clichés eliminated. Hear and attend, O reader. I think you will find it most enlightening. I call it "Midnight in the Palace."

"Midnight in the Palace"

Snake Woman had left a call to be awakened at midnight exactly. The youth serving as corridor guard had stationed himself by the window at the end of the gallery so as not to miss the signal. Now the chief priest, face freshly scrubbed, long hair combed out straight, is ready to begin his nightly prayer vigil. These days, sleep is the last thing he has on his mind, nor is there any lack of sincerity in his prayers. Grave trouble stalks the land. And the Tlatoani? He only cavils. He only temporizes. Impolitic are his strategies. Captious are his arguments. His spirit just lies there, tattered and raggedy.

Snake Woman shakes his head sadly. "O by whose hand is it we will bloom? By our own face, our heart, our spirit, either we will bloom or we will wither. We will become as a green land or a desert without even a puddle. Can we sprout? Can we flower? How will it come to pass lying thus in deep shadow, withering beneath the dry, black cloud of self-deception? Who is so blind? Whose spirit will not freeze as this great city slides back into its muddy womb? Hubris! Well it won't be the first time Mexico follows incompetence down paths that lead to defeat."

"Now, now, sir, chief priest and secretary of state, why don't you stop complaining and start praying?" comes a squawk from the window. Snake Woman's spirit nearly pops loose.

"Quauchi, my dear and disrespectful little monkey. Where hast thou been?"

"My, my. Don't we see clearly tonight. How much of that stuff did you swallow, anyway? You could probably pat my head and we'd both feel it."

"Pat your head? Ah, well ... you know ... you look funny—that is to say, odd, peculiar, strange. Like a tarantula with an incompetent haircut."

"Eight legs or two, I'm not handsome it's true ... Neh, neh. Forget it. Not important. I've got some delicious gossip, sir judge. O my, you should have seen our ruler's face when they brought the news. He was terrified; he was astounded. Could be his brain is in a rut, for he can only think to ask what kind of food they eat. The Spaniards, that is. He wants to flee; he wishes to flee. O how he needs to hide himself. He desires to take refuge from the gods. Secretly he says to himself, 'If I can just get into a cave, I'll be safe.' 'Too late,' say the soothsayers, 'and anyway you can't hide from the gods.' You know," said Quauhchi thoughtfully, "could be the wizards are only taking vengeance on him—feigning wisdom they never possessed. Now there's a thought."

Snake Woman is no longer amused. "Not another word, Quauhchi. You go too far. I can have you exorcised with a snap o' my fingers, you know, and it will be a goodly sheaf of years before you are able to return. By insulting the Tlatoani in this manner, you curse as well his father and his grandfather and all that great and glorious line of Toltec ancestors."

"Toltec ancestors? Don't make me laugh! Revisionist twaddle! Surely you have not forgotten the old union—how they shoved your illustrious grandfathers into swamp water up to their necks, forcing them to eat insect eggs scraped off the grass. Not to mention those fabulous "cakes" made of dried algae? Ahuahutle, remember? And the women. I can hear them now, begging piteously for a few scraps of rag to cover their naked flesh. O my. All that bare butt marching off to slavery. Quite a sight, wasn't it?"

Shopper is beginning to lose his temper. "Correct, Quauhchi. Quite right. And now look at us—absolute rulers of the One World. It is a great shadow our warriors cast across Anáhuac, a pall of terror from the Huaxtec to Guatemala. Now our treasuries overflow with—"

Quauhchi breaks into a mighty cackle. "O yes, and you can't even eliminate little Tlaxcala just over the hill. Tell you what," he whispers. "Do something about that scrawny Tlatoani, and maybe your luck will change."

"Treason! Treason!" whispers Snake Woman and is about to ring for the guard. But then he thinks better of it.

"O my, the odor of goodness," sighs Quauhchi. "Dear gods, the smell of virtue. Not terribly pleasant, Mr. High Priest. So thoroughly uninteresting all that, what do you call it? Morality? And such total dedication. Gahh! How absolutely boring. Well, you'll never change. A pleasant good-bye to you."

Snake Woman feels more than a little dizzy. Can it be the draught is, indeed, a little too strong tonight? He walks quickly to a shelf and picks up a handkerchief-like piece of cloth and a small obsidian blade. Holding the rather dirty looking rag under his left ear, he makes two quick downward slashes in the earlobe. As the blood runs out, he stands looking at the ceiling rather like a man standing in front of a urinal. Then with a rather irritable, even violent motion, Snake Woman pulls off his gown and sits bare-bottomed on a pile of fresh nettles lying in a corner of the room. He stares at the wall and begins to pray:

"O rain, O sea, O Lord of the far and also of the nigh, O you by whom we live, O night, O wind. We know you've already made up your mind, because only you can see the inner nature of all that exists—including the rocks and the trees. Thus, that which a man might do to stir up your anger, to precipitate your wrath, is not really his fault."

"Perchance our ruler is unbalanced, perhaps even a coward, At least we know he is not a pilferer—neither is he a pervert. Open his ears, open his eyes, set him on the path ..."

Later, Snake Woman stands at the window, watching a fleet of merchant canoes pull out of the boat basin. For a long time he studies the design formed by fading ripples reflecting the full moon. So lovely, it catches at the heart. "What have we done to deserve such glory?" he asks the night. "By what noble act have we earned all this? Such a sad land for all its beauty. People go about their business in a bit of a daze, don't they? Are they asleep? Are they awake?"

A child is carried up the steps. The tired priest waits. It has been a long day, and he has gashed a finger on the obsidian. He waits. Is it but a vision? A little smoke that gets in the eyes for a time? Indeed, surely it would be best if our Lord came right away. He with the beard and the coat of greenish feathers. The sooner the better.

Finally, when it seems certain the sun will once more emerge victorious from his all-night battle against the stars, the High Priest Good Shopper, Snake Woman, magistrate and regent of Mexico, lies down for a little rest.

Hopefully, friend reader, you have spotted the "history" clue buried in the bowels of the above tale. Do you not recall my earlier remarks regarding the various rulers and their o'er weaning urge toward territorial expansion? Do you not see how the notion forms a chain binding the generations together, and expressing the changing character of our government? Now that, my friends, is how history is constructed. Father Argon disagrees. He says the idea is amateurish, poorly written, badly expressed, and barely worthy of an undergraduate paper. However, I shall not allow myself to be discouraged by critics, no matter how skilled they may be. I've been through that before—and more than once.

Now let us step onto truly solid ground. This much I can tell you with absolute certainty. The Spanish army would not have entered our nation like a sled on a track greased with chicken fat if certain events had not taken place two years earlier. To wit, an opening wide enough for all creation to pour through began to spread apart its gates all along our eastern borders.

Since the beginning of time, the east side of our beautiful and life-giving lake had been dominated by our league ally, the city of Texcoco. This eastern area was known as the Acolhua country. In the Christian year 1515, its great poet king and philosopher, Lord Coyote Fasting, died without naming a successor, though he had sons aplenty. Strange that a man of brilliance like C. Fasting would not bother to consider the consequences such neglect would bring about. Ah well. Wisdom is rarely wise enough to protect the all-confident seer from a cock-askant view of the ability of others—especially offspring.

Three, probably legitimate (more or less) sons, were the main contenders for the throne of Texcoco. The youngest, twenty-one-year-old Small Corn, was loaded with ambition but little else. He thought it might be enjoyable, or that is to say, diverting, to run a kingdom. Then came Communal

Snake, leaning whichever way the wind blew—a man standing always in the center of the road. Vanilla Orchid was another story. He strongly desired the removal of Texcoco from the Three City League. Small Corn kept whining that the league constitution proclaimed him the new king. "Is Moteuczoma my uncle or yours?" he *qujmjtalhuja* (nagged, complained) at his brothers. "Is my mother the sister of Moteuczoma or yours?" he pouted.

"May the gods prevent that particular succession," said the Acolhua knights, "and if they won't, we will." For once, they had Moteuczoma "over a barrel," to use Fr. Aragon's phrase. From his uncomfortable position bent o'er the barrel, Moteuczoma saw to the appointment of a militarily undistinguished but very studious and thoughtful younger brother named Braided Plumes. My general, Baron Fertilizer, was put in charge of the fleet carrying the coronation party across the lake. I was at that time assigned as his orderly, and during my visit to Texcoco, I got to know the whole crowd over there. Braided Plumes was crowned by the Mexican prime minister and then quickly murdered. So much for the life span of students, intellectuals, and other nice fellows in Anáhuac.

And so the ancient and honorable Acolhua empire was ripped apart, torn asunder, dissipated like smoke. It was gone forever. Vanilla Orchid took his followers, a not inconsiderable number of very tough troops, and camped them up in the hills within striking reach of Tenochtitlan. They would prove of some value to the Spaniards later on.

Ah, yes, O ho. Let me now elucidate a principle of history that neither Aragon nor the Pope himself can quarrel with. Here it is: insolent hubris in a ruler will always unchain government's most destructive tendencies. Acolhua would still exist had not Moteuczoma insisted on exclusive rule over all Anáhuac. His pride led him to scheme endlessly for the downfall of the Three City League and personal control over all the land. He would brook no competition. O arrogance! O insolence overbearing!

In the Christian year 1517, rumors "winged with baleful prefigurations of doom" (I wish I had said that.) foreshadowing the imminent return of Quetzalcoatl, the true god and holder of every title and mortgage, absolute and undisputed owner of Anáhuac, reached the Tlatoani in Tenochtitlan. Next year, the Christian year 1518, Juan de Grijalva dropped anchor off the coast near the future community of Villa Rica de la Vera Cruz—The Rich Town of the True Cross. Of course, the place was, in actuality, nothing more than a windblown, insect-infested sand spit. It was called Hummingbird Beach.

The trusty and serviceable sycophant Pinotl was sent as ambassador to Grijalva, but for all his trouble, climbing up and down the passes of East Mother Mountains, he was presented with nothing more than a handful of green glass beads. Compared with our people, Spaniards are paltry, mean, and very cheap. This fact is indisputable, and no one in all the earth will deny it.

Back in the capital, the beads were handed to Moteuczoma who, paralyzed with fear, had hardly the strength to question Pinotl as to the possible identity of these floating characters. "This is it," sounded a voice from the back of the room.

The Royal Council of Four was immediately assembled and joined by some other local kings. This group wrote and proclaimed Mexico's very first policy with regard to the Spaniards, and so it is only fitting that a competent student of history should attempt to name them—at least as many as he can recall.

Small Corn, nephew of Moteuczoma, was there, but his statements were largely ignored, coming as they did from the mouth of that callow youth.

He Who Flattens the Earth (an ancient title harking back to pre-foundation days), ruler of Watertown, was present.

Ecatempatiltzin (descended from the Ancient Land of Heroes) was there as well.

Sir Fertilizer, my own noble general, great diplomat, and great soldier, ruler of Yellow Plant City and brother of Moteuczoma, was there in the room. It was Fertilizer who, as the last Tenochca Tlatoani, oversaw the end of organized government in Anáhuac and Tenochtitlan as its capital.

Quetzalaztatzin (Sun Under the Earth) was present.

Armory Chief, (Tlacochcalca) direct descendant of the world-renowned poetess Five Flower and one of the last to stand at the battle for the streets of Weavertown, was there.

Fire Feeder, descendant of Tezozomac who is known as the first "emperor" of Mexico, also joined the assembly.

Serving as conference chairman sat Tlilpotonqui, "Snake Woman," secretary for foreign affairs, chief priest for Tenochtitlan.

Also among the councilors was the famous military tactician Eagle Swoops, under whose authority the Mexica nation finally dissolved into a mere brotherhood of knights, the "Teuctli," a classless, stateless, band of warriors fighting in the service of the gods only. According to Aragon, such paramilitary groupings were common throughout the history of his land.

91

As has been noted, *Cuauhtemoc* is translated to Spanish as Falling Eagle or Eagle Swoops. What more fitting name for a leader of the doomed. Well, he was there at the conference, armed to the teeth, and no one dared blink an eye in complaint.

After opening prayers, Snake Woman called the meeting to order with some startling remarks, capped off by the presentation of the green beads. There they all sat with eyes downcast, all too conscious of their dignity, hesitant to do so much as glance in the direction of the sacred beads. Snake Woman spoke again.

"To this most august company in all Anáhuac is given the task of determining the identity of the newcomers. Now the great tragedy plays itself out. Now the future is unfolding. Now perhaps the time has come to offer him the kingdom that he has returned to reclaim." "O ca, ca," whispered Eagle Swoops, all the while staring straight ahead at the wall. And then he leaned very slightly toward his assistant ruler, Eagle Vision. "If they wish to make him a present of Tenochtitlan, that's just fine, but not Weavertown. Weavertown is off limits. The Yellow Plant Causeway is defended by allies. As for the western bridges, well, we can take our chances there. We'll destroy them if necessary."

Eagle Vision's expression changed not a wit. He only raised one finger from the table as a signal of assent.

Chapter 13

Last Night in Cempoal—August 15, 1519

Lately Marina's sleep is fitful and dream haunted. Lying there on her mat next to Cortés, strange images appear before her. Though quite certain she is perfectly conscious, still the young dreamer seems unable to move a muscle. A woman appears in her dream-hallucination. Marina sees her dressed all in white, going about weeping and crying out. Loudly does she sob, bitterly does she wail as she walks back and forth. "My beloved sons," she says, "now we are about to disappear. O my sons, whither am I to take you? How can what is about to come to pass have befallen you? My beloved sons, how you will tremble at the fate that will soon catch up with you."

With a sob, Marina snaps out of that hypnogogic state. Lying there rigidly, staring into the darkness among the ceiling beams, she groans aloud. "O how real that white woman seemed. O what can it mean? What have I done?"

Cortés reaches out to hold her, but Marina rolls over on her side avoiding him. "Only a dream," she sighs. "Nothing more than a dream."

Stung by her rejection of his embrace, Cortés responds crudely. "Oh yes? No doubt some vision of your devil gods. Of course, they would be troubling your sleep these days."

With a heart sunk down to her feet, Marina manages to turn and face him. Now she is angry and grows a bit reckless. "Troubling *my* sleep? And what, I pray you, my lord and master, troubles yours? As for me, I am a Christian. I believe in the mercy of our Lord Jesus Christ." Marina lowers her head and the tears stream down into the lap of her nightdress.

Cortés sits up and begins to speak in that official voice of his, the one he uses to calm men in a tight spot.

"Now, Marina, calm down, please. There is really no need for hysteria. Of course, you're a Christian, and your faith cannot be doubted. Believe me, no one would dream of questioning your sincerity with regard to this

S. L. Gilman

matter. However, all of us experience lapses, and it must be remembered that your formative years were molded by pagan beliefs. Of course they will come back to haunt you from time to time. How could they not? Now here is what you must do. Tomorrow, go see Father Olmedo and discuss this little problem. He will surely know how to handle the situation and perhaps ... no, certainly, you will be pestered no more by this ... old-fashioned stuff."

"Yes, sir, of course, I'll do that," Marina replies in a small voice.

"So then, we've got an early call in the morning. Perhaps it would be best to try for some sleep. I bid you good night." Cortés leans over to kiss her cheek. In spite of the prevailing mood, the touch of that soft flesh arouses him, and so they make love, albeit without much enthusiasm. *Well,* thinks Cortés, *this is nothing new. All my relationships end in bland disinterest. Usually, however, I'm the one suffers emotional burnout—not the woman.*

Chapter 14

Moving Toward Mexico

"'The lot is now cast. Let fortune take what turn
she will,' as Caesar said in passing the Rubicon."
Spanish historian

Cortés has decided to use Cempoal as a staging point for the invasion
of Mexico. Fat Cacique insists the route via Tlaxcala is the best way
to go. "The Tlaxcalans," he says, "are great friends of ours. They loath
and despise Mexicans even more than we do. You can't go wrong in
Tlaxcala." This prophecy proves more than a little flawed. Fat Cacique
sends along fifty of his best fighting men and two hundred tamimes to
pull the cannon.

And so, on a day in August, the little army sets out in good order,
cavalry and light infantry leading the way.

Up beyond the front range of East Mother Mountains, on a barren and
icy cold plateau near a place called Cocotlan, at last the Spaniards enter
the country of the Mexicans. The pass leading up to the plateau is higher
than any in Spain and is named Nombre de Dios. As far as the troops are
concerned, God can have it with their compliments.

"For heaven's sake, Hernán. Get hold of yourself." So exclaims a shocked
Father Olmedo at a dinner among the chiefs of Cocotlan. Carried away
in a mood of patriotic and religious enthusiasm, Cortés is demanding that
the priests abandon their idols and the practice of human sacrifice. Father
Olmedo quickly jumps in and shuts him up.

"Where do you think you are? These are ignorant savages, liable to
commit some ungodly outrage against our holy symbols—not to mention
the ill will you're creating here."

With an irritable grunt and recalcitrant twist of the mouth, Cortés clams up and remains grim-faced throughout the meal. He cracks a smile at last when Frank de Lugo's large mastiff growls like a lion and the Cocos panic. The Totonac allies take advantage of the situation and deliver a strong lecture on Spanish power and the danger of getting crushed in the jaws of their godlike horses and dogs.

A few miles further, the army runs into a wall of stone and cement. It seems to stretch the entire width of the valley. The entrance is constructed so that it doubles on itself, making it necessary to turn a couple of corners in order to get through.

"Totonac say this wall made to stop Mexicans, keep them out of Tlaxcala land." Marina disappears into the opening.

"So then, shouldn't there be some sort of garrison around here? A guard, anyway?" Alvarado takes his mare right up to the wall and taps it with his knuckles. "This thing is like iron," he says. "It would take a cannon to knock it down."

"Yes," murmurs Cortés. "When it comes to engineering, we're not dealing with amateurs here."

"The Tlaxcalans are not going to defend this place," del Castillo whispers, his hand on Sedeño's shoulder. "No, they've got something else planned for us." Sedeño, by the way, is the richest man in the outfit. He not only owns his own horse, but a Negro and a load of bacon as well, items not to be purchased for any money. He's not sure he'll live to enjoy any of it.

A crowd of valley inhabitants, including a couple of high-ranking Coco officials, gather round Cortés. "Sir, we beg you," pleads one of the nobles. "We know you're going on to visit our natural lord, the great Moteuczoma. Why then do you attempt passage through the land of his enemies?" The official turns to the villagers and taps the ground with the butt of his staff.

"Why, why, O why?" the crowd echoes like a Greek chorus in embroidered cotton.

"They are certain to be evilly disposed toward you and will do your people much harm."

"O, you will die there by the road. You will not survive. Why, why, O why?" sing out the villagers.

Cortés ignores the warning and the men move through the opening. Once on the other side, the troops reassemble in attack order: cavalry in front, followed by infantry, and then the cannon under Orozca (sturdy veteran of the Naples campaign) coming behind. The women, baggage, and camp servants bring up the rear, back there at a little distance.

Cortés turns and studies the wall for quite some time. Finally, he wheels his chestnut about and gives a great shout, "Only follow your standard, the Holy Cross, and victory will be yours!"

Chapter 15

Tangling with Tlaxcala—August 20, 1519

"Indeed, if wounds had exempted us from duty,
few of us would have been fit for it."
Spanish ranker

From Cocotlan forward, only Nahuatl is spoken, and Marina sticks close to the captain. At midday, a group of Tlaxcalan soldiers enter camp with a customary "welcome to the battlefield" message. Cortés greets them cheerfully, and the well-dressed and well-armed warriors wear big smiles as well.

Cortés speaks up. "Listen, fellows," he says. We're really not looking for a fight. All we're after is free passage through your land so we can pay a little visit to Moteuczoma over there in Tenochtitlan. Not far from here, as I understand it."

"O right, right. No distance at all. Maybe two, three days at most. But what can you possibly want with that little degenerate?"

"Oh, we just want to have a word with him. We understand he is an old enemy of yours. Maybe we can take care of the situation for you."

Marina shakes her head in disgust as she delivers this message. She tries to modify it a bit but without much success. His lack of understanding surpasses all. Nothing of tactful converse has he learned from el Cid, he of the splendid beard. These are nothing like our coastal drudges. The pouring out of blood in war is the very life spirit of this people. They want no one fighting their battles.

The Tlaxcalans burst into gales of laughter. "O my," chuckles their leader. "So its peaceful passage you want. You only want to stroll across our land, yes? Actually, you'd do better to run. Well, you shall have something akin to peace. After you've been boiled with spices and thoroughly consumed, I think you'll have all the quiet time you can handle."

The ground ahead is broken and rocky—not particularly suited for cavalry operations. The men know the surrounding hills are chock full of Tlaxcalan warriors. They stand around shifting their feet restlessly. "What the devil are we doing here? How did we get into such a mess? We're all dead meat."

Bernal the swordsman knows exactly how he got into this mess and now finds himself waiting to die up on a cold plateau. "We came here to serve God, and also to get rich," he says, a line for which he will long be remembered. But tell me, is Bernal really prepared for his own death in combat? That first startled glance at the feathered shaft sticking out of his chest? Who is that anyway? Hey. Those are my own ribs. O Dios mio! That's me! Sure, sure. All that's somewhere in the back of his mind, but so what? Nobody thinks about that sort of business when he signs up. Then it's just: get me off these damned islands. Hanging around the Little Florida without a casserole to squat in, chasing whores, playing chess with the bums in Columbus Park—some life that is.

The scouts come in and report. Cortés asks for an estimate of numbers. Dominguez lowers his head and then looks up and faces the captain.

"Maybe ten, twelve thousand: archers, lancers, swordsmen," he says, "maybe more. Hard to say."

Cortés nods grimly. "Like it or not, we've got to move out of here. There's flat ground ahead, and we'll be able to use the cavalry. Horsemen, remember this: try to charge in groups of three. For heaven's sake, don't stop to thrust with your lances, and don't aim to impale any one. If your lance gets stuck, they'll jump on it and drag you down. Just point at the height of the eyes and keep going till you're clear. The idea is to scatter close formations, break up the jam. Then the infantry will be right behind."

As the army picks its way forward across the pitted and boulder-strewn valley, the advance guard stops and points out some thirty or forty warriors just ahead. The Tlaxcalan fighters remain perfectly still. They stand there like statues, only staring at the Spaniards and leaning on those dangerous double-headed lances of theirs.

Cortés, ever the diplomat, still trying to negotiate his way past Tlaxcala, sends the troops forward at double-time with orders to take hostages. Warriors as hostages! The absurdity of the notion strikes Marina dumb.

But the Tlaxcalan squad is only a decoy. A body of nearly three thousand fighters sallies out from behind the boulders and attacks with considerable fury. As always, archers make up the front line. Cotton wadding protects the Spanish foot soldiers fairly well, but the horses begin to look like pincushions. Cortés' little army is almost swallowed up before Orozca can bring the artillery to bear.

"Grape and chain up the fundament!" he yells. This terrible ammunition, along with musket fire, forces Tlaxcalan ranks to fall back. Strangely, the army of Tlaxcala seems more disciplined and more efficient on the retreat than when attacking. It departs the field in perfect order, fighting every step of the way.

September 2, 1519, Tehuacacingo, province of Tlaxcala—the men fit for service manage to stagger into the usual formation, a few half-chewed bones plus tortillas their only breakfast.

"Look men," says Cortés, "compared to our army, these Indians are a bunch of amateurs. Sure, they're well trained in that flint weaponry, but tactically very limited. It looks like they've got only a single trick up their sleeve: lure us forward with a small force and then fling the whole lot at the flanks. The old bait-and-switch game. We can handle it. Just keep your eyes open."

Proceeding on the march, the cavalry spots two bodies of warriors waiting on the plain ahead. "There must be six thousand of them," the scouts report, "and dressed to kill."

"Not funny," someone in the ranks remarks.

"No, I mean you should see the uniforms. Tiger skin capes. Huge helmets shaped like the heads of eagles and covered with feathers. Most of them carry white and red flags. I think it's the symbol of the country, or maybe the general's device. Listen to that!"

The air is split by a noise something like a million wild geese sounding off in a million separate keys, conch-shell horns probably meant to deafen an enemy. Then come the whistles, shrill as stuck pigs. And the battle cry: "TLAX-CAL-A, TLAX-CAL-A, TLAX-CAL-A."

Cortés calls a halt and sends for the royal notary Diego de Godoy. "Diego. Good man. As official notary, I want you to go tell those troops that we require only peaceable and amicable conversation and that we wish to consider them as friends and brothers. Don't forget to bring some paper and your royal stamp." adds the captain. "That always makes a big impression. Marina, take my horse and go along. Let there be no misunderstanding."

Looking pale as a sheet with a slightly greenish overtone, Godoy sets off up the valley. Marina rides beside him; the prisoners are just ahead on foot.

"These people don't harm messengers," Godoy keeps telling himself. "We're not in France, for heaven's sake. It's going to be all right." Still—

what wouldn't he give to find himself back in Santiago, draped in an office armchair watching cigar smoke curl toward the ceiling.

Three officers stroll out of the ranks and wait for the delegation. The world has never seen the like of their battle dress. Each warrior's helmet is decorated with the feathers of a different bird—quetzal, trupial, and red macaw. Gold pendants hang about their necks, and at their sides are tied flint knives with finely worked and very elaborate gold handles. Their cloaks are magnificent, better than any seen in Moorish country or in India. There is the yellow Xolotl head decoration, the Quetzal feather banner with golden eyes, and the blindingly blue cape put together entirely of cotinga skins.

For a moment, Godoy forgets his nerves. He can't help thinking, *these look like parade clothes, but they're not. Obviously this bunch is ready to fight, and not in the least loathe to wreck all that high-price couture. Just look at that blue!*

Godoy clears his throat and speaks. Marina translates.

"I have a message for the general called Fork-in-the-Road. Is he present here?"

"That's me," says the warrior in blue. "I am Sir Fork-in-the-Road. What do you wish to say to me?"

Xolotl cape looks at him. "Wait a minute. Wait a minute. That's not you," he announces. "I am the real Fork-in-the-Road."

"O, frog feathers," says the third. "It is I who am Fork-in-the-Road,"

Marina and Godoy look at each other. Godoy's mouth opens and closes like a fish out of water.

"O they are only acting like *choteadores*, what we call wise-guys in Nahuatl. Go ahead. Repeat the captain's message."

Godoy follows diplomatic procedures without much enthusiasm. The pessimism writ large across his heart and surely his face is bound to promulgate failure and personal extinction. When the communication is delivered, the three officers make a big show of squinting in deep thought. One strokes a meager goatee, the others scratch their heads and stare up at the clouds.

"Now that's what I call a generous offer," says quetzal banner to blue cape. "O generous beyond all generosity," comes the reply. "Good friends, we will need some time. A little time to think things over. Surely this will prove acceptable to your brave leader?"

Godoy finds it hard to concentrate under the gaze of blue cape's dark and haughty eyes. The polite tone of the conference, however, begins to relax him a bit, and after awhile Godoy believes he will, most likely, return to camp in one piece.

No sooner do the two envoys turn away from the Tlaxcalan horde than a great din of horns, drums, and whistles rends the air. Godoy jumps in the stirrups and nearly falls from the saddle. He and Marina twist their necks and look back, but the army has not stepped an inch forward. Anxious to get out of there, they both break into a gallop. The clamor follows them all the way inside Spanish lines, but still the Tlaxcalans have not budged.

The Spaniards are deeply impressed by what they perceive as a civilized military code. "French troops wouldn't behave so courteously," somebody says in wondering tones.

Once the envoys are safely home, the Tlaxcalan six thousand begin a slow movement forward. These soldiers constitute a somewhat reduced *xipil,* or division, in European terms.

"Santiago and at them," screams Cortés, and the Spanish army echoes his cry. Artillery blasts away. Many Tlaxcalans fall beneath the barrage, but soon the Spaniards find themselves in a familiar situation. Once more they pursue a fighting retreat, and once more the battle carries them into broken terrain where the cavalry is near to useless. This time Lord Bumblebee sets his trap with a huge reserve corps hiding up in the pines to either side of the valley. With the troops already engaged below, the numbers approach twenty thousand.

Chapter 16

Alligator Division Funks—August 23, 1519

"And indeed, when you come to think of it,
had the British army consistently waited for
reserves in all its little affairs the boundaries
of Our Empire would have stopped at Brighton Beach."
Kipling

"Those Castilian fellows have been to school," says Multiplier. "Perhaps we ought to get down there."

General Bumblebee shades his eyes and quickly darts a glance at the sun. The general often expresses himself in ancient tropes.

"In Mecatlan
My lords, the yucca drum lies croaking
To the sorcerers house
Did the sorcerer drop
It's not time to come out disguised"

General Noble Savage has charge of the eight thousand-man Alligator division. He lies stretched out on the pine needles, staring intently down at the battle. Just now, he is trying not to voice an emotional complaint, or better, attempting to express a complaint in unemotional terms.

"It's those animals," he says, the strain of self-control roughens his voice. "Those damned great beasts, giant deer, or whatever they are. Without them, the Castilians would be lost, trampled down like grass, swallowed whole. We could roll them up like a mud ball."

"Animals? Animals, my stinking outhouse!" grunts Bumblebee irritably. "Sir Noble, it's the tubes, the tubes! Especially the gold-colored ones. That's what's tearing the troops to shreds. Maybe we can find a way to smash them up. They are guarded mostly by low-land tlatlacolli, mere coastal trash."

"Yes," answers Multiplier, "but the tubes embody a concept which our people are unable to grasp. They cannot be comprehended, and thus their existence is uncertain. The giant animals, on the other hand, may be gods, and yet they are also flesh. Everyone understands that. Everyone must want to kill them."

Bumblebee nods. Multiplier is no soothsayer, only a military man, but he's always had that contemplative nature. His view seems visionary, truly wise.

"I think you may be right, Sir Multi. What could be closer to the truth? So then, killing of the giant animals is hereby declared an important objective and will be highly rewarded—amount to be decided post-battle." Bumblebee is thinking hard. *A close-up operation if ever one was planned. I'll need the best.*

"Hai, courier!" his voice carries low beneath the pines. "We'll attack on my flag. But first find me Sir Stony's company." Expressing nothing more than a little pre-battle irritability, he adds a short, *soto voce* clause, "the little bastard. He's never around when you need him." Stony is of the shorn-headed Otomí class of warriors and known as a great captain.

Motionless as a pair of rocks, Noble Savage and Multiplier stare at the general. Do their ears deceive them? There in quarters close as a honeycomb, they have just heard their commanding officer insult and seriously damage the heart of General Noble's one and only son and thus also of the father.

"Whoever shames me knows me quite ill." Sir Noble is almost crying. "And I had considered you a great advisor."

Bumblebee can only turn a deaf ear to his own words. Nothing more to be done.

"Amanteca are our foes," he intones the old war hymn.
"About me place yourselves in battle form
There's going to be war
About me place yourselves."

He motions toward the top of a tall oiametl fir where his signals aide shakes out the huge red and white banner of Tlaxcala. The reserve armies pour down the hillsides and join the battle.

Even at the distance of a half kilometer, the Spaniards are assailed by an ear-bursting din: drums, whistles, conch horns, and above all, the battle cry TLAX-CA-LA, TLAX-CA-LA.

"All right, young jaguar, get me a full company of archers stationed along the side of that broken ground there," Bumblebee tells his teenage courier, student warrior, intern, what have you. "And stretch them out a man's length." The general does not have to raise his voice. These battle leaders know how to communicate below the racket. Bumblebee slaps the boy on the back. He takes off like an arrow.

"This could be embarrassing," says Alvarado with a little laugh. "How are we supposed to get through that?"

"Oh, my dear fellow," Cortés answers. "Why such pessimism? It'll be slow going but with God's help—and we know he's on our side—we'll carry past this mess to the flat ground."

"Company close up," he shouts, "Tight column formation."

The archers are at too great a distance to do the men much harm, but once more the horses are punctured.

"Santiago," exclaims Alvarado. "I hate to see the animals take this kind of punishment. It's really upsetting."

Cortés is keeping a close eye on the infantry formation. He does not answer.

De Leon comes riding up behind the infantry trying to get to the forward line. Not wanting to break the tight formation, he twists La Rabona this way and that, almost trodding on the heels of swearing soldiers. Finally, he squeezes in between Cortés and Ávila.

"So what's up?" asks Cortés.

"Orozca wants to know if he should put some cannon on those bowmen."

"No, no, they're spread too thin. Be a waste of powder and shot." He leans closer to de Leon. "Better just stay in line now."

"This is as flat as it's going to get," says Cortés to no one in particular.

Bumblebee holds his army back. Multiplier and Noble Savage and son are nowhere in sight. Well enough he knows the reason for their absence. Has his incontinent tongue lost the fight? No! He will take one or more of those great beasts by himself and in his own way. He knows exactly how to do it. Better go now. The pitch seems about right. Bumblebee signals his horns for a sustained blast and moving out front, starts the hard, down-valley run. "Waste of powder" no longer worries Orozca. The guns blast and warriors go down in a blood-soaked tangle. The Tlaxcalans ignore their losses and crowd in for the kill. No more space for a cavalry charge now.

"Argh," yells de Leon, "those damn lances go through armor." With a tremendous backhand swing of his blade, he decapitates the warrior who stuck him in the leg, but he can't get the double-headed spear out of the metal. It swings clumsily and de Leon begins to lose his seat. Aguilar aims a mighty two-handed blow and catches the haft at a forty-five-degree angle with plenty of wrist, as if he were trimming a tree branch. The spear breaks cleanly, tearing the leg wound only a little.

"Ay!" screams de Leon.

Bumblebee drops to his stomach. *Just like my barbarian ancestors*, he grins to himself. *On our bellies in the melee, fighting for those phony Toltec snobs and peanuts for pay. They'd have gotten nowhere without us. No one could touch us then. Neither can they lay a hand on me now.* He wriggles and squirms through the flailing feet of men and horses, slashing his way toward the heart of the struggle.

So dense is the howling mob there is barely room to lift a weapon. Pedro de Moron pushes in with three other cavalrymen. Contrary to accepted tactic, he is trying to clear a path by thrusting with the lance. Several warriors jump on his weapon and drag him out of the saddle.

"Help me, God," he yells. "I'm down. O Jesus, I'm dead."

Bumblebee, squirming along through the dust, works his way among the churning feet and from a prone position takes a cut at de Moron. Some person or some horse crunches down on the shield strapped to his back causing the blow to miss its target. Bumblebee pushes himself up onto his knees and delivers a mighty uppercut to the neck of de Moron's horse. The flint blades nearly sever the mare's head and she drops dead on the spot. While some Tlaxcalans are trying to drag the body off, Alvarado yells, "Get the saddle, get the saddle." A number of Spaniards jump on and manage to cut the girths. The thing is clearly valuable, for at least ten infantrymen are wounded in the foot-to-foot combat around the dead animal.

A squad of the stoutest swordsmen, crowding close to the center, manage to break apart the Spanish infantry formation. These chaps make up the heavy infantry, and "heavy," we quickly note, describes more than military convention. Only the stoutest and heftiest warriors in the land wield the huge club-sword, a tool that makes warfare in Anáhuac such a thoroughly bloody business. The weapon is nothing more than a large bat lined about with razor edged obsidian blades, but at close range, nothing alive can stand up to the thing.

Sometime back, the great ruler Water Eggs was nearly cut in half by the killer tool. This occurred at Pouchtown during the disastrous invasion of Tarasca in '78. They managed to get him back to Tenochtitlan still breathing, and amazingly, he lived another year. The *maqhuáhuitl* is, without doubt, the most effective offensive weapon of pre-ferrous times, yet against Europeans, it is somewhat disadvantaged. Its razor sharp blades are extremely brittle, and if wielded against iron, they snap off, leaving the swordsman with nothing more than a wooden club capable of inflicting a few deep scratches.

"Close up there. Close it up," shouts Cortés, riding behind the action, wildly swinging that expensive Toledo sword. Then he picks a target and dives into the fight. He slides the blade into the throat of a warrior wearing a jeweled headband. Cortés is Cortés, and so his brain can't help churning out a quick appraisal. *Those stones look valuable,* he thinks. Others close to death merely review their lives.

European troops are trained in close-order maneuver. They learn to hold a line, form a moving wall of deadly pressure. Soldiers of Anáhuac only attack in mobs, unable to bring their forces to bear efficiently. In the hand-to-hand clash, Spanish iron is directly pitted against American obsidian—perhaps for the first time. The black stone chips fly in every direction.

Fighters of Anáhuac know well that death in battle brings luminous glory. Their blood poured on the ground carries perfect redemption, for themselves and for all mankind. The Spaniards, on the other hand, are only frightened out of their wits, literally. The great black razors slash in from all sides. A split second's distraction means certain end, and so they fight like animals, or like madmen. The Spanish are frantic, and they are quicker for their weapons slip smoothly through the air. Time and again, iron punches home through brown flesh, and the brown bodies pile up underfoot. Tlaxcalan swordsmen begin to give way before the hard, tempered metal, and the Spanish line manages to close up. Cavalry ranks form in the cleared space and charge again and then again. From time to time, a lance butt stands erect and moves forward in an arc as a trooper clears his point. Finally, the Tlaxcalans begin moving backward, shoved into one of their famous fighting retreats.

Historians speak of the ferocious Afghan tribesmen, far more intimidating on the attack than when attacked. Then they run away, it is said, "like wearied wolves who snarl and bite over their shoulders." Not true in Anáhuac. The warriors of that land are just as dangerous in retreat as attack, and much better organized.

The Spanish horses follow, but only a short distance, for they are very tired. At last, the Tlaxcalan forces leave the field, disgusted and more than a little irritated.

Cortés sits drooping a bit in the saddle. "Jesús," he exclaims, "I'm really thirsty." He resists the temptation to help himself to a slug of wine. "It's water we need, not alcohol."

A couple of officers ride up looking baleful and beat. De Ávila has lost his helmet, and Lares holds up a broken pinkie sticking out from his palm at a near right angle.

"Somebody take a swing at you?" asks Cortés."

"No, I slammed into one of those little mesquites, or whatever the hell they are."

"Get it set in camp, or you'll never duel over a woman again."

Lares can't help sporting a grin. "What camp would that be, sir? Are we stopping here? God knows we need the rest."

"No, Lares, we've got to keep going. We can't afford another fight in this place. We've lost horses; we've lost men. Could be a lot worse next time. We're bloody damn lucky, actually."

"Look, Captain," pleads Ávila. "It's getting dark. The men are in bad shape. There's no water. Nothing to eat. We need rest, and we need it pronto."

Cortés' eyes flash but his voice remains calm. "Ávila, my old friend, if you want to stay here, feel free to do so. For that matter, anybody wants to go back to Villa Rica is welcome to leave. Give me ten men, just ten men who know how to obey orders, and I'll take Mexico. Ten men who understand discipline—that's all I need." Ávila drops his eyes and shrugs as Cortés turns away.

Within the next league, the land flattens out into fields of corn and maguey plants thickly strewn with neat farms and villages. The army halts for the night in a pleasant little town on a cool running brook.

"Pretty enough place," says private Pacheca, after looking around the empty houses a while. "But a man can't eat paving stones. They've carried off the chickens—beak, feathers, and feet."

"Hold on," breathes Acosta, pointing up the street. "What do you call that?"

"I call them dogs. Coming in for the night. Look, there're even some pups. Quite a few it looks like. All right, keep it slow and quiet. Oh, man, we eat tonight! What's better than fresh boiled doggie?"

On the following day, Chief Bumblebee sends Cortés a peculiar message. Bumblebee's words may draw a chuckle from you, reader, but the Spaniards find its combination of impertinence and intimidation unsettling.

"That great and holy creature killed in performance of its sacred duty has been divided in many pieces, each dispatched to a different province of our land and each will be studied assiduously by our priests in order to determine whether its nature be beast or immortal or a little of both. Rest assured the remains will not be eaten and will be treated with the greatest respect."

On the long walk back to town, Fork-in-the-Road's bearers move in close to Bumblebee. The latter is hardly in the mood for conversation but is interested in what Fork-in-the-Road might have to say.

"You see the way they fight, good Sir? In straight lines, so that the strength of one is as the strength of many. They take prisoners but then let them go! It seems quite sacrilegious."

"Neh!" answers his commander. "They just don't want extra mouths to feed."

"Well, they could sacrifice and skin them there on the field as Mexicans sometimes do when far from home."

"O for the sake of god, Sir Fork-in-the-Road! Do they look like Mexicans to you?" Bumblebee is silent for a while. "No, it's something different. Tricky little bastards. Mayhap Moteuczoma is right. Could be they've come to take the whole damn land—in the name of that Feathered Serpent, that Topiltzin … gahh!"

At the edge of town, the defeated warriors take down their hair and let it swing loose, a signal to the people. "Ah," they sigh. "This means we have sustained losses, heavy losses." Bumblebee, however, enters the city with hair still tied in the top-knot. He has had, after all, his own personal victory.

That night is the most uncomfortable the Spaniards have experienced since landing on the continent. There is little enough to eat, no salt, and no cooking oil.

"Tough," says Cortés. "Well, I guess Indian fat is good enough for dressing wounds, but I don't suppose anyone wants to fry a meal in it."

Up here on the plateaus of central Anáhuac, close to eight thousand feet above the level of the sea, cold winds blow down from the high sierras and cut across the barren landscape all through the night. "Human beings without a roof above their heads," ponders Bumblebee, "must shiver helplessly till our father Tonatiuh, the sun, appears on high once again. Now there's a thought worth dwelling on," he tells himself.

Cortés and Marina have not been together much during the last couple of days. As the two of them lie there shivering, their eyes tangle and old feelings seem to revive. It would be nice to cuddle up for warmth, but Cortés, fearing a night attack, will not take off his armor. Marina reaches over and grabs his beard in one hand and his hair with the other.

"The greaves," she gasps. "At least remove the greaves."

"That won't do any good," Cortés is close to whining. "The cuirass drops much too low. It would be extremely uncomfortable."

"I don't care. I don't care. What would el Cid do? He of the magnificent beard?" She tightens her grip on his hair and shakes his head with both hands.

It would not occur to the captain that his libido has been drained by the day's activity and the intense crises of leadership he has passed.

"Well, merde." With a snort audible throughout the camp, Marina turns on her side, back to the captain.

"Marina, my dear friend and helper, won't you at least give me a good night kiss?"

The woman turns over in a flash and clamps her mouth to the captain's. She forces his lips open and nearly sucks the tongue out of his head.

"Oh, dear God," Cortés moans. "O saints in heaven."

Marina moves back and stares at him with shining eyes. Then she wraps her arms, her legs, her self around that cold armor as though it were his very flesh.

After a couple of days of uneasy quietude, the army shivering and hungry and depressed, Cortés sends Marina and Duka, along with some soldiers, to deliver a letter to the chiefs in their lair at the capital city of Tlaxcala. Cortés knows well the Tlaxcalans are illiterate, and Marina can't read either. Duka will read the thing and Marina will translate. The letter represents the formal approach, a proper and necessary procedure or standard requirement in the application of the rules of international diplomacy.

Chapter 17

Lunchtime in Tlaxcala—August 25, 1519

"Turkey with small chilies, turkey with yellow chilies,
turkey with green chilies, white fish with yellow chili,
gray fish with red chili, tadpoles with small chilies,
small fish with small chilies …"
Nahua Menu

Chief Fork-in-the-Road sits with the letter in one hand and a dart in the other, looking moueishly about, wondering how to phrase his next remarks.

"Gentlemen," announces Marina, "as we have requested time and again—O we have begged and pleaded—even 'till spit ran dry and our tongues blackened. All, I say, all we desire is unobstructed passage across your lands. Courageous Tlaxcalans, you have done your very best. O how bravely you fought, even facing the frightful cannon's deadly roar—and more than once. So now, how about it?"

Sir Fork-in-the-Road speaks haltingly, trying to make something up as he goes along, but improvisation is not his strong point. Fortunately, a servant picks the right moment to make an entrance. He carries a large tray loaded with hors d'oeuvres.

"O! O!" Fork-in-the-Road yips with relief. "Tamales." He leans over the plate and inhales deeply. "I hope they are to your liking, for you see, they contain nothing of meat—only green leaves of the … the …" He turns to the servant. "You, there. What do we call this vegetable, anyway?"

"Only the broadest leaves of the huauhquílitl plant are used, my lord, and thus the finished product is known as *quíltamal*."

"Really? Can this be correct? Hearken, O bag of trash, when I want detailed information regarding the culinary history of Anáhuac, I'll look it up! So, as I was saying, on this day we eat them in honor of Ueue Teotl, our father the old fire god, without whom we could not warm ourselves or cook, or burn wood …"

Bumblebee grunts softly. Just now, the god of fire holds little interest for the general. He sits there bandaged from wrist to shoulder, badly burned when he stumbled over a hot cannon during the recent battle. Despite the discomfort, Bumblebee waves his bandages before the council. "You can see who is the real hero here," they seem to say.

Fork-in-the-Road leans back in his ocelot-skin seat. Unlike the other official mats: the bear skin, coyote skin, mountain lion skin, and the plain reed mat (which carries the most prestige of all, doubtless another reminder of simpler Chichimec times), this one's got a good strong back rest. He knows he's in for some lengthy oration and overblown rhetoric.

Bumblebee ignores the Spaniards and directs his attention solely to the other officials present: Fork-in-the-Road, Stony, Guaxobcin, Tepeyaca, Multiplier, and Noble Savage. The last couple ought to be tried for treason, but their families are too powerful. O to see them locked up in wooden cages deep in the basement storehouse, down among the squash seeds, chilies, and dried ducks. As things are, though, he can only consider a quiet little assassination. He is angry enough to do the job himself.

To Fork-in-the-Road's surprise, Bumblebee keeps it short and to the point. No decision can be made regarding the Spanish request until the priests have been consulted. Send over an opinion-appeal immediately, and we should hear from the temple around noon tomorrow.

As the lords rise and leave the chamber, a majordomo type stands before the now empty ocelot chair. He begins reciting something that sounds like a list. His tone gives new meaning to the word "monotonous."

"We're to stay the night," says Marina. "That's the dinner menu we're hearing now."

"Gophers with chili sauce, maize gruel with wrinkled chia, red maize gruel with fruit and chili, maize gruel made of tortilla crumbs covered with small chilies …"

"O they are only bragging," whispers Marina. "Pretending to be rich as Mexicans. They don't have a tenth of all that. But don't worry. We won't starve."

Chapter 18

Implementing "Diplomatic" Procedures—August 27, 1519

"For in truth they thirsted mightily for gold;
they stuffed themselves with it; they starved for it;
they lusted for it like pigs."
Tenochca historian

A couple of days rest at Bumblebee's ex-headquarters (the town of Tehuacinpacingo itself) does Cortés little good. He comes down with some sort of fever, and Father Olmedo is also quite ill. On a night patrol, no less than five of the horses stumble and go down. A stumbling horse always presages bad luck, but five at once? The men believe big trouble is close at hand. And indeed, history clearly presents us with some excellent examples of the tripping horse-bad luck connection. One of the best is found in the life of Sam Houston. On the very day Sam received (at long last) the sacrament of baptism and acceptance into the body of Christ, he was overheard damning his horse, in God's name, to hell for all eternity. That unfortunate animal had stumbled on the trail home from church. Margaret and the minister were present. They forced the president of the Republic of Texas to get down on his knees in the mud and pray for forgiveness.

Like desire after love, dreams of gold and glory have faded from Spanish hearts. The men only want to go home. Especially restless are the ones with houses, plantations, girlfriends, and prize cocks back in Cuba. A ranking noncom reports that the soldiers are beginning to hold very "querulous language."

"Damn that two-timing hustler," says A. Cruz, shivering over a meager fire. "How in God's name did we ever let him talk us into scuttling those ships." Cruz darts his eyes around the black circle of night. "Trapped," he says, "like flies in a web." A. Cruz takes a breath and wrinkles his nose.

"Smell that? It's brimstone. We're stuck here in the devil's pitch of this evil land. I ... I can't even say my prayers anymore. Last night I went to bed and I couldn't even pray. Oh, screw it. I gotta go urinate."

"Urinate? What kind of word is that. That's a word you use in front of a doctor ... or your old aunt or somebody. Not around your buddies. Jesús!"

"All right, then, I'm going behind that tree and make *pi pi.*"

"Pi pi? Who says pi pi? I'll tell you who—fancy whores trying to come off respectable-like. And those fops with the big ruffles. Look you! Look you! Just say, 'I'm gonna go take a leak.' Now that's the perfect phrase. Neither vulgar nor silly."

"Mirad, mirad, look here, my friends," whines W. Colón. In fact, he is close to tears. "We've got to have a word with the captain. I think we've tempted God once too often. He's been reasonably merciful up to now, but it's imprudent to tempt him too far. At present, there is hardly a hope of escaping the stew pot."

Nuzi Duka, standing just beyond the fire's glow, throws a couple of words into the pensive silence. "Pedro Carbonero,'" he says, and the men are startled.

"What? Pedro Carbonero? What do you know of Pedro Carbonero?"

"Egyptian infidel," somebody snarls.

Nuzi is offended. "I'm as much a Spaniard as anybody here. Who was it buried the wine and the host back there? The captain gave me that job. Me, and me only."

"Wine and host? What wine and host? What are you talking about?"

Indeed, Sr. Nuzi, that is somewhat peculiar. You claim to have buried a quantity of sacred materials along the trail up from Villa Rica, and yet only one historian notes it. Our lone eyewitness describes the excavation of a number of wine jugs or barrels, and that's quite an inconvenient load to cart uphill through enemy territory. Bread wafers, on the other hand, are near to weightless, consecrated or not. What's more, army clergy usually manufacture and bless the host right there in the field. All that's required is an iron tool like a tiny waffle iron with two long handles. Heat the iron, drop on some dough, squeeze the handles and there's your bread wafer. What need to hide them in a hole and cover them over with New World earth? Perhaps Father Olmedo's oft-expressed anxiety that pagan hands might mishandle and defile the holy materials has some bearing

---

* Peter the charcoal maker: a troublemaker, an Oilenspeigal-like figure in Spanish folklore.

on the matter. And there is another possibility. Can it be that Cortés, in a moment of insecurity, anticipated a retreat and wanted to make certain mass would be available to the troops? And so, our daring and intelligent leader first destroys the material means of escape—the ships—and then concerns himself with the spiritual welfare of his men? No, no, the entire business defies understanding. With a sigh, we admit its inscrutability and drop the subject.

"And I tell you now," Nuzi goes on, "it is Pedro Carbonero who put us in this hole from which there's no getting out. We've been mad to let him finagle us into a position from which there is no escape."

"The Gypsy has it right for once. We had better do something but quick. We ought to spread the word. We should start for the coast first thing tomorrow."

Rumors of disaffection reach Cortés, and so, dragging himself out of bed, he makes plans to address the situation. He calls a meeting of the officers.

"The men seem a little depressed lately," he says. "There's little enough to eat, and everybody's got a puncture or two. Tomorrow we'll put 'em to work. That'll take everybody's mind off old Pedro." *Yes. Tomorrow I'll set the men to burning a few of the surrounding villages. A little pillage and destruction. What better way to perk up a Spanish army?*

Frowning deeply, Marina approaches Father Olmedo. "Tell me, dear Little Father, who can he be, this Pedro Carbonero that everyone speaks of?"

"Peter the charcoal maker? O my dear child!" Father Olmedo throws up his hands with a laugh.

Unfortunately, Bumblebee and his lieutenant Sicutengal choose that very evening for their temple-sanctioned night raid. The expedition is a disaster for both sides. True, the Spanish artillery can't find the Tlaxcalan attackers, but neither can those worthies zero in on the Castilians. In utter chaos, they wander about in the dark tripping over tent ropes, clattering among kitchen utensils, and causing panic among the horses. Cursing Spaniards blunder into some sort of formation but it is too late. The Tlaxcalans have given up and left the scene.

Back in camp, after a morning foray, Ávila takes the exhausted captain's bridle. "Quite a nice bit of country hereabouts," announces the captain. "Corn, beans, squash, those tomato things. Not a hand's breadth of land uncultivated."

"I say, chief." Ávila puts in impatiently. "Fifty or so fancy-dressed Tlaxcalans came in this morning crying crocodile tears. Well, there they are. Crouched out in the dust begging to be forgiven for past evil doings, and swearing to high heaven they'll never fight us again. It appears to me—"

"Is everyone asleep here?" Alvarado puts in mildly. "I think we're being taken for suckers. Do you know what those boys have been up to? Just ask the Cempoalans. Sicutengal has a whole division stationed over the ridge." Pedro raises his nose to the west. "He's only waiting for a signal. Our Tlaxcalan guests have been relaying info as to our strength, guard postings, number of horses, all that."

"Right," says Cortés. "We know what to do with spies and traitors. They'll soon see what manner of men we are."

Marina looks up sharply and catches Cortés' eye. He quickly glances away, stomach achurn.

"You have certainly done very wrong in opposing us," Cortés addresses the Tlaxcalans, "and in refusing to destroy those dreadful idols and accept the Son of Our Lord as your savior. Yet it pleases me to be your friend and pardon you for your sins."

With these remarks, Cortés orders the entire fifty arrested and their hands cut off. Some only have their thumbs removed.

The maimed notables are sent back to Bumblebee. When they arrive in that deplorable condition the chief takes one look and kicks the nearest household slave with all his strength.

"All right, all right," he shouts. "They want to come through Tlaxcala? So let 'em come. See if I care!" Pouting like a schoolboy, Bumblebee retires to his tent. "As for me, the skin of my posterior will not detach itself therefrom." Thus does he mumble from behind the cloth.

Nuzi's attitude is not so accepting. He keeps visualizing those thumbs arcing through the air. Just now Nuzi is out behind the camp throwing up his breakfast, meager as it was.

Marina, on the other hand, stands paralyzed in front of the chopping block. A light breeze seems to blow through her ears. The little hairs begin to vibrate and itch as though some tiny insect were crawling around in there, or some parasite out of a foul pond.

"What are they doing to my people, my people, my people?"

"Who said that?" Marina sticks a pinkie into her left ear and scratches furiously. Then she shakes her head. But the tickle won't go away.

Ruy Diaz el Cid—is he of my people? When Ruy Diaz el Cid, he of the magnificent beard, took prisoner Count don García Ordóñez, he pulled out only part of his beard, not the whole … broom. But my captain, who is of their very same blood, he does not do this. No. He amputates limbs, which is a thing without honor.

What are they doing to my people, my people, my people?

My people? What in the name of Kuk'ulk'an does it mean, my people? My people live in a city by the sea. Far away from this place—another world.

Do the Castilians take some great joy in this butchery? I don't think so. Such horror only brings out their grayish pallor—that dreary, colorless complexion of theirs. They look like underdone dough cakes. And the black ones are obviously over-cooked, perhaps even burned." Marina stares down at her hands. *"But look! Our skin is just the right shade. Wrought in copper. Shiny and warm like the polished metal, like the skin of a gumbo-limbo. So these are my people? All the brown ones? Including, I suppose, the ones who only clean the outhouses.*

The next morning some Mexicans show up in camp. Five members of the aristocracy, coutured to grace the pages of a Tenochca fashion mag, stroll casually into the little town. They trail behind them a larger than usual conglomeration of servants, priests, and some disheveled persons of indeterminate seer-savant status.

"Captain Cortés," says the chief delegate. "How splendid an occasion this is—I mean to find your countenance shining, yea, verily glowing after such a long illness. You were stricken with some fever, I believe?"

Cortés waits for the translation and then answers in an off-hand manner. "Oh, it was nothing serious, but thanks so much for your concern." *These fellows manage to keep track of our every move,* thinks the captain.

"If it would please your grace," says the ambassador, "clearly it is, ah … mucho molestia." The Spanish words strike Cortés and Marina like a bolt from the blue.

"Many of our people are deeply interested in the arts of healing. What medicines, pray tell, were utilized in the alleviation, the suppression, the elimination, that is to say, the cure of your fever?"

Cortés looks at Marina with ill-concealed impatience. "So tell him," he says. "Tell him."

Marina begins. "Certain fruits of the Cuban hillsides—"

"Oh, it is not I who require this knowledge," the ambassador quickly responds. "I am far from expert in the field of potions and purgatives. Rather it is these." With a contemptuous toss of the head he indicates some old ladies standing close by, "our esteemed, if rather unkempt and not overly sanitary, guild of herbalists who lust after such information."

At that, he reaches over and tries to grab a grinning crone by the shawl. The woman, however, has dropped prone in the dust where she remains just out of Lord Dressed to the Nine's reach. He solves the problem by inserting a foot beneath her belly, and by means of a mighty kick, brings her to a standing position.

"Whee," shrills the old lady, and then she announces to her cohorts, "damn good thing I'm not pregnant."

"Oh, that's a good one," her friends cackle loudly. Oxyria has always been a great wit, a veritable genius of the adlib.

Cortés is beginning to feel a bit tired. He pulls off the bag of fruits he wears at his side. "These grow in the mountains of Cuba. They are used against fevers of all kinds."

The ancients all gather round and lay hands on the bag. After a couple of sniffs they spread the contents out on a rag they have placed on the ground. "O gracious," they cry. "Tepetomatl (manzanita) Nothing more than tepetomatl. Ay, ay, ay."

Cortés and the Mexican emissaries agree that their business is of more import than the ravings of those old bags, and so they ignore the crones and once more resume serious diplomatic bickering.

"It is the wish of our supreme Tlatoani," begins the ambassador, "to become a vassal of the great King Carlos and to pay an annual tribute, the substance of which is to be agreed upon. You may rest assured the amount will not be piddling. Our Tlatoani greatly desires to greet you himself at the court of Tenochtitlan. He feels obliged, however, to deprive himself of that pleasure in consequence of the poverty of the country and its bad roads. The which are near to impassable."

Once more an exhausted Cortés feels like packing it all in. How on earth is he supposed to respond to this nonsensical set of lies.

A cry from the old herbalist distracts the company and gives him time to think—but not for long.

"Tepetomatl! Tepetomatl! That stuff wouldn't cure a dog's diarrhea."

Cortés expresses his gratitude to the great monarch for the presents and his offer to pay tribute to the Spanish sovereign. Then he makes an odd request. He wants the Mexican ambassadors to accompany the Spaniards to Tlaxcala. No treaty has yet been made with that country and he wants the Mexicans present when those arrangements are finalized.

While the Captain is deep in conversation with Moteuczoma's ambassadors, General Sir Bumblebee himself shows up with about a half company of fully armed warriors. They strut toward Cortés and the Mexicans in parade formation, conch horns blaring, whistles shrilling. All are rigged out in blinding white cotton uniforms decorated with bright red designs. The Mexicans are stunned but needlessly so, for the Tlaxcalan delegation is a peace mission—albeit one of haughty and somewhat nerve-wracking demeanor.

Here, then, is history in the making. Mexicans, Tlaxcalans and Iberians: deadly enemies, now come together on a bleak and chilly plateau of a great continent. In deep shade beneath the massed clouds of summer, they will address problems, ancient and contemporary, and for once no blood will color the outcome (except for that of sacrificed slaves). Words now spoken, notions put forth, ideas exchanged round this old bone yard of a battleground may forge a link, or even two, in a chain of actions binding worlds together for all time.

The ancient plant specialists encountered earlier are holding a querulous sidebar argument, practically under the feet of our official diplomatic reps. Let us listen in. (It should be of special interest to those readers concerned with efficacious herbal products and dietary supplements.) The ladies are known (in Greco-Hispanic translation) as Oxyria, Hymenosepalus, and Pigweed.

Pigweed: "Tepetomatl. It is ruddy. It has berries; it has a berry. It is a … a round tree? It is of average size. It becomes ruddy; it produces berries; it produces a berry."

Oxyria: "Madame, your profound knowledge of the natural sciences passeth all understanding. I can only kneel at your feet. Who can say? Perhaps yet one more brilliant jewel will plop from your lips."

Pigweed: (in self-deprecating tones) "Well, you can make a pretty good pie from those berries, and they're not so bad against fevers caused by urinary infections."

Oxyria: "Neh! Look at that man's color. Take a gander at the scaling beneath the eyebrows, the black hair covering his hands. No, he is recovering all right, but slowly, very slowly. I mean over a period of many years, and from something far worse than bladder problems. What he needs is a good dose of necutic ground together with—"

Pigweed: "Necutic. It is only a thick root. It is ground together with xoxocoyoltic. And also its name is oquichpatli. It is required by one who has harmed his genitals or—"

Hymenosepalus: "O my, the great book of knowledge speaks once more. Well, go on then. Finish the recitation. Leave nothing amiss. Harmed his genitals or—"

Pigweed: "Harmed his genitals or has expelled semen in his sleep."

Oxyria: "All right, all right. Enough with the euphemisms. That medication cures one ailment only and it ain't wet dreams. It is meant to take the curse off any one they have frightened—that is, ah … catching him in the act. It can be pretty scary, you know."

Pigweed: (face now ruddy as any manzanita) "… is drunk with acidulous water or with plain water. Xoxocoyoltic is also an eye medicine. It is applied only as a dry powder when the eyes are flesh-filled."

The big conference for the purpose of serious discussion and interchange of ideas between Mexico and Tlaxcala never takes place. "Feh," say the Mexicans. "Gahh," exclaims Tlaxcala. Both sides find the idea unbearable.

"O *Malintzin*," say the Tlaxcalans to Cortés. "Had we but known who, and what you are, we would have gone down to the coast and invited you up here. We would have swept the roads before you from the beach to Tlaxcala City."

Marina looks startled, and this is rare, for she never displays any sort of emotion in public. Wide-eyed, she glances over at Cortés.

"What? What was that? By what name does he call me?"

Marina relaxes a bit, for she has an acceptable explanation at hand. "Well, Captain, it is simple enough. The *tzin* sound is put at the end of high-ranking and royal names and since it cannot be added to Cortés, they have tacked it on to my own name. *Malintzin*. Perhaps they only mean to say "Marina's boss." At any rate, that will be the manner by which you are known around here."

The next morning Cortés gathers both armies, Spanish and native American, including every servant, slave, cook, bottle-washer, and camp follower, and delivers a mighty sermon on the evils of idolatry. Father Olmedo not being present to cool his Christian ardor, Cortes "lets it all hang out." When he finishes, the local chiefs seem pensive.

Sir Bumblebee the Elder, who is quite blind, expresses a certain curiosity. He wants to run his hands over Cortés' head, features, and beard. This the captain permits.

Finally, Bumblebee the Elder speaks up. "Look here, my good friend," he gently begins. "We are only too happy to believe in your god, his mother,

her son—and all the rest of those holy godlets?—of whom you speak. O my, who would not believe? O virtue glowing! O sacred beauty!"

"On the other hand," continues Bumblebee the Elder. "We must also stick with our old time religion. And this includes the ancient custom of human sacrifice. Failure to observe these ceremonies will lead to fire, famine, flood, and revolution. So, we'll just have to add your gods to our own holy pantheon. And thus we arrive at a perfect solution. Now, if you don't mind, we'd rather not hear anymore on this subject."

Go on, go on, thinks old Bumblebee. *They're waiting for you down in Cholula. See how you like things down there.*

Part III

Peering Over

Chapter 19

Marina in Cholula—September, 1519

"And I certify to Your Highness that I counted from our
vantage point in the said city, four hundred and more
towers and all of them are mosques."
H. Cortés

I, Marina, am now a slave of the most despicable sort and truly in bondage,
for I tied the cords with my very own hands and bound them tightly about
my heart. In youth, I would whisper, "O sir, today I am not well and would
really not like to do that, sir, so how about a nice game of Parcheesi?" Or,
"Painalla plays the barracks today and O what an afternoon of thrills! Can
we not attend the match?"

Well, my own heart is the master now: a master that will not be
ordered about from bucket to well. How can I stir my own self with some
yearning look of love? Can I bat my eyes at my own soul and expect it to
faint away with desire?

A sin so great as mine, Tlazolteotl has not the power to forgive, but she
would permit me to die. Of this I was certain, and so, spattering myself
with bloody dust, I wandered out into the courtyard, into that place where
swords flashed thick as blow flies about a corpse, and blood flowed like
water, turning the dusty earth to red mud.

And on that spot, I received exactly my due—life, empty and pointless;
time, silly and useless. O salvation most dishonorable.

Suddenly the loyal Bernal stood there before me, holding next to his
face an upraised and dripping sword, its hilt not a hand-span beyond
that ridiculous mustache. The combination was irresistible. Certainly I
laughed in his face, but the sargent only thought me hysterical. He heaved
me across a shoulder and ran over to one of the big doors. Of course, they
were barred from the outside for no Cholulan would be permitted to exit

alive. After a great deal of banging and cursing, somebody on the other side recognized Bernal. Then the gates opened a bit, and I was shoved through into waiting Spanish arms.

What a fuss they made over me. Of course, from their point of view, I had done the work of a great hero. "She must have got trapped in the courtyard," they told the captain. "Acting out her part to the very last. What a woman!"

But now I see the pen doeth outrace the mind. Perhaps it would be best to go back a bit. It seems only yesterday we entered the gates of that city.

"Get a load of this place," the men exclaimed. "It's bigger than Granada, and every bit as beautiful."

"My goodness, just see the huge number of street beggars," remarked Cortés. "Like any great city in Europe. A sure mark of high civilization, those mendicants."

The men all craned their necks about like a bunch of village tourists on pilgrimage to visit the holy places. Remember, it was Cholula that gave refuge to the Great Lord of Ways on his flight to the sea. Soon every Spaniard grew silent, nurturing the same disturbing thought: perhaps, after all, we are not dealing here with unmitigated barbarism. I must admit my own heart swelled with pride at the sight of those awestricken Spaniards gawking about with their bumpkin faces.

In the city, Cortés always introduced me as a valued assistant, and so I was given a separate apartment in the court of a large palace. While walking about the streets that evening, I fell into conversation with a woman of rank who begged me to accompany her to her house. She hinted darkly of a plot to kill all the invaders, and that if I were to save my life, I should not hesitate to follow her home. In return for this information, she requested only that I marry her son and become part of the family.

I have no recollection of that evening stroll through the streets of Cholula, my mind as blank as a freshly plastered wall. Or perhaps turmoil it was, too intense to bear, that blotted out all thought. A massacre of Spaniards! Why should my fate be so permanently sealed to theirs? And what of Cortés? My emotions with regard to the captain remained a mystery to my own heart. Did I feel love for this man? Or was it only his power and strength that attracted me? And even in this I had spotted great gaps and omissions. No, most probably it was his mind that aroused me, despite Tlazolteotl's murmurings. Such great dreams wrapped in superior intelligence. O noble taco! O irresistible enchilada!

When I arrived at our compound, the Captain was not in, but at midnight he sent for me. Did he never sleep, this man? In this alone, he seemed almost godlike. I put on a gown and dragged my feet across the court.

Lately the Spaniards had taken to referring to all the people of Anáhuac and even beyond as "esta raza," (this race) as if we were all one. What an absurd notion, yet it stirred within me an uneasy feeling akin to horror, worse even than when the team forced me to steal cookies from grandma's jug, and I had to wait a day and a night for retribution. "Esta raza? Esta raza?" What can it mean?

In Cortés' quarters, a few Tlaxcalan officers, all in civilian garb, sat about smoking cigars and looking smug. Also present were a number of Cortés' officers, and a council was in progress.

"Ah, Marina. Sorry to disturb you," said Cortés politely. "What news in the city?"

"O my captain," I began, and I spoke with my eyes pasted to the floor tiles. I could not raise my head and look him in the face. "The Tlaxcalan chiefs claim to have seen pits being dug at strategic points throughout the city and lined with sharpened stakes, thus making it impossible for the cavalry to pass through the streets."

"Yes, this much is already known." Cortés sat back in his chair while Alvarado emitted a sharp little laugh. Leaning back with legs crossed and arms folded, Cortés appeared to be looking down his nose at the Tlaxcalans, a sure sign of unease.

"Listen. This is no joke," announced de Tapia. "The priests have this very afternoon dedicated six children to the great god of war, what's his name?"

"Huitzilopochtli," said I. "The Hummingbird on the Left."

"Yeah, that's the one." Then he threw me a look as if to say, this woman knows too much. Why is the enemy living here in our very midst?

"Anyway, the Tlaxcalans say there can be no surer evidence of treason, and I am inclined to agree. They request permission to enter the city with the six thousand-man division now camped outside the walls. Not much time remains, they say."

"Hmm ... well, well. Marina, extend to these gentlemen my deepest gratitude. They must have been considerably discommoded in the gathering of this information. Please assure them the Tlaxcalan forces will most definitely be put to use—but later, not tonight. If trouble comes, we will not be the ones to precipitate it."

The caciques complained a bit. "Such a strategy seems defensive in style," insisted the Tlaxcalans, "suited to forces surrounded and seriously pondering surrender. Here we have a sure thing," they said. "No reason to hold off."

"No, there will be no holding off, my friends," Cortés answered. "Your troops will be put to full use. If there is an attack, no one is to leave Cholula alive." At this remark, Tlaxcalan heads nodded with satisfaction.

"No one but women and children, that is," continued the Captain. "Any warrior—Cempoalan, Tlaxcalan, or my own Spaniards—caught doing harm to child or female will be punished to the full extent of the law."

O my, I thought. *Now speaks the great and merciful Ruy Diaz el Cid; he of the magnificent beard. Like his hero, Cortés would spare the helpless. Nor would they lose any limbs to the Spanish steel.*

After the Tlaxcalans had shut the door, he turned to me again. "Anything more, Marina?" O yes, there was more all right. Plenty more.

"Well, my captain," I said, "today I met a woman of Cholula whose husband is commander of a division. Right now he is in the hills nearby co-coordinating Cholulan troops with those of Moteuczoma. The Emperor has sent two oversize divisions, fully twenty thousand infantry, to lead the attack on your forces here."

The two Cholulan priests Captain Cortés had summoned only confirmed this news. They told Cortés something that caused him to frown deeply. The emperor Moteuczoma, they said, had remained in a sad and frightened state of constant vacillation since the arrival of the Spaniards, and the oracles had kept him in such confusion. But now they had twisted his head once more, convincing him he must straightway fight the Spaniards since really they were only men not gods, and that Cholula would be the final grave of his enemies.

O such a mixed up little emperor. In the beginning, faith tells him the Spaniards are truly gods. Then doubt moves in his heart and they become only men of flesh and blood. Around and around he goes, gods to men to gods and back again. From what I have seen, it is possible to say the minds of Christians are not much different. No, really, it is not much different for the Christians. Back and forth they twist, passing with eyes ablaze through greed and fear and hatred of their own god, and then they come to a halt, dwelling softly for a little while in humble faith and sweet humility. And there they remain until, once again, something stirs the doubt within. Perhaps it must be so for all humanity, followers of Christ and Ciahuacoatl and Kuk'ulk'an alike.

Then, for the first time, I spoke unbidden and revealed the rest of the information gathered in my association with the woman of Cholula. I raised a hand and finally managed to look up at Cortés.

"Sir," said I, "they have cut a great number of poles and attached leather collars to them. It is by means of these devices they plan to march us as prisoners into Tenochtitlan. I can testify to this before God, for I myself have seen these instruments. Yes, with my own eyes I beheld them. Furthermore, they plan to cage a few Spaniards and keep them here. A prize for the Cholulans, you understand." Clearly I spoke and clearly I heard myself say these words, and yet all the while my mind seemed to run along two paths at the same time, so that I could not see my feet and knew not where they stood.

De Godoy turned red of face and flung his hat to the floor, but before the men could begin their usual complaints, the captain raised his voice, and inclining his head toward the grinning priests of Cholula, reminded everyone there were foreigners present. Next, he nodded in my direction before addressing the two temple officials. He began with a deep and heavy, if somewhat affected, sigh.

"Gentlemen, gentlemen," he said in tones as mild as one would use in communicating with a sick child, "you've got a beautiful town here. Too bad your sense of hospitality is not so finely designed and delicately wrought as the architecture. Well, fear not. We will burden you no longer with our unwieldy presence. In fact, we're taking off in the morning. Bright and early. Can you be so kind as to provide a couple of thousand men to help transport luggage and artillery? Yes? Grand. Oh. Splendid. Let us gather together in the temple yard for a little farewell ceremony. Of course, all your leading citizens are also invited. Till tomorrow then. Don't be late."

Before the door had shut behind the Cholulan chiefs, everyone began talking and shouting at once, and so it became difficult to make out more than a few scattered words and phrases.

> "... fall upon us as we leave the city ..."
> "... just a real cup of coffee. Not that damned acorn juice."
> "... past the traps and out of town? Never ..."
> "My God, what'll I tell his mother?"
> "... got a biscuit. Don't drop it."
> "... just another bunch of Indian lowlifes."
> "Who? You mean Mexicans?"
> "Yeah. And then there's Mexicans ..."
> "Bah, Mexicans. Who the hell are they?"
> "... haven't even seen them and already you're soiling your pants."

Cortés explained the policy that must be advanced if ever they hoped to get home alive, and that was to strike such a sudden and terrible blow that all in this land would be frightened into passivity. They must be shown that Spaniards can no more be crushed by weight of numbers than they can be fooled by simple-minded duplicity.

When Cortés outlined his plan for the morrow, there was emitted from the mouth of our valiant Captain Alvarado that strange little chuckle of his, something like the growl of a cat just as his teeth close on the rat's neck, or mayhap like the snap of a dry twig on the forest floor, or maybe more like two twigs, or perhaps ... O no, impossible. No use attempting to describe that ghastly sound. Only the pen of a great poet like our Packstrap of Painalla (who, since retirement, composes full time) might capture some part of the spell now cast over the hearts of the Spanish officers. Then that crowded place seemed like a great empty cave and all was silence. Then I heard Packstrap shout in my ear "out of bounds," but I know not if any other heard it.

Finally, Cortés ordered the men to bed. "We've got a good four hours of sleep remaining, and we ought to take advantage of every second."

Down here in Painalla, I have come into possession of a clock and can now comprehend most fully the keeping of time. It has little or nothing to do with the cycles of Citlalpol or the sun's passage across the horizon or the elliptical path the ruler walks from his inner sanctum to the temple entrance. Time, we see now, is a mechanical process set in motion by God at the beginning of creation. And it goes on and on in a straight line forever and ever. No adjustments necessary.

That night was one of terrible anxiety for the Spanish army. The captain did not close his eyes even once during the remaining hours of darkness. Every horse stood saddled and bridled and ready for service, and every soldier lay down with his arms. But no assault came.

With the first streak of morning light, Cortés had arranged everything. The gates were barred and guarded and the guns placed along the avenues outside. As the yard grew dense with citizens and tamemes, Spanish soldiers remained hidden in the shadows under the temple porticos. Anyone with eyes could understand what would soon take place, but the Cholulans never caught on. O the fools. They had all been protected for so long they no doubt saw themselves as invulnerable. The sun showed itself for just a second over the fourth step of the Teocalli and all that great crowd in the square were, for a moment, blinded. And then they were all struck down by the sword. In a great killing like this, the Spaniards don't waste much time with stabbing. They slash downward at the point where the neck meets the shoulder and the heavy steel penetrates to mid body. At least that's the way it begins. Then when the victims stop running about and lie down in despair, they must be decapitated or dispatched with a downward stab through the back. At any rate, there was a great deal of blood. I was there in the middle of it but not a drop of that blood, not a speck, was mine.

And so, the one who should have perished lives on, but not for long. Not myself, but all Anáhuac came to an end on those temple grounds. If indeed Ce Acatl Quetzatlcoatl had returned, why would he slaughter his own people and push over his own image? No one could think of an answer to these questions, but I knew well the answer. All things, both good and bad, follow on the will of God and do so in accordance with the way we on earth behave. And so, in response to my treachery, a great emptiness opened before the land, and out of the hearts of the people all faith drained away like water down a roadside ditch.

Chapter 20

Approaching the Dream World—November 8, 1519

"Clearly, the book of Acamapichtli held a true
prophecy. There it lay like a crisped offering,
its edges all burnt black and blown to the wind—
and yet the prediction came true."
Carlyle Duka

"O Malinche, Malinche. These glorious presents our Tlatoani sends you,
saying how grieved he is that you should take so much trouble in coming
from a distant country to see him, and that he has already told you that he
will give you gold and silver for your Teules on condition that you will not
approach Mexico. Alvarado turns to his company with a jittery laugh. "Oh,
yes. That's the way to keep us out. Threaten us with gold and jewels."

Late that afternoon, Marina crouches by a little creek washing out
some clothes. Cortés has told her more than once that he will provide
her with a servant to perform such duties, but she always says, "Thanks,
Captain, but I'd rather do it myself. Nobody around here knows how to
dry and fold these skirts and huipiles. There's a trick to it."

Marina frowns and suddenly whirls about. How long has Nuzi Duka
been standing there staring at her back? Both of them freeze there like river
rocks with eyes, only gazing silently at each other. Marina's skirt is quite
damp and it clings to her rear end. Nuzi is stunned by the view. *Isn't it
amazing,* he thinks. *The sight of a body, an ordinary human body, can inspire
a man to want to reproduce. Well, I suppose that's the way it was planned,
but really, it's quite bizarre.*

Finally Nuzi picks up a pebble and tosses it into the quiet backwater
where Marina has been working. "You know, señorita," he says quietly,
"perhaps we have more in common than either of us realizes."

"Oh, really," answers Marina.

132

"Yes. I'm aware you asked Little Corn for a private meeting with someone in the city. I'm not certain who. My Nahuatl isn't quite that good. But one thing is certain. Cortés knows nothing of this particular development. I think we'd better, uh … watch each other's backs, don't you?"

Marina seems paralyzed in place, wet laundry still in hand.

A little pause and Nuzi continues, "Marina, Marina, my love, you are truly an amazing woman. How on this earth did you manage to get the book away from those two sets of hands. Bright Water, well, that's not such a miracle, but Cross Hunter is as hard-headed as they come and a direct descendant of old Acamapichtli himself."

"O Sr. Duka, those things would only disgust you, anointed as they are with human blood."

"Bloody or not, those pictures cannot be permitted to circulate among the people at this time."

"Really? Is that so? And what danger lies in a few pages of cartoons even if, indeed, composed by the very first Tlatoani—which notion is probably nothing more than the product of someone's imagination working overtime?"

Duka's Gypsyish complexion seems to thicken: turning opaque and purple, like the wings of a cowbird reflecting inconstant sunlight. "Marina," he whispers, "don't try to play games with a Duka King." Marina can hardly keep from laughing. *So where,* she thinks, *are the rest of your subjects?*

"So, then," Duka goes on. "We know the book of prophecy predicts, in no uncertain terms, the return of Quetzalcoatl this very autumn. Moteuczoma ordered Bright Water and Cross Hunter to destroy this evidence, but they chose instead the road of treason. The fact that they asked Olmedo to baptize them is pretty much proof of that."

Now Marina is humming to herself and looking up into the trees.

"They planned on turning the book and the city maps over to Cortés. Somehow or other that incomparably brave and infinitely resourceful maiden Marina Zazil Ha knocked those plans into a crooked hat. Now, as for the book of Acamapichtli, I can't really …"

Marina stares into the green branches. *A virgin, he calls me. Well, that's sweet.* A hand seems to rest on her shoulder impelling her to speak.

"It is already destroyed, burned to a crisp, the ashes buried in mud, according to orders as originally issued."

"And of this you are certain?" asks Nuzi? But answer comes there none. Nuzi leans back and looks up at the great cypress limbs overhead. The sudden move brings a touch of dizziness. He groans softly and pinches the bridge of his nose.

"So this means … what? We're on the same side?"

Chapter 21

Entering the Fantastic—November 9, 1519

"For I dream not, nor start from my sleep, nor
see this as in a trance."
Moteuczoma II

The meeting between Cortés and Moteuczoma takes place in the borough of Xoloco at the city end of the Yellow Plant Causeway. Later, Alvarado will build his house on the very spot. Tenochtitlan's sister city, Weavertown, is represented by its Chief of the Armory and ruler, Eagle Vision. The encounter is not as dramatic as might have been expected. In fact, it verges on the silly.

"Is that you?" is all the captain can think of to say. Moteuczoma's greeting is little more creative.

"It is so. I'm the one."

Later, however, the Tlatoani waxes more poetic. He bows his head and speaks in humble tones, his words barely audible yet infinitely expressive.

"Our Lord you have arrived on earth; you have come to your noble city of Mexico. You have come to occupy your noble mat and seat, which for a little time I have guarded and watched for you."

What Moteuczoma had to say on that occasion is already well-known. His words have been written into plays, explained by academics, and published in ever so many languages. What need to review them here? 'But it's quite interesting,' you protest. Very well, then. Here are a couple more lines from that speech delivered in a room in the palace of Water Eggs.

"I do not dream that I see you and look into your face. Lo, I have been troubled for a long time. I have gazed into the unknown whence you have come—the place of mystery. For the rulers of old have gone, saying that you would come to instruct your city, that you would descend

135

to your mat and seat, that you would return. And now it is fulfilled, you have returned."

All of the council of princes are there and hear every word of Moteuczoma's peroration, yet none are convinced. In the echo of that speech, the Party of Doubt comes of age—in Nahua style: It hardens. It grows firm. It crystallizes.

Then Moteuczoma motions Cortés to follow and leads the Spaniards to the lodgings that have been chosen for them. These rooms are in the palace of a deceased relative, Water Eggs by name. A raised platform is assigned to Cortés and for the rest, thick mats with little canopies over them. The whole of the palace is light, clean, and airy with an entrance through a great court. Little do the Spaniards know that the palace of Water Eggs is Moteuczoma's treasure house, and the walls around them are stuffed with gold and silver and jewels. When made aware of it, they will tear the place apart without a thought for the consequences.

Moteuczoma avoids looking into the face of Cortés unless he is speaking to him directly. Then he turns gracefully and stares directly into the captain's dark and hooded eyes. His own are not so dark, but seem to glisten with a golden light. Their expression is extraordinarily benign, mild, and pleasant. Now he takes Cortés by the hand and leads him to a bench against the wall. A couple of officers nudge their comrades, causing a minor disturbance to the rear. There, against the opposite wall, sits that old hunk of Moroccan furniture the Captain had presented to the ambassadors down on the beach ... when? It seems like years since that first meeting aboard ship. Imagine dragging that ancient monstrosity sixty leagues uphill. Little do the men know that within months they will be lugging entire ship sections up through those miserable passes.

With little or no ceremony, Cortés begins speaking on the subject that is uppermost on his mind—the making of a royal convert. When Marina begins to translate, the Tlatoani looks at her sharply and then settles his gaze on the middle distance. Gorgeously decorated, the big apartment might do for a reception room in an Oriental palace, except the ceilings are lower. Its walls are hung with cotton drapes stained richly in every shade of dye. Clouds of incense pour out from censors, thus diffusing the room with delightful odors. Moteuczoma seems to fix his eyes on some gorgeous feather-work drapes wrought with figures of birds, insects, and flowers. To some, the glowing radiance of their colors compares favorably with the finest tapestries of Flanders.

Moteuczoma listens to Cortés the preacher with the nicest attention, yet the second his jaw stops moving, the Tlatoani claps his hands and announces dinner. He does not wait for a translation of Cortés' last line.

"And now, gentlemen," he says, "I will leave you to your refreshment and then perhaps a little rest? You must surely be a bit fatigued after your long journey from the east."

"Oh, not us," Cortés pipes up saucily. "Spaniards never suffer from fatigue. We just don't get tired."

Moteuczoma looks around, pleasantly taking everyone in with that benign gaze of his. "Well, Malintzin," he says, "perhaps we can meet again for a little conversation. After you have taken your ease for a while, that is." Then the Tlatoani, with the deepest of bows, withdraws from the room along with his escort of nattily attired nobles.

Cortés is left standing around "with his teeth in his mouth" as the saying has it.

But then in comes the food—great heaping platters of it—mostly pieces of a large local fowl called guajelote (*turkey*), which, as was later learned, is the cheapest and most plentiful meat in the land. The guajelote is a large bird, bigger even than a goose, and quite domesticable. There is a wild version as well, which is a little smaller and not quite so tasty.

And here we are lead into some important considerations regarding the foods of the land of Anáhuac. A number of historians, none of whom were present, have claimed the Spaniards never really grew reconciled to the "peculiar" Indian cooking but found it only barely tolerable. Nothing could be further from the truth. It was relished—that is, when the good stuff could be obtained. This problem is simple enough. Not every Indian chef is a culinary genius, and when stale, old, or over-spiced or under-spiced, their creations can be execrable. Certainly, as much can be said for any cuisine on earth. No one, for example, has yet to find a decent meal, reasonably priced, anywhere in the vicinity of Salamanca. The situation can be directly related to the town's large student population, for students and Gypsies make up the most fertile grazing ground for cheating merchants and restaurateurs. This is true in any part of the world.

The basic *delicioso* of this country is as simple as it is tasty. Take a fresh-made maize tortilla, spread on some mashed and then refried local beans, add some guajelote slices or pieces of fish or venison, or only a few chunks of onion, and then sprinkle on some bits of red or green chili and fold the tortilla into an envelope. Oh, believe me, there is no more savory snack imaginable. It is not clear, however, if the Indians themselves have always consumed this concoction. It may be something the Spaniards invented along the trail to Tenochtitlan. To name the dish, the Spanish takes the past participle of the word "envolver," (to wrap), adds the Nahua "chili," and somehow comes up with "enchilada."

True, the historians are correct to a very limited extent. There are a few who are unable to tolerate any form of spicy dish. These individuals have a difficult time in southern parts. For them, one can only wish relief and a long and happy life amongst the isles of Hibernia.

"I suppose they are all related—I mean the Spaniards who have been showing up on our shores from time to time over the last few years." Moteuczoma seems quite cheerful in the morning. "For example, the batch who put in an appearance on the Tabasco coast not so many seasons past. Their Captain's name was … yes, yes, Grijalva. Of course. An older man with blue eyes and a very black beard. And O yes, that poor young Balboa, the one who lost his head down "Where Seas Almost Meet." We've never been properly apprised regarding that business. And you must forgive my somewhat over-eager curiosity if I express a desire to know something of the rank of these officers who accompany you. That is to say their position and … uh, hmm … what do we call it? O yes, military occupational specialty—their jobs within your organization."

Cortés begins by introducing Pedro Alvarado as his second-in-command. *Let's wing it a bit,* he tells himself. "Alvarado was in charge of the conquest of your old-time enemy, the city of Cholula." Moteuczoma responds with a thin smile. *My old time enemy, eh? Does this half-cooked, semi-aristocrat, talented though he be, think he can trick me with his off-beat revisionism?*

Then Cortés works his way through Sandoval, Ordaz, and the other officers present. Moteuczoma is a highly educated product of a nonliterate society. His powers of memory are developed far beyond our own. Before the morning is over, he knows the name rank and function of every officer among the Spanish troops.

Moteuczoma beckons to Cortés. "Come up here and take the right hand side of my bench. Then speak to me of your land, its government, its religion. And describe, as well, the beauties of its scenery, mountains, valleys, rivers, and sea shores."

Cortés jumps at the opportunity but unfortunately jumps up on the left. Immediately a wall of hands emerges and gently steers him over to the other side of the Tlatoani. Moteuczoma knows he is in for a religious harangue. *O well,* he thinks, *a minor inconvenience. Could be he'll say something revelatory.* The speech, however, merely bores the Tlatoani and also proves a little irritating.

"You know, Cortés," says Moteuczoma with a frown, "this whole business troubles me. I've already heard through my ambassadors of those things of which your sacred mass consists. We, it is true, consume the flesh of our fellowmen given in holy sacrifice. But answer me this if you can: Is it not more fitting to feed on the flesh and blood of a fellow creature, than on that of the creator himself? This is a great puzzlement to me."

"Oh, come, come," whispers Father Olmedo. "He's only pretending to be stupid."

"Well, Of course, your priests have explained the whole business to you in terms far beyond our poor powers to add or detract," says Moteuczoma, "but meanwhile, we'll stick to the old gods of our ancestors. Any other course would risk famine, flood and fire, sooo ... lets drop this discussion for the length of your stay. It can do no good for either of us. But do not take offense. No doubt your gods are every bit as holy as ours."

Just here, the Tlatoani rises and begins distributing among the poorest soldiers the most elaborate and valuable gifts, rich cloths, gold trinkets, and some heavy gold collars hung with large and beautifully made golden shrimp. Of course, the common soldier is concerned only with finding an opportunity to melt down those lovely products of the goldsmith's art into good solid ingots.

The Tlatoani's generosity, combined with the obvious delicacy of his emotions, begins to soften the iron-hearted Spaniards, and on the way out, all remove their hats and make him the most profound obeisance. Back at quarters, the men speak among themselves:

... fine breeding ..."

"And such courtesy and ..."

"Consideration. Yes, that's the word ..."

"This man commands the greatest respect. Of that there can be little or no doubt."

"... gentle eyes and sensitive countenance."

Cortés appears not quite so sanguine. "Nuzi," he says, "here we have neither the plain and rude republican of Tlaxcala, nor are we confronted by the effeminate church-going Cholulan. This is more like some old Greek city-state—Sparta maybe." To Alvarado, he speaks of more practical concerns. "It's been six days Pepe; I think we have to make a move. As stiff-necked and intolerant as Spaniards are, well, if he should get at odds with us, he's strong enough to wipe every trace of us off the face of this land. He can no longer be permitted to run around loose. But we need a reason, some kind of charge."

"How about those nine Spaniards dead on the beach at Nauhtla?" Nuzi pipes up. "Including the gallant Escalante himself. How's that for an excuse? We can't prove the Emperor is responsible, but so what?"

"Nuzi, my lad, you're a genius."

Chapter 22

The Arrest—December 19, 1519

"The idea of employing a sovereign as a tool for
the government of his own kingdom,
if a new idea in the
Renaissance, is certainly not so in ours."
American historian

Now Cortés understood very well that if he did not remove the Tlatoani from the influence of his advisory board (Council of Princes), they would, in the shortest of shrifts, force the leader to summon troops for an attack on the Spaniards in the city. And so, Cortés had no choice but to separate Moteuczoma from that element and place him under arrest. General Fertilizer went into captivity with the Tlatoani and Sir Small Corn. Half the kitchen staff and servant corps accompanied them, and so their surroundings in the Spanish quarters were the same as that to which the high ranks were accustomed. They bore no resemblance at all to those fetid prison cells in the basement storage rooms.

A frazzled and careworn Cortés stands leaning against a wall waiting for mass to finish. Preacher Olmedo drones on. "I am the savior of all people, says the Lord. Blest be our Lord of the Flowers. Blest be his holy name. Blest be his most precious blood. Blest be the great Mother of God, María most holy. Alleluia, alleluia, alleluia. Now let the victor's triumph win. Now let the strife be o'er. Let the song of praise be sung. For this we pray in the name of the Father, and of the Son, and of the Holy Spirit."

Now Cortés proceeds to Moteuczoma's throne room in the company of his best officers, the crazed but fearless Alvarado, Sandoval, de Leon, de Lugo, and de Ávila. He has sent notice to the Tlatoani that he is on his way to pay him a visit. No point in alarming the ruler with an unexpected entrance.

"Why would the Teule want an audience at this time? Why now in particular?" The Tlatoani is almost whining. "Can it be he blames me for the deaths of his comrades on the coast?"

When the Spaniards are ensconced in the throne room, Moteuczoma begins speaking in a jocular manner.

"Well, well, Sr. Cortés. I've been meaning to ask you—how do you find our little Mexican women? Do you think them attractive?"

"Oh, Majesty, they are lovelier than the flowers blooming in your gardens and smell even better."

"Ha, ha. Cortés, I am beginning to like you more every day. So tell me, dear sir. Why have you not yet found yourself a wife here in the city? It can't be that you are—. O no, no. Of course not. What an absurd thought."

Is the Tlatoani indulging in some sort of subtle insult? Marina, who is versed in all the double entendre and hidden meaning in the Mexican tongue, thinks this entirely possible.

Cortés answers with a laugh that echoes the Tlatoani's own. "Oh, Your Majesty. Unfortunately I already have a wife back in Cuba and my religion forbids taking more than one woman in marriage." Marina rolls her eyes around. Moteuczoma glances at the two of them. Barely able to cover a grimace, he looks down, again stroking his thin little goatee.

After a minute, Moteuczoma throws up his hands and heaves a great sigh. "O religion, religion. Indeed faith can be burdensome at times. Well, maybe you're right, Cortés. After all, why buy a duck when eggs are so cheap?" This last Marina is able to translate almost literally.

Then Cortés speaks up, taking the company completely by surprise. In a mild and neutral tone, showing not a trace of anger, he accuses Moteuczoma of plotting the destruction of the Spanish-Totonac settlement guarding the port down at Nauhtla.

"In addition to this provocation," continues Cortés, "we understand that your officers are even now plotting our immediate destruction. Such being the case, we should be forced to defend ourselves and this great and beautiful city of yours would end up as a broken pile of rock and rubble. In order to prevent the destruction of the city, Your Majesty, it would be best if you came to live with us at our quarters where you will be treated with the greatest respect. On this you have my word."

Turning pale as a ghost, Moteuczoma listens to all this with profound amazement. "Since when," he blurts out, now flushing red, "since when was it ever heard that a great prince like myself voluntarily left his own palace to become a prisoner in the hands of strangers!"

"Oh, Your Majesty, will not go as a prisoner. You will be surrounded by your own people and perform your daily duties as usual. What we're talking about here is simply a change of residence from one palace to another."

"Listen to me, Cortés," says the astounded Moteuczoma, eyes cutting from side to side. "Surly you are aware that I have a legitimate son and two fine daughters. Take them as hostages for me if you will, but for the sake of god, do not expose me as a prisoner to my own people."

Meanwhile, the noble cavalier Vasquez de Leon appears on the verge of apoplexy. Pulling a dagger from his belt, the overwrought cavalryman begins to shout. "Enough, enough. No more playing around with this barbarian dog. It's sickening. If he doesn't come along this very second I'll plunge my dagger through his throat." A little froth appears on the lips of de Leon.

Cortés breathes not a word. Apparently he believes such tactic is appropriate for the situation.

The deranged De Leon makes a rush for the Tlatoani. Moteuczoma's guards move not a hair. They appear to show little interest in the defense of their king. It is the Spaniards who jump forward and drag de Leon away from the throne.

The action described above serves to shake the Tlatoani's resolution. He is in tears now, looking desperately around for some support or even a little compassion. None is forthcoming. "My hour has come," he sighs. Then in barely audible tones, he agrees to accompany the Spaniards to the palace of his great uncle Water Eggs.

At this point, a few remarks regarding the behavior of Moteuczoma seem appropriate. His grandfather, Moteuczoma I, Moteuczoma Heavenbound, would have left his blood soaking into the cushions, say the historians, rather than surrender abjectly to the invaders. On this occasion, Moteuczoma II proved himself a moral and physical coward, they insist. Actually, this is not so sure. Perhaps there are two kinds of bravery in both the moral and physical realms. The first is thoughtless and instinctive, usually accompanied by rage and temporary loss of reason or self-control. Mexicans warriors are thoroughly acquainted with this emotion. They call it "battle rage."

Now the Tlatoani Moteuczoma was as Mexican as they come, but there was something out of sync in his Mexicanism and at odds with it. Brave enough he was, but his courage was of the second variety. That is, he was of the type that needs to first peg his guts to a sticking place, and this requires time and mental preparation. Many a brave man or woman can be startled into ignominious behavior if not given sufficient time to call on their inner resources. And this is what happens to Moteuczoma. The twisted, ominous face of de Leon, the screaming threats and naked dagger, all roll through his brain like a great peal of thunder. In deep shock, the Tlatoani consents to accompany Cortés to the Spanish quarters just down the road. Here, the captain tells his officers, the ruler will be unable to rally his nobles, and they are quite unlikely to attempt anything without his personal orders. Cortés has spent his only resource—the courage of his troops—and with that coinage buys himself a bit of time.

Moteuczoma gives orders to prepare a litter for his transport. He announces his intentions to the head steward and other household attendants.

"Ahem … I am planning to stay a few days with my Spanish friends." Moteuczoma is having a difficult time keeping his countenance from expressing the deep sense of shame and horror he feels. "We will simply walk the short distance to Water Eggs's palace. I go voluntarily, see? I go of my own will. Cortés is my dear friend and bosom pal, so there need be no tumult of any kind. See that the streets are cleared and kept free of any overly curious rabble." And so, the caravan sets off down the road. This incident occurred on a day in mid November in the year 1519.

In such manner is the seizure of the great Moteuczoma accomplished. He brings with him to the Spanish quarters his wives, all manner of servants and chefs, and his diplomatic staff. He takes a bath every day.

Oh, yes. The Tlatoani is comfortable enough and, of course, he remains in touch with current events in Anáhuac. The Acolhua, the eastern defense line just across the lake has evaporated. The Tepaneca cities now swear allegiance to Charles V. The Chinampa cities to the south are in open revolt against their Mexican garrisons.

But now, in the palace of Water Eggs, Moteuczoma drapes himself in ignorance. It covers him like a magic veil and only good cheer passes its invisible weave, and much humor. A kind of tenderness slips through where nothing of politics or considerations of empire can penetrate. And this tenderness is felt by all coming into his presence.

Chapter 23

Smoking Tree—January, 1520

"And one cannot deny that, as he reflects on the progress
made by the Aztec in knowledge … he must admit their claim
to a higher place in the scale of civilization than that
occupied by barbarians."
Prescott

The knight who led the raid on Nauhtla is called Smoking Tree, and he is
one of Moteuczoma's most trusted military advisors. Lord Smoking Tree
holds the titles "Lines Tactical" and "Plans Strategic," and rarely does
he—no, he *never*—makes mistakes like that dreadful foul-up at Nauhtla.
How was he to know so many Spaniards were in there defending that filthy
hole? How was he to know?

How? Because that's his job, that's how. Defeat due to insufficient
intelligence. Ye gods! Those gum-chewing whores in the market place will
be giggling over this one for quite a while. Well, Smoking Mirror, that
tricky barbarian, could simply osculate his posterior at high noon on the
temple steps.

At the evening meal, Smoking Tree is interrupted by a delegation
from Tenochtitlan. Out of the woods they come, making a great racket
with drum and horn. The general is outraged. He stands and shouts at
the leader.

"Thou who art here. *In axcan tlaxiccuj*. Take heed. Who dost thou
think thou art, screaming and howling into my camp, which happens
to be localized in the very heart of enemy country? And who will defend
you if an attack should materialize? Those musician-degenerates thou hast
dragged along?"

The leader of the intruders cuts the general off. He has some rank of
his own and is not intimidated by the ravings of General Smoking Tree.

"I must remind you, sir, of the written and well-established law forbidding such accusation without direct proof. Homosexuality has never presented problems of a general nature in our army. Only individuals are affected, and they are perfectly safe so long as they quietly remain within their spirit-lined category."

"O buttocks," responds the general.

The recently arrived official turns and snaps his fingers calling forward a servant in feathered livery. That individual holds out a fancy-carved box, which he has carried all the way down from Teochtitlan. It contains nothing less than the great seal of Moteuczoma. General Sir Smoking Tree takes one look, and his heart sinks to near colonic levels. *Well, it was a pretty good career,* he thinks. *So let 'em bust me out. They can't take away my pulque rights. A little place at Acapulco with a good view of the Southern sea. Glass in hand. Ocean sunsets—.*

Smoking Tree's musings are interrupted by the voice of the recently arrived official who is making another speech. "Summoned you are. Called to appear before the great Moteuczoma, First Speaker of Tenochtitlan, and you are to depart immediately, regardless of hour, weather, or unfavorable omen."

Smoking Tree looks at him expressionlessly.

"Ahem," continues the recently arrived. "The band, you will be interested to know, will remain here for the purpose of building morale. It will add professionalism and authenticity to the celebration of the day on which the statue and the banner of Paynal is raised up on the altar. And that day is upon us even as we speak."

"Yes, I suppose the boys will be happy to have a bit of a spree," says the general without much enthusiasm. "It's a little breezy for walking around naked, but I suppose we can dress some of the chaps up in skirts and huipiles to play the women's parts. We don't have enough paper to lay out the path of "He Who Hasteneth," so sticks will have to do. After all, there's a war on. I'll go make some arrangements. We'll leave for the city first thing in the morning." Smoking Tree heaves a sigh and turns to go.

"No, no, good sir," shouts the recently arrived. "My instructions say something to the effect that we make our departure with no more delay than required to consume a small snack."

The General has already started down the path to his tent. Without turning around, he raises a hand. "In the morning," he says. "First thing in the morning."

Next day, the entire company, including three of Smoking Tree's officers, Coatl, Quiabuitle, and one whose name is forgotten for all time, move up the trail leading to the eastern escarpment. Three days later, they find themselves up on the cold plateau, just out of the pass the Spaniards call Nombre de Dios. Here the company runs into a cold, thick mist. The stars are invisible and navigation is tricky. What's more, a fierce headwind comes up in their faces, rolling down the slopes of the volcanoes that rim the southern side of the valley. Does Smoking Tree hold authority over this expedition? Difficult to say. Nevertheless, he gives orders to camp in the shelter of some huge boulders that line the trail, and no one contradicts him. Just in front of the rocks is a rather large patch of prickly pear, so if they are stuck for a while no one will starve.

The General steps around a boulder to relieve himself and finds a suitable cul-de-sac between two rocks. He turns about and almost stumbles over Moteuczoma's rep. That worthy has followed Smoking Tree straight into the little alcove.

"What in the underworld—," gasps the general. "One doesn't expect a great deal of privacy in this man's army, but here you go too far."

"I must inform your person, sir," says the rep. from Tenochtitlan, "that he is … he is … well, under arrest, to put it bluntly. When we reach Texcoco, he must be bound to prevent any attempt at escape. Now then—"

"Over my dead body." Smoking Tree grinds the phrase out harshly.

"Then, sir, you must give your word not to make a break for it at any time during this voyage."

"Sir, you speak like a man with an orifice of paper. Why should I try to get away? Am I afraid of my speaker? Moteuczoma loves me. We are like brothers. Now if you will please excuse me."

Moteuczoma's rep throws a quick glance over his shoulder and then grabs Smoking Tree by the arms. "Listen," he whispers, "everything hinges on did you or did you not attack Nauhtla under orders from the speaker?"

"But of course the speaker ordered the attack. Would I go into battle without such a direction? There was tribute due, and I was ordered to collect it. What could be plainer?"

"And were you informed of the presence of Spanish troops in the fortress?"

Smoking Tree only frowns deeply.

S. L. Gilman

"No, no, of course you weren't. Listen, General, it would be best to deny any communication with the speaker during the last couple of months. Right now the situation in the city is extremely ... fluid, we might say."

Fluid, eh, thinks the general. *What in creation does that mean? Ah, maybe he's working on some kind of diplomatic maneuver designed to outwit the foreigners. Not my cup of atole. With our numbers, we ought to be over 'em like ants on a dead tlacahuachitl. Well, we'll talk it out when I get back, the Kid and I.*

"Fine, fine. Whatever seems best," says the general impatiently, "Now my good sir, if you'll please excuse me?"

Smoking Tree and his officers enter the throne room dressed in capes of nequen, a rough cloth made from maguey fibers. It is designed to cover up fancy clothing, feathers and the like, thus avoiding any semblance of competition with the royal finery.

When the group is admitted, Moteuczoma doesn't bother to look up.

"No, no," he announces, "I have nothing to say to these gentlemen. Just ... take them directly to Cortés." He waves a limp-wristed hand, a gesture in the classic Pontius Pilot mode, dismissing the officers. Cortés is considerably more long-winded. First he delivers the usual pre-punishment justification speech, full of references to trust betrayed, fairness double-crossed, love and affection freely given and then stomped upon.

"So, then," he adds, "the punishment for murdering Spaniards is death. You are hereby sentenced to be burned alive in front of the king's palace. Judgment to be carried out immediately." And then aside, "Don't just stand there, Marina, translate, translate."

"Hold on a second, Sir," pipes up Diaz. "This business of *immediately* may not work," he says. "There ain't enough fuel to burn a chicken unless you want to try immolating 'em with charcoal 'cause that's all we got."

"Not to worry," says Captain Ávila. "There's plenty of fuel. Just across the patio in the whaddyacallit."

"The Tlacochcalli," says Marina.

"Yeah, whatever. The armory. Spear shafts. Good, solid, wooden spear shafts, and spear throwers. There must be thousands of them in there."

Cortés gives orders for the armory doors to be broken open.

A young man wearing the sash of a Shorn guardsman blocks the portal. "Halt!" he yells. "Where do you think you're going? Nobody gets in here without an order from the Tlatoani, or Snake Woman, or Swooping Eagle, or Smoking Tree, or —"

"Listen young man," says Cortés via Marina (the lady is right up front, as usual), there's no time. We're under attack from Huexotzinco. Out of my way this instant."

"O sure, and my grandma's coming on the double with a meat fork. You need an order, I say. Officer of the Day! Post number three," he yells.

"Look here, kid, out of the way or you'll get your head broken along with the woodwork," says de Ávila stepping up so that his writhing lips are but a centimeter from the guard's nose.

"Don't worry. I'll take the responsibility," yells Cortés, and the door goes down.

The prisoners are led out with bound arms. In the courtyard they begin singing:

> "Dispatch me to the place of mystery
> From the turquoise boat
> his words come down
> And I have told the omen-lord
> That I shall go"

There are no stakes to tie them to so they must kneel by the heavy stone benches just in front of the main entrance. Wooden spear shafts are snapped in two and piled up around the four men. When the fires are lit the singing stops, but all four prisoners remain quite calm. Marina returns sedately to the palace and walks on through to the kitchen. Nuzi Duka stays where he is on the edge of the crowd. He does not wish to appear weak-kneed and unmanly, so he forces himself to watch the spectacle. Never having witnessed an auto-da-fé in extremis, Nuzi does not know about the order of burning. First, the skin begins to blister. Then body fluids rush to the surface to cool it down. Next the system of heart and lungs so admirably conjoined for the purpose of transporting living vapors goes into shock—but, unfortunately, the shock is not severe enough to cancel the pain. Neh! *Ya basta*, as the Spanish say. What can it profit us to review that dismal horror in detail. Such treatment will not add a jot to the value of this history. We need only mention that they died there, and they died silently. There were no screams, no groans, and no moans. Not a peep out of them. The reader who would comprehend something of those Mexicans of old should know this: Passive fortitude in the face of hard death was the great virtue of Mexican soldiers, and it was the glory of their lives. Yes, perhaps its only glory. Well, that and the poetry.

Chapter 24

A Thicker Plot—January 21, 1520

"If it were done when 'tis done, then't
were well it were done quickly."
Shakespeare

When the odor of burning animal matter reaches the nose of Nuzi Duka he grows very nauseous. Nuzi turns on his heel and heads for the palace door as rapidly as dignity will permit. He walks through an empty anteroom and then comes to the main hall, which is also deserted. Next he passes through a small chamber lined with huge jars of oil, chilies, and grain, all arranged there for quick and convenient use by cooks and serving personnel. The smell of foodstuffs does nothing to alleviate the crawling discomfort in his stomach. Immediately on entering the kitchen proper, Nuzi steps over to the stone trough built into the wall for the purpose of collecting garbage, and into that receptacle he vomits heartily and noisily.

Marina is at the main sink, kneading a ball of masa (*corn meal and lime for making tortillas*). Lately she has assumed some of the duties of meal preparation, for such occupation helps compose her mind and gives relief, for a moment or two, from those dizzying personal, social, and geo-political conflicts swirling through her mind.

"Ah, no. Ah, my God," Nuzi gasps. Marina stands tall, back as straight as a good arrow, her spread hands grasping the edge of the sink.

"Insuportáble." Nuzi chokes out the word and then turns and spits in the trough. "Insuportáble," comes the gargled repetition. Marina's head tilts back a little. She seems to be staring up into the corner, that dim geometry shaped by the juncture of wall and ceiling. Up there among the shadows, say the folk, dwell some of the nastiest little creatures in the land.

"These Spaniards are neither human nor animal," he says, "only devils cast up from some black pit. They must be stopped—these monsters must be brought to an end ..." Nuzi trails off with a gurgle.

Marina does not turn about and face him. Clouds remove themselves from the face of the sun and a beam of light enters the room by way of a slit window high in the wall. It lingers for a second in Marina's braided tresses and then goes on to catch the countenance of Nuzi Duka. His round eyes, black and Romish, break it into a thousand shards, and they glare forth raging like those angry warriors twinkling away in the night sky. As for her part, Marina remains silent. Well, almost silent. Only two syllables does she breathe out. "Poison?" she says and the word seems to curl up a little as it dies on the kitchen air. "Venón?" comes the whispered query. Ah, venón. At the sound of it Nuzi Duka's eyes blaze brighter still.

And in this manner does that rebellious urge, long buried in the depths of their souls, come into the light. It grows there and it flourishes. It begins to bear fruit. It waits quietly for fate to reap the harvest.

Chapter 25

Speaking of the Fiscal—February, 1520
(162,000 pesos de oro or
6,300,000 U.S. dollars)

According to St. Roger l'Agendiste: "He who would survive lengthy spates of boredom, who would endure and even flourish in very dull times, requires two important qualities: an unflagging will in the pursuit of amusement and, also, a keen nose for diversion." In these characteristics, the people here can be said to hold much in common—that is, the visiting "Spicas"* and those homebred "Anáhuacos" the Spaniards call Indians.

In both Spaniard and Mexican, gaming is a deep-rooted passion and it is through indulgence in this pastime that they all manage to put out of mind the dreadful situation in which they find themselves. The Mexicans are hanging about, dolefully contemplating the downfall of their great empire; the Castilians are also a bit crestfallen for they know well that the breaking of only a few canal bridges will trap them there in the watery city of Tenochtitlan.

The Spaniards remove many a good drum head and cut these stiffened skins into small rectangles called *cartulinas*. These are marked all over with special symbols and used in a kind of sorting game played for golden stakes both large and small. Yes, Cortés, in order to raise the spirits of his men, has divided up some of the gold. The amount given by the very generous Tlatoani, plus the treasure stolen from behind the plaster walls in the main hall of the palace comes to 162,000 Spanish pesos de oro. The value of that amount in American dollars has been figured in terms of nineteenth century prices. Certainly it would be worth more today. This much, however, can be said with certainty. When the gaming ends,

---

* from a first magnitude star in Virgo said to be fifteen hundred times brighter than the sun.

153

most of the common soldiers find themselves as penurious as the day they departed the motherland.

And now, murmurs arise among the troops. "Who dealt this mess?" Mexía quietly demands.

"What? This hand? This hand's of fortune's issue," de León responds.

"What's more, those chains don't belong to you," Mexía adds quietly, still trying to avoid a fuss. Captain de Leon feels no such compunction. "Oh, come off it, Mexía," he shouts with a laugh. "Whose neck are they hanging on anyway." He grabs for his throat in a gesture of mock violence. "Argh, yeah, it's me alright," and the men around begin to giggle. Mexía reaches for his sword but de Leon throws his hands up. "Whoa, whoa, hold up. You don't want to do that compadre. You wouldn't stand a chance."

But Mexía draws his weapon and death walks into the room. Fortunately, Cortés enters at the same time. He permits them to stick each other a couple of times, and when a little blood runs, puts an end to the fight.

The Mexicans, it has been noted, gamble a bit as well. They play a bowling game using golden balls and gold objects d'art standing as pins. Often Cortés attends Moteuczoma with his 150 or so guards, and he and Moteuczoma, with his own 150 or so retainers, play together at the golden game called *tlotolque*.

"O Malinche," calls out Moteuczoma. "We mustn't let Tonatiuh keep score for he has a tendency to exaggerate the count," and then he coughs delicately not wanting to accuse Alvarado of outright cheating. At this, all the Spaniards burst into nervous laughter. They are starting to feel the walls of the old palace closing in.

"O Malinche," says Moteuczoma to Cortés, "Such a long time it's been since I have prayed to the gods of my fathers. It would be a good thing if I went to the teocalli. It would show my friends and relatives that I live among the Spaniards by order of my gods and by my own choice."

"Well, that presents a tricky situation," answers the Captain. "In so doing you must understand that it will be my business to see you commit no act which might be considered dangerous to the Spaniards. I'll send a guard with you, and they will be under orders to kill Your Majesty at the first sign of commotion."

When this is translated, Moteuczoma gives a little shrug and then nods in what can only be called a patronizing manner.

"And another thing," adds Cortés, "there will, of course, be no human sacrifice."

Moteuczoma's mouth slowly turns up into a three quarter grin. "No, no," he says, "clearly not. Would I be so foolish as to antagonize your sovereign and your god in such manner? Not to mention yourself," he adds, goatee raised toward the heavens.

Then they all file out into the courtyard, Moteuczoma with his usual pomp and feathers and Cortés accompanied by the usual 150 infantrymen and four officers, de Leon, Alvarado, Ávila, and de Lugo—the ones with "blood in their eye," as the Spanish phrase has it. And so, as already mentioned, they form a column and enter the courtyard. Years later, John Prodigal talked about the events of that afternoon.

"Now, therefore, if patience will allow, the author will describe something of that walk across town to the Weavertown temple precincts. Yea, and though it risk stomach's ease and peace of soul, he must once more call to mind the streets of that splendid city 'ere the place was dashed to pieces. For now the blood-soaked ruins are covered o'er, and even the lakes, so they say, are drained off and only muddy fields of corn remain."

"After a left turn on the Tlacopan road, we see just to the right the palace of that very famous war leader, Eagle Swoops. The edifice is skirted with a left onto Tecpantzinco Avenue, which wide and well-paved thoroughfare continues the length of the borough of Cuepopan. Arriving at Necoc Zixecan (guard post at Weavertown bridgehead) Moteuczoma's litter is recognized, and the column is quickly passed into the precincts of Weavertown. A few rods further, and the main road (no longer called Tecpantzinco Avenue) curves off to the northwest toward the main marketplace. The entourage turns left sharply on a narrow side street, which passes through the canoe basin a square south of the market, thus avoiding its crowd and confusion.

"And there they all are, climbing the steps of the temple of Huitzilopochtli, the Hummingbird on the Left. Once at the top Cortés and Father Olmedo turn a deathly shade of white, for there on a large stone altar lie the bodies of four individuals."

Cortés reaches for his sword, but Olmedo covers his hand even as it grabs the pommel. "No, Hernán," he gasps, "patience, good sir, we must be patient."

Back in the palace, Moteuczoma is in an extraordinarily good mood. He lavishes presents with that special generosity of spirit, which seems to be his birthright. Gold and silver plate, mantles embroidered with gold thread, fancy capes adorned with the feathers of rare birds—all this he distributes graciously among those who had attended him at the teocalli.

Chapter 26

Comparative Theology—February, 1520

"You might as well try to convert Jews without the
Inquisition as Indians without soldiers."
Don Diego de Vargas Zapata Ponce de Leon

Of course, Cortés cannot let those four gutted and headless corpses simply rest in peace. No, they only inspire him to harass Moteuczoma and regale him with pleas to the end that the Tlatoani should permit the baptism and conversion of everyone in the land. In the midst of these contentious theological discussions, at the point where argument assumes the aspect of threat and the countenance darkens, Moteuczoma makes a proposition. From out of the blue it comes, a piece of stunning illogic, a veritable non sequitur: he offers Cortés one of his daughters, and the best looking one at that. In the language of the sacred sport he "elbows a hook" at the Captain, thereby discommoding him greatly. Oh, it's true, he proposes a legal marriage, and at this, Marina's face grows very still, very solid, like brown clay baked in an oven.

"See, Malinche. I know what you need," says the Tlatoani, and his palms come up in imitation of that statue of the Buddha, which, of course, he has never seen. Cortés can hardly keep from staring about in amazement, but he manages a straight face. "Why, Your Majesty, that would be a great honor," he says, not wanting to offend Moteuczoma with a refusal. "But of course … surely, you can understand … er, ah, my religion … it would be impossible … unless the girl first be baptized in the Holy Spirit, cleansed of the sin of Adam and Eve."

Marina translates to Nahuatl. "My Lord, he says he would, indeed, be greatly honored, but first the lady must be cleaned up: washed free of the filth of the first mother and the first father."

"O baptized … yes baptized … certainly baptized," responds Moteuczoma. "Well, you must know, Malinche, that in this land, all infants are 'baptized' at birth. I mean with actual holy water, sacred water, blessed water. Without it we are prey to our enemies—the big mossy-heads, the big excrement and ashes types." Moteuczoma leans forward with raised forefinger like a lecturer at some Franciscan college.

"We worry a lot about the filth that covers a baby because of the manner of its conception," he says. "All life springs from corruption, and human conception is nothing more than fertile dirt transformed into a baby. The new child must be cleansed of it and also rehabilitated and reassured." The Tlatoani raises both hands and also his shoulders. "Only consider the great danger the little thing has recently passed through. O such a fright he or she has endured."

Cortés makes a little moue and looks over at Father Olmedo who only shrugs as if to say, "Captain, my captain, you're the one with the facile tongue. Surely, some kind of answer will occur, and maybe it won't be too far off. Please remember, you were warned against the pitfalls of importunate evangelism."

Cortés breathes deeply. Oh, surely he can find the right words. Yes, certainly he can. "Good water purifies the body," he says, "that's true enough—but it can't clean the soul. Has Christ been dipped in your water? Does it come from the River Jordan?" *Oh, this is too complicated,* thinks Cortés, and changes tack. "Mechanical washing … that's not where it's at," he says in a herald's voice as though announcing something.

Moteuczoma has a ready response. "O Malinche. By you it seems we can do nothing right. I tell you we wash the newborn very thoroughly and the mother, too. And what's more we also clean her house for her." Here Moteuczoma gives a little laugh and a little wave of the hand. "Our mat-maker folk say it's Nappatecuhtli does the job and he often uses fresh dew. Now how much cleaner—"

Now it is Cortés' turn to raise a hand. "The body counts for nothing," he exclaims with a shake of the head, which makes his beard move. "You see, it is the spirit that must be made clean. We are all born soaked in original sin, drenched inside and out with that evil, and if a child dies before its soul is purified by baptism, which is a sacrament, it is dragged into purgatory."

"Original sin" causes Marina to frown deeply, but finally she comes up with "huehuetlatlacolli" or "old sin."

"Wait, wait. Dear young lady." Moteuczoma raises a hand. "What was that other word? "Pecado?" Yes, "pecado." That's Spanish for ground-up meat, is it not?"

"No, that's 'picadillo,' my sweet little ruler, but of course 'pecadillo' can mean 'minor sin.'" Marina pauses for the length of three heartbeats, and then she stands as tall and straight as she possibly can. When her voice emerges it is harsher than usual and has within it a touch of Spanish iron. "The best way to translate 'pecado,' Dear Little Lord, is 'tlatlacolli,' spoiled, corrupt, rotten, damaged goods."

Moteuczoma stares out into the room but sees nothing and his lips seem to form those words: spoiled, corrupt, rotten, damaged goods.

With a shudder that makes the feathers of his mantle squirm, Moteuczoma comes to himself. "O Malinche," he says. "Such a pessimistic view of life. Surely, man is not born evil, only a little dirty. True, later in life, the tlazolli he commits sticks all over him like glue, and finally he is so covered with corruption there is nothing nice left to see. But we are not born that way. Just look at the little babies. They don't get drunk, do they? And they don't take lovers one after another. No, no, after a good scrub they are very pure, as pure as can be."

When this is translated, the lay cleric Juan Diaz can no longer contain himself. "O blasphemy!" he cries. "Blasphemous lies and heretical nonsense. The souls of unbaptized children are like coals, like clods of earth. When it comes to unbaptized children, God's procedure is immutable. He imprisons them all in purgatory because of the sin that is within them."

At this, everyone in the room turns to look at him. The Mexicans, the Spaniards, and the two or three Tlaxcalan attachés who happen to be present, all turn and stare at Juan Diaz.

In his fifty-page *Contemplation* (as he calls it) of Spanish religion, Prodigal ends on a note of resignation.

"Oh well. Perhaps a reduction in length will prove beneficial for the comprehension of this most extensive tale, so extensive, indeed, it seems to go on forever. Only witness the theological haggling in our own parish and the absurd liturgical compromises that result. Why nowadays, the priests wave in our very faces a round, shiny device suspiciously reminiscent of Tonatiuh, the sun. True, the thing has a holy cross embedded at the top, but it is tiny, very small indeed, and who knows what Gregory VIII would say if he should come to mass and catch sight of that peculiar symbol."

At any rate, it will suffice us to know that after some hand-wringing in the throne room and even a few tears shed, Cortés wins a concession. Moteuczoma will not change religion, but he will convert a building. One of the smaller temples to Hummingbird on the Left is to be cleaned out, redecorated, and rededicated to the Christian god and his three parts. When the job is done, everyone files up the temple stairs to partake of the first mass. Everyone attends: Spaniards, Mexicans, Mexican priests, and the previously mentioned Tlaxcalans. For a nonbeliever the howling and screeching up there is near to unbearable. Perhaps the Spaniards know which god they mean to worship, but Mexican priests are not so sure. They simply lead their followers in the old prayers to Hummingbird on the Left, and these do not blend well with Paternosters and the Te Deum.

Chapter 27

Dabbling in Politics—late February, 1520

"Are we at war?"
Moteuczoma Xoyocotl

In the mountains east of Texcoco, the rebel Vanilla Orchid ponders little brother Little Corn's escape from Tenochtitlan. "O sure," he tells his chief of supply who happens to be married to an ex-wife, "Little Corn knows well the depth of my contempt for the 'Kid.' He hopes to use us. He wants to put his own juvenile butt on the Sacred Mat. No, no, brother of mine, 'twill never happen." Orchid leans back and blows a smoke ring toward the west. "That town belongs to me," he says. "We ought to think about a base in the lake. Maybe Tepetzinco Isle. And we need to get a note to our beloved, if somewhat hairy ... amigo? Is that the word?"

Vanilla Orchid frowns in concentration so that his brows meet. "Look here," he says. "These cigars are better than ours. Are there any left?"

"No, I'm afraid not, my ruler."

"Hmm ... well, I don't suppose we can have a free Anáhuac and Cuban cigars as well."

Marina is in the throne room when a messenger from Texcoco is ushered in. Also present is Sir Noble Bean who holds the title "Chief of the Amory." He is trying to talk Moteuczoma out of inaugurating the festival of Toxcatl.

"Look here, friend ruler," he enunciates grumpily. "It's only asking for trouble. All those people in the courtyard. There's bound to be a misunderstanding. Mark my words—somebody's going to cry before this is over."

"O come, come, my dear sir," replies Moteuczoma. "Are we at war?"

Noble Bean bows out with a mumble and growl. Moteuczoma strokes his wispy goatee and looks benignly down on Marina. "Well, my child, my little Malinalli," he asks, "what think you of all this?"

Marina speaks, and the guards look at each other with startled faces. The young Spaniard Orteguilla also takes on an expression of puzzled concern. Orteguilla has picked up quite a bit of Nahuatl and so Cortés has assigned him as a sort of page to the ruler (or ex-ruler, as the reader pleases). What is now being communicated, however, is somewhat over his head.

"O the glory of it all," Marina sweetly articulates the Nahuatl trope. "All honor to the gods. May they reign forever in their true home. Perhaps some small celebration?"

Moteuczoma peers intently at the girl and then looks about him. Nothing but frozen faces on all sides. The Mexica present know that Marina speaks in huehuetlatolli, "old men's speech," which sometimes means the opposite of what it says. "O the humiliation of it all," might be a more accurate translation, and "small celebration" might be interpreted as "large disputation."

"Ah, yes, of course," Moteuczoma is barely audible. "Perhaps we might time it to coincide with Toxcatl—"

Cortés interrupts with a growl. "You are aware, Majesty, that I have been in communication with Little Corn?"

Moteuczoma pulls himself back from the contemplation of doom. "Ah, yes. Yes, indeed. All too aware. 'Show up here with an army,' goes your message, 'and your king's life will be forfeit.' Moteuczoma taps a few fingers on the arm of his chair. "Hmm, well, I can understand your methods," he shrugs, "In a tight spot one uses what's available," and then he grins broadly.

Cortés frowns and replies with a touch of vindictive humor. "Then certainly, Majesty, you will recall my reply to Little Corn: 'Neither the life of this city or your own are of any consequence to me.'"

Moteuczoma only laughs.

When the interview is officially ended, Cortés, still growling, puts a bold proposition before the ex-Tlatoani. "Give me one Xipil, no, a mere half division. Alongside my Tlaxcalans, they'll be sufficient. I'll put an end to that puny pretender once and for all."

O my love, thinks Marina, *"Your" Tlaxcalans. "You'll" put an end—*. A sneer springs to her lips, and she can barely repress it.

Looking extremely serious. Moteuczoma raises his right hand as though swearing an oath. "No, Malinche, that won't be necessary. I still have many friends among the Acolhua nobility. They'll handle Little Corn. Of course," he sighs, "this is only a stopgap measure. The bite of Vanilla Orchid will be much more venomous than that of Little Corn."

Walking back from Herb House, Marina is more than a little distracted. They won't permit Little Corn to show up in this town. That much is certain. No, certainly not, for then what would become of that little Tlatoani Moteuczoma Xoyocotl? Would that he drink the "water of shame." We should all drink it, but granny says it's not too reliable. "A person might die of fear having seen that which does not exist," she says. "On the other hand, he might fail to note the real thing and thus step off a great precipice."

Standing there on the corner of Tlacopan and Tecpantzinco, Marina shrugs. Then she crosses Tlacopan and enters the palace of Water Eggs through a servants' door. *Atlepatli* is pretty good stuff, they say, and very certain. Painful, but certain.

Chapter 28

Extortion—March, 1520

"No, no. Montezuma handed over the kingdom 'in obedience less
to the dictates of fear than of conscience.' That's what Prescott said,
but what he meant by it is any body's guess."
Carlyle Duka III
conversation at P. J. 's Deli (Third Ave. branch)

And yet, the ex-Tlatoani Moteuczoma Xoyocotl, Moteuczoma the Younger,
the Cadet, that is to say, the "Kid," still had within him some crafty guile
and more than a little strategic know-how. Only a short time ago, the
reader will recall, Moteuczoma was chained to a wall, and there the proud
Tlatoani was observed weeping his eyes out and wailing loudly. Now, see
what he has wrought even from that place where he lives as "impotent
captive." From behind his prison walls, Moteuczoma aborts and prevents
the invasion of Tenochtitlan by Sir Little Corn, and then he succeeds in
cutting off food supplies. He secretly orders the city markets closed, and
the Spaniards grow very hungry, indeed.

Now here is where the great Baron Fertilizer comes into the picture, and
the handling of his case was a great mistake on the part of Cortés. One day,
after a meal of shoe leather and dried roots, the captain asked Moteuczoma
to reopen the markets. That one claimed he couldn't do it, not from captivity,
at any rate. He said, "Now, why don't you release my brother, Sir Fertilizer,
and he can perform the market opening ceremony." Cortés agreed and
Fertilizer went out into the city where he opened not a single stall much
less the whole market. The release of this great warrior seemed to transform
Mexica morale, and confusion gave way to purposeful action. Moteuczoma
was pronounced "executable," only he was, of course, unavailable.

But let us return to the throne room where on that June day in the year
1520, Cortés, emboldened by the easy defeat of Little Corn, once more

importunes the ruler. This time he wants Moteuczoma to acknowledge the sovereignty of Emperor Carlos V. To this, our depressed and morose Tlatoani agrees, making a fairly long and now ubiquitously (one might say promiscuously) published speech of abdication. It begins, as always, with the standard introduction, "Long have we Mexicans known we are only caretakers here," followed by many a reference to discredited mythology, Aztlan, Godland, Quetzalcoatl as true owner, Cortés as Quetzalcoatl, etc., etc., so forth and so on. That is to say, those notions hardly anyone still believes, for everyone knows Cortés is no son of god but only a human being like everyone else. This address, it is said, was unusually compelling, causing the dissolution in tears of all who heard it. Well, it's true they all wept, but for very different reasons. The Mexicans cried for their lost empire; the Spaniards did so because they were under great emotional stress and often cried at the drop of a hat.

While all are milling about preparing to leave the throne room, the palace chiencuauhtli (marsh hawk) starts swooping about up among the ceiling beams. The Spaniards stare at the bird in admiration remarking on the beauty and flight of the creature. Moteuczoma wants to know what all that enthusiasm is about, and so Alvarado explains. "Well, Monty," he says, "er ... ah ... that is, dear little lord, in our land we tame hawks and fly them from our hands. It's a great pastime and a terrific hobby. I'm sure you'd enjoy it."

"O really!" exclaims the "ruler." "How delightful. O Malinche, I will have the bird captured and perhaps one of your officers can teach me that art. What a splendid diversion," he says, and then his face twists around in a half smile—or perhaps it is only a sneer.

Chapter 29

'Twixt a Rock and the Obdurate—April 2, 1520

"The good ruler is a protector—one who carries his
subjects in his arms, who unites them, who brings them
together. He rules, takes responsibilities, assumes
burdens."
Mexica commentator

In his brilliant guide to power politics, young Niccolo di San Casciano includes
some good advice for a bold conqueror, but Cortés did not heed it.

Of course, we all know how Niccolo came up with those clever notions
of his, all the while living in the depths of bucolic poverty, drinking the
cheapest red wine, arguing politics with the butcher, and playing penny
ante through the day. Yet the man was not drowned in that flood of adverse
fortune. O no. Up he floats on inky leaves and points out to the mightiest
princes on earth that he, Niccolo, he too knows the score.

His advice to the conqueror: always make friends in the priesthood.
As usual, the sage of San Casciano illustrates the principle with an apt
and appropriate example from history. When Duke Valentino wanted to
secure his conquests in Romagna, he had to ask himself a question: would
a new successor to the papacy prove friendly? Or would he try to take
away what old Alexander had given him (namely permission to move in on
Romagna)? The answer was straightforward. Why take a chance? Secure
the election of a toady to "Peter's Place" and do it by winning over as many
of the College of Cardinals as possible.

Now let us scrutinize the actions of Cortés in the light of San Cascino's
intelligent advice. Yes, well … the exam won't take long, for plainly Cortés
did not follow it. A country will often abide silently any abuse to its civil
institutions, but it is never wise to tamper with religion. Father Olmedo
understood this and tried to warn Cortés against the priestly power, but to no

avail. Once Christian icons were placed in that little out-of-the-way temple of Hummingbird on the Left the place was defiled and revolt a certainty. In other words, the die was cast, the milk spilled, the camel's back broken.

Cortés, de Leon, de Ávila, and a couple of others are on their way to see Moteuczoma when young Orteguilla rushes up in tears.

"They're gonna cut the bridges, Captain," he gasps. "Then they'll attack the palace."

Orteguilla stands there, eyes swollen, mouth agape like a flushed and red-streaked marble work titled "*Terror*."

De Leon wraps an arm around the boy's shoulder, and Cortés takes his face in both hands. "Easy, my boy," he croons. "To what oweth this daunted mien, both nonplused and lachrymose?"

Orteguilla stands looking at Cortés, a statue with blue eyes and movable lips.

"It's Marina, sir." Another tear courses down his nose and takes a right at the nostril. "They've been telling her things." Orteguilla's round blue eyes grow wider still. "Oh, Captain," he whispers, "this morning I went to tend his lordship as usual and found the door barred to me. 'We're having a meeting,' they said, 'and so?' I replied. 'I always attend the Tlatoani at meetings. Sometimes I take notes. You know … like a secretary.' 'Not this time,' they said. 'No foreigners today,' and the door was slammed in my face … or anyway the curtain was dropped."

"*Calma, mi hijo, calma*. We'll handle it from here. Straighten up now. Ah, that's better." Cortés gently pats a cheek so damp indeed, that his touch stirs a small tidal wave among the sprouts on Orteguilla's upper lip. "In we go," he announces and links arms with the boy.

"O Malinche, Malinche," says a depressed Moteuczoma, once more slouching on the Seat of Tenochtitlan. (To the which he was, of course, no longer legally entitled. Moteuczoma had signed the state over to Cortés, who then gave it back under the suzerainty of Carlos V. The captain is, after all, a student of law, and he uses legal form whenever it serves his purpose.) "Everything you were warned about is now coming true," Moteuczoma tells him, "I mean that which was predicted. I tell you this out of regard for the safety of the Christians and for no other reason. The gods have threatened to desert the city if the Spaniards are not driven out or sacrificed on the temple altars.

"What is more," Moteuczoma reportedly adds, "I have only to raise my little finger and every 'Aztec' in the land will rise in arms against you." Now, this last remark is found in the works of many a reputable and prestige-loaded New World historian, hardly born, and certainly not present during the conversation here recorded. It is, however, incorrect. Only later, considerably later, was that derivation from the mystic caves of Aztlan chosen to name the peoples of Anáhuac.

Cortés does a good job of covering up his confusion and uncertainty. He doesn't even glance at the officers standing near him. He tells Moteuczoma he'd leave the country at the snap of a finger if only he had some ships, but he has no ships.

Moteuczoma looks away and begins studying his fingernails. "If this is necessary," he shrugs, "well, perhaps it's not."

Marina does not bother to translate; she only stares clay-faced at the captain.

"There is another step I must regretfully take, Your Majesty," says the captain. "You will have to accompany us. That is to say, come along with. You must, after all, be presented to his Majesty Charles V."

Moteuczoma stares at Cortés, and his eyes glitter like chipped obsidian. "Oh, really," he says, "well, tell me, Malinche, how long to build the ships you need?" Cortés starts a reply, but Moteuczoma interrupts with a laugh and a wave of the hand. "You see, it won't be necessary, Malinche. Actually you already have four, five ... what? O maybe nine ships at your service, Malinche, and you can go home."

Marina stumbles over the translation as though her tongue were frozen.

Any injury to that organ, however, must be very new, for lately Marina has been bending the ear of Cortés with all sorts of information. Sir Fertilizer, she says, is organizing an attack on the day of Toxcatl, the services for which will be held in the palace courtyard, right here outside the door. What's more, a Spanish fellow by the name of Pícolo Narfakhid has landed at Hummingbird with eighteen hundred men and orders from Carlos V to take New Spain away from Cortés. Actually, he has no such orders and his men number closer to eight hundred. Furthermore his name is not Pícolo but Pánfilo—Pánfilo Narváez, a cohort of Velazquez. Yes, they are very nervous there in the city of Tenochtitlan. The men sleep in their armor, and the horses are saddled and bridled even through the night. Sgt. Diaz has written a recollection of those days. It is quite beautifully expressed, except he makes everything seem very romantic and adventurous—which are sentiments he probably did not feel at the time.

Cortés sends a letter off to Narváez declaring his joy at learning that a friend from Cuba is here, and that he has the best interests of Carlos V at heart. He goes so far as to ask Narváez if there is anything in the way of supplies that his men might need to make themselves more comfortable. And that offer goes whether or not they are Carlos's subjects. "But why," he adds, "didn't you let me know you were coming, and why have you been attempting to suborn people already of my camp down there in San Juan de Ulua?" Narváez reads this aloud to Lt. Rodriguez and then turns and speaks as though he were addressing Cortés, himself. This confuses Rodriguez a bit, but then he catches on.

"Watch out what you're saying that you and you alone are the conqueror of New Spain," says Narváez, nearly nose to nose with the Lieutenant. "You know very well you have conquered nothing. The land is the Emperor's to give, not some back pasture of Medellín." The commander grunts in a satisfied manner. "Now get somebody to write that down, Lieutenant." Ah! An insult directed at background and heritage. Narváez will be deliberately offensive at every opportunity.

And now, a strange procession appears on the Yellow Plant causeway, headed by Pepe "Behind the Door" Solis, who is a town official down at Veracruz. He leads a group of coastal tamemes, each of which bears a stunned, exhausted, and wide-eyed Spaniard trussed up and tied to his back. "Oh, mi madre!" breathes Ávila and not one can articulate a more appropriate response.

"So anyway," says Solis, and he is not even breathing hard, "when mayor Sandoval heard Pánfilo was coming down from Cempoal with eight hundred guys and a bunch of cannon, first thing he did was put up a gallows on the road (standard Spanish response to crisis). Turned out it was only three, and here they are. Father Guevara in the collar there, somebody Amarga or Amarga somebody, and the secretary Vergara. And as I said, here they are. The good Father tried to get Sandoval to surrender the town and was kinda rude about it. 'Hey Vergara, show him the papers, show him the papers,' he kept yelling and finally the mayor said 'you know what we do with paper in this country,' and then he had 'em all tied up like chickens and shipped up here on the backsides of these bearers. Pretty funny, eh?"

Cortés unties these gentlemen himself all the while making soothing noises. He loads them up with gold and leaves them satisfied as fed pigs in the sunshine, albeit a bit stiff and sore from their peculiar journey.

Chapter 30

Talk in a Garden—April 15, 1520

"So you could not kill the king yourself."
Aeschylus

In this month of spring, the rains have not yet commenced, and the air is clearer than white wine. And, oh, the stars! Those twinkling would-be killers of the sun march across the sky in perfect step. In full parade dress and with dazzling precision they go.

Marina looks up into the branches of a big cochiz tree growing in the palace garden. *"Tecotlauh, tecujtlacotlauh,"* she is whispering. "It relaxes one, it calms one. It lowers the stars of night." Marina is carefully translating some Nahuatl educational material dealing with fruit trees, trying to improve her Spanish. Why bother at this time? Well, she has a studious or scholarly nature, that's all.

"Atzaputl xochicualli, qualonj, iectli … the fruit of the atzaputl is edible, good, fine, sweet, agreeably sweet. It is yellow like a child's excrement, very fine texture."

"Oh my, isn't that appetizing," says Nuzi Duka from his seat on the barrel of a brass four-pounder, the one pointing streetward.

Marina pays no attention. "I eat the atzapotl; I bite it, I dissolve it, masticate it in my mouth. I swallow it, swallow it whole, take it in one bite … ah me," she grunts, "with Cortés gone to the coast, there's not much point. There'll be no masticating, no swallowing, no dissolving." Staring up into the branches Marina is practicing the use of the Spanish present participle.

"No, we'll have to put it off. What's the word? *Aplazar?* Yes, postpone."

"Well, Father Olmedo took five bearers and quite a lot of gold." Nuzi seems to be hurrying his words, as though stuffing them into the open spaces between the stars. "Certainly enough to turn the heads of those men Nárvaez brought along. They don't think much of him, anyway. People say the fellow was a good soldier once, but now he's out of date, not at all hep and a rotten leader. The only one Velazquez could get. The only one dumb enough to take on Cortés."

In tones of wonderment, Marina speaks very slowly. "Aplazar ... did you not hear ...?"

"My God, they're already fighting over Moteuczoma's presents. Nárvaez took 'em all and made a public fuss about listing every feather and frill. 'Better not be anything missing,' he announced, and then he refused to hand over a copy to his own accountant, his own man, no less!"

Marina only stares into the night but Nuzi flows on, a regular Indus of information, a veritable Danube of data. "Well, you can imagine how that went over. When the accountant objected, Nárvaez had him arrested. According to the secretary, Vergara, they're shipping him back to Spain. Oh, and when Mr. Oblanco remonstrated with Nárvaez and said something favorable to Cortés, he was tied up and also tossed on board.

Marina turns and regards Nuzi with her usual ceramic face. "And this is what?" she hisses, "Only cowardice? Or something that runs deeper ... like absence of honor." This last she only mumbles, but Nuzi hears her.

Nuzi frowns and goes on talking. Now he is in flood stage, a veritable Volga of vituperation pouring off his tongue. "Honor? Oh honor. Well, once before you told me I was without honor. Me and all my ancestors. You were cursing me out in this language," Nuzi tilts his chin at the city round about, "but I'm sure that's what you said. In these parts, it seems all insults are directed at somebody's family tree. Tell me, young miss. Why do you speak Mexican when it's not necessary? Good heavens, you fling about the most poetic insults and always in Mexican. Bah! The slave speaks the master's tongue, is that it?"

In an attempt to wound her with words, Nuzi may have gone too far. At first, Marina just stands there. Slowly her upper lip hardens. It curls into that irritable-nymph-in-plaster look. Finally, she speaks, and what she says is clear enough, yet truly enigmatic.

"So you could not kill the king yourself but had to let a woman do it."

That's what she says, and Nuzi is taken aback. Well, that's an understatement. He is unmanned by those words. His head starts to spin. Certainly he's heard that line before, but where? Oh, of course, Clytemnestra to what's-his-name—the boyfriend? No, no, the chorus to Aegisthus. Right. Agamemnon is already dead. But, how would she know? Nuzi looks up to the stars, but they seem to be swimming around up there. They float about raggedly, as in an ocean of tears. Nuzi Duka is certain that he will never again see the towers and spires of Salamanca, his beloved college town.

Chapter 31

Prodigal Days

"What's untied at Whitsuntide."
W. Kelly

Pentecost or Whitsunday: Christianized "Feast of the First Fruits," or Shavuot—starts on the second day of Passover. Since Shavuot falls on the sixth day of the month of Sivan, or the fiftieth day after the first day of Passover, the holiday was given the name "Pentecost." Associations with "whit" are speculative. The word is defined as "the smallest amount, a small sharp sound." Example: the arrows hit the planks with a "whit, whit." From *"Book of Holidays"* (author unknown*).*

Down on the coast, Lt. Rodriguez swears he will cut off the ears of Cortés and roast them for breakfast. When Cortés learns of this threat, he understands that Narváez and his officers are only a bunch of blowhards, and so he plans to attack them down there on the beach. Cortés always claimed the assault was launched on the eve of Maundy Thursday, but according to my calculations, Whit Sunday is the more likely date. This most holy of days, it must be remembered, celebrates the anniversary of Moses coming down from Mount Sinai carrying the Ten Commandments.

The feast of St. John the Baptist has also been mentioned (which is, of course, my own name day, I mean myself, John Prodigal) but it seems certain that was the day of Cortés' triumphant return from the coast. Some have claimed Boxing Day as the proper date of Cortés return from the coast. That holiday, however, falls in December, and actually, it commemorates Cortés' review of troops in Tlaxcala before the final assault on Tenochtitlan.

And here, we plainly note that "historical fact," in its myriad detail, is confused and difficult of authentication. Chimerical is its nature, and it can't hold a candle to the eternal verities, the Platonic infinities reflected in those ancient and noble holiday names.

Now, then, friend reader, are not these little explanations of mine of considerable historic interest and educational value? And are they not more entertaining than some horrific and bloodstained tale of an intra-Spanish bru-ha-ha in a coastal swamp? In that one, suffice it to say, Cortés comes out on top. Intrigued by the odor of gold, the men of Nárvaez turn their noses and all their equipment toward the captain and join his cause.

Chapter 32

Post Toxcatl—May 27, 1520

"On this day fell the flower of Aztec nobility. Not
a family of note but had mourning and desolation brought
within its walls."
American historian

Cortés sets his captives free and returns the horses to their owners. This last order sends a wave of discontent through the ranks. Diaz, for one, complains when he has to surrender a good horse with saddle and bridle, two swords, three poniards, and a shield. He had hidden it all somewhere out in the woods, thinking his booty would go undiscovered.

Alonzo de Ávila and Father Olmedo take Cortés aside for a man-to-man talk.

"Look here, chief," says Ávila, holding tight to the tourniquet wrapped about his arm. "Looks to me you're not yourself. What are you trying to do? Imitate Philip of Macedon?"

"Good grief. Philip of ... Oh, my sainted ..."

"No, Hernán, it's not so far out," says Olmedo in somber tones. "Whenever Alexander's army achieved some noble victory—"

"Oh, Alexander. I thought you said *Philip*. Well, that's something else again," answers Cortés, his lips soaked in sarcasm.

"After he achieved some noble victory, he was more generous to the vanquished... Aye, all the gold and valuable presents he turned over to the other army...quite appearing to forget his own men—the ones who made him what he is today." Ávila does not worry about the weakish grammar in this sentence. He knows what he means.

Cortés draws a deep breath as though to launch one of his lengthy diatribes on patriotism and morality but thinks better of it. Instead he unloads another one of Narváez' donkeys and passes out the shiny contents.

When Cortés arrives back in town, there is no one on the causeway. Prodigal was in the city during his absence and knows the reasons for those deserted streets, and they are not pretty to think about.

Alvarado enters the guardroom only a few minutes after the captain's arrival. Cortés is still in full armor, and his face is distorted beyond recognition. What comes out of his mouth is something between a roar and a groan.

"I had no choice; I had no choice," cries Pepe Alvarado. "We couldn't get anything to eat. Fertilizer never opened the market. You should give him a piece of your mind."

Cortés jerks off his helmet and flings it in a corner. He grabs Marina by the arm and pulls her close but does not look at her.

"The attack was made upon *me, upon me* I tell you." Alvarado is very earnest. "It was Montezuma's friends trying to get him free ... and ... and we thought the Narváez bunch had finished you all off down there."

Cortés takes a deep breath. "Now, now Pepe, let's go easy here. But ... but you must have had a reason for attacking that unarmed crowd."

Alvarado is somewhat soothed by the captain's new tone. Earnestly, eagerly, he looks into the face of Cortés. "Oh, Hernán, I certainly did. I had it from the best sources that they were planning an attack in the middle of the ceremonies. I only wanted to be on top of it."

"Sources? What sources are we talking about."

"Well, Little Corn for one, and—"

"Little Corn? What the hell? He's locked up in the basement."

"Yeah, but he's still got connections," Alvarado nods eagerly. "And also Marina here. Marina knows everybody."

Cortés looks down at his hand. He is still gripping Marina's arm. He moves toward the door, half-dragging the girl along with him.

"Remember, that cannon went off by itself, Captain," shouts Alvarado at his back. "Made such a hole in their ranks, they stopped cold."

"And the springs, the springs, Captain." Cortés has turned around and now faces the room. De Lugo is speaking. "We needed water real bad, so we dug a hole in the courtyard and fresh water came shooting out, just like that. Oh, Captain, can't you see?" de Lugo says. "Plainly, what we've done merely reflects the will of the Almighty."

"Oh, glory be to God for all his mercies," pipes up Diaz. "Amen," the troops sound off in unison.

Cortés' old enemy, that inveterate quibbler Fra. Bartolomé de las Casas, writes that it was avarice and greed prompted Alvarado to attack the Toxcatl celebrants, but the author doesn't think so. Alvarado only acted out of terror, and it was a very bad action indeed—worse than Cholula—for here, women were involved and even some children.

Chapter 33

Increments of Incompetence—June 12, 1520

Just about lunchtime on February 9, 2001, the submarine
U.S.S. *Greenville* completed a fairly complex surfacing maneuver
off the coast of Hawaii. Unfortunately, she came up directly beneath
the hull of a Japanese fisheries training ship, the Ehime Maru.
The accident, which killed nine fishermen, resulted from
a series of careless errors on the part of captain and crew.
These were procedural mistakes, piled one atop the other,
they were perfectly timed, perfectly synchronized for disaster.

The Captain remains extraordinarily irritable and more than a little peevish. When a messenger from Moteuczoma shows up, he shouts him down. "Get him out of here! That dog! Where's the food he promised?" and then later: "Why should I kowtow to this traitorous dog? Wasn't he dealing with Narváez on the sly?"

This author has made something of a study of the character of that Spanish hidalgo, Captain don Hernando Cortés, and assures the reader that the captain's irritable mien and ill humor owe but little to considerations of eminent doom. No, no, the man is merely suffering from a case of wounded vanity. On the way up from the coast, he was heard expiating on the subject of his power and influence in Tenochtitlan and of the smoothly running organization he had established there. The old line troops merely sniggered quietly, but the new men were eating it up and now Cortés feels he has lost face with the army. If there is anything better calculated to put him in a rotten mood, the author can't think what it might be.

In the time-honored manner of young men before battle, Cortés' troops turn to thoughts of girls. Actually, it is the captain himself who instigates, albeit unwittingly, this not particularly constructive frame of mind.

Feeling himself in need of consolation, he asks squad leader C. Cruz to run across to Tacuba and retrieve doña Isabel from the house of her uncle, the Tlatoani over there. Doña Isabel is Moteuczoma's daughter. She had been stashed in that town for safe-keeping while Cortés' little expedition dashed off to the coast in search of Narváez.

"Is he boffing her?" asks A. Cruz with real curiosity.

C. Cruz is lacing up his boots. "What?"

"I said, is he—"

"Yeah, yeah, I heard you. Why must you be so crude?"

A. Cruz is not merely curious, he is genuinely interested. "You know, I don't think the captain is … ah, residing with Marina anymore."

"Well, that's a little more appropriate. Better nosy than nasty. Yes, that's correct. Marina sleeps in the kitchen these days. These days Marina lives in the kitchen—running chow production for the whole outfit. The squad was helping for a while, that is, until we ran out of chow."

With whisper, wink, and nudge Cpt. Ordaz approaches Cortés. "I say, Captain. While we're at it, how about fetching over the rest of that bunch. You know, cousin what's-her-name and the others."

Cortés looks at him for a long moment. Quietly, he speaks. "Captain, those girls are not to be passed around. Is that clear?"

Ordaz pales and takes a backward step. "Oh, señor," he gasps. Then, recovering, he calls out to Cortés who has turned away. "And, sir, maybe they can bring along a few chickens … a turkey or two, no?"

Less than three hours after commencing his mission, squad leader C. Cruz staggers back into the courtyard of the palace of the grandson of Moteuczoma I. He is dripping blood and cursing mightily but without much originality. "Oh, those dirty rotten, low down, no good, miserable, lousy …" he manages to grunt out and then changes the subject. "Who's got a drink?" he wants to know.

The type of misfortune C. Cruz experiences along the road back from Tacuba is really nothing new in the annals of war, but it serves to illustrate a principle: defeat and death by incremental incompetence. In peace as well as in war, wherever humans gather to implement complex social, political, or technological operations, there the scaly visage of "incremental incompetence" will often pop up. In the case of C. Cruz at the Tlacopan Bridge, Cortés himself is found depositing the primary layer. "Go get my girlfriend," he orders with a kind of exhausted indifference to the tactical difficulties involved. And then, he sanctions de Ordaz's untimely request for extra women and poultry. Now the plaster of inevitability begins to set. Next squad leader C. Cruz builds up the mess with a goodly load of hubris. Cortés has a reputation for listening carefully to suggestions by his line troops, but Cruz never questions that order for procurement. Hand on hilt, he is suffused with soldierly pride. Soaked past saturation, he drips it all over the place. Indeed, an order of the merely stupid sort Cruz might very well contest. Add an element of deadly danger, however, a real threat of extinction, and he is sure to respond with respectful alacrity. And that's the way they are in the New World, these haughty soldiers of old Spain and later the Creole-born as well.

Passing directly in front of the courtyard of Water Egg's palace is Tlacopan Blvd., a main thoroughfare leading from Hummingbird On the Left temple and out onto the lake. Between the temple gate and the foot of Tlacopan causeway no less than five canals wind across the western borough of Moyotlan. They are used mainly for commercial deliveries. The town of Tacuba, also known as Tlacopan, is situated just above modern Chapultepec on the west side of Lake Texcoco.

Turning left on Tlacopan, Cruz and squad make their way through thinly scattered groups of citizens going about their business in civilian clothes. No one gives the Spaniards a second glance. We know right away that disaster struck on the return trip, for Diaz tells us the girls were present. Actually, the word "struck" here represents a seriously inadequate euphemism. Defeat and death on the causeway, accuracy demands, was plainly called down, subpoenaed, summoned, yea, verily it was sent for. About two hundred meters short of the city, Cruz notices that the ground at his feet, or rather the crushed and pressed caliche they have all been trodding, has suddenly disappeared leaving a watery gap about three meters wide. The last bridge has been removed. The final bridge before the island of Mexico-Tenochtitlan is no longer there. Squad leader C. Cruz stands, hands on hips, looking about. On either side, some canoes are slowly cruising past.

"Hey there. You fellows." Cruz shouts out and adds a series of succinct gestures. "Take us across, will you? We can pay. See here," he yells while waving about a small pouch. Thus does C. Cruz address the paddlers, anticipating the manner of a British colonial officer demanding assistance from the native. His answer comes in the form of a rain of darts and arrows, and he is struck in the arm just above the wrist—that is, the arm attached to the hand that holds the bag of coins. The bag he drops, of course, and it falls to the white dust at his feet. In that instant Cruz is nearly brain-dead but one thought manages to get through—retrieve the money. He stoops in time to catch a missile in the right thigh. "Ay!" he screams, and then the brown bodies pile on and a rope goes round his ankles.

C. Cruz claims he doesn't remember what happened next. "They forgot to take my sword," he says. "I guess I just got it out and started swinging." What's more, he has no recollection of crossing that cut in the causeway, and no one remarks on the state of his clothes, whether wet or dry. Nor does history remark on the fate of the squad, those seven or eight men Cruz commanded. No doubt the subject is too painful. In the course of the war over seventy Spaniards are captured, sacrificed, and their limbs consumed by Tenochca officers and clergy.

After interviewing C. Cruz, Cortés sends Ordaz out with three enhanced companies, four hundred troops, to reconnoiter the Yellow Plant causeway. Four hundred is a peculiar number for a Spanish detachment. Perhaps the captain has been influenced by Mexican military organization. Obviously, he is feeling about for a safe way out of town. But Ordaz's force gets only one hundred meters past the gate before it is intercepted and shoved back. Twenty-seven men are lost in the retreat. What's more, the Mexicans have rebuilt their stores of rooftop ammunition, and the streets are bombarded every time a Spaniard shows his face. The Toxcatl massacre has infuriated the Mexicans beyond endurance, and now open war has come at last.

Interlude ...June 30, 1520,
Retreat from Tenochtitlan

> And the heart must pause to breath
> And love itself must rest.
> Byron

Now, friends, we really ought to glance at the sources and try to determine how much of our story remains untold. The death of Moteuczoma comes next, of course, and we will leave its presentation to Prodigal's graceful Nahuatl. The retreat from Tenochtitlan, which occurred just after the ex-Tlatoani died, is commonly referred to as "the night of sorrow." It has been described many times. Just about everyone who got out alive and came across pen and paper has given us a version. All of these writers agree that the dreadful slaughter on the Tlacopan causeway came about through mishandling of the business of the portable bridge. Knowing that one or more of the causeway bridges had been destroyed, Cortés ordered some timbers knocked together, which, when thrown across a gap, would permit the passage of men, cannon, and horses. One hundred and fifty Spaniards and four hundred Tlaxcalans were assigned to the job of moving this thing about. Cortés formed up the army just before midnight, June 30. Marina and Moteuczoma's daughter, Luisa, were certainly among the vanguard, for both made it to the mainland before the last bridge went down.

So, then, here comes the army out from the city, led by Sandoval, Pulido, de Lugo (he of the large mastiff), de Ordaz, and de Tapía; the women are in their midst. The makeshift bridge goes across the open cut. Most of the cavalry tromps over, and finally the heavy guns creak and grind their way across. It is raining now, and there is a lot of yelling in front. The second bridge is broken, and they need the portable span up forward and they need it immediately. Oh, they'd bring it up on the double except the bloody thing won't come loose. The weight of horses and heavy cannon has jammed the beams into the rocks and while a couple of picks and a shovel might pry it loose quickly enough, how is it possible to stand around digging under that cloud of arrows thick as poison gnats? So now the army is trapped on the causeway between the first and second bridges. Finally, the second aperture begins to fill up with baggage, cannon, wounded and dead, men, women, and animals, and that's how the rest of them get across—clambering over that grim wreckage.

As pointed out earlier, the events of "the sorrowful night" or the "melancholy night," however one wants to translate *noche triste*, are well known wherever scholars gather to chew over those events along with their churros or fat-free cranberry muffins. And at these conferences, if a metaphoric jumble can be forgiven, the most heavily gnawed bone of contention is still the question of casualty rates in the disaster at the bridges. Prescott says that most events in the history of the conquest "are reported with the greatest discrepancy." Well, readers, that assessment is correct, yet it carries about it the ring of understatement. Take Cavalier don Thoan Cano, for example. He estimates the slain at 1,170 Spaniards and 8,000 Indians—more than the entire allied army—and he was there; he witnessed the whole business. Our friend Bernal Diaz, a fellow who usually takes pains to be accurate, seems to have lost his head over the numbers. There were 120 men in the rear guard, he tells us, of which 150 died. A few lines later the number rises to 200.

Here is a list of casualty figures provided by some other historians of the era:

	Spaniards	Indian allies
Probanza	200	2000
Oviedo	150	2000
Camargo	450	4000
Gómara	450	4000
Ixtlilxochitl	450	4000
Sahagun	300	2000
Herrera	150	4000

We note that just three of the conquest historians are in accord, and each writes from a very different perspective. Cortés' biographer Gómara, a chap who never set foot in the New World, says 450. Correct, agrees the historian Fernando de Alva Vanilla Orchid, a descendant of the great Texcocan rebel. And Diego Muñoz Camargo, a citizen of Tlaxcala working in the 1580s, is the last to concur. Well, perhaps 450 comes close to being the right number. It is certainly enough of a loss to put a serious dent in the Spanish army of conquest in central Mexico. One thing seems fairly certain: no one in the rear guard survived. These were the troops of Narváez who insisted on trying to escape with their gold, hand-dragging it across the causeway. All were killed, the treasure sunk in Lake Texcoco—most of it, anyway. The Tenochca and Weavertownies probably repossessed a number of pieces. And there were other items that went down in those turgid, murky, midnight depths. Lost as well were Cortés' handwritten diaries of the conquest to that date. What would be their value today? Oh, they would be worth more, yes, far more than all that deadly load of yellow metal.

Between the retreat and reinvestment of Tenochtitlan occurred a number of events that have been abandoned in time's dim storerooms. One of them points up Anáhuac's ambivalence toward Europeans and their technology, and so it will be re-illuminated here.

Followed every step of the way by the slings—not to mention those deadly arrows—of its fortune, the broken army finally staggers into Tlaxcala. In the big council chamber, old Fork-in-the-Road makes a speech in support of Tlaxcala's alliance with Spain. Bumblebee the Younger, son of the general who almost stopped the Spaniards (and might have had he not been abandoned by Alligator division) is violently opposed.

"O youth," remonstrates Fork-in-the-Road the Elder. "What's the matter with you, son? When has there ever been such prosperity in our country? When have we ever had so much land available for the planting of corn? Why, we even have salt now whenever we want it."

"Salt? Salt? You value salt over liberty? Why you old fool …" Bumblebee the Younger shouts out the insult, but now he has gone too far. The guards grab him by the tilmatli and drag him out onto the porch. One good push sends him tumbling down the hard stairs. "Hah! O hah! There he lies totally shamed," exclaims someone in the crowd. They are all standing on the porch, looking down with interest. "There he lies, hit repeatedly in the face with a rabbit. O the shame of it all. O think of the disgrace." Cortés has nothing to say regarding this business. He just stays out of it.

At Tlaxcala, the men only sleep and they eat and they dream of home. The captain, however, has no intention of taking them there. He is already planning the reoccupation of Tenochtitlan.

Now, students, we must do a little retreating ourselves: back in time a couple of months. We have to make this jump if we want to be in time for Prodigal's presentation of the "Death of Moteuczoma." The maneuver should not prove disconcerting for anyone. Surely the modern reader is already quite accustomed to literary time twisting. We are, after all, familiar with such creations as "Benjamen Butto by F. Scott Fitzgerald, a story which proceeds in reverse—if that's not a contradiction—and screenplays like Mitch Leison's *"Hold Back the Dawn,"* flitting about as it does between present and past, quick as an eye-blink. And let's not forget Majal Roddenberry's TV drama *"Andromeda."* That one bats time around like a cat does a mouse.

Part IV

Slipping Over

Chapter 34

Prodigal Knows Something
about the death of Moteuczoma

In a letter to the Holy Roman Emperor, Cortés claims the ex-Tlatoani requested to be taken on the palace roof so that he might calm the raging warriors below. Well, friend reader, he never did. Cortés was, in some ways, an honorable gentleman, but not so in his presentation of important occurrences in history. What Moteuczoma really said is this: "Who me? Up on the roof? O, Malinche, surely you jest. Why should I have anything more to do with your schemes? Listening to you is what got me into this trouble in the first place. I'm going to die now and so are the Spaniards." Then he thought for a minute. "Should you survive, though," he added, "take care of my children. They are as precious jewels to me."

Sometime after the Holy Office at Coahuila saw fit to acquit me of all charges of blasphemy (I was accused of erecting on my roof a large cross and hanging it with chilies for drying), I began telling someone the story of the death of Moteuczoma as I had witnessed it. Never before had I related those details, nor had I dwelt upon them, no, not even in those restless shallows where sleep is strange—I mean when furies come to visit just before the dawn. But that day was different. It was born in fearful revelation, a notion shocking as the August sun. Something came to me. *There are no gods of literature*, I thought, and then I groaned aloud. And there are no holy laws applicable to the arts of composition, and above all, no heaven-made standards by which aesthetic matters are judged. All this I saw in a flash. Oh, it was clear as a brook, and so, against doctor's orders, I headed for the cantina and a very small glass of *sotol*. There, in the dim public room, I told the story of the death of Moteuczoma. I told it to Nacho Bé, and before it was over, he laughed in my face.

189

When Bé was born, his people still practiced head compression, and so his physiognomy formed a single curve from brow to chin. How repulsive he seemed in that instant.

Nacho raised both hands in the air. "O, O," he said. "Truly, I meant nothing by it. Only you sounded a bit like Clytemnestra, you know."

"Clytem …," I managed to breathe and then was silent.

Eyes cast down to the tabletop, Nacho spoke softly. "An old Greek woman."

I could not stop myself from looking around in shocked surprise. "But here there are no—"

"I should say rather, a Greek woman of old."

"What? O *tzintlantli* [buttocks]! Literature! I might have known. No doubt some goddess who murdered a family member.

"Well, not exactly. She was a queen, and she stabbed her husband. Then the lady stood in the flow of blood and claimed it was very refreshing. 'Like a spring rain,' she said."

"And … and it seems to you I drew satisfaction watching the life pump out of Moteuczoma? O for god's sake, Nacho, there is no comparison. The Tlatoani lost his life's blood by way of the nose. I thought I'd made that clear. Neither Spanish steel nor Mexican stone came near to touching his flesh."

Nacho turned on me those round and pitiful eyes. "There must have been some misunderstanding," he whispered and then had the good grace to vomit on his feet—and mine as well.

O demon of digression, stand back. I know thee, and thy name is Procrastination. I will gather my wits now, pal reader, and return you to the city of Tenochtitlan and the palace of Water Eggs.

June 29, 1520. A combined force of Tenochca and Weavertown warriors are knocking down a section of wall around the palace; they are also up in the tower setting fire to the place. *It's time to go find my commander and rejoin the outfit,* thinks I. Aya, what a clamor! Some warriors are trying to break through the roof, and the hammering is noisy. Del Castillo is making such a fool of himself, throwing around those literary allusions of his. O what a pretentious character. "We are like unto Hector of Troy," I hear him proclaim. "O better than Roldan," he announces. Now, of course, I know Hector quite well, but the identity of Roldan has never been of much interest. The name puts one in mind of gray skies and cold drizzle.

At night, loud voices, not missiles, come sailing in over the walls. Some are singing, others recite lines of poetry. Cortés smiles grimly in the firelight, and his teeth show through his beard.

"What's that?" he says, and every head in the room rises. Even the badly wounded perk up their ears.

Marina also grins, but her teeth do not show.

"Only idle threats, sir. They are singing of the cages waiting where you will be fattened up. They are singing of the spices to be used for cooking your arms and legs." Cortés only laughs and rubs the back of his left hand. Tapía is standing there behind him. "How about that hand, sir? It doesn't look so good."

Cortés doesn't even glance at the offended appendage.

"Nah," he grimaces. "I'll tie the arm to my buckler. Be stronger that way."

Of course, on that day my Spanish was not adequate for on-the-spot translation, and so I have reconstructed these conversations from memory. As noted earlier, a Mexican's memory is his bond.

In the morning, Cortés tries to negotiate a passage out of town but finds himself engaged in a screaming match with some Mexican warriors. "You know," he shouts, "the king still loves you … this is rebellion …"

"O Malinche, don't be such a tlalalacatl [goose]," the warriors answer. "You're running out of everything, while we just get stronger. You're finished, Malinche."

Cortés shouts right back, "I will make of your city a heap of ruins and leave not a soul alive to mourn over it." Diaz waves his sword in the air. "One Spaniard is worth a hundred Indians," he screams, and the Mexicans seem to understand him. "So what?" they are jeering. "The bridges are down! *Hayai*, the bridges are down! You're not going anywhere." Such language sends the men of Narváez into a *fahmixtl* [tizzy]. Of course, Marina talks to everyone, but she should stay away from Narváez' notary, that Vergara. He can do the Spaniards no good. Perhaps Narváez' soldiers will fight Cortés, but they will never ally themselves with Mexico.

De Lugo often complains about the way Alvarado's knife lies on the table. Custom older than Caesar dictates the cutting edge should never be turned toward a fellow diner. "That's making me nervous, "says de Lugo.

Alvarado raises blond eyebrows. "I didn't know you were such a stickler for etiquette, Frank. A regular Hervé [Miss Manners] of the Indies."

De Lugo's left eye is closed for now. His right is a black stone embedded in bluish dough. "That guy's a *maricón* [homosexual or sissy]," he says in puzzled tones. "You calling me *maricón*, Pepe?"

"Come on, kids," Cortés interrupts. There's work to do. First, the planks for the bridge, and then we'll get *him* ready to go. Cortés inclines his head toward the door. "He'll go in front with the women."

"He'll go to hell with a knife in his gut."

De Lugo also nods at the door. "Yeah, wha'da we need *him* for?" he rasps.

Cortés shakes his head. "Most of the boys are crazy about him."

"Yeah," giggles de Morla. "They think he's their father."

"He goes," Cortés states it firmly. "But I'll tell you this: 'ere we depart this place, the emperor Moteuczoma will be a Christian. You have my word on it."

When Moteuczoma died, I managed to leave the palace of Water Eggs, and I went looking for my old outfit. We already knew that Moteuczoma had been declared persona non grata and that my Baron Fertilizer was installed as the new Tlatoani. We did not know that every one of the allies had deserted us. Yellowplant City, Flowerfields, Sedgegrass City, Potcrack, and the southern "beyond" towns like Roughtree, Harvest Point, and that lovely resort community and favorite of Cortés, Near-the-Trees (Cuernavaca)—all gone over to the enemy. Only Weavertown remained loyal, and yet it was Weavertown that brought us down in the end.

It happened thusly: the defense of Fort Xoloco on the Yellowplant causeway was assigned to Mexico, and it was our responsibility to hold the place. When, after a great fight, Xoloco fell to the Spaniards, Weavertown accused us of cowardice and incompetence. O what a great lot of irritable carping they indulged in! O such a lack of patriotism they displayed! Finally, our warriors could no longer hold up their heads. They were forced to hand the image of Hummingbird on the Left over to the Weavertown priests, and then there was nothing much left of our Mexico. Soon the common people began leaving the city in their thousands. It was the northern route they chose, up the Pack Frame causeway, as if they were heading out into the desert, as if they wanted to see again their ancient home in the Godland. It is to the north. O, O it is to the north.

But that came later, almost a year later. In the last days of June, the attacks on Water Eggs palace went on relentlessly. On June 30, 1520, Moteuczoma departed this earth. Now, perhaps, I will describe the manner of his death. It happened when the Spaniards were unable to throw off their discouraged air, and some were wandering about aimlessly.

Chapter 35

Prodigal Postpones
the Tale of the Death of Moteuczoma

"I perceive an endless string of congruences
So perfectly undiluted in their correctness
They defy reason,
Nor will they permit religious interpretation."
Son of Eagle Swoops
College of Santa Cruz, Weavertown

The uncanny, untimely, and eerie demise of the ex-Tlatoani must be considered carefully. It must be studied in the light of the new philosophy of miracles promulgated at Santa Cruz, Weavertown. Well, it wasn't exactly promulgated—more like expurgated.

The poem above, composed in Nahuatl by young Eagle Swoops II, perfectly embodies the new notions. Unfortunately, it got its author expelled from the college. "I could have changed the whole idea with a Latin rewrite," said the young noble, "but that seemed like an awful lot of work." And , he tendered his resignation without further ado. Franciscans are broadminded, it's true, but when young Eagle applied his "Holy Coincidence" theory to the creed of Nicaea ... well, that was the straw that finally finished off the camel. He should have remembered: the miracles in that statement are *im tlaaujilo*, (outside the sprinkled area; that is to say, out of bounds.)

The young student probably wouldn't have lasted much longer anyway. The Viceroy didn't like the idea of educating the son of a rebel traitor (the Franciscans didn't mind). Eagle Swoops the Elder had, of course, been executed for treason by Cortés. This happened down in the jungle on the road to Honduras. "Yes, yes, I admit it," Eagle Swoops had grunted after they burned his feet a while. "I have certainly entertained thoughts

193

of jumping the Spaniards here in the woods—but as for an actual plan? Don't be ridiculous. My friends and I are just as hungry and exhausted as you all."

"Can't take chances," said Cortés, and then he had the chief and his cousin from Tacuba strung from a big ceiba.

"What a fool [*tlalalacatl*] I was," said Eagle before he died, "to put myself in your faithless hands. And in my own city of Tenochtitlan!" (Of course, it wasn't his city at all; it was our Mexico.)

"Who me? Are you talking to me?" said Tacuba, looking down his not inconsiderable nose. "Of course we thought about it, but we did nothing … nothing," he added bitterly. "Now I'm happy to die here next to Cuauhtémoc."

But all this is digression within a digression, which is the most slovenly variety.

Picture me, rather, seated in my garden in the evening coolth. I am deeply immersed in a copy of that favorite of Cortés, the poem of el Sayeed. Suddenly there comes a pounding at the gate, accompanied by a loud shout.

"Hey, Champ! Champ! Open up. I've got the hats. The little hats for All Hallows."

"Not here, Yanach. They go over to the church."

"Father says they go to you."

I arise suppressing a curse but not the sigh that goes with it. In the few seconds it takes to reach the gate, I am vaguely aware of a crunching, popping sound, but there is no room in my head. In my head, there is room only for Alvar Fañéz. He is boosting el Sayeed up onto Bibieca for the last charge. With a shake of the shoulders, I throw off this little fantasy, and suddenly the air is filled with a great tearing, crashing noise. Now the gate is open, and so is Yanach's mouth. I turn in time to see my garden bench disappear in a cloud of splinters, a rain of chips—O a great many little pieces. A big limb of the misquijtl (mesquite) tree, which shades my yard, has come crashing down exactly where I was sitting. Yanach understands before I do. With countenance aglow, he lifts his arms heavenward. Then he drops to his knees and begins crossing himself. I only stand there shaking.

Well, friend, that's it. That's the miracle. "Oh, no," the reader will mutter confidently. "That's only 'the breaks' [cualli quijtlanilia]," what the Spaniards call *coincidencia*. Coincidence? Perhaps. But a very holy one. A very sacred one. What if I had delayed four seconds getting to my feet? What if Yanach's wife had not grabbed a hot pot handle, said, "Ay," and put some butter on it, thereby delaying her husband by fifteen seconds? Backward, backward winds the string, nigh to infinity. What if the little marsh hawk had not flown down from the rafters in the palace of Water Eggs? Then many young Spanish nobles would have died there in Moteuczoma's chamber. What if the rats had not shown up in Sludgemud Street that last day in Weavertown? Then I would be already dead. I would not have almost died here in Coahuila so that Yanach might witness it and be greatly inspired. Yanach would have gone on drinking his daily liter of sotol and most likely his consumption would have risen to two liters per day. Then Yanach would not have been admitted to Santa Cruz College, where he was ordained and rose to be the Bishop's right-hand man.

Chapter 36

Prodigal speaks of the
Death of Moteuczoma—May 21, 1520

"With a board between his shoulders
And at his breast another,
And at the sides these joined together;
They went under the arms
And covered the back of the head.
This was behind, and another
Came up as far as the beard,
Holding the body upright,
So that it leaned to no side."
Attack on King Bucar
Poem of El Cid

"Father O. is in there all right," says the guard outside the chamber, "but I don't think he's getting anywhere."

Cortés nods and pushes his way in.

They are all gathered around Moteuczoma, who is leaning back on a pillow nursing a migraine. A servant enters with a bowl of yaupon tea. In a corner, more or less out of the ex-Emperor's view, preparations for officer's mass are underway. Orteguilla, considered the least sinful of the company (his fantasies regarding Marina patting tortillas while half naked are not public knowledge), is permitted the pouring of the wine from ciborum to chalice.

Fr. Bartolomé leans in close, brandishing a crucifix. Moteuczoma gives a yelp, a small, despairing screech, and tries to wave it away. "And now what do you want from me?" he cries.

Young Orteguilla is leaning over him as well. "O my ruler," he says, "this is the sign of man's redemption on earth as well as in heaven, and you must embrace it."

"*Aya!* Trouble me no more with false words and promises. I have but a little while to live, and I will not now desert the faith of my fathers." Moteuczoma sits up straight and takes a sip of tea.

With an irritable shrug, Bartolomé begins the liturgy of the mass. Grim-faced, he spreads his hands over the oblation. "*Hanc igitur ...*" he intones, and that's all we hear of the Oblation of the Victim, for the rest is repeated silently.

"Fine. Just fine," Cortés whispers. "So we'll take him along as a heathen—as the bloody heathen that he is."

"*Quam oblationem tu, Deus, in omnibus ...* vouchsafe in all respects to bless, consecrate, and approve this our oblation ..."

Kneeling by the bed, Marina whispers, and her voice breaks into something like a giggle, "O sir, they plan to take you along even as a heathen." Moteuczoma answers softly, "Have no fear, child."

"*Nobis Corpus, et Sanguis fiat ...* so that it may become the Body and the Blood of Thy most beloved Son, our Lord, Jesus Christ."

Bartolomé kneels and holds up the host for all to adore. Now he would launch into the liturgy of the Eucharist, except there is an interruption. Suddenly he finds himself stretched out on the cedar floor midst a welter of bread, wine, and clanging silver plate. You will remember the little marsh hawk living in the palace? Well, she has flown down and attacked the glittering paten, causing Bartolomé to knock over the makeshift altar. The bird rakes him once across the nose and then disappears among the rafters. Now Moteuczoma is on his knees, gathering all the wine-soaked bread he can reach and shoveling it into his mouth. Marina screams loudly, grabbing her hair with both hands.

"See that," he gasps, spouting purple crumbs in every direction, "I, too, can be a martyr. O it's not the whole world I save, true enough, but only a group of very ordinary Spaniards. The common people. The simple ones. Isn't that correct? Aren't those the most worthy of all?"

He goes on chewing and swallowing while Marina stands there clutching her head; the Spaniards are also paralyzed—from the neck down, they are quite dead.

Father Bartolomé is the first to regain his senses. He wants desperately to preserve the holy accouterments from further desecration. On his knees, he scoots over and picks up the fallen chalice. Next, he reaches for the paten but is interrupted by something very wet and very warm running down behind his coat collar. He puts his hand up and brings away blood. The blood of Moteuczoma. From the nose of the ex-Tlatoani it pours out in twin rivers, splashing over his expensive tilmatli, over the rich flooring, the sacred Catholic vessels, and also the holy Catholic priest. Moteuczoma closes his eyes and lies down in the wine and blood.

"Hey, Pepe, what the hell … is he dead?"

"Beats me," Alvarado shrugs.

"What are you talking about? How could he be dead?"

"What's he saying?" Cortés whispers.

Moteuczoma's lips are moving, but Marina's are curled up. She glares fiercely at the captain.

"Oh, sir," wails young Orteguilla, "I think the emperor is dead."

Cortés is very impatient, "Yeah, yeah, but wha'd'e say? wha'd'e say? Some curse …?"

Marina's lips loosen up like wax in the sun. "O no, O no, sir, nothing like that." Her eyes are very wide. "He says, 'Remember, Malinche, you must take care of my dear children. After all, it's the least you can do.'" And then she bows her head.

Cortés opens his mouth, but nothing comes out. He tries again, and this time he is too loud. "Get him changed," he almost shouts. "They've got to see him."

The men only stand around looking worried. Cortés doesn't take his eyes off the dead ex-ruler, and his eyes are very strange. Today we see it all clearly. In that moment, Cortés was living in a dream world. In that moment, Cortés was caught fast in some literary ghost land, trapped in that swamp where medieval poetry empties its drains. And he was bound in there by notions of heroism and also by syntax of a delicate and poetical nature.

"Get me some poles," he rasps, and his look drills a hole in the body of Moteuczoma. "No, wait. Boards. Of course, boards. Boards would be better. About a meter long."

Then Cortés turns to Alvarado, "Hurry, Pete. We've got to brace him up and get him on the roof." Alvarado only stands there, and he appears quite unsteady—a feather, it seems, could knock him over. Somebody else goes for the boards; I think it was Orteguilla.

As to the last words of Moteuczoma, Marina does not report them accurately. Perhaps she, too, wants to revise history. Here now is the true and final statement of Moteuczoma Xocoyotl, the eigthth Tlatoani of Mexico-Tenochtitlan:

"Auh intla çan maceoalli ... Our common people, even those born in Lucky One Deer ... they should be made to dress in rags and also muddy huauraches. As it is, the upper classes, our nobility ... well, they simply do not stand out clearly enough."

Chapter 37

Prodigal and The Rats of Sludgemud Street
August 11, 1521

We came here only to sleep—
Only to dream.
It is not true that we came to live on the earth.
from a Nahuatl poem

When the month of Hatchit was already here, the Spaniards returned to our valley. We first spotted them digging a ditch in old Coyote Fasting's backyard. They wanted to dig a canal from the palace grounds to the lake so that they might launch their boats in safety. There was an enormous labor force over there, maybe six or seven thousand Tlaxcalans. *That's a lot of barbarians,* we thought. That's a lot of savages. We shook our heads and frowned, though nothing was said.

When Moteuczoma died, Baron Fertilizer became Tlatoani, and when he died of the plague, Eagle Swoops was the new Speaker of Tenochtitlan. He was the first Weavertownie to rule all of Mexico since Lord Paceabout over fifty years earlier. Eagle Swoops sent Captain Dog and the Youth and also the Shorn Guard over to the east shore, that is, the Acolhua shore. Those troops began attacking the lake towns that were supplying Cortés. This caused great confusion, so Cortés accepted the help of the traitor cities, Chalco and Cholula. They got in good with the Captain by begging and pleading for forgiveness. "We would never have attacked you," they said. "We never wanted to kill any Spaniards. The Mexicans made us do it." O clearly. O of course. Blame it on the Mexicans. They all did that. Whenever something upset the Spaniards, it was Mexico that took the blame.

Around the south shore and up into the Tepaneca they came, and we fought them every step of the way. We fought them at Near-the-Trees, at Rabbitboro, Excavation, and Wickerbag. We fought them at Skinny Coyote and at Stickswitch, and when the west side causeways fell, and then the city of Tenochtitlan was cut off completely.

In the second week of the siege, young Caretaker reported to the Tlatoani with some bad news. "The water pipes have been smashed," he announced. "They must have found the springs."

"O ho," answered Eagle Swoops. "That's no trick. They've got Malinalli after all."

"Yeh. Whose side is she on anyway?" Councilman Noble Bean seemed quite irritated.

"Well, she's still passing us information. Such a lovely girl," sighed Fertilizer Jr.

"O I don't know. I've seen better" Said Prodigal.

The Tlatoani shook his head and then smiled ruefully. "Hard to believe, but she still works closely with him. Always at his side. Goes everywhere with him."

"But they don't sleep together anymore," Caretaker piped up. All present studiously ignored him. "I could be wrong," he shrugged.

"Well, gentlemen," said Eagle Swoops pensively, "we Mexicans were trapped on this little island once before. In those days we lived on algae cakes and bug eggs. Now we'll eat 'em again. Only this time with chili. There's plenty of chili downstairs."

According to our sources, there was a great argument going on in the Spanish camp. It seems the men were tired of hanging about on guard duty in the cold and drenching rains. They wanted to take the city with one grand attack. Cortés was against it, but the officers prevailed. And so we got ready for them.

Alvarado and Cortés were to attack along the Stickswitch, and once in town, they would break up and penetrate by parallel streets into the Weavertown market. Alderete, that bureaucrat leading one of the groups, took his company in too rapidly, and we fell back as they advanced. One after another, they carried the barricades, and Cortés could hear their cheers of victory. It made him quite nervous. "Too fast, too fast," he was saying. "We don't know all the canals, and we can't see what's going on," and that was perfectly correct. Cortés got off his horse. He took a squad back to reconnoiter Alderete's route, and there on the Anthill he was stopped by a canal: a connector canal that Alderete had not filled in properly. He had only thrown in a little rubble, and now it was open again. O yes. Those Spaniards were all so eager, so greedy for glory. No one wanted to be detained by such an ignoble job as filling in a ditch. Of course, we hit them then. We poured out of the buildings and out of the side streets. We killed a number of Spaniards and shoved the rest into the water. Cortés only stood there watching from the other side. When the horns blew retreat, they went into camp at Anthill City.

It was a clear night, and we could hear Cortés yelling across the lake. "How many fucking times do I have to tell you guys! When you cross a canal, you fill the fucking thing in before advancing. Bloody idiots!"

O victory how delicious thou art—albeit insufficiently nourishing for the support of our bodies here on the earth. The Spanish limbs were all eaten up (by officers only, of course). The siege continued, and now famine stalked into the heart of our city. Even so, there was fighting every day around the market or the temple grounds, and the paths there grew quite slippery. Broken bones and torn-out hanks of hair lay around under foot. At night, the worms wiggled about in the cluttered streets. The water was dyed with blood. Even so, we drank it. We drank it salty with blood.

O but what doeth it profit the student of history to dwell on war's gory details. Everyone already knows it's a nasty business. In the long run, only the numbers and the names are of any real significance. Only the numbers of casualties, the division names, and the names of the places where battles took place—only these have real meaning. You writers of times to come—those who would follow me down the ages—you would do well to remember it.

Cortés called for Orozca his artilleryman, the one trained in Greece. By means of the cannon, he would force us out of the houses. He would drive us from street to street. He would herd us along until there was no place left to go. Of course, Cortés knew his cannon would destroy the city of Tenochtitlan, and he didn't like that idea at all. "How many times did I tell them?" he exclaimed. "How many times were they warned?" he said to the officers. Then the Spaniards dragged in a Lombard gun and set it up at the Eagle Gate. Captain Sir Greenyear was in the courtyard behind the ocelot statue, and I was crouched down right under the wolf's belly. When the gun went off, it became dark and smoky. The columns slowly collapsed in a great cloud of dust, and the fighters back there were forced to leave. But Greenyear just stayed exactly where he was behind the statue. He didn't move at all. "I'm getting out of this," he said, and he looked up at the sky. That frightened me, but I only crouched there staring at him. Greenyear shook his head. "I've got women in the house," he said, "and some kids, too. They have to be moved. Let's go. The troops are only behind the temple."

We picked up the children and the beloved women and took them to Greenyear's mother's house in Sludgemud Street. This move was made by way of the Little Canal, the one that passes between some buildings and goes through the family property of the young Otomí Sir Flagstone Butterfly. The town seemed very quiet, but once we heard a great whirring sound, and suddenly it was as if a deep yellow cloud appeared above our heads. A great rain of spears and arrows was coming over the houses and down on the waddy-ya-call-'ems, the brigantines in the basin. We just kept moving, and soon I began to understand that I was very empty. My legs felt like jelly, and I knew that if I lay down there would be no getting up again.

We saw no one until we were in the barrio of AsYetNowhere. The Young Men's house had been set on fire, and it was still smoldering away in the gathering dark. From out of the smoke came a squad of Weavertownies, and they were leading some prisoners off to where they would die: a place called Tlacochcalco. But it was all so very quiet. There was not a peep out of anyone. Those warriors were not cheering. There was no crying out, no shouting, and no singing. We also remained silent. We only sat there in the canoes and watched them tramp across the bridge. The footsteps faded off, and I think for a short while my spirit abandoned its body—but then it came back again.

"They were Spaniards," I said wonderingly. Sir Greenyear chuckled softly, but for a minute I thought it was my stomach complaining. "O Sir Prodigal," he said, "surely you jest," but even then, I knew it was only sarcasm.

"You know, sir," I said, "that temple is visible from just about everywhere. Their friends out on the lake will see the whole thing, heart-extraction, all of it. That's a notion, isn't it? Ought to cheer our boys quite a bit."

Now Greenyear seemed very serious. He certainly wasn't smiling. "O yes, clearly," he said. "That plus a good meal would cheer them up considerably."

From Sludgemud it was easy getting over to the Packframe. We saw the women off on the causeway, and then we returned to the house. The place seemed deserted. What a surprise awaited us! Seated there against a wall in the front room was old Bellringer himself. This Bellringer was a great Otomí warrior. He would go into battle hefting those big paving stones and the Spaniards would begin to duck for their lives. Bellringer really despised the Spaniards. He had absolutely no respect for any of them. "Who are these barbarians," he would yell. "Who are these little men. Come on, Mexico!"

Now he had a thigh wound right on the spot where people are bled, but it didn't seem very serious. We gave him a formal greeting, but Bellringer just sat there grinning. I think I was staring at his feet.

"I had to eat them," Bellringer began to laugh. "The straps were fine, but the soles proved indigestible."

"Dear, little sir," said Greenyear. "Can you tell me what happened to my company? We left the boys here, but …"

"I ordered them out of the neighborhood," he snapped. "I told them to take up their shields and go find something useful to do." Then Bellringer stared over at some pots on the hearth. "As for me, I can't walk anymore." He said this very bitterly, and when he moved his leg, we could see it was badly torn at the calf.

For some time there was only silence in the room. It was very quiet there in the front parlor of the house on Sludgemud Street. Finally, Greenyear spoke up, "You know, gentlemen," he said, "I don't think war is as much fun as it used to be."

Bellringer frowned deeply. "My good sir," he replied haughtily. "I resent that remark. The gods resent it. The state of Mexico resents it, and the city of Weavertown deplores it." Then Bellringer thought for a minute. "And besides," he added, "it's all wrong. We've had some very good times in this fight. For example … for example," Bellringer managed to lean forward a little. "O you should have been with us in Ayacac. There was an old woman in a house, and when the Spaniards broke in, she threw water all over them. She threw it right in their faces." Bellringer raised both hands and smiled broadly. "It was the only weapon she could find. O you should have seen them, water dripping all down those ugly cheeks and into their beards."

"O yes. Very true," exclaimed Greenyear. "And the dike at Yellowplant! Remember? O my, that was good thinking. The timing there was just exactly right."

"Ayá!" we both agreed, albeit somewhat weakly.

"Eagle took half the Tenochca nobility and put them in work clothes. They were digging holes in the dike all day long, and the Spaniards never got wise. Thought it was a maintenance crew. O and didn't they trot when that cold salty water came up." Greenyear clapped his hands and began to laugh, though it sounded more like grunting. "There they were, staggering around in the dark, lost everything—food, powder—had to go back to Texcoco for more stuff." Now all three of us were smiling. We were all smiling broadly when the ceiling came down. The Lombard's of Spain had caught up with us there in Sludgemud Street.

When I awoke I wasn't sure how long I'd been unconscious, nor was it really certain I was back on earth. Greenyear was not present, but this hardly mattered since I had forgotten all about him. Across the room sat Bellringer, leaning against the wall as usual, only now he appeared to be deceased. I never thought of trying to move; I never thought of anything. I just sat there a while, and then something caught my eye. It was a dead rat, and it was lying right in front of me. It was quite large and healthy looking, and it was lying right there between my legs. *I've got a knife,* I thought, only I didn't, so I pulled a stick out of the rubble and shoved it into the throat of that rat. I sucked out as much blood as I could, and then I poked a hole in another place and sucked out some more.

After a while, I got my legs loose and tried to stand. O such a headache. A ceiling beam had fallen on me and beneath it ... yes, beneath it was another rat. I drank some more blood, and then I could see rats lying everywhere. They were all over the place. "O ha!" I said. "It's like the search for peyotl. The first one must be consumed, and then the others will reveal themselves." I picked up several by the tail, and I picked up Bellringer's good Spanish sword. "My clothes are gone," I said, and this was puzzling, so I leaned against the wall and thought about it. There was a rag with a big hole, so I stuck my head through it and went out into the street.

The Spaniards were already in the neighborhood, and I can tell you, friend reader, I was dealt with in an honorable manner. They took the sword away and gave me something to eat, but I held on to the rats. And there on a roof terrace, in that very street, Cortés himself stood talking to Eagle Swoops. He was standing close to the Tlatoani, and he was stroking his arm continuously. The Snake Woman, Goodshopper, was present and also Lord Bodybare, the Chief Sacristan. Cortés was talking to the nobles about the gold. "Is that all there is?" said the captain. "That load you paddled in this morning—surely that's not the whole of it."

"May our lord captain hear me," said Goodshopper of Tenochtitlan. "We don't fight in boats, we don't even go out in boats. It's not our specialty. Only the Weavertownies use boats, so it must have been them."

"Goodshopper, what the devil are you talking about?" said Eagle. "Who does that stuff belong to anyway? We were captured, we brought it in, we turned it over. Nothing more need be said."

Then Marina spoke up. She didn't wait for the captain; she just went ahead on her own. "You will produce two hundred pieces of gold this big," she said while moving her hands in a circle.

"Well, I don't know," said Snake Woman. "Perhaps there is more. Maybe some commoners took it away. Could be some poor woman has it up her skirt. O but you'll search for it. I'm certain it will be found."

The conference up there on the roof dealt with the surrender of Mexico. The date was One Serpent in the year Three House, or August 13, 1521.

Chapter 38

Marina in Coyoacan

"On August 13, in the year of our Lord 1521, our great city of Tenochtitlan was finally reduced to bloody dust. Perhaps I should bend my mind to describing those events, but I don't feel like it. The memory of such destruction gives me gas on the stomach. My own punishment, however, was delayed till after the Fall. First it took the form of humiliation, wretched and enduring. Cortés installed me in a *seraglio*, no term is more appropriate, a house in a neighborhood called Place of the Skinny Coyotes.* O but I was not alone. All "wives" belonging to army officers were put away discretely and kept out of sight of the newly arrived Spanish officials."

We had with us the mysterious masked lady known only as doña Inez. Because of the pox there was, in those days, a plethora of masked women throughout the land. But this misfortune was never discussed. To bring it up would have been rudeness unspeakable. With us, as well, was doña Isabel, daughter of the dead Tlatoani Moteuczoma and wife of Cuauhtémoc. And also doña Francisca, sister of the great Lord Coanacoch of Texcoco.

So there we all were, walking about the rooms and gardens of that nice little house in Skinny Coyote with our bellies stuck out before us, doing our best to keep from colliding with the verandah pillars and climbing in and out of porch chairs in the mode of ancient cripples. But we were well kept and well fed and served on silver plates from the royal cupboards.

On the day before the birth of my son, I received my first visitor. That is, if we do not count our crew of witches passing themselves off as midwives.

When he appeared in the doorway, I felt my face freeze harder than the top of Popo and my lips grow numb—as they used to do in those tiresome

---

* Coyoacan - future home of a number of fateful characters in Mexican history: Diego Rivera, Leon Trotsky, Frieda Kahlo.

teenage years when something made me really angry. And yet there was joy as well. I know there was. I felt it under my fingernails and around the little holes from which my earrings hung. Yet I could hardly breathe.

"O, O Bernie," Was that me speaking? "What a great pleasure to see you. How is everyone … ah, that is to say, how are things going …?"

Bernal stared fixedly at the floor. Of course he knew exactly who it was I wanted news of.

"Oh, the captain seems to be doing … well, pretty good. Regulár. Asi. So, so. Like that. You know he gets less sleep now than back in the field around Tlaxcala. Busy, busy."

It crossed my still petrified brain that Bernal was trying to make excuses for Cortés' failure to visit me here in my confinement.

"Well, let's see. What else? There was a little unpleasantness over the gold shares, and Cortés got stuck in the middle of it. But that's all settled down now. The officers and soldiers had gotten a bit nervous about what the gold shares came to for each man. I forget how much it was, but it must have been mighty piddling for no one would accept it. So then they blamed the treasurer, what's-his-name, Alderete. That one turned and put the whole thing on Cortés. Said he had taken a second fifth for himself and also a tremendous deduction for the loss of horses. The Velazquez crowd who, as you know, never much liked Cortés, started writing clever and sort of poetical style insults on the walls of his house. Lines like 'We are more conquered by Cortés than Mexico by us.' Or … Oh, yeah. 'We are not the victors of New Spain but the vanquished of Cortés.' Then the captain added his two *maravedi*. 'A white wall is paper for fools,' he printed in giant letters. Not bad, eh? Politics. Politics. It's getting dicey around here. Sometimes I wonder if Cortés can hold on, you know?"

By now my face was well-melted. Bernal must have seen my drooping mouth and scrunched up brow. For a bringer of cheer, this is not the right tack, he must have noted.

"Ahem … ah, yes. Well, it's all circus and tragedy, you know—the whole thing from start to finish. Oh, right. You'll get a kick out of this," Bernal choked out, desperately trying to change the subject. "There are now three del Castillos in my outfit. Talk about confusion. It was nicknames that saved the day."

Now, I—poor, fat Marina—perked up a bit. Knowing more about army shenanigans than any woman alive, I was already giggling in anticipation.

"For me they settled on Castillo 'the gallant.' Oh, not because I'm so brave or anything like that. It's the snazzy way I've been dressing lately." Then he held out his arms and turned about. "Hmm ... well, maybe without the sash. Oh, to hell with it."

"The second one is extremely slow of speech and takes an age to answer a simple question. And then he usually comes up with some rattling absurdity. Him they call Castillo 'the thoughtful.'"

I was trying to swallow a bit of water from my bedside jug but only succeeded in spraying the bedclothes, Bernal, and part of the ceiling. "Ay, señor," I gasped. "Por favor!"

"Now the third one is very smart and ready in all he says. Trouble is he talks so fast no one can understand a word. Him they call Castillo 'the prompt.'"

"Ooh, Bernie. My stomach," was all I could get out.

"Yes. Well, I suppose I better get going. I'll tell the captain you're doing all right. Anybody laughs with such spirit can't be too far down in the dumps."

That's the way I remember my last personal conversation with Sr. Bernal Diaz del Castillo. Perhaps some of it is not quite accurate, but as I say, that's the way I remember it, and I have done the best I can.

Good old Bernie. Not, perhaps, the brightest candle in the hall, but such a storyteller. Such a shaper of words. "Circus and tragedy." With a snap of the tongue, he names our land. I inscribe it, but he names its spirit forever. That night I fell asleep in the midst of a giggle, or at least I think I did. This much is certain. Whether real or imaginary that laugh was meant to be my last here on the earth.

When I, the pregnant one, became aware of labor pains, the midwife said my "moment of death" had come, and so they washed me, penciled on some eyeliner, combed my hair, and swept the room where I was supposed to suffer—only it wasn't that bad. They said, "You must be in terrible pain" and tried to make me drink ground-up possum tail, which I refused. When the baby finally showed up, the old lady screamed in my ear at the top of her lungs. "You have fought a good battle, you are a brave warrior, you have captured a baby." The racket gave me a headache, but the boy seemed to enjoy it all, and I must admit to a touch of pride in his equanimity.

A few days later, Cortés came to see us. He did not so much as glance my way but stood staring at the child who was, in color, about halfway between he and I. Finally the captain turned and looked out the window into the streets of Coyoacan. The place was in pretty good shape having escaped the bombardment. Still gazing outward, as though his mind were fixed on the planets or anywhere but the room in which I lay, the Captain began to speak.

"I want the boy baptized with the name *Martín*, after my father, you understand," he said in tones reminiscent of a judge sending a pauper to debtor's prison. "Later, he will be taken to Spain and his name inscribed in the lists of the nobility." Then he added with a barely audible mumble, "it's his birthright, even as a bastard."

"I have no objections," I managed to croak, but discordant emotions nearly tore my heart apart. Then he glanced my way with a sneer as if to say 'what matters your opinion?' and turned back to the window.

But there was more, much more involved in that naming, that Spanish nobility business, than met the ear. Breathes there a boy who does not live to light his father's eyes with pride? Cortés had brought his parent nothing but disappointment and remained heartsore because of it. He had not finished his education. Like a boy dropped out of the *calmecac* and forced to earn his living as a woodcutter, he was consumed in shame. His victories, great as they may have seemed to others, did little to alleviate this pain. Childhood hurts can never be soothed. They remain buried in the spirit forever.

"Orders are to take the native women away from their Spanish husbands and return them to their rightful families." Slowly the voice of Cortés came back out of the haze. "Trouble is none of them want to go. When parties go searching for these women, they hide in the basements, the attics, wherever. Father O. tells me they don't want to go back to idolatry, but he's a little biased. Oh, well. Can't say as I blame them. Spaniards have always been great lovers," he said without a trace of humor. I kept a straight face, but it cost a bit of effort, I can tell you.

"Now the Church is starting to complain about the way we do business here. They say the Pope doesn't like repartimiento. It's just plain slavery, he says. Well, I'm writing Charles today. No more Salamanca lawyers, no more intellectuals, no more bookworms in New Spain. They only stir up trouble. Anyhow, the pressure will be off any day now. It seems both Charles-the-Holy-Roman-Emperor and Pope Leo are in big trouble. A couple of renegade heretics trying to change the world. Huh. German, of course. What else? Well, Pope'll burn 'em if he can catch 'em."

Cortés continued his harangue for quite a while. Spaniards have mouths like magical echo caves. Throw in a word or two, and they come back in endless repetition and variation. I knew, of course, that Cortés was deeply disturbed, or he would not have been carrying on so. After a while, he sat himself on the edge of the bed and took the baby's hand.

"It's de Olid. My old compadre. My paisano." said Cortés, slowly shaking his head. "He's staged a revolution and taken over the government in Honduras."

"Honduras? Ah, Higüeras. That's a long way off."

"Still I must go, and yet I am unable to go." Cortés clutched a handful of beard. "It means leaving behind in this city some of the most influential nobles of the old empire. Cuahutemoc, Tacuba, Popocatzin, Tlacotzin. Eagle Swoops swears there is nothing going on, and Vanilla Orchid paddles all the way over from Texcoco to vouch for him. But who will vouch for Vanilla Orchid? Bah, it's impossible!"

"O nothing to it," I answered lightly. "Just take them with you. What trouble can they cause on the trail?"

Cortés' eyes widened. He looked at me a long time. I only smiled knowingly. Finally, he took his leave in a most courteous manner.

Years later, the events in Higüeras reached my ears. What a strange lot are these gentlemen officers. Las Casas and De Ávila went first to see what was up but were immediately captured. De Olid's soldiers demanded their execution but Las Casas broke into great gales of laughter. "Listen," he said to Olid, "Why don't you just send me back to Mexico. I've got a job there, after all." De Olid replied that he was overjoyed to have such a brave man for a companion and didn't choose to part with him. "Well," answered Las Casas, still laughing, "Watch out I don't kill you the first chance I get."

One night at supper, one of the soldiers fell on Las Casas who pulled a knife, grabbed the attacker's beard, and cut his throat. He yelled for help, but everyone was too busy eating to pay attention. Then Las Casas ran off into the bushes. At any rate, this is the story as I remember it. It may contain errors that are due to a lapse of memory. It should be noted that our people also went in for mealtime assassination but without so much fooling about. The Spanish gentleman would rather play the saucy clown, all the while walking the most slippery and jagged edge he can find.

Much of the story came my way when I was once again living in Painalla. Cortés gave me a great deal of money and bought a nice farm for me and my mother up on the north end of town. Interested parties have made a big fuss, comparing my homecoming with a great scene from the Bible: the one where Joseph finally meets up with his brothers and graciously forgives them for selling him into slavery. I suppose my reunion with mother was something like that—in public, anyway. What could I do? Kick her in the cula and chase her into the woods? In the town square, I forgave her. At home, she was put in charge of the kitchen where she serves me very well as a cook. Mother always knew her way around a kitchen.

My husband, Juan Xaramillo, is rarely home. He prefers living here and there and around, and I certainly have no objections. I have made life here rather uncomfortable for Juan, something like a bed of red ants. The unpleasantness of his person makes respect on my part an impossibility. I am grateful for his womanizing, for such behavior prevents him from annoying me.

We were married on the way down here. In Jalapa or some place near there—on the army's route to Honduras. Cortés picked out Xaramillo as my husband right after he took little Martín and sent him back to Mexico. My head was swimming when the baby was taken away, but then I began to laugh. So here is my punishment at last, I thought. Well, it's about time, I thought. At least the gods do not call for my own death. After this, I felt very little pain, only a kind of stupid relief. Finally, my spirit was released. At last my own hands grasped my fate, and I could not help but rejoice. It was finished.

The captain? Before he left to go back to Spain, a couple of rumors about him came my way, and I must admit they are difficult of credence. They said he had grown quite stout and red of face. What's more he was sleeping away a good part of the day, even when on the trail. Does that sound like the old Cortés, always on the move, checking guard posts at all hours of the night, and in battle moving like the wind across every part of the field? Ah me, ah me. *Así es la pinche vida*. Of course, it must come to us all.

And, now this may not be true, but they say the government in the new City of Mexico had begun some mischievous activity in the hopes of getting rid of Cortés. His enemies assailed his character with the foulest imputations...he was a homosexual; he was a child molester; he planned to shake off his allegiance and establish an independent kingdom in New Spain. This, frankly, is the real reason he left for Spain, not because he was homesick for the land of his birth. The authorities in Mexico, greatly alarmed at the charges, apparently appointed a special commissioner to investigate him, and that's when he took off. He left from Villa Rica, and his going was a great spectacle. Both Mexica and Tlaxcalans gathered in their thousands to get a look at him and his festive retinue. He took along with him several Mexica and Tlaxcalan chiefs, including a son of Moteuczoma. He brought as well a number of birds of gaudy plumage, wild animals, jugglers, dancers, acrobats and buffoons. They say the Emperor Carlos V received him very warmly and even visited him personally in his sick room when he lay ill with a bit of fever. Carlos also gave him the entire valley of Oaxaca, but he wouldn't make him governor of New Spain; and that's what he really wanted.*

My property contains the ancient ball game center where we all used to play as children. I have never found time to visit the place.

---

* After devoutly confessing his sins and receiving the sacrament Cortés died on 2nd December, 1547. He had made a second trip to Spain and on the way back to Mexico came down with severe case of dysentery in the port city of Seville. Some friends moved him tothe nearby village of Castilleja de la Cuesta. where, worn down by the disease, he gradually expired. He was 63 years old.

Part V

What Happened

Chapter 39

What Happened in Coahuila or
The Sins of Coyote

April 16, circa 1540, Spanish mission in Coahuila

Wildflowers are blooming everywhere and Mother Earth glows like a rainbow. Clouds move along, their passing shadows turn the land into a kaleidoscope. Lupus shifts to indigo, and as the cloud shapes slide across the land, patches of orange figwort seemed to chase each other over the fields. Opuntia and the poppies, though, don't change very much. They are already so deeply saturated in red and gold.

The work party finishes slipping the new church door onto its hinges and then swings it shut to check the fit. *Hupah!* shout all, for it has been a half day's work and perspiration flows like ... what? "Like the wine of labor," suggests Prodigal. Yes, well that's the metaphor came to his mind at the time, but of course, he was younger then.

The Father asks all to bow in thankful prayer to St. Joseph, who is the patron saint of carpenters, but then holds back, first wanting to note if the door can be opened smoothly by a single Christian. Ambrosio of the Well, the colony's ironworker and developer of boiled squirrel with the yellow rather than the red chilis, begins to complain, gently but with a touch of bitterness.

"Father, if you'll just consider a minute ... there's not really much carpentry work in this—merely a bunch of planks cut to length." With that the woodcutters give out with a low rumble like the sound of hoofs from a distant bison herd. Father John only looks puzzled.

"But the iron work," Ambrosio goes on. "Those great hinges, squeakless in their perfection, with the pins that come out in a jiffy. And the lock plates!" Without quite touching the surface Ambrosio stretches out a hand and spreads it lovingly over the chased metal. "Here's the letter Tau, chosen by Innocent himself. I need hardly mention, it stands for reform.

And there's the arm of Christ. I know there's supposed to be another one, but … well … anyway … and there's the bleeding heart, and that thing that looks like a prickly pear, I don't know exactly what it is." Ambrosio's embarrassed eyes drop earthward, but then they rise again. "These are the symbols of your order, Father. Our order. The Order of the Friars Minor, all made from bell scraps. The cheap one, I might add."

Oh, good grief, thinks Father John but keeps the thought to himself. *These are new Christians,* he remembers. *They take everything very, very seriously.* "But … but, 'Brosi," says John, "there isn't any saint for the forge, not a Catholic one, anyway."

Young Charley Pacuache, of the Nogal River Pacuache, now pipes up. "Yes, there is, Father—there really is. He lived a long time ago, and he was a Frenchman called St. Servitus."

"O no, O no Charley," says a fellow in a green leather helmet tied about the neck with leather straps. "Servitus was Armenian. Armenian, certainly."

"O what are you saying?" snaps Charley. "His family name was Tongre, and he went to the council at Rimini … when? Father, when?" He whirls toward Aragon who seems unable to respond, and then he whirls back to face Green Helmet. "Three hundred and fifty-nine! That's when! Does that seem like an Armenian to you? With a name like Tongre?"

"Such a goose he is," says Green Helmet, making his eyes cross. "Tongre wasn't his name. It's the land where he was a bishop. Isn't that right, Father?"

But Father John remains wide-eyed and jaw-sprung. *It's the Latin,* he thinks. *We shouldn't teach them Latin. The smart ones pick it up all too fast. I'll have to give some serious thought to the curriculum. Changes may be necessary.*

At almost exactly midnight Aragon comes awake in his narrow bed. His eyelids literally pop apart. Those eyes don't feel very well, either. They are quite irritated—as if a lot of Coahuila sand had worked its way under the lids. *No more rest tonight,* he tells himself. *Clearly, my sleep doeth break from me. Let's see, I've had … what? Just short of three hours.* "Actually, that's better than average." He says this last aloud and then reaches under the bed for the manuscript. Pen and ink are on the table, and so he must get up to fetch them. "Idiot!" This is pronounced yet more loudly. "*Mene, mene, tekel upharsin.* You'd better watch yourself. Do you think you can write in the dark?" When there is some light in the room, good Father John opens the Chronicle, full title: *Seraphic and Apostolic Chronicle of the Holy Cross School of Faith-Propaganda of the Valley of the Circumcision of Our Lord* (which is the place where most of these scenes occur).

For the previous November, there is an entry paying special tribute to, and offering prayers for, the wellbeing of the Tlaxcalan friends and helpers. They are the ones, John recalls, who pointed out the meteor shower. "At least fifty spheres of light, which seem as stars loosed from their moorings," they said. "Wake up Father! Wake up! They are falling all around Lampasas Spring." This seemed a clear indication of the spot where the mission church should be built, so in the morning Father John assembled everyone at the spring. He bade the congregation pray the Alabado, giving thanks to the Lord for the new harvest of souls—only nobody showed up. Well, anyway, not very many. Finally, the Tlaxcalans took some candles, some silver cups, and a white gown up into the Carmen Hills and brought back "our Pachale and our Chaguane."

"It should be remembered," emphasizes John, "that these Tlaxcalans were allies of Cortés, and as such are exempt from taxes and from compulsory service, and yet they gladly share our burdens and even more, for they are the scouts and forerunners."

When all were baptized, Father John spoke to them through the interpreters (those ubiquitous characters always hanging around the frontier, of whose actual linguistic abilities no one seems very certain). He told the Pachale and the Chaguane that he had been sent by the king to instruct them in the Christian doctrine. They would be taught how to farm, how to wear clothes, and to be polite. What's more, His Most Catholic Majesty would grant them official possession of the land, including the use of the waters and the forests.

Only a few days later, Aragon awoke to an empty campsite. The 150 or so neophytes gathered near the mission had fled—taking the livestock with them. At first, John was quite disheartened. "They came to me! They came to me!" he wailed. "They are the ones who begged me for baptism, to live among them and teach them," a complaint involving a certain amount of exaggeration. But soon the priest recovered his equanimity. He got on a horse and followed the people up into the Carmens, where he seemed to have shamed them into returning to the mission. And that's the kind of man this priest of God turned out to be: thoughtlessly courageous, fanatically dedicated, filled with loving charity. As for the stock, a few cows and horses had already been eaten, of course, but there was no help for that.

Father John realizes he has forgotten his blotting materials and rises to fetch them. Sliding to the left, his foot strikes the table leg just between the left little toe and the next one over. John gives a little grunt, but the worst is yet to come. When the human foot is caught in that sensitive spot, there is always a second wave of pain, worse than the first. It begins exactly when the first wave is subsiding a bit. John's mouth comes open, and he finds himself on the floor—the injured part gripped in both hands. As the pain fades, he leans back against the wall and slips into a sort of trance. After a while, daylight begins seeping in through all the building's little cracks and gaps.

"*Pst, pst*, Father, you up?" comes a voice from beyond the window shutter. "I saw the candle's gleam and figured you were awake." Gregorio Ibn Chan pushes the shutters open. "Father, did you tell the Cacaxtle they could take some goats? 'Milk for the kids' they said. Milk, Indeed! Food, land, irrigation… more earthly conveniences than those Indians are able to appreciate. What's more there is little or no gratitude for …"

"Greg, Greg, please. Let's take this to the kitchen. I must have a tea."

Prodigal's adopted daughter, Ana, who is trying to stoke the fire, is caught in a sudden gust of smoke and begins coughing violently. Catching sight of Aragon, she manages to control her heaving little lungs, "Oh, Father," she gasps, "We're almost out of flour."

"Can't be helped kid. They're faster than we are—get to the mesquites faster, strip the pods faster."

For Del Pozo and Ibn Chan, the kitchen is actually off limits, so they stand outside and poke their heads through the window casement. "I think we need soldiers," says Ibn Chan. "A garrison. Maybe fifty men to serve as a halter for those barbarous Tobosa and the other savages who molest this dominion of His Majesty."

John raises a hand patiently, as if to slow down this discussion, which takes place much too early of a weekday morning. He crumbles some dry brown yaupon leaves and drops them into the pot. (*Ilex vomitoria* is a short-leafed shrub growing just about everywhere. It is loaded with caffeine and in taste very similar to the famous maté of South American renown.)

"And who will carry a letter to Mexico?" he asks.

"The Tlaxcalans! The Tlaxcalans!" Ibn Chan and del Pozo sound off simultaneously.

"No, no, we need the Tlaxcalans," says Aragon. "We've got to keep professional carpenters on hand. At all times."

"One might as well try to convert gentiles without soldiers as Jews without the Inquisition," says little Ana, whose father was a Sevillano.

"What we really need is cloth," says Aragon, "a couple of hundred varas. Preferably blue. If we could dress them all in new clothes ... well, anyway, the chiefs and leaders, it would certainly encourage them to behave decently. All we have to give them now is beads. Silly blue glass beads."

"That's about all they deserve," says Ibn Chan bitterly. "They are to Jesus our pastor as was Judas."

What a shocking thing to say! Father John claps a hand over his mouth in a gesture he has picked up, the traditional Native American startle reaction.

Suddenly the church bell begins to ring, only it sounds a little strange. The pull ropes are not connected, so someone must be striking the rim with a stick. Not a smart idea. It's a good way to crack the iron.

In the scrubby shadows at the edge of a plowed field, Gosata and Ouchcala stand shaking their heads. "Grapes!" exclaims Ouchcala. "The woods are full of those things and here they're growing 'em."

"Well, it's like I've always said. Agriculture makes men stupid. All right, let's go around through the back."

A voice reaches down from the bell-tower and into the kitchen. "Better get out here, Father. I think maybe we've got visitors."

At the rear of the church, just beyond the northeast corner of the back wall, where wild pin oak and prickly pear come closest to the mission grounds, stands a line of about thirty-five people. The men are armed, but not heavily. "Horses. Where did they get horses?" says Prodigal quietly, and his hand comes up to cover his mouth. Indeed, there are three good horses in the middle of the line, and each is loaded from stem to stern with small children—toddlers to ten-year-olds. *That's a twist,* thinks Prodigal.

A man's voice rings out, some sentence, some phrase, maybe only a greeting. The words sound harsh as a war cry, but there is no sign of hostility, no spear shaking, bow waving, or the like. Ambrosio glances over at Aragon and is taken aback. The good Father has turned white as chalk, white as the morning clouds drifting overhead.

"What is it? What did he say? " the ex-Aztec asks.

Father only grimaces and waves a hand as though shooing gnats.

221

"I mean the words. The words, dear Father. That is, what do they signify?"

"Nothing, nothing. *'Tu maman porte bottes de l'armée,'* that's all. Your mother wears army boots."

At that moment young Ouchcala is on the receiving end of the dirtiest look imaginable. "Idiot! What's the matter with you?" Gosata whispers harshly. "I told you to be nice. They have horses." Ouchcala shrugs and looks at the ground.

Too shocked to make much sense of the father's words, Prodigal turns temporarily stupid, or "wooden lipped," as the Nahuatl has it. "Now, dear Father," he says, "Spanish army footwear, while not particularly pleasing in the aesthetic sense, is certainly world-renowned as the most durable, well-constructed, cleverly stitched, versatile, and hardy foot-covering in existence. Why they can actually be used to hold water and if one employs the hot rock technique, it is possible produce a bit of soup or stew. But Father, you knew my mother well. Why, you presided at her funeral. She was laid to rest in the finest silver-trimmed sandals with ..."

Father Aragon throws him a look of scorn and begins to growl. He is actually growling as he speaks. "French? French? *C'est impossible.* The French here in New Spain? That's illegal! How can it be? Are they hiding somewhere?" Aragon hitches up his robe and starts across the scrub in back of the church. Walking through the bushes, Aragon takes the cross from around his neck and holds it forward like a banner. *"Bon jour, bon jour, mes frères. Vous parlez Francais? Eh, bien! C'est merveilleux, merveilleux!"*

Gosata of the Titskanwatits answers with a little laugh and a toss of the hand. "O not very well, sir. We learned a few words only." Gosata is wearing the most charming smile in his repertoire.

Seeking specific intelligence on a possible French presence in New Spain, Aragon asks the least intrusive question possible. "Have you journeyed far, my friends?"

"Quite a ways, quite a ways. But of course, we always take our time. Try to enjoy the trip." At that moment, a woman comes up and stands next to Gosata. She is perhaps no longer a teenager but quite attractive—that is if one likes the style. Ocoya wears a mini-skirt—a wraparound affair reaching to mid-thigh. Her bare breasts are painted in concentric circles from base to tip. Her hair is particularly nice. It falls down the side of her face to shoulder length and from the top down it is decorated with stones woven into thongs. Just under her left shoulder and almost out of sight hangs a baby, a precious little round-faced creature that looks just like her mother.

"Tell me, *mon ami*," (Aragon knows better than to ask the man for a name), "That sweet baby, does it belong to you?"

Gosata answers with a sigh. "Yes, yes, she's mine. I had to take her in, if only to keep her from making a fool of herself."

"What? Who? the baby?"

"Yes, yes, and the mother too. Look at the way she stands there. You can see she's somewhat boy-crazy," he says, shaking his head. "Of course, she's quite nice. Look at those breasts. Not very large, it's true, but so beautifully arranged. And how jauntily they protrude." Father Aragon's armpits grow damp. Perhaps Gosata's words, plus the womanly image before him, are somewhat responsible.

Gosata proposes a feast that very evening, and Aragon wants to contribute some beef. "Beef?" says Gosata, "O, you mean those things like hairless buffalo. Yes, well, buffalo is quite good, but tonight we have something better: fresh deer meat cooked the old way—in a pit with snails and blackberries. Hmm, too bad the grapes aren't ripe yet."

During the meal Aragon can't help looking around for Ocoya and the baby. In his mind's eye he can see the baby's face. The image provokes unconscious liturgical urges within his soul. *If I could get hold of that baby, I could baptize her,* is the theme running through him. *And the mother. The mother, too.* But they are nowhere in sight.

"No, we don't live anywhere in particular," Gosata is saying. "We like to move around. Sometimes we get in the mood for a trip and go down to the beach—eat oysters, gaze at the ocean, you know, that sort of thing. So there we were strolling around the shallows, some with nets, some with gigs, when we ran into these Frenchmen. Said their boat was wrecked while chasing a whale." Gosata shakes his head and shrugs his shoulders at the same time. "Anyway, they were in real trouble, so we stuck around and lent a hand, showed them this and that. We stayed over a year. *Mon dieu,* I don't care if I never see another oyster. Then we moved up here for the nopales, but of course, it's too early. Well, we knew that."

"But ... but ... it's a long way to the coast; how did you come? Not from the east?"

Gosata smiles that charming smile of his. "No, no, that's no good. Too many mountains. One picks up the Palm Tree right at the sea. A place called Bouche Petite. Only follow it up to the fords, turn south, and here we are."

Aragon looks puzzled. "So the Palm Tree is just to the north?"

"Not very far, but of course, there are no palm trees around here."

Aragon is mumbling to himself. "That must be the Great North River. I've never seen it, but the Tlaxcalans have. So it goes down to the sea. And in the other direction? Going upstream?"

"Oho, nobody knows where it comes from. Maybe all the way down from heaven."

Like intermittent lightning, images of Ocoya and her baby flicker through the priest's brain. He would like to ask for them, but that would be humiliating, and so, as a good Spanish citizen, he focuses once more on those geopolitical concerns, which have been nagging at him since he heard the French language shouted across his backyard.

"And ... and the Frenchmen? What became of them?"

"O they were feeling better, so they took off. Toward the land of the Cadodacho. Claimed there were some really big lakes up there, and they could follow them home." Gosata shakes his head. "I don't know. We've been pretty far north and never saw any big lakes."

Prodigal sits by the fire wishing he had some implement with which to pick his teeth. "Quite tasty," he says, "but rather sloppily served. Juniper bark does not fine dinnerware make."

Bé, the Yucatecan, responds with a glaring non sequitur. "This language ... I don't know. Its Coahuila all right, and yet ... take the word *haidjcogonai*. In these parts they all say *coyotl*. Nobody says *haidjcogonai* around here."

"Nobody says nothing around here," states Yanach. "Aragon hates those weird little stories of theirs. 'Writ by the devil for the gentile trade,' he says. Come on Ana. Don't be scared. Take a swallow of this," he says, holding up the jug.

Ana raises her imperious little head. "That sir," she says, "would be unnecessary. A Christian has nought to fear from witchcraft nor from necromancy."

"What witchcraft? Oh, my dear child!" Prodigal exclaims. "These people have an overactive imagination, that's all. It's the drugs. Up here? Probably mountain laurel."

Gosata of the Titskanwatits waves a finger back and forth in a gesture of negativity. "No, no. No more red berries. That stuff is dangerous. We

224

switched a long time ago—like everybody else. Now we buy only the best. From up on the river near Happenstance Place." Ambrosio and Prodigal eye each other blankly. Well, it could be true. But Gosata has more to say. *"Haidjcogonai huehuetlatolli. Im Mexica coyotl im tlalli tlatoanj. Passez moi le vin, s'il vous plaît."*

Everywhere one goes in this New World a little Mexican is spoken, so nobody is surprised to hear those Nahuatl words—but Bé understands their significance. *Haidjcogonai* is not Nahuatl. It's an archaic Coahuilan word meaning 'Coyote the landowner.' Its roots are buried in an earlier age, an age when everyone believed Coyote was the world's proprietor and his permission was always sought before changing hunting grounds.

"Man, that's really old," mumbles Nacho Bé.

Among the Titskanwatits, naked old ladies like to sit close to the fire with a buffalo robe or a bearskin thrown over the head. This campsite is no exception. One old woman has been coughing for a while and finally everyone turns to look at her. "Haidjcogonai'la," she says. *"Haidjcogonai'la ha-nanoklakno'o."* (In Coahuilan, the 'la' and the 'o' only mean: These events did not happen to me, they were told to me. This is a story and you can believe it or not, as you like.) "Coyote was going along, it is said, when he happened to climb a mountain. Down below he saw a large camp, and in the last hut he heard someone weeping. Coyote went down and entering, said, "What's the matter?"

"The woman said, 'All this camp off in this direction has no people. An evil one has killed them all.'"

"'Well, you can stop crying,' Coyote said. 'Tomorrow I'm going to fight him.'"

"Then the woman went out and made the announcement. 'Coyote says he will fight the monster tomorrow.'"

Prodigal's attention begins to drift. This story doesn't interest him much. But an overactive imagination, now that's real trouble. An overactive imagination can sometimes change reality. It doesn't happen often, but it happens.

Now a thin breeze rolls up the narrow creek bed. It brightens the embers in every hearth and campfire across the Valley of the Circumcision of Our Lord. The old naked lady pulls her bearskin tight across her shoulders and goes on with the tale of Coyote and the camp of no people.

For a change, Ocoya is well-covered from the waist up. In fact, she is wearing two shirts, a long-sleeved blouse of sheared skunk skin (skunk hunting, indeed, certainly no job for amateurs!) arranged so that the stripes run down her arms from shoulder to wrist, over which she wears a vestlike affair of plain, carefully tanned buckskin. She sits almost in front of the fire so that the youths gathered before her see only a dark shadowy form. Ocoya speaks. She also tells that strange old Coyote story.

"'Now listen up, Madame,' said Coyote. 'Tomorrow, when I fight that creature, you must watch me closely. There'll be no running away.'"

"'Very well,' said the woman

"That night, before he went to bed, Coyote went down to the river and cut himself a stick of really hard wood. Then he burned it black and put it away."

Burned it black and put it away, eh? says Ocoya to herself. *Now what's that supposed to accomplish?*

Meeting uneasily, the full Committee of Four Hundred for Religious Affairs (really just twelve socially prominent individuals), is deeply concerned with the coyote-wolf liturgical question. Why, O why was that ancient and incomprehensible tale on everyone's mind last night?

"Why? I'll tell you why," exclaims Ouchcala. "It's because everything is up in the air and hidden under the bushes." No one minds Ouchcala's mixed metaphors. They are all quite used to his manner of speech.

"Do we go for the horses or not? Can we get back across the river without breaking our necks—not to mention every pot we own? Can we …?"

Gosata wants to heave a sigh but he doesn't. *Ouchcala only belabors the obvious,* he thinks. "One must consider the source," he says. "All these problems stem from Coyote's misdemeanors. The evidence is plain. When that monster comes out of the woods, red on top, black from the waist down, as usual," Ouchcala draws a flat palm across his waist, "the women all run screaming out of town—doing exactly what they were told not to do. Now it's all over. Coyote does what he always does. Absolutely nothing. Will he lift a snout to fight that evil creature? No, he lets the wolves do his killing for him. Well, that's an old story, isn't it? And when the wolves leave? Who takes the credit? Right! Exactly! I think it's time that fellow's influence in our community was circumscribed."

"No can do," pipes up Ocoya, and her very serious-looking baby seems to agree. "We can't do that. It's too dangerous. As long as the meaning of the stick remains hidden, we can't change anything."

"The stick? What stick? O the damn stick. No one knows what that's all about," grouches Gosata.

"Perhaps the local brown robe here can tell us. He's a holy man, after all. Could be he holds possession of that knowledge."

"That little brown robe? Why should he help us? Unless he is very stupid, he must know we've been thinking about his horses."

Ocoya speaks with a little shiver in her voice. "He wants to do some water-of-life ceremony. Only god knows the reason, but this desire is very strong in him. He wants to do it to me and the baby. If he can solve the mystery … well then, I will permit it."

"O that baby," groans Gosata. "That baby doesn't even have a name."

"Well, maybe it's time we got her one."

When Ambrose of Milan was appointed governor of Aemila-Liguria (372 AD) most of Italy remained dedicated to the proposition that God and Christ were co-substantial, that is, made of the same substance—not merely a similar substance. Soon Italy was embroiled in a great philosophical struggle testing whether that country, or any country so dedicated and so consecrated could long endure. A public debate on the subject was held in the future parking lot of the La Scala music hall, and when the crowd threatened to get violent, Governor Ambrose himself stepped in to calm them down. Suddenly, a child's voice rang out shouting, "Ambrose for Bishop!" and the mob grew quiet, even thoughtful. "Who me?" responded Ambrose. "I'm just a Roman citizen. Why, look here. I'm not even baptized."

On 7 December, 374, however, the reluctant Roman, now officially baptized, finally accepted the See of Milan. He soon found himself putting pen to paper on the very subject: the meaning of baptism as a sacrament. These views included the notion that original sin could be canceled out through faith alone—no holy water, no ceremony, no priest required. Quite a progressive idea that, very … what? Hellenistic? Humanistic? Thoughtful? Certainly very independent of unreasoned tradition and indigestible superstition. On the other hand, Ambrose was no saint (at least not for another twelve hundred years). When the Christians of Callicium on the Euphrates burned down a synagogue, Emperor Theodosius was all set to punish them. "No, you don't," screamed Ambrose by mail. "Violence in the pursuit of a religious cause is no sin." The Emperor backed down and the culprits were released. His anti-Semitism was of no interest to the Milanese. They were, however, a bit irritated by his book,

De Virginibus. "The Bishop's unremitting stand on female virginity is depopulating all Northern Italy," said his detractors, but of course that was an exaggeration.

Father John Aragon, like Ambrose of Milan and other intellectual churchmen, is often found operating in conflicting modes: Christian charity vs. block-headed orthodoxy. Aragon never got the opportunity to express any anti-Semitism, it's true, but once he set fire to a chipmunk in order to prove a theological point. That's right. This gentle and charitable Christian man tossed a small creature belonging to God into a blazing fire. He was trying to explain the torments of Hell to a congregation of Mexicans and his Nahuatl was not yet up to the job. Hence, the chipmunk immolation.

Now the good Father kneels in his little office on the left end of the transept praying for guidance. When Ocoya and the Committee first approached him with their spiritual trade-off plan, Aragon was horrified. No, no, he thought, a half-nude woman and a talking coyote, just the sort of pagan absurdity no priest should get involved with.

"Interpretations belong to God," he told the Committee and quickly realized he had just paraphrased a line from Genesis—fortieth chapter, eighth verse. "Do not interpretations belong to God? Tell me them [your dreams], I pray you," said Joseph, the Godly shepherd of Shehe, to his dungeon-mates. These were Pharaoh's chief baker and his butler, who were in there for mismanagement of one kind or another. Then Great Pharaoh himself had a dream—something to do with cows: fat-fleshed and healthy ones being devoured by some skinny and ill-favored ones. On the recommendation of his ex-convict butler, Pharaoh sent for Joseph, who barely had time to shave and change clothes before appearing in the throne room.

Now, cows don't eat meat, reasons Aragon, much less each other, and so this Coyote business is no more ridiculous than Pharaoh's dream. *Twixt a cow and a coyote, moral and ethical disequivalences are not inferable,* thought Aragon, who had taken a couple of courses under Jesuit professors. "All right, I'll do it," he said to himself. "In God's name, I'll do it." But some problems of protocol still remained to be settled.

"Can you relate the story in French?" asks Aragon, "For more accurate comprehension, you understand." The question is greeted with stunned silence.

"Well, how about Nahuatl, then?"

Gosata nods his head in an understanding manner. "Don't worry, good sir. The woman will speak very slowly, very clearly. To take effect, however, it must all be heard in our tongue. That which you call Coahuila."

"To take effect?" Aragon repeats the line and rolls his eyes at the ceiling.

"Haidjcogonai'la ha-nanoklakno'o," the woman begins.

Yanach leans against the door trying not to yawn. *Coyote was walking along again was he? I wish he'd get a horse, that Coyote.*

Prodigal glances at the statue of St. Francis feeding a bird, the little wooden effigy sitting atop the breakfront. *A church office,* he thinks, *What a strange place to be listening to this stuff.*

Aragon is drumming his fingers on the Chronicle's wooden cover. *Here it comes: cuts the stick, burns it black, puts it away, etc., etc. many wolves, blah, blah, and then the wolves went away.*

The tale teller pauses, and Aragon thinks the story is finished. He already has an answer to the stick question and only its manner of presentation remains problematic. Wait a sec. What's this …?

"Yanjidxilda'an 'hedan'ok' o-c'ou yadjox'an-de'-la nawe'l…" the old lady continues. "Then coyote went off a way and, running back, shouted, 'Come quickly! This camp is burning!' But nothing happened. Again he went off, and, running back, shouted, 'Come quickly the camp is burning,' and nothing happened. Three times he did this, but nothing happened."

"E'kla holau-'a'lak ha'nada hengwa'dan 'hedan'ok 'o-c'ou yadjox'an-de'-la nawe'l' noklakno'o …"

Yes, yes, I've got that. Three times he did that—and then the last time?

"Ha'nadjidjxileklakno'o … Then the last time he went off and, running back, shouted 'Come quickly! This camp is burning!' Then many people ran out, it is said. Then they gave Coyote a pretty woman for his wife, it is said."

There is another stunned silence, only this time the mission residents are the ones who can't think of anything to say. Aragon opens his mouth a couple of times, but nothing comes out.

"Yes, yes, yes," Gosata sighs. "Of course, you are laughing at us. Who wouldn't laugh at us? Indeed, the world is much bemused at our plight. 'Come out, come out, the camp is on fire.' O heavens above and below! How ever did we permit ourselves be taken in by that slippery creature?"

Sounds good to me, thinks Aragon, *awfully close to confession.* "Oh no, oh no, my friends. This is all perfectly understandable," he says, throwing his hands in the air. "The devil can fool almost anyone." Then Aragon explains all about Moses. Moses was a man with a real power stick, he tells them, not some little homemade imitation, which, by the way, Coyote knew wouldn't work, and that's why he put it away, never to be heard from again. Moses' stick, though, was infused with the power of the Lord of Hosts. Right in front of the Great Pharaoh of Egypt, God turned it into a long snake, and the shock nearly made Pharaoh jump out of his skin. Out in the barren desert Moses tapped a rock with it, and a great spring of fresh water leaped forth. "This was at Kadesh, or maybe it was Jebel Musa, but the point is …"

Yes, the Committee of Four Hundred for Religious Affairs understands the point. Coyote is a failure. Coyote is an impostor, a real flop. Well, that's what they've been saying all along. The brown robe's interpretation is far from perfect, but it's reasonably satisfying. The Titskanwatits all nod a few times and sigh a little. Ocoya agrees to the baptism ceremony. As she understands it, the holy water sprinkled over the baby's head will drown the evil spirits within. The child will be named Abra after the consecrated virgin of Poitiers. Ocoya doesn't know how very young the saint was when she died.

If one considers the surface of our planet as an integrated system of interlocking ecologies, the Valley of the Circumcision of Our Lord can be said to occupy a position on the montaine-prairie transition zone along the southernmost edge of the Great Plains of the North American continent. Every once in a while, in fact, a few members of the plains buffalo herd come drifting down, but they don't like it very much. Too many thorny plants mix in with the grasses: Opuntia, Mammillaria, catclaw, barrel cactus, horse crippler all make getting a bite to eat quite a risky business.

But, good sir, doesn't all that prickly vegetation indicate a rather dry climate?

Reader, as ecological insights go, that's a good one. Oh, it's dry all right, but it's no desert. Average rainfall amounts to twenty inches a year. Much of it falls in the months of April and May, but there is never a true rainy season. Sometimes, in September, a hurricane wanders inland out of the gulf, and the low pressure dumps a series of heavy downpours on the land, making the valley look like Malaya in monsoon season. But this is very rare. Mostly there are two sources of precipitation in the Valley of the C. of O. L.: arctic cold fronts—howling wind and violent thunderstorm quickly changing to freezing rain (temperatures can drop thirty-five degrees in little more than an hour)—and warm fronts, which are usually just cold ones that have run out of momentum. Then they back up to the north bringing warm air and a slow warm rain that seems to go on forever.

On the day of the baptism, a Sunday, warm front weather is in the process of arriving. First come the thick layers of stratus cloud, and everywhere in the valley people can be seen throwing glances at the sky.

10:30 am. Yanach and his wife walk out their door, headed for church. Noting the weather, they turn and lower the shutter on the lone front window. Yanach puts on his cap.

10:45 am. Father John and Ocoya are sitting in the office. The baby is also present. Aragon seems a little downcast. He has come to the realization that the mother cannot begin her Christian initiation this day. She will only hold the baby during the ceremony. "When Philip was preaching down in Gaza," says Aragon, "he happened to run into Queen Candace's chief eunuch, who was—"

"Chief what?" interrupts Ocoya. When this is explained, Ocoya seems more than a little stunned.

"Anyway," the priest goes on, "after Philip opened his mouth and preached Jesus to him, he immediately asked for baptism. From this, we take it that the sacrament cannot be administered to adults without some previous religious instruction. That is, not unless they are on the deathbed— in which case it is okay." Before becoming a full Christian, Aragon explains, Ocoya must spend a while as a student, a catechumenate.

When she understands this, Ocoya looks quite relieved. She will be long gone before anyone can turn her into a cate ... catechuli ... whatever.

11:00 am. Father John is preaching from the pulpit, but there is a moment's hesitation. He seems to have forgotten the Nahuatl word for *dry*. Ah, *huaqui*, of course. "Dry-shod, you brought them through the waters of the Red Sea to be an image of the people freed in baptism," he says, and goes on to talk about St. John the Baptist standing in the River Jordan.

11:12 am. "Born of water and the Spirit," Aragon intones the Latin and all across Coahuila it begins to rain.

When the holy water touches little Abra's head, she frowns deeply and throws a dirty look in the direction of the congregation. Prodigal sits there thinking about the blood and the water, which flowed from the wound in the side of Christ.

"Misa est," announces the priest and the worshipers rise to leave.

6:00 pm. It is growing dark and the rainfall rate is definitely on the increase. Aragon is beginning to worry about the church roof.

"No, no, Father. I'm sure it'll be all right," says Bumblebee of Tlaxcala. "That leak we had … we boxed it in and extended the overhang so—"

Son of Bumblebee interrupts his father. "Right, that's right," he puts in. "Water can't get in there anymore. And that design for the dome—the interwoven branches plastered over—that was my father's idea. That will never leak."

Aragon stands looking out the mess hall window.

"Maybe we should start building an ark, eh, Father?" says Prodigal with a smile. Across the courtyard Aragon sees Ambrosio coming through the downpour off the roof over the office door. The sight of that deluge makes his stomach churn so he comes up with a biblical reference. Talking about scripture always makes him feel a little better.

"Abraham," he says joyfully. "Of course, Abraham. He too is a symbol of baptism and eternal life. When Abraham's descendants—oh, they were numerous as the stars—finally got into the promised land, didn't they first have to cross over the River Jordan?" John's voice trails off and a look of concern ripples across his face. Prodigal knows what's going on in the Padre's mind.

"Ah, no, Father," he says. "That can't happen again."

"No, of course not, Prodigal my friend.

The impossible "that" of which Prodigal speaks refers to is a rainy weather incident five years before, when a clan of the Paiaguanes got tired of working in the fields with no dancing and no enemies to eat. They waited for a good downpour and when the river flooded, the clan crossed over in buffalo-skin boats. When the Tlaxcalan search party caught up, the Paiaguane just stood around on the north shore shouting insults and making obscene gestures. Of course, they were too far away for the gestures to be very effective.

"You know we can't keep them Father."

"But just long enough. She agreed to be baptized."

"I don't know, Father." Prodigal frowns. "These Titsksanwatiks are true nomads. Keep them under a roof and they'll only die." . *Not like the Indians around here*, thinks Prodigal. *Our crowd gladly sell their souls for a square meal and a hut.*

The mess hall door opens and Ambrosio comes dripping in. "Father, I've been looking all over for you. I'm afraid we got some trouble, Oh man, have we got trouble."

Prodigal gives out with something like a grunt, but Aragon raises his chin and looks Ambrosio in the eye. A fatalistic sense fills his being from head to boot tops, and his look is very mild.

"What can it be, 'Brosi?" he asks.

Ambrosio is gasping a bit now, as if only just realizing how short of breath he is. "The horses, Father. It's the horses. They're gone. They're missing. Like, not there anymore."

Chapter 40

What Happened in Coahuila or
The Sins of the Father

"In the City of Querétaro, New Spain, on the sixteenth day of February, 1542, His Excellency Señor Don Porfirio Flores de Repente, Count of Coruña, governor and captain general for His Majesty in this province of New Spain, and vice-president of the Royal Audencia that is located there, etc., said that he had been informed of some very mysterious doings involving witchcraft, devil worship, and treason at, and in the environs of, the mission of the Valley of the Circumcision of Our Lord, and even across the Great North River along the road to the Tejas, which region, acting as a buffer against foreign incursions into the mining areas of this province of New Spain, should be protected at all costs."

Accordingly, the Count of Coruña issued permit for an expedition to the north, utilizing funds and personnel contributed by the Holy Office of the Inquisition at the city of Mexico, and that for the safety of their persons, he granted that as many as twenty soldiers might go with them. And it appears that, conforming to said permit, these religious and eight of the said soldiers set forth on the eighteenth of October last.

On arrival at the Valley of the C. of O. L., an oath was at once administered to Sr. John Prodigal, former resident of Petlacalco, and to Sr. Nacho Bé, formerly of Dzibichaltun, Yucatan, and various others. They were sworn in due form, in the name of God and Holy Mary and with a sign of the cross. Under this oath they all promised to tell the truth. (No written record of the testimony of these individuals is found in the archives of the Inquisition)

Here is the actual testimony:

"Well, of course, you see, that would be impossible," states Father Diego Ibarra, MD, of the order of San Francisco. "After questioning the patient and giving him a most thorough exam, I conclude that Mr. Prodigal suffers from an ulcer—peptic or duodenal. Prodigal himself knows this, and whenever possible takes small meals at more frequent intervals. And never does he touch chili—neither green, red, yellow, small or large, dried or smoked. With what motive then would he string huge amounts of that fruit and place them to dry up on his roof? Draped over a wooden cross, says the charge? Oh, it's not exactly a charge? I see. Well, charge or no, cross or a clothesline—he just wouldn't do it. Oh, by the way, since we're all here together, I think we should offer up a quick prayer for Father John's safe return. Hopefully he'll soon be here to greet us."

"My name is Nacho Bé," states Nacho under oath. "I was never given a Christian appellation; I suppose because 'Nacho' sounded Spanish enough to suit the priests."

"My profession is librarian and scribe."

"I have been away from home and family for twenty-three years. Cortés himself hired me at Champoton, where I was attending a conference. This was in March of 1519."

"Born? Where was I born? An excellent question, my lords. Well, I can tell you I was born very near the old city of Dzibichaltun, but the name of that province is lost forever. They say that when old Grijalva stepped ashore he asked the name of the place and the chief answered, 'Sorry, I don't understand you.' Somehow, the words sounded like *Yucatan* to the Spaniards. Another great Castilian explorer claims the land is named after the little mounds in which yucca is planted. Yucatan. So you can take your choice. It's between a vegetable and a misunderstanding."

"O Your Reverence, yes. I am aware that Father John is not here at this time. Yes, I am informed as to his whereabouts. Well, more or less. Somewhere on the Sabinas, I believe."

"No, my lords, I wasn't particularly surprised," states Nacho Bé. "Horses are getting to be quite a big deal up here. Stealing them is rapidly becoming an art form. Even the naked Indians of the prairie are working to lay hands on them, but ours was the first really big horse heist in Coahuila. No, what surprised me was that they left behind three good animals. Oh, yes. And our ancient mule, which, if truth be told, was already pretty much retired and out to pasture. The mule we used to pack a few supplies, but unfortunately, when we got up there, we had to cook the poor old thing.

Turn her into stew. None of us are really hunters, you see. Not very good ones, anyway. We had trouble enough getting her butchered, though Prodigal managed to dispatch her all right. He remembered how to cut a throat cleanly enough."

"Yes, I know the whereabouts of Father John," states Prodigal. "Well, within ten or twelve leagues, anyway. He is among the rancherías, between the Sabinas and the Great North. He visits there quite frequently. Tending to the gentiles, you know."

"What route did we choose? O good sirs, there was little or no choosing to be done," answers Prodigal. "We went north. Due north 'till we came to the Sabinas. 'There's no getting across this,' I said to the Father, and hearing it, he waxed very wroth. Never had I seen the Father so angry. His face took on a purple, splotched look, but just as he opened his mouth to speak, out stepped two Indians from behind a bush. Members of the Assares nation they were, and they told us of a place downstream where many islands lay in the river. 'The channels between them are quite narrow,' they said, 'and it is easy to get across.' Father John kneeled down and began a prayer of thanks. And then you could have felled the lot of us with a broom straw: the Indians were also kneeling, and they were repeating the Our Father in the Latin tongue. Father John finished the prayer without batting an eye, and then he asked the two Assares if they had been baptized.'

"'No, no, not us,' they replied."

"Finally, it was determined that their knowledge of Catholic ceremony was the product of observation. Apparently they had been dropping in from time to time and hanging around the mission. In other words, they had learned about Christianity by spying on us. They were, however, very reluctant to cross over the river. It seems a friend of theirs, a fellow who liked to call himself Augustín, had gone over in order to tell those people something about the new religion and had been killed there."

"My name is Ambrosio of the Well," states Ambrosio under oath—and also under oath sworn in the name of God and Holy Mary—"I was born in Barcelona, home of the great bard, Ausias March."

"My profession is blacksmith and iron worker."

Ambrosio looks around with a puzzled air. "Yes, I know he's not here. Not right now. Where? Yes, I know where. He's up among the rancherías along the Great North. Trying to start a mission up there."

"No, sir, he probably doesn't have permission from the Father President in Queretaro but ... well, you see, it isn't exactly a mission. There isn't any church. It's more like a medical center. He has some people helping him. Some are Christians, but not all. There is a woman ... very intelligent ..."

"Ah, the trip up. Yes, clearly ... yes, that's right. I was the first to spot the thorns. Huge masses of them, big bundles, rolls of it: green briar or cat's claw spread along the river trail. Oh, we knew ... we knew what it meant; we'd seen it before." Ambrosio seems a bit choked up. Is he about to burst into tears? "Ah, yes, thanks my Lord. A glass of water ... yes, please."

"Well, of course that was later. We traveled all the way to the Great North River and not a trace of the Titskanwatits did we spot. In fact, we saw no one after the Sabinas. Not a soul in all those what? ... twenty or thirty leagues? As to that Great North River, well, just then it must have been a half league wide and there was no getting across it. No, not by any means. Even Father John could see that. 'We'll wait,' he said. 'We'll wait till the river goes down.' So ... with nothing better to do, we began ambling down-stream in the vague hope that maybe the Titskanwatits couldn't get across either. That's when we saw the thorns. They put them there to try to stop it. They thought it couldn't get through. Like a barrier ... stupid heathen notions." Now Ambarosio is weeping in earnest.

"Good sirs, perhaps I can explain," interrupts Prodigal. Taken aback at the depth of Ambrosio's emotion, the inquisitors make no objection.

"It's demon smallpox, you see. Demon smallpox pursues them. When the Indians flee for their lives, they strew thorns along the path behind them to impede its pursuit. If the disease attempts to follow and runs into the sharp spines, the evil thing will be broken and lose all its power. That's what they believe, but of course, we understand what tragic nonsense all that business is. Anyway, from that moment Father Aragon forgot all about the Titskanwatits. 'There are people dying out there like beasts in the fields,' he said. 'Dying without knowledge of Christ. We must find them. We must redeem all the souls we can with holy baptism.'"

Prodigal doesn't mention the words Nacho Bé hurriedly whispered there on the trail.

"Some say it's the holy water itself carries the disease, that it's some kind of poison."

"Well, he doesn't have any with him."

"Oh yes, oh yes. He always carries a few drops."

"About a league further down we came to another stretch of flat and muddy water with trees sticking out of it," continues Prodigal. "'This must be a feeder creek,'" we said, and turned south looking for a place to cross. At last we came to a line of great cypresses, their roots clear of the water. It was a lovely spot. The trees had just come into full leaf, and the sun shone through, casting a cool, if rather splotchy, light over everything. There was an elderly woman there, seated on the ground leaning against a tree. She was in the first stages of the disease, and they had surrounded her with thorns in an attempt to confine the evil. They had left her a jug of water but no food. Well, certainly she hadn't much of an appetite just then."

"So we moved the brambles aside and Father John got out the holy water. The woman was lying there groaning softly, but when she caught sight of Father with his little bottle, she quickly animated herself. 'What the—!' she exclaimed, 'No you don't. Get that stuff away from me. That poison has done enough damage around here,' and she stood and leaned against the cypress trunk with her hands out as if to protect her face. Then she clutched her head and moaned. 'Oooh,' she breathed harshly."

"Father John almost dropped the bottle, so surprised he was. 'Have you already received … the water of life? Have your people already been baptized?' he asked in tones verging on the querulous."

"'No,' the woman answered, 'but there's a lot of it going on somewhere around here, that much is clear. And it's killing the people.'"

"We put the woman up on Father John's horse. She was still able to hold on all right, and in fact, she liked it. Being mounted up on a horse seemed to calm her fevered body and spirit. 'We'll take her home,' said Father. 'There are bound to be others in need of salvation.' Father led the animal himself, and in a minute, he spoke to us in Spanish. 'Maybe later,' he said. 'Yes, later when she's closer to death.'"

"'But Father, they don't always die,' said Nacho Bé. 'I didn't die, and neither did Prodigal here.'

"'I didn't get it.'" Says Prodigal.

"'No, but she'll think she's dying,' remarked Ambrosio. 'She'll wish she was.'"

Inquisitor #one heaves a sigh of compassion and taps his pen on the table before him. "Very true, very true," he says. "Our gracious creator, knowing the little consistency of these miserable Indians, from time to time visits them mercifully with an epidemic of smallpox. Especially when a baptized child dies—then it is cause for rejoicing, for the soul of an innocent one has been saved from the thorns of paganism. Yes, God has chosen it to be a beautiful flower of the celestial paradise." Both inquisitors #1 and #2 nod their heads and look over at Prodigal as if inviting comment.

"Yes, certainly. But, of course. O clearly. Well, anyhow, as previously mentioned, the old woman we picked up was only in the first stages of the disease. This is fever, headache, and aching joints, especially in the small of the back. I mean right here, at the top of the hips, where the lumbago tends to get us older types. Later it becomes something quite different. In his poem entitled 'Aoc Vel,' in the Spanish, 'No Longer,' the noble son of the warrior hero Eagle Swoops, I mean the poet-philosopher Eagle Swoops the Younger, describes the course of the illness with accuracy and sensitivity. Let's see if I remember how it goes."

> "In Toptwist there in a deep ravine,
> Spread over the people like a covering,
> Like a blanket of ..."

"No, no dear lords, that's not quite right. The years roll on, and I begin to suffer from old-timer's malady. Well, dear me. I have it written down some place. Ah, there it lies, right before my eyes. Now among the—"

"Hold on a minute there, young man. Just hold on," interrupts inquisitor #1. "That Mexican to whom you refer, Eagle Swoops of Weavertown, was, as the world knows, tried, convicted, and hung for treasonous action against Charles V of the Holy Roman Empire who reigns as well, I need hardly add, as King Charles I of Spain. Nothing, but absolutely nothing that criminal had to say, can possibly interest this board of inquiry."

"Forgive me, kind lord, but I do not speak of that well-known pervert and sociopath Eagle Swoops the Elder, but rather of his son. I mean Swoops the Younger, the talented scholar and Christian philosopher." *No need to mention the young student was booted out of Santa Cruz U. for shooting his mouth off. These chaps weren't even around back then,* thinks Prodigal.

Inquisitor #1 waves a deferential hand, which gesture Prodigal interprets as a carry on signal, and so he does.

"Among the clergy these days," he says, "there seems to be some loss of language skills, especially with regard to the Nahuatl tongue, so I will translate going along. I beg your patience."

"Just like a covering; covering-like spread the pustules
On the face, on the head, on the breast, etcetera,
Like a blanket of pain, and of suffering a plethora.
No longer could they walk, no longer could they rise,
No longer could they stretch themselves out on their sides,
No longer could they stretch themselves out face down,
No longer could they move their bodies around,
For when they bestirred themselves,
Much did they cry out."

"Clearly the author is a youngish person. The somewhat self-indulgent thoroughness of expression, the dedicated attention to horrific detail, all indicate a talented if somewhat immature mind. We conclude, therefore, that the piece was composed long before it was written down at Santa Cruz—most likely during young Swoops' recovery. This would have been at Toptwist, where the plague finally died out. It will be recalled that the first case of pox occurred in the community of Cliffwhip, and then it moved on to Chalco. Next it came to be prevalent in Teotl Eco and after three months—Mexican months, that is, or sixty Spanish days—it went diminishing toward—"

Inquisitor #1 pushes back his chair, causing a nerve-wracking squeak which makes everyone jump a little. "Sir, sir," he interrupts. "What on earth? Does any of this bear on the inquiry at hand? I really don't see how."

"O pardon, Your Reverences," says Prodigal. "I am only trying to explain why things are so very different up here in the north, up here in the 'Godlands.' O pardon again, lords. I mean up here in the Chichimeca. Nothing godly about it. Certainly not."

"You see the tribes in these parts are certain the pox is a deliberate attempt to murder the people. Yes, murder. By means of poison in the holy water. We Mexicans were not so naive. We watched the Fathers in their robes, and we saw they did not die. We knew it was a contagion and so we stuffed our corpses down the wells, and still the Spaniards did not die. The Spanish God must be stronger than ours, we thought, and that's all there is to it."

"Father John? That man is a saint. No, he's an angel," states Ambrosio del Pozo. "I mean, whichever ranks higher."

"Oh, no. He knows there isn't any cure, but the Father has found that simple nursing care can save an awful lot of lives."

"Only my opinion. Correct, sir, correct," sighs Ambrosio.

"Well sir, we tried to get the old woman home, but she died before we got there. She was pretty old, and she died just from the fever—I mean even before the rash broke out. You know, sir, the fever and pain subside a bit and they think they're on the mend, but then comes that itchy rash spreading down the arms and on the cheeks and then across the stomach and then the back and then the thighs—"

"Yes, yes." interrupts Inquisitor #2. "The great Bishop Margolis teaches that smallpox is a test, and man is meant to bear it just as Job stood up under God's trials in times long past. Now, this does not mean we can't do a few things to help relieve the suffering," says #2 in a nice show of humanity.

"Yes, sir," says Ambrosio. "Well, Father John brought us in there. We went in. The first of those spread-out villages covers about a league, and there are a couple more rancherías close by. You could smell them before you got there. That stench came right through the woods—those stinking, scrubby woods they've got in those parts."

The brother of the Reverend Father Diego Ybarra, MD, is married to the Countess Luiza Calderon, a second cousin of Margaret of Parma whose son, Alexander Farnese, might someday become King of Portugal, so no one interrupts when the doctor speaks. Just now, he believes it necessary to counteract the rather fatalistic aura floating around the room. He means to present a sort of early pre-Enlightenment, semi-rigorous look-see at the dreadful disease we know as *variola major*.

"'The odor of rotting flesh' of which Mr. del Pozo speaks," says the doctor, "is exuded by the suppurating cankers which ulcerate the body of the smallpox victim. They begin with reddish maculae spreading across the cheeks, abdomen, and anterior sides of the limbs. In three or four days these itchy lesions give rise to small round bumps, which turn into clear blisters. Very slowly the blisters fill with pus. Soon the face is unrecognizable, a swollen mass of running sores. The fever rises while the head and joint pains return with doubled vigor. Sometimes pustules form in the mouth, the throat, and membrini mucosa of the trachea making the swallowing of food and water an impossibility. Coughing can cause tracheal hemorrhaging so that victims often drown in their own blood. Patients sometimes die, as well, of lung failure, poisoning of the liver or severe intestinal colic. After a week, if the patient is still alive, his or her pustules mature and then split open and dry into dark scabs."

The information the good doctor articulates there in the mess hall at the Mission of the Valley of the Circumcision of Our Lord is not new to the people assembled. The complete and concise manner of its presentation, however, seems to freeze them all in their seats. The doctor goes on in a somewhat lighter tone.

"Well, if you're still here when the scabs fall off, you'll probably make it. But you won't be so pretty anymore. Of course the Indians of our New World are more susceptible than us. This may be due to the fact that they are all descended from the same tribes: the ancient Hebrews. We Europeans come of more divers ancestry."*

"And so we stood there in the plaza area," states Nacho, "I mean the little cleared space where they hold their dances and such, and we started arguing history. I know it seems absurd, but we were all a bit overwrought, and Prodigal still had blood all over him from killing the mule. 'If it wasn't for Leo, we wouldn't have to be in this shit hole,' someone was moaning. 'No, it wasn't Leo,' somebody else said. 'It was Julius. Julius II.' And so we stood there with wet rags wrapped around our heads, trying to keep the smell of death out of our nostrils, and we were arguing about the Popes."

"'1512, one thousand five hundred and twelve! Pope Leo declared the Indians human beings and entitled to—'"

"'No, sir. It was Julius. Julius said they were descended from Adam and Eve, and thus they could be saved by God's grace, and that's what we're doing here.'"

"'Just a minute. Hold on. The Encomienda came under the Laws of Burgos, which was when Julius was Pope—1512. Now, I know that's right because—'"

"'That's what I said! That's what I said! Julius! Julius, not Leo!'"

"Father John wanted to say something, but that wet rag kept getting in his mouth. Finally he removed it and just stood there, holding the thing in his hand and shaking his head. It really didn't work very well, and anyway, after a couple of days you couldn't smell a thing anymore."

* The notion of genetic homogeneity as a factor in disease susceptibility is currently in vogue in anthropological circles. author

"You see, the disease had struck so hard there was no one to take care of the sick. There was no one to hunt or fish or build fires or carry water—or bury the dead. We figured there were as many died of hunger and thirst as killed by the pox. And those miserable little huts of theirs … it was pretty bad in there. The people rolling around in agony, tearing their clothes with their own hands, just trying to get some air on those burning bodies. Why, they couldn't even get up to relieve themselves—fouling the blankets and the clothes and then tossing and turning in their own filth." Nacho spreads his hands on the table and looks down at them. "O yes," he says. "We had our work cut out for us."

"O yes indeed, your honor, our work was cut out for us," answers Prodigal, and then he looks up and sighs. "Think of the little brook," he says, "how it runs along and flows into the stream. And the stream flows into the river, and the mighty river rolls along forever. Well, that's how our days went: one sliding into the other, into a single endless day. We never forgot to pray, though—thanking God for the good weather."

"Father had taken on the duty of distributing firewood around the rancherías, thus killing two birds with one stone. The firewood was badly needed, of course, but so also were the sacraments of baptism and extreme unction. So the Father was about a league down river when we got the news from Chief Waopira. We always called him Plácido because of his calm manner in dreadful adversity. The chief had sent word he was ready to die and wanted baptism and the sacred oil of extreme unction. Only he didn't call it the 'sacred oil,' he called it 'God's poison.' Well, Father came in just at dark and we told him, but we left out the poison oil part."

"Father John was exhausted. His eyes were a pair of red lamps and his knees shook as he stood there. But in a minute, he began quoting James in a joyous manner. 'Is any man sick among you? Let him bring in the priests of the church.' Then he smiled broadly and raised an admonishing forefinger. 'Not the local wizards and witches, mind you, but priests of the church, and let them pray over him, anointing him with oil in the name of the Lord, and if he be in sins, they shall be forgiven him.'"

"'All right boys,' he told us, 'get going. Take over a crucifix, two candles, and a spoon. You know the drill. I'll be right behind you.' Of course there was no point in mentioning to Father that it was dark and that it was late and he was already on his last legs, as were we all."

"Chief Plácido had a hut bigger than average, but still it was packed to the rafters with kinfolk from across the river. They were all camped out in the scrub, but drawn by a desire to witness the healing rites they were curious enough to brave the odors, miseries, and general unpleasantness in the 'downtown' area. These relatives had already been observing the native priests dancing and singing to the spirits, and now they would watch the Christian ceremony.'"

"'None of these people are sick,' said Nacho. 'I don't know if this is such a good idea, all this mob in here.' Father John arrived just as the Indian witches and wizards were filing out, and I think he was a little taken aback. 'Don't mind us,' said the wizards with a touch of sarcasm. 'We were just leaving.'"

"I set up the candles and the crucifix and also the spoon. Father John took out the chrism, the sacred oil, and the Eucharist, which he always carried with him. He once told us it was a sin for a priest to go around without these items. Anyway, so it was ordained by St. ... er, uh, St. ... O you know, the patron saint of brewers.'"

"St. Boniface," smiled Inquisitor #2.

"St Boniface. Right. A German. Well, when the Father came in, those people standing around backed up just as far as they could. They almost disappeared into the walls. And suddenly there was quite a bit of room in there."

"'Through this holy anointing,' Father began the Latin, 'and by his tender mercy, may the Lord pardon you what sins you have committed by sight, hearing, speech, etc., etc.,' Plácido remained wide-eyed through it all, and when the Father was finished he spoke up. His voice was so very weak we had to bend over to hear. Not 'Brosi, though, he doesn't speak much Coahuilan anyway."

"It was quite a long speech for a dying man, so I'll give you only the gist of it. 'When a smallpox victim pulls through,' said Plácido, 'we give the credit to our good spirits. The failures we blame on evil demons. The Christian God, on the other hand, deals out both the gift of life and the pain of death. The same God—get it? Now, that's real omnipotence. He should be worshipped with all diligence!' insisted Plácido. Then he went on to outline some of the causes of God-wrought death."

"1. The eating of coiametl [Tayassu tajacu-wild swine] on the sixth, thirteenth, twentieth, and twenty-seventh days of the moon.
2. The eating of slain enemies on any day—this one made Father very happy.
3. The taking of poison via holy water and sacred oil."

"This last Father John found extremely depressing. He grew very quiet and seemed to shrink into himself. We walked out into the plaza, and for a while we all just stood around out there. That night, as I recall, there was a full moon. Father John was bent over like an old man."

"O, you know how it is, my lords. When food and sleep are scarce, small problems take on gigantic proportions. Ambrosio, for example, well, out there in the moonlight, he fell into a rage. 'I told you so! I told you so!' he gargled between clenched teeth. 'These Indians are not like us. They're not capable of understanding. It's a waste of—'Brosi must have noticed Nacho and I looking at him rather closely, for he stopped in mid-sentence. 'Oh, you two,' he added. 'Well, of course you two are different.' After that, nobody said a word. Nobody slept and nobody spoke—that is, until morning when there was plenty to talk about."

"About sunrise we heard a lot of shouting and wailing and other sounds of mourning, and we figured there were some new dead somewhere. Father John got to his feet. 'Whoever it is certainly hasn't been deceased for long,' he said. 'We can still administer the sacrementium exeutium. Yes, we can still save a soul or two.' The sun was directly in the Father's face, and his eyes looked … strange. Yes, and very tired."

"Well, there were some new deaths all right but they were not plague related. A nephew of Plácido, a man called Big Dog, had smothered his two children, stabbed his wife and then turned the knife between his own ribs. He had decided they should all die before they could be baptized. He didn't want his family showing up in the afterworld with scarred and disfigured faces. 'Even the wolves will scorn our rotten bodies,' he was heard to say. I'm certain the Father was much disturbed by all this, but I don't believe he said very much. We just went back to work. I mean that grim round of duties in the settlements: cooking, feeding those who could eat, cleaning the huts, burying the dead. Each day seemed longer than most people's lives."

"Well, sir, you know, it's difficult to say," states Ambrosio. "Everything got confused. Plácido's relatives, the ones from across the river, well, they started getting sick, and a couple of the old ones died. Last rites? No, I don't recall Father doing—"

"Well, you see we found the Titskanwatits, or anyway—"

"Baptism?"

Ambrosio is having trouble keeping up with the flood of questions regarding the Father's pastoral functions. "Baptism. Well, that would have been tricky. We had run out of holy water from the mission a long time ago, so Father had brought some up from the river and prayed over it and blessed it. But then he knocked the jug over." Ambrosio shrugs his shoulders. "It was an accident. I remember he was standing there. He was watching the holy water soak into the earth of Coahuila. No, he didn't fetch any more. Did he cross himself? This I don't remember. I know he put the Eucharist, the chrism, and the spoon back in his duffel. The crucifix? I don't know what happened to the crucifix. Did we think it strange? O my lords, we were too busy to think anything."

"Yes, the Titskanwatits. Well, they never made it across the river, you see. They came down with the pox and couldn't travel anymore. I think they're all sick up there. I mean the whole region, in every direction. I think they've all got it."

"I don't know, sir, Maybe they were trying to get back to the mission. I don't know where they were going. What was left of the Titskanwatits showed up outside the village, and Father and I went out to meet them, to get them set up. Oh, we found out what happened to our horses. Their old friends, the Lipan, had run off with them. They were bragging they'd killed one of them in the battle, and most likely they ate him. Maybe that's how they got sick. Who knows? Ouchcala was dead, and Gosata was dead, and there in front of all that pathetic bunch stood Ocoya, her own self."

"Clearly she'd had the disease. On both cheeks you could see that cluster of scars like a spiral, as if the pits had been made on a potter's wheel. But otherwise she looked pretty healthy. This is when Father John became ill. No, no, not the pox. No, of course not."

"Yes, exactly, sir. It was more like a fever of the brain. At first Father was very glad to see her, but then he found out the baby was dead, that woman's baby, the child he had baptized. So then he collapsed right there on the trail. He fell to his knees in front of her, and he began to weep."

"Was he praying? I don't know, sir, but he sure was weeping. And he was sobbing. Dear Lord, what can I say? I only know what I saw. There was a look came over that woman's face. You know, I've seen that look before. It was like … like the Madonna. Like the Madonna in a painting. Well, she took a step forward. Then she stretched her hand out and placed it on the Father's head, and he quieted down right away."

"That night we all slept soundly. The dead were already sleeping, of course, and even the dying got a good night's rest. Yes, all of us. We all got some peace and quiet for a few hours. In the morning I felt very well, as if we were finally free and any minute Father was going to tell us to pack up, that we were all going home. I think Prodigal and Nacho felt that way also, sort of like there was something nice about to happen. But, really we were only fooling ourselves. We weren't going anywhere on that day."

"Oh, the Madonna." Ambrosio is grinning with embarrassment. "She took off down-river with Father John. There's this place she knows. We were long out of mule-meat so John, er, uh, Father got some teenagers, three boys and a girl, and he organized a hunting party. The kids weren't quite up to it yet, but John said … I mean Father John said, it would do them good. And actually, they were quite successful, that is, if you like armadillo."

"Come to think of it, that's right. There were no deaths, and there were no new cases. Yes, I guess we were right. I guess that was a good day after all.

Chapter 41

A Smallish Miracle

"Is the secrecy of the confessional compatible with the
mutual confidences of conjugal love? ... Have no secrets
which cost too much in the telling and then you will have
no cause to fear the gossip of the vicar's wife."
George Sand on celibacy

Along the lower-middle stretches of the Great North River, or perhaps
more accurately, the upper-lower part, there are a couple of very heavily
wooded areas. Giant *avevetl*, what we know as bald cypress, live there with
their feet right in the water, and directly behind them, and even alongside,
stand the black willows, cloaked in their medicinal bark. The medicine is
salycin, an ingredient of aspirin. The compound provides the only relief,
albeit temporary, from the pain of variola.

On the south side are found the northernmost groves of *nuez
encarcelada*—pecan. In fact, one can travel north as far as the polar cap
and not see another pecan tree. Heading east, however, the distance is not
so great. Cottonwood and persimmon, hogplum and candalia, along with
a countless variety of woody plants and shrubs add to the vernal lushness
of the place. It has a tropical look, though it's well within the temperate
zone. The parakeets, however, don't seem to comprehend such latitudinal
niceties, and neither do the ocelot and the coati.

Grateful for the shade, the little hunting party from upriver is camped
on the first terrace, just above the slow-moving current. In less than half
a millennia, this very same location will be used as a fording place by
those attempting to engage in the great search for employment. I mean
that illegal hunt for a better life in the northern reaches of the continent.
For now, though, only our small, mixed-race group of would-be hunters
is present.

They're positioned a good five meters back from the campfire. If the seating arrangement seems unorthodox, rest assured it is necessary. Firelight attracts mayflies. They swarm around it in their thousands, great clouds of them, and it's easy to breathe in a mouthful of the fluttery little beasts. And for John Aragon, the day has already presented its quota of strangeness.

It all began that morning with the business of the eggs. Scouting around the scrubby plain just above the river, the youngsters heard the nasal *Chip-churr* [accent on the second syllable] of the local quail, the species we know today as *Callipepia squamata*, the scaled quail. The nests of a large covey were soon located. The nests were full of eggs, which the teenagers joyfully brought back to camp. After all, everybody loves eggs, raw or boiled, it hardly matters.

"Oh, eggs," exclaimed Aragon, and immediately his stomach began to rumble. "Too bad we don't have an onion. And some mushrooms."

"Onion? Mushrooms?"

"Xocanacatl. Menanacatl."

"O menanacatl. There's plenty of that. Up here on the flats it grows all over the old buffalo turds. *Jima'shka*. It's the same thing. Wait. We'll be back in less time than it takes to peel a squirrel." Ocoya stood there, hands on hips, shaking her head, while the girl, a sixteen-year-old, covered her face as if to hide some giggles. Then she took off after the boys.

Nomadic people usually eat their eggs raw, but Aragon fried his in a pan with the mushrooms. After breakfast he felt a little queasy. *Quail eggs are awfully rich,* he thought. With a small lurch his stomach put him in mind of some bad tamales he had bought once on the street in Coyoacan. *"Sellers of bad tamales ought to be prosecuted to the law's fullest extent,"* said Prodigal in those years long past. *"Filthy tamales. And some are broken, and some are tasteless, frightening, deceiving, swollen tamales. Tamales stuffed with chaff. No, they shouldn't be permitted … foul tamales, sticky, gummy, old tamales, cold tamales, exceedingly sour and stinking …"*

Too many of those really unsavory street-market items spinning through his brain were beginning to cause a little nausea, so Aragon thought it might be best to get up and move around a bit. In the pecan grove he seemed to be puzzling out a theorem. "It's all done through arrangements in space," he was saying in a very thoughtful manner. "I can see the space between the trees. Quite amazing, really." Ocoya came up and looked at him closely. "Oh, don't get me wrong. The trees themselves look marvelous," he told her, "with limbs so sharply limned and standing there encased in air. But the distance between them is really extraordinarily obvious."

249

"You didn't know there was a distance between trees?" responded Ocoya. "O my poor blind baby," she said with a laugh.

"Eggs cooked in metal. Are they very tasty? Very strong?" asks Ocoya, sometime after supper. She is glad they are sitting away from the light. Ocoya gets uneasy when she thinks the world is looking at her scarred cheeks.

"What? What do you mean?" Aragon is leaning over, peering at her.

"Only what I said. Why are you staring at me?" she breathes and claps her hands to her face.

"Ah, no," says Aragon very softly. He wants to reach up, grasp her wrists and take her hands down—but he only changes the subject. "That was a nice job the kids did today, wasn't it," he says with strained cheerfulness.

The youngsters had managed to put a couple of arrows into a young doe, but running her down and dispatching her proved exhausting. Now they are stretched out, sleeping like the dead. "Tomorrow they're going to try something different," says Aragon. "Going after those big gar. *Uitzitzilmichin*, I think. I don't know what it is in Coahuilan. Anyway, fishing. Fishing is usually quite amusing, isn't it? Then we have to clean them, split them, and build a smoking rack. Isn't that how it's done?"

Ocoya is staring at the ground. "Yes, that's how it's done," she says, but she doesn't look up. Ocoya isn't much interested in the upcoming fish barbecue. Grief makes concentration difficult, but the subject of Abra's death must be discussed. There are some rather important ramifications to the demise of that baby. Hard forces are let loose in the land, and they seem to coalesce around this simple-minded priest. Care must be taken or civilization-as-we-know-it might just disintegrate, disappear. It's already pretty well screwed up.

Such an unlikely power-figure this little brown robe. Ocoya hesitates. She knows he feels responsible for the death of her baby, and she doesn't want to frighten the fellow yet further afield of his wits. Finally, Ocoya sighs and sits up straight. She decides to take the bull by the horns.

"Abra was very brave," she whispers, "O very brave. First came the diarrhea, and you could see the child was annoyed, but she didn't blame anyone, not me, not anybody." Aragon is looking out at the fireflies darting over the river. They're amazingly bright, multiplied by their reflections in the quiet waters.

"Then when the fever started she cried a little. Well, who wouldn't? Before those red patches showed up on her skin, I myself became ill. We were in the same bed, lying there together, but I don't remember much.

They told me she just closed her eyes and died. 'There were no pustules,' they said. 'She went to the afterlife still looking good,' they said."

For John Aragon, the skittering lights along the river are now multiplied maybe a thousand times, refracted in his tear-filled eyes. Those tears begin to roll down his cheeks, but he weeps silently as if words, cries, groans were thoroughly inadequate, perfectly useless things. Ocoya gets to her feet. *Yes, this is what I wanted,* she thinks. *But now what?* Aragon sits on a fallen cottonwood, one hand holding on to the stub of a broken limb. Ocoya steps around and falls, kneeling before him.

"O brother," she says, shaking her head. "I mean, little friend." Ocoya reaches up and takes his face in one hand and with the other she grasps his knees in a time-honored gesture of supplication. "You must understand," she says. "There is no judgment here. No one is at fault. It is only that your path has been changed. That's the most important thing. You must take a different road now. Can you understand? Listen, it happens." She releases him and shrugs her shoulders.

Ocoya sighs and turns her head to look at the river. Her hair brushes across his knees, and though he wears that woolly brown robe, Aragon feels a peculiar itch as far up as his solar plexus.

"It may be you can no longer live among us here in this land. The power in you is far too strong for this place," she says, and then begins musing softly to herself. "But where will you go? How will you live?" she mumbles.

Aragon is on his feet now. "You know, Ocoya," he says, and he is almost in tears again. "Really, I can look out for myself. I'm a skilled person. I can build a house; I can sow; I can reap." Yes, the tears are definitely flowing once more. Ocoya doesn't know if she wants to burst out laughing or go over and wipe his face.

"O sow! O reap!" she sneers. "That's a big help." *But the fellow said something else, didn't he? He can build a house?* Ocoya ponders. Silence descends on the river. The breeze has died, and for some reason even the little frogs have shut up. "A house," says Ocoya. "A house may be the way." At that moment a large fish, maybe a blue cat, breaks the surface and comes back down with a loud splat. "O yes," says Ocoya pointing at the river. "Listen, will you? Even the fish agree with that one. Yes, you must build a house, and we will live in it. That will change everything."

Seeing the look of horror on Aragon's face, the woman begins waving a hand in front of her face, a gesture of negativity. "No, no, no," she is adamant. "Nothing like that. Only a roof, a roof over our heads. Come on. Let's move under the pecans. This is very important, and I don't want to wake the kids."

"But ... but, Ocoya, that would be ... inappropriate," says Aragon. "Council of Elvira in 302. That's Canon XXXII, to be exact. 'No bishop, priest, or deacon is to have any woman living in the house with him unless it is his mother, sister, or aunt,' and at Neo-Caesaria in Cappadocia they weren't so sure about the brother-sister part, and that's because St. Paulinius—"

"What's a deacon? What's a bishop?" Ocoya raises her arms so that her breasts point straight at Father John's eyes. She takes a step toward him and those two little bulges in her shirtfront catch the leaf-filtered moonlight for a second. Tracking them makes Aragon cross-eyed. "O who gives a damn," she says. "Listen to me, little brother. There is a debt owed me." She grabs the pinkie of her left hand with the fingers of the right and shakes them both close to his face. "One baby. One female child. Well, a boy would be all right. You and your god took my Abra away, and you will bring her back. In the name of the Wolf-Who-Led-Us-Up-From-the-Center-of-the-Earth you will do this."

Aragon kneels down in last year's leaves. "Ocoya, oh, Ocoya," he pleads. "It wasn't me. I didn't do it. I couldn't do it. Maybe it was ... maybe it was Coyote," he says.

Ocoya is firm. "No!" she says rather sharply. "Coyote is a scoundrel, a trouble maker, and a fool, but he doesn't do things like that."

Aragon is frowning at the river. Kneeling there with bowed head, he recalls a certain day, a spring day in Salamanca. It was in a tavern called *The Angry Duck* just off campus—1517? 1518?—oh, what matter. Aragon shakes his head. He was kind of depressed that gorgeous spring day, and so his friends were pouring beer down his throat. One of those young men, in fact, the least articulate, the least intelligent, the one most likely to flunk out, came up with a line Aragon had never forgotten, one he'd always tried to live by it. "When God lays a hand on you, it's useless to keep dwelling on your inadequacies. When God tells you to do something, who cares whether or not you are good enough."

Ocoya looks down on him. Then she reaches out and places her hand on his shoulder. She gives a little push, and Aragon topples back into the leaves of last year. No, it's true. This man can work no miracles. She sees that clearly, now. But maybe between the two of them they can perform some sort of miracle, even if it's only a minor one. She lies down next to him and presses her face to his so that their noses are touching.

Addendum

Chapter 42

Tejas in Our Time

"Blessed are they that have not
seen, and yet have believed."
Book of John

August of the common year two thousand and nine is perhaps not the hottest on record but it is certainly the muggiest. During these weeks of deepest summer, poison ivy thickets grow shoulder high along the Manos River. First named by Spanish explorers "El Rio de Las Manos Perferadas de Cristo" (River of the Perforated Hands of Christ), it was long ago shortened to just plain Manos. Even regional historians with reference books spread open before them have trouble locating the original nomenclature.

Those of you from northern climes may have seen a patch or two of the above mentioned poison weed, may even have accidentally plucked a few leaves in lieu of sanitary materials and suffered a bit. The thickets on the Manos, though, are truly dangerous. If sundried and inadvertently fired, the smoke can cause painful death for people and stock.

On summer nights, the odor of burning insects rises from the lamps of fishermen beneath the cottonwoods. Little smoke puffs form as mayflies in their thousands, maybe millions (who can count?), vaporize themselves on the hot Coleman lamps. Boulders large and small sweat like pigs along this river in August, but a soul could catch its death of cold. That flaky white stuff on the mud only mimics snow—chilling to view and positively disgusting to step through. Pale, crunchy little corpses of sizzled flies are piling up in widening circles around each lamp.

An elderly gent wearing a clerical collar seems to be getting quite a kick out of the beastie-filled night. Yes, he muses happily, merely an expression of raging, relentless libido: the creator's seed cast freely upon the ground.

The pastor, if such he be, seems to have a dramatic turn of mind. What a clever little notion. And so aptly put. It brings a few seconds of blessed relief and the joyful fellow's diastolic probably drops a few points.

"Stupid. Idiot." (Is the good man revising his position?)

"The birds you like to track through this dense and twisted brush would certainly disagree those bugs are a waste. Bah. Nasty goat."*

"Cabron," he whispers softly.

The old Christian soon manages to shut down these negative subvocals but can't prevent an image from rising to his mind's eye. It is the greenish-stained cover of Milton Navarre's *Franciscan Mythopoesis and the American Pox*, the old copy, the one he'd found at the yam-seller's stall (she handled a few books on the side) in the campus market at Kolomyya Tech. When? Was it 1946? '47? Milton, Milton. Such a sweet guy—such twisted notions. Relieved of temporary restraint, the old man's internal acids resume their treacherous business among duodenal tissues.

On the bluff above, a crushed lime road runs parallel to the river. Taken either direction it leads into clicking, buzzing night. Just atop the path down to the river, however, stands a single lamp post. Here a short stretch of concrete fronts three small edifices. In this place, the sticky black forest walls retreat. Untamed nature climbs into a back seat and stays there. Civilization prevails. Well, perhaps such statements smack of hyperbole.

Actually nothing in sight seems to partake of those advantages of sophisticated society: environmentally integrated architecture, well-designed place settings, etc.

In fact, the little buildings jar the eye. Number one (right to left) is an oblong structure put together with slabs of some light corrugated metal. A low wall of woven steel strands like a stiff and useless fishnet surrounds the area. On its gate hangs a plaque reading "Chainsaw Art for Sale." Ah, a center for aesthetic expression, a place wherein the race's oldest longing is made concrete. (Something awry with that metaphor, but it will have to do.)

Nevertheless, the art world should be praised. Of all man's fossilized and crusty institutions, it does the least harm here on the earth. Never do *famine, sword,* and *fire*" crouch for employment beneath its banner.

---

* The term has little meaning in English. It is, rather, a literal translation of a word in one of the divine's mother tongues (might as well admit his profession now. What is there, after all, to be ashamed of) the one he uses quite frequently now since it is the first language of 23 percent of his flock.

Riots in Paris? Come, come. Wrapping the Eifel Tower in green plastic may have offended a few French nationals, but not all, by no means all. A happening in Tejas? What happening? Oh, of course, the reference is to the great sponge made to suck up Lake Selwin P. Johnston. Certainly the fish-kill was unconscionable, but all water was quickly squeezed back into the lake, which was then restocked by state authority.

Building number two is a small, inconvenient store of some sort. Posters in garish tatters block the windows. The narrow shelves and counters within are so jammed with useful products that little space remains for the business of transaction 'twixt seller and sellee. Perhaps a jug of pickled things could be shifted just a bit in order to make room for leisurely conversation and warmer social interaction. No, no. Such advice from strangers in this torrid night would offend or appear unseemly.

But wait. Standing in front of this emporium, resting on a narrow base, is a wooden square covered with print. The light barely touches it. One must cross the road for a better look.

Ice
Beer
Worms
Art

Absurd. Impossible nonsense. No, look. See the painted letters. Though applied many a rainstorm, hailstorm, green, black, and blue norther past, still clearly visible. Hmm … Perhaps a chunk of ice wrapped in cloth and applied to the temple would be comforting as this equatorial night wears on. Fortunately, no use for the other items mentioned can be found at this moment. Few outsiders would care to meet the challenge of a trip through that cloud of winged beasts hanging about the entrance light.

Building number three is the cleanest. Made of white painted boards with a steeply pitched roof it forms a longish rectangle. The large double doors stand open to the night and through the screens some figures are barely visible. A man wearing a dark suit appears to be clutching a woman in tight embrace, but it is her back, which presses against the dark figure. His arms, wrapped around her body, jerk up and down like the wings of a panicked chicken. Suddenly she snaps forward from the waist, fingers clutching at empty air. Strangled sounds like tearing metal escape her throat. The woman gags and spews up some lumpy substance as bats swoop and crash into the screen doors.

So then, on a muggy night in August, when wild grape vines canopy the cottonwoods and black crickets pile up under a street light, a resident of the town of New Prague named Gracie Dally is choking on the body of Christ and requires a Heimlich maneuver.

Gracie's boss, His Eminence Guillermo A. Trachtenberg, bishop of the diocese of Central Tejas, is unaware of the distressing event taking place almost over his head. Father Gil is down on the bank tending a line set with live bream, or perch, as all finny little unknowns are called in these parts. The priest has always laid odds on live bait. To what avail chicken gizzards spread with Peter Pan? Of what use corn flakes soaked in Big Red and then squeezed into little balls? Such gimmicky notions are only propaganda designed by river rats to confound the tourist.

The bishop crouches on an old tractor tire just north of the big loop where Garlic Creek joins the river. Forked stick jammed firmly in the mud, rod butt held between his new Reeboks, Trachtenberg does not twitch a muscle, does not creak a joint, perhaps he does not blink an eye. This last would be hard to note since he sits at the edge of the fall of lamplight, almost in darkness. Fishing this river on summer nights is a problem. An angler stationed too close to the lamp risks a lung full of those wiggly bugs.

The bishop's two companions eye him warily. They would stroll naked through a mesquite thicket rather than interrupt that unnatural stillness. If the old man's body shows no sign of life in the next hour or so, one or the other will work up the nerve to sidle over and check his breathing.

The office of the diocese of Central Tejas is not located here in this small agricultural community of New Prague, but upstream about thirty miles (by road) in the state capital at Mirabeau. Father Gil's fishing buddies live here though, and so does Gracie Dally.

D. J. Lornsby and Billy Gates Haldwell and the bishop are a trio, but the two younger men have never visited Father Gil in the city. Their affection seems bound up with the jack oaks and cedar thickets and the slow brown Manos down here in New Prague County. Neither one is Roman Catholic. Billy Gates serves as deacon at the New Braunschweig Church of Paul, and DJ practices a gentle and unassuming faith in fine Caribbean rum.

For both men, the relationship with Gil Trachtenberg reduces to a peculiar formula: 50 percent unconditional love plus a 50 percent mix of awe, uneasiness, and abject fear. The fear is not so easy to explain.

Bishop Gil is a humble man with a single quirk. The slightest reminder of advancing years seems to injure his spirit in some way. Try to take his arm, perhaps to assist him up a flight of stairs or maybe out of a limo door. That obsidian-eyed stare will quickly freeze your well-meant impulse—turn you to stone right where you stand—like it did Billy Gates at the PDQ checkout (but that's another story).

Both Lornsby and Haldwell are descendants of the first American settlers to arrive in this part of the world. The province of Tejas was at that time one of the most northerly reaches of the Spanish empire in the New World. At first, the Alcalde, from his office at San Anthony de Bexar, refused admission to the Americans. This official knew trouble when he saw it coming. A few well-placed bribes cleared the way, however, and soon new settlements appeared on the Manos, the Dedo (river of the Extended Finger of San Pancraz of Phrigia), and the Wadi-al-Lupi (today's Guadalupe).

The good folk of Tejas soon turned to face their long-time enemy of the north, the Commanche, a small but powerful military nation with an incomparable light cavalry. These warriors were soon attacking the new Anglo agricultural communities. Of course the Anglos kept horse flesh every bit as good as the enemy's, but they were not so foolish as to attempt battle in open country with these highly skilled fighters of the plains.

Just glance back a few generations. There you see a company of volunteers lining quietly, if not calmly along the shelter of a creek bank. The men know this tactic will allow for few if any casualties, but the knowledge does not slow the racing heart or moisten dry mouths. Slightly dazed by some tricky, shifting maneuvers on the field in front, each tries hard to focus on the shrill whirlwind weaving closer, closer still. Now a growing vibration across the prairie covers sound clearly audible only a minute ago, like the splat of tobacco juice striking dead oak leaves.

Ho hum, oh, for the good old days. They are briefly spoken of here only to point out something of the character of the fine folk of present day Central Tejas. Families once possessed of knowledge and skills necessary for survival along a dangerous frontier, though still unfailingly brave and courteous, now amble about town with greatly diminished reflexes. This condition manifests itself in their pathetic attempts to manipulate through four-way stop signs in good order.

Chapter 43

Fruit of the Carya (Pecan)

"Due to the unusual configuration of the Dedos River,
virtually encircling the peninsula of Nueces Ridge."
General information regarding the first
commercial use of *Carya illinoinensis*.

There is a perfectly good gravel road leading down to the river, but will the bishop ride? Of course not. He prefers to walk. This means a steep climb back up the bluff. Lornsby and Haldwell worry about the old man's heart but, as usual, keep such concerns to themselves. Precisely two hours before that moment when Gracie Dally's spirit and/or body will reject the host, the three men stroll out under suburban trees carrying their fishing gear. They will stop at Moro's on Manos to buy bait.

"Oh, hey, almost forgot," DJ is rather frantically brushing a sticky web from his eyes. On summer nights the arachnids of New Prague outdo themselves, stringing their insides across fantastic spaces, between porch pillar and curbside tree, for example.

"Oh, yeah. Geez, I almost forgot. Maxine called last night. You weren't around. I guess she wanted to talk to somebody from home."

Billy Gates checks the sky. Clear as bouillon despite the humidity. "So how's little sister doing. I know she's plenty sick of Monclova."

"That's an understatement. She's working on a deal of her own now; she told me to tell you. Milt Navarre wants her to go into business out of Sabinas. Oh, yeah ... what happened with the onions? I didn't want to ask."

Trachtenberg stops dead in the street and the others drift to a halt.

"Oh, man, that was close but ... no cigar. Sixty thousand pounds of onions packed and ready to go. At six cents for Max that would have at least got her out of there."

"So?"

"So? So it fell through, so. She'll make it now, though."

"With Milt? He's kind of a ... well, kind of a nut, isn't he? Of course, with his money ..."

Now the bishop speaks rather sharply. "Milton Navarre is not a nut," he exclaims. "It's just that he has some rather strange ideas."

"I guess," mumbles DJ. "Anyway, they were in Musquiz and ran into some Tonkawa guy who's gonna put them onto a pecan source. Very good nuts, very cheap. Personally, I don't get it. I thought he hated Indians."

Billy Gates frowns and looks puzzled. "I don't think he hates Indians."

"Well, anyway, this is one Indian he likes."

The group discovers it has stopped in front of Moro's. The bishop, both hands in the air, waves them back from the doorway. He wants to choose the bait alone, in that state of perfect *satori* he uses only for picking fish. Any other application of the principle would constitute a mortal sin, a clear and obvious violation of the first commandment.

Billy Gates turns to DJ. "See, it's the right product at last. That's what it takes. Now we're talking in terms of dollars per unit, not pennies, you know? The whole thing gets more practical. You can begin with smaller volumes and still stay alive."

DJ shifts the rods to his left hand and looks blank. "You mean pecans?"

"You got it old buddy, pecans."

"Mexican pecans?"

"Just as good as ours."

"Well, that's the point. Where's she think she's gonna sell Mexican pecans? Not in Tejas, that's for sure. Look around. All we got is pecans. There's nothing as good as our Choctaws."

"Maybe not in Tejas, but Tejas ain't the whole country. They'll sell up north all right." Billy Gates is not exactly whining, he merely sounds a mite defensive. Slouching there on the corner of Masaryk and Chavez he begins to pout a little.

"No, they won't neither. That market's all sewed up. All they buy are those tasteless Georgia papershells. That's all they know."

"Well, maybe they'll go for a really good pecan for a change."

"Damn it, Billy Gates, that's not how it works. Those people in ... in ..." DJ knows there are a number of states one encounters traveling north, but not a one comes to mind ... ah, Minnesota. "Yeah, Minnesota!

They wouldn't know a good pecan if it bit their ass. They just don't care. The old companies—"

"Listen DJ, what do you know about it? Who made you the big pecan expert anyway?"

Father Gil stands before Moro's door, bucket of perch swinging from his left hand, the right raised as if in benediction. He listens very carefully to the debate.

"I guess I know a nut case when I see one," DJ mumbles.

The priest frowns deeply. *Doesn't sound so good,* he thinks. *Definitely on the edge again. Seven months between drinks. Dear God, depression is not an acceptable lifestyle alternative to alcoholism.*

What is needed is a miracle, but DJ may have already had his "sign" for the year. It happened during his second day of detox at the combination suicide, alcoholism, drug abuse, and depression ward (also spousal abuse and teenage pregnancy center) at New Prague County Hospital. DJ was seated spiritless and nigh to brain-dead in front of the rec room television set when a commercial advertising medicine for "your cat's urinary tract" slowly began percolating its way through the gray and dimly lit channels of the back-brain and up into the frontal lobes. Once arrived at that place where they might be consciously considered, those words "cat's urinary tract" turned and attacked DJ mid-body with wave after wave of wrenching nausea. There followed an hour of vomiting and dry heaves as bad as any attack of mal-de-mer. DJ, now very much alert, tried twice to get help but was unable to travel more than a couple of steps beyond the bathroom door before his stomach turned him back.

It was very odd. When the nausea subsided, DJ found himself drained of all symptoms of post-binge drinking. What's more, his spirits were up. He felt normal, stable, and relaxed. Yet the fellow gazing calmly out of the bathroom mirror seemed not quite recognizable. Who the heck is this guy? For a minute DJ didn't get it, but then it dawned on him. The chap in the mirror was that other DJ, the one he'd thought about often in the past: the Diego James Lornsby who had attended New Prague schools, grown up, married, and raised a family with never a taste of alcohol.

The bishop was supposed to be in the building for a scheduled counseling session but didn't answer the page, so DJ sat himself back down in front of the TV set. One of those Saturday morning fishing shows was on—this one taped out at Chisel Creek Park in the next county north.

DJ knew perfectly well such shows were rigged, but those fake yells and expostulations the guides came up with, he found thoroughly delightful.

"Oh baby, did you see that? Did you see the size of that thing?"

"Whoa … can I hold him … Can … I … hold him?"

"Whoo boy! Whoo boy! Oh brother. Unbelievable. Oh man, we're talkin' ten pounds here!"

Or the lovingly whispered, "Come on now … come on … ease on out of there, honey. Oh yeah …!"

But all that was last Christmas. This is August and the warranty on DJ's little miracle fast approaches its expiration date. And yet … perhaps DJ's experience should not be regarded cavalierly. The strange events at the hospital last December bought him quite a bit of time, perhaps a life's worth. Too many of those long, slow recoveries and the process turns into a meat grinder. No one comes out in one piece. The great Christmas escape can thus be seen as a major triumph for Diego James.

Bishop Trachtenberg steps off Moro's porch holding out the bait bucket. DJ stares fixedly into the plastic pail. From the back of a thousand-yard stare, Billy Gates ponders. *A nut case he calls me?* His eyes remain fixed. Should he focus in some direction, something worse will happen. At last DJ heaves a great sigh and looks up at the companions.

"Oh man," he breathes. "I don't know what the hell that was all about. Shoot. Let's go fishing. Sorry you guys. Don't know how I come to make such a fuss over a bunch of pecans. Let's change the dang subject."

"Suits me," says Billy Gates.

The gravel path down to the river begins just behind the church of Our Lady of the Pillar of the Village of New Prague, but the peculiar event we viewed through the screen door has, of course, not yet taken place.

Above the unmetered cacophony of crunching footsteps, DJ puts a question. "What was Milton doing in Coahuila, anyway?" he asks.

"Oh, he's always poking around in libraries and archives and people's old letters," responds Father Gil. "Especially in northern Mexico." *Such a thorough researcher. One wonders why he can't get his facts straight,* thinks the bishop.

"Yeah," says DJ. "I know he's supposed to be a great scholar. So where does he get all those weird ideas about history? It's like he thinks all the wars, revolutions, famines, and floods on earth are preordained."

"Yes, yes. Along with the messianic destiny of the Plantagenet family and all the rest of that white-bread crowd. Well, his family's from Bucks

County, and they winter in Vero. What other attitude can be expected? But that's not the heart of the matter, DJ. No, he's what they call a Revisionist, with a capital *R*. He can't help it. It's part of his makeup. It's in his blood and bones."

"Yeah. He'd revise the Ten Commandments if he could." says DJ.

Father Gil cracks a big grin. "He'd revise the Magna Carta if he could get away with it."

"*Webster's Dictionary.*"

Billy Gates remembers college days. "*Roget's Thesaurus,*" he adds and gets a laugh. The three walk silently on toward the river for a while and then Billy Gates says, "What did you all think of *Anna Karenina*? Of course, it's always a problem turning out even a passable screenplay based on a great novel."

"Garbo certainly captured the essence of Anna," replies DJ, "but Vronsky was not so convincing. March has always been overrated."

"Quite right. But who would you choose for the role today? De Niro?"

"De Niro. Bah!" thunders the Bishop. "Oh, talented, yes, of course. Genius? Well, most certainly. But when it comes to taste and judgment, the man's a perfect idiot. An incarnation of the Capote proposition: the more brilliant the actor, the dumber the individual."

As the little group tops a rise in the gravel path, the river below can be heard gurgling along in the deepening twilight.

Not all discussions dealing with that monarch of nuts, the richly delicate and savory pecan, have ended as peacefully as the one here reported. There was once a nation brought down, engulfed, its people scattered in diaspora. And all in the name of Central Tejas pecan fanaticism.

The original inhabitants of that area had been wandering around as hunter-gatherers for about ten thousand years, since the end of the last ice age. They were deeply attached to their way of life and of a profoundly conservative turn of mind. By the end of eighth century AD, those sophisticated societies of ancient Mexico had reached fluorescence only a few hundred miles to the south, yet the nomads of Central Tejas had not yet taken up so simple a tool as the bow and arrow. Apparently it was just too trendy to suit them.

A great many generations later, when Anglo settlers arrived, the Titskanwatits (known today by their Waco name, *Tonkawa*, the ones who stick together) were still living in the area, though they had been forced to drift north a bit in order to escape the Mexicans, Spaniards, and Apache, who were always on their heels. The settlers found them to be a friendly, easygoing lot, quite capable of turning on some charm when it suited a purpose. Not even their practice of cannibalism disturbed the Anglos, for the Tonkawa ate only Comanches (and a few Waco). The tribe was given many opportunities to occupy good land and take up agriculture as a way of life. These offers were always rejected with horror.

"Why the hell can't they settle down and go to work like everybody else?" yelled DJ's great, great grandfather.

"And if Santyany had a spout, he'd be a teapot. Come on, Ruben," answered his wife.

Living in one place went against Tonkawa religious precepts, and as for farming? Well, there you had true blasphemy, an unspeakable disrespect for the creator's orders. Unwilling to take up spade and hoe, they were soon tagged with the label, "welfare case." This was unfair. The Tonkawa were gainfully employed as pecan traders. To be sure, they often sold settlers their own nuts, but this was all right since the labor saved made the price worthwhile. Then some Anglo farmers discovered local pickers using age-old methods of harvesting. They were sawing off whole limbs and often knocking over entire trees. Agriculturists throughout the land were enraged.

"But this is the way we've always done it," wailed the people.

"Not no more you ain't," came the response.

Ultra-conservative people unwilling or unable to change with the times often pay a dreadful price for such intransigence. The Tonkawa proved no exception. They were rounded up, driven off the land, and out of Tejas forever. Worse things befell them in later decades, but those events occurred outside of Tejas, so they won't be retold here.

Chapter 44

Confessions of the Dragon Lady

"For real reception of the Blessed Sacrament it is
required that the sacred species be received in the stomach."
Catholic Encyclopedia

Bishop Trachtenberg stands quietly in the little church of Our Lady of the Pillar of the Village of New Prague. Clouds of dust raised by the pickup that rushed him up the hill have not yet settled, and some of the fine grains of white caliche seep in through the screens. Father Glück has walked up the aisle with broom, mop, and bucket. The part-time janitor, young Johnny Diaz, walks over and takes the equipment out of his hands. "Where's Gracie?" asks the bishop. "Right here, Father," comes the dark voice of dark-haired Grace Yancey Dally, lying more or less out of sight in the front pew. It should be noted that the bishop prefers to be addressed by his simple pastoral title: Father. "Your Eminence" is saved for official occasions.

"I'll be okay in a minute. I don't know what happened. I'll be fine."

I'm not so sure, thinks Trachtenberg. *What the devil does it mean? God forgive me. Of course, it doesn't mean anything.* Gil remembers the words of a valet parker at River Heights. "Grace Dally? Oh, put her on the payroll. You can't go wrong with Gracie. Worked her way through State running booze into Sardinia." (Not the island, the county in northeast Tejas.) "Up home they used to call her the Dragon Lady. You know, it's still dry up there."

Oh, certainly, Grace will be okay.

"Gracie, Gracie," says the bishop. "Coughing up the host is not a sin."

Why would he say that? thinks Grace.

"What an hour for confession," says the bishop with a shake of the head. "For goodness sake, it's past supper time." Gracie looks up at him, the corners of her mouth turned down. "All right, Gracie. Just rest for a minute, and then I'll call a cab. Give me your car keys; we'll get it to you later."

Gracie lies there looking up at him. Suddenly she pops upright. "Okay," she says.

Back in the little vestry room the bishop puts his phone away and turns to Father Glück. "What's going on, Father?" he asks.

"Right, right," answers Father Glück. "Of course, you are her confessor but ... well, she seemed very distressed. Personally, I felt it came under the heading of the most minor delectatio morosa. Barely a class E."

"Delectatio morosa, eh? Go on Father."

"I suppose she thought it was rather minor herself at first, so she went to Absolution Online. Well, you know how efficacious that is. Why the French chef's association is on there all day long trying to get gluttony removed from the deadly sin list." The priest clears his throat and looks out at the darkened screen doors. "It was some sort of 'ethnic epithet,' I believe they call it now." Father Glück stares down at his hands. "I'd best not repeat her exact words. Apparently she referred to someone as a Mexican of low intelligence, and as far as I can gather, she was actually alone at the time."

"Ah, Father. Perhaps it would have been best if you'd sent her to me."

"I concur, Your Eminence."

"Father. Call me Father, Father."

"Father. Right. Well, Father, given your uh ... background, perhaps she felt it might be awkward." Glück raises his palms as though making a plea.

"My background? You mean she thinks ... how amusing!"

"Well, Father, we all ... well, your fluency in Spanish for one, and also the first name." Glück doesn't want to mention skin tone and eye color.

Johnnie Diaz enters carrying the monstrance and ceborum. *He's not Mexican?* Johnnie almost grunts aloud. *I don't believe it. Sounds like pure Norteño to me.*

Now the Bishop is helping Father Glück put away the communion things. While setting the monstrance in its cabinet, he happens to glance down. The host in reserve—that's what's supposed to be in there, but it doesn't look like diocese altar bread. Diocese bread has *ecce homo* stamped on it—behold the man—supposedly what Pilate said when Christ was presented for judgment. A little too medieval for Trachtenberg's taste, but the contract with Kleindeinst & Kleindeinst was arranged before his time.

The Bishop holds up a wafer and catches Father Glück's eye. "Free sample," says the priest. "A chance to save a few dollars," he says with a giggle. "There's the rest of the package. Right there on the table. Oh, I suppose this business of accepting free samples when one knows no purchase will be made might be considered unethical in some—"

But the bishop is reading, "Cowie's is committed to producing the very finest altar bread. Because of a special sealing process applied only minutes after baking, we can offer breads that are virtually crumb-free. Rolls of 250, 500 and 1000, Cowie's Crumbless, Inc., (www.corpumats.com) 711 Place Bonnebel, Metairie, 70005, LA."

The bishop is pensive. *Metairie, eh? It can't be … can it?* Looking again at the wafer, Trachtenberg sees it is incised with the initials MN—Milton Navarre—with a bar across the top. "Listen Father," he says, "How did you get word of this free sample business?"

"It was an ad, Your Em … uh, Father. Through the mail."

"I'm taking this package with me. Oh, wine. Did you receive any wine from this company?"

"No, Your Em … uh, Father. Just the bread."

Chapter 45

Man's Best Friend

Behavioral History: a statistical comparison of recorded events without reference to sequence or synchronicity, cause and effect. Goals: a better understanding of the relationship between those events and human behavior.

Lying as it does on the very edge of the Great American Desert, forest and swamp to the east, the city of Mirabeau is oddly placed for a regional capital. Until very recently the city was quite isolated. Closing day for the frontier was nigh at hand before the Union Pacific decided to lay some north-south track, thus connecting Tejas with St. Louis, that ancient jumping off place for western exploration. But things are changing fast. All the freeways in and out are now completed, giving citizens … oh, maybe three years of good travel before the roads overcrowd and begin to break up.

An overgrown country town Mirabeau may be, yet it has always held a few extraordinary cultural advantages. Food, for example. The area is a world center for savory smoked meats. Pork ribs are tasty enough to eat straight from the pit. No need to drench them, as they do in St. Louis and Cincinnati, in sticky, gooey tomato sauce. Mirabeau is celebrated, as well, for its distinctive version of the cuisines of Mexico. Developed originally at a restaurant on the lower-upper part of the Great North River (not as some scholars contend on the upper-lower part), the #1 dinner was designed to satisfy the healthy appetites of workers on the Southern Pacific railroad. It soon spread worldwide but is actually edible only in Tejas. New York, Paris, London, all advertise the #1, but they can't produce it. Nevertheless, desperate Tejans abroad have been known to frequent these establishments. "Better than nothing," they say. "At least the sign outside reads 'Mexican,'" they say.

As for the life of the mind in Tejas, well, that's a subject especially germane to this tale. There is, in little old Mirabeau, a great university. Established in 1867, Tejas U. gradually developed into an important academic center—albeit in the middle of nowhere. And this, too, plays a part. Isolated academic institutions, no matter how splendid, seem to breed a special tolerance for conservative and even reactionary viewpoints. Not that they are favored, no, not at all. It's just that they are accepted and paid attention to, as they would never be at Harvard or Yale. Professors of strange repute and peculiar credentials (Ulaanbaatar University Press, Kitchener College of the Humanities at Khartoum, etc.) are hosted and present their works before world-renowned scholars: Capaldi, Browning, Carter, Stevenson, Peterson, oh, the list is long.

Today a number of academicians and other interested parties have gathered in the great hall of the Selwin P. Johnston Center for Behavioral History. Dr. Milton Navarre is presenting his latest study, title: "Pox Mexicana: Demographic Catastrophe or Franciscan Myth?"

It's a bright and coolish morning, long past Labor Day, but Navarre still wears his white linen suit and a silver-stitched Malayan-batik tie. Well, why not? He isn't in New York after all. The behavioral history center is about 10 degrees south of that city, perching almost exactly on the 30th parallel.

Introductions are short. What can one say about Milt Navarre minus the terms of controversy (which no one here would dream of using). Preliminaries must, of necessity, be abridged. On the stage, Navarre takes off his Raybans, but he doesn't pocket them. They will be used to emphasize important points: waving, tapping on the podium, and so forth. But now, lest the thread of an important argument be lost, or a vital point missed, perhaps it would be best to pay closer attention to what he is saying.

"And that's been the case since October, 1992, which month, we will recall, saw the five hundredth anniversary of the beginning of Castilian civilization in the New World. What's more, in the last fourteen or fifteen years we note a considerable increase in the number of studies devoted to the original chroniclers, with special emphasis on their accuracy. Well, I'm glad to see they're beginning to catch up." Navarre looks up smiling, and the audience actually responds with a laugh.

"A careful reexamination of the sources indicates that the smallpox epidemics of the sixteenth century produced no demographic catastrophe in America, and that the estimates for population reduction—one third to one half—are absurdly exaggerated. These figures are propaganda. They represent an attempt by the Order of the Friars Minor, the Franciscans, to promote 'liberal' reforms in New Spain. Granted, some of these polemics are beautifully written, but they are myths. Dramatic mythopoeia."

A few audience members nod in agreement, but mostly there is silence in the hall.

"Nobody was better at it than Fray Beneventes. 'The afflicted one,' the Aztecs called him, most likely because of his ragged appearance—the usual Franciscan mistrust of anybody in fancy clothes. Well, down in New Prague County where I live, they still use that term, only they pronounce it differently. They say *'flicted*. 'You 'flicted, man.'"

A few titters, not many, rise in the academic air.

"Beneventes says that the terrible plague began at Cempoala, carried into that place by a black slave, a fellow called Eguia, Francisco Eguia. Well, the later accounts agree, Gómara, Del Castillo, Codex Ramirez, Alva Ixlilxochitl (Vanilla Orchid), who was, parenthetically, a descendant of the Mexican traitor, Vanilla Orchid, all relate this story. But there's a problem here. Those writers ..."

Now Navarre is tapping on the podium, a rhythm to match his words.

"Get their ..." tap, tap, "... information ..." tap, "... from ..." tap, tap, "... Ben-e-vent-es ..." tap, tap, tap, "And Beneventes was writing a fable."

Navarre leans an elbow on the podium and flourishes a forefinger.

"That's why he needed a nig—"

"Ahem! [cough, choke]." Navarre takes a sip of water and goes on. "He needed a black man—to complete an allegory, albeit a strained one, for the Biblical account of the Ten Plagues. A Biblical connection was a must, or no Spaniard would believe him. Yes, there was smallpox in North America. Yes, there were a number of deaths, a bit of suffering. But the impact of smallpox on this continent was no greater than in Europe. A mortality rate of, oh, under 5 percent."

And there one has, if not in a nutshell, in a shot-glass, Milton Navarre's revisionism: one scholar's view of a significant event in the history of New Spain. Bishop Trachtenberg can't help shaking his head. Climbing into the old Caddy he is still shaking it. Navarre's critique depends entirely on an interpretation of Beneventes' *History of the Indians of New Spain*. But that's a mutilated version: some Spanish bureaucrat's notion of what Beneventes *ought* to have said. Why the fellow was wrong about the date when the Franciscans arrived in New Spain, and he even messed up a description of tortilla making. After forty years in Mexico, would not the *Afflicted One* know how to make a—?

"You want some lunch, Father?"

"No, I don't think so, Automedon. Just to the office, and then you go and get something to eat."

Passing by the sports stadium, Father Gil is still shaking his head. Actually, that stadium draws negative reactions from a number of folks in this community. A few Christmases past, when all the students were away, a wealthy regent and sports booster named Irving Franks ordered the felling of the many ancient live oaks surrounding the place. The university needed parking space for a new expansion program. But of course this is not the reason for Father Gil's gentle negation, there in the back seat of a well-kept '82 DeVille. The early autumn air, he notes, is saturated with confusion.

And clearly, if confusion reigns here in the present, this *now,* which can be seen and touched, then events a half-millennium old must be obscured indeed. For example, there's the business of the double manuscripts. Several of the conquest authors produced two versions of their work: one sent hurriedly off for the king's perusal and the deconstructive efforts of clerks and bureaucrats with their red pencils—and then the author's own rewrite, lying out of sight in a trunk for generations. Bernal Diaz' second version of the *True History* wasn't in print until 1904. That's what happened to Beneventes' *Historia* that Navarre puts so much stock in. Really, it's only a bastardized version of his *Annals*. In the case of Beneventes, the accurate version came first, but the principle is the same.

Confusion drips from the lampposts, from the spreading sycamores, and from the backs of dogs in the alley behind the cathedral of St. Cyril. The campus dog pack at Tejas U. will play a role in the resolution of the events here related, so a few words outlining its character won't be out of place. The term "pack" brings to mind a stereotype not really expressed in the behavior of this bunch. The dogs are neither barbaric nor vicious, noisy nor aggressive. In fact, a kind of disinterested friendliness of demeanor, even courtesy, is noted by all who meet them. Well, not all. Motorcyclists coming down the alley run their legs through a toothy gauntlet. But, of course, the racket of mufflerless, two-cycle engines will provoke misbehavior in any organism with ears.

Ricocheting about in a style to match the ambient disorganization already mentioned, are the thoughts of His Eminence Bishop Gil Trachtenberg. Didn't Cortés himself, in a letter to Charles V dated May 15,

1522, write that many chieftains were dying of the smallpox "distemper?" No names are mentioned. Cortés hated putting in writing the names of the great royals opposing him. And anyway, he probably couldn't spell them. But Diaz speaks of the deaths of Sir Fertilizer, "the lord who ejected us from Mexico" in the Noche Triste, and also his son, little Water Eggs. Sixteenth century native annals, such as the *Crónica Mexicayotl*, also tell a dismal story: Bumble Bee the Elder, Morning Sun, Captain Dog, Paving Stone, Greenyear, Flagstone Butterfly—all dead of the pox. Clearly, the upper classes succumbed readily to the disease. What then must conditions have been among the common people living, as they did, in much closer quarters?

Bishop Trachtenberg is shaking his head again. He is distressed by Navarre's use of his Franciscan library privilege. Milton's card should certainly be revoked. Father Gil tries to remember if he still knows anybody at St. Bonaventure. How about Allegheny? Who in that crowd still lives in Allegheny? Can it be, the bishop asks himself, that Milt's on diet pills again? That would explain a lot. He throws money around like confetti when he's taking diet pills. He'll buy anything.

Father Gil feels certain the dogs can provide some information regarding this situation. Yes, the dogs can tell us. In the rectory, the bishop changes into an old-fashioned brown cassock, and then he steps out the kitchen door into an alley. The dogs are not in sight, but surely, they're around somewhere. Taking advantage of the unforeseen hiatus, Trachtenberg leans against the limestone building blocks with their fossil imprints like the cast of an ancient relief, and he begins to pray:

"Hear my humble prayer, O Lord, for our friends the dogs, especially for the ones who are suffering or about to be put to death for cause or for no cause at all. May their sacrifice be written in the Book of Angels, and may they be remembered forever in Heaven. And for those who must execute that sacrifice, for them we entreat thy special mercy and pity."

"In the name of the Father, the Son, and the Holy Ghost. Amen."

Two alleys intersect at the northwest corner of the cathedral complex, and the campus dogs have made this intersection their headquarters. Catching sight of the bishop, their leader ambles up to see what's going on. Unbeknownst to Father Gil, this animal has a name. "Gunther," the street people and graduate students christened him, and they tied a red bandanna about his neck. That item of haberdashery, however, has long since been lost. Gunther is a more or less white, well-set-up Labradorish type with an intelligent face. Only mildly curious, he watches the father dig a hand into the pocket of his robe. The sight of a paper bag, however, makes him sniff the air, and now the other dogs draw closer. The father takes out a handful of Cowie's one and one-eighth-inch diameter altar wafers and hands them to Gunther, who gobbles them down with a wag of the tail. Now the others crowd in for a share, but Trachtenberg, with frowning countenance and raised hand, halts them, and all step back a pace.

With a sigh, Father Gil seats himself on the concrete coping beneath the spread of a big sumac tree. The sumacs, really just large weeds, hang over backyard fences all down the alley. Along with the elms and hickories, they turn dreary commercial vistas into shaded garden walks. Even the rows of garbage cans and dumpsters seem placed there to enhance the ambiance like decorative vases on a mantelpiece.

Father Gil is sitting there under the sumac with his head in his hands. The dogs are present also. Gunther's concerns involve interaction with his friends and cohorts holding converse in "alley doggish." The father's thoughts are not so sanguine. Hopefully the ideas flooding his head are only self-indulgent, crack-brained imaginings. He hopes so. He would rather be paranoid than right.

Gunther and the bishop look at each other. "Well, amigo," the dog seems to say, "if there are no more treats forthcoming—not that it's the only reason we've been hanging around, you understand—but, well, my friends and I will be moving along now."

"Oh, sir dog," responds the bishop, "words cannot describe my joy at seeing you sitting there in shiny-coated good health. Pray for me, sir dog. Pray God will forgive this vile act. I had no choice, you see. I had no choice.

Chapter 46

Amend the Dilemma

"We cannot have it both ways,
and no sneers at the limitations of logic."
I. A. Richards

Standing in the doorway of the office of the diocese of Central Tejas, Milton Navarre lights a cigar and comes up with a line of poetry. "Why are your cheeks so starved, and why is your face so drawn?" he recites. "Why is despair in your heart and your face like the face of one who has made a long journey?"

"Oh, yeah?" responds the bishop. "Why is your face burned from heat and cold, and why do you come here wandering over the pastures in search of the wind?"

"Excellent. Excellent, Gil. Though your hair departs, your memory remains intact—up to and including Hittite poetry."

"It's not Hittite," says the bishop with downturned mouth. "It's Sumerian. Third millennium."

"Ah, dear Gil, I beg to differ. The epic was created during the proto-literate stage of the archaic phase of Sumerian civilization, but it wasn't written down for several centuries. Hence the confusion, especially among scholars less meticulous in their research."

Now Milton offers the bishop a cigar. Trachtenberg looks askance for just a heartbeat, and then he accepts. Negative little gestures smacking of hostility are only irritating, the priest knows.

"Well, Milt, I asked you to drop in because I want to talk to you about Cowie's Church Supplies. That was a rather … I don't want to say outrageous … a rather strange decision. And the *MN* stamped on the host—for heaven's sake, Milton!"

Navarre slumps in his seat looking shamefaced. "I know, I know. That wasn't my idea. Plácido is responsible for that one."

"Plácido? In Musquiz? Yeah, but you did it, Milton. Plácido is down in Musquiz."

"No, I'm afraid he's not. He did the design and had the mold manufactured. All on his own."

Now it's the bishop's turn to slump in his chair. "You took a dedicated Titskanwatits herbalist, a known witch, and you put him to work in, in … what is essentially a food service business?"

"And his family."

"How did you get them in?" Trachtenberg asks, but Navarre only shrugs.

"So then, Milton," says the bishop softly. "You'd just as soon get Cowie's out of your hair? Isn't that correct?"

"Gil, Gil. Oh, my friend," says Milton with a laugh. "Perhaps a good-sized contribution to the diocese will help restore your faith in humanity. Listen, I'm gonna make that contribution though your cynicism flood the Vatican. No faith required, Gil. None at all."

"That won't be necessary, Milt. Just get hold of your broker or your agent or whoever and get rid of Cowie's."

"I will. I will. Eventually, my friend, eventually. But it can't be done right away, you know. First of all, there's the Tonkawas to consider. They run the company now, you know. In fact, they *are* the company."

"Listen to me, Milton," says the bishop, and his eyes are obsidian chips like the sharp black triangles set along the edge of an Aztec maqhuáhuitl. "Your actions put your soul in danger." Navarre blows smoke at the ceiling and rolls his eyes.

"*Macula peccati*, Milton. A voluntary act contrary to the rule of right reason. The sin remains until penance is completed. Here's the penance, and there's the phone. Make the call."

"Don't you quote Aquinas at me, you old … macula peccati, my foot! I am, sir, a direct descendant of Henry Plantagenet. Henry II, who, as we all know, told the church just what was what. I, my dear bishop, will do the same."

"Yes. Henry also did his killing second hand."

"Nobody died, Gil. Nobody died. Oh, I suppose you're referring to that Becket business. Pure myth. The worst sort of calumny. It never happened."

Trachtenberg takes a couple of deep breaths and decides to light his cigar. He is having an unpleasant reaction to the events of the day, and it's all culminating in this interview taking place in the office. A desire for revenge (and we note it regretfully) for the fright Navarre has given him, now floods his being. Reveling in sinful thought ... a class A if ever there was one, and surely he knows it.

"And we go back a lot further than that," Milton raves on. "Where do you think my name comes from? We fought Charlemagne at Pamplona in 778, and we beat him good at Roncesville Pass in 806. My ancestor was knighted by Enico Arista, first king of Pamplona, and when he died Garcia II made us Barons and—"

"Very interesting. Very interesting," interrupts Father Gil in the mildest of tones. "And now if your highness will pick up the phone and call whomever it is that needs to be called in order to divest yourself of Cowie's Crumbless, no further action will be taken. And I want you to go to New Orleans, pick up the Tonkawas personally, and escort them back to Musquiz. Very easy. San Anthony de Bexar to Monterrey, then take a bus."

"Aargh!" grunts Navarre, waving his hand in the air while the match flies across the room. Father Gil watches to see if it affects the rug in any way. (That rug is a kilim from Asrou, and while not expensive, certainly hard to replace). Milton Navarre places the cigar between his teeth once more and prepares to light it.

"Dear Gil," he says. "In the first place, I don't ride busses across Coahuila," and then he laughs in a rather forced manner. "The church is big business, Gil. You know that. Real estate, the market, all of it. So you understand what I'm talking about when I tell you Cowie's is a big money maker. I suppose it was a mistake getting involved but ... well, there's nothing to be done about it just now."

The bishop stands, holding out his cigar as though it were a scepter, and his expression is not pleasant to behold. "You will make whatever arrangements are necessary to begin negotiations for the sale of Cowie's Crumbless. You will do it now from this office—or else."

"Ay!" gasps Navarre, and another dead match hits the rug. The professor can hardly believe his ears. "Or else? Or else what?"

"Or else you will never again step foot in a Franciscan library. Every Franciscan collection from Kalamazoo to Kyoto will be closed to you, including the Library of Congress, La Crosse, Giles Lane in Canterbury, Hunt Street, and of course, St. Bonaventure."

Navarre's eyes grow wide. "You can't do that. You wouldn't do that."

"Oh, I almost forgot. Makarska Archive on the island. What's its name? Visovac. Right? When I'm done you won't be able to get on the ferry."

"But you can't—"

"Oh, no? See this button? One little push and I've got Zagreb on the line."

"Oh, the Capuchins, who cares about them?" says Milton with a weak little wave of the hand. "That joint isn't very well organized, anyway," he adds shakily, and shaky-handed he finally manages to get his cigar relit. The bishop only sits there looking at him.

Milton gets up and paces the floor. Puffing furiously, he mumbles through the smoke clouds. "It's after five in New York. It'll have to wait," he says, and then he stops in front of a bookcase. "Oh, Hume. The brainy boy of Berkwickshire. No doubt he talked like an Edinburgher. Unpleasant sounding accent if ever there was one. And kind of old hat, wasn't he? Even C. S. Lewis wouldn't quote him anymore." Navarre shakes his head. "Lewis and his miracles. Oh, that's right, he's dead, isn't he. Hmm, speaking of the miraculous, Guillermo, here's an idea for you."

Navarre turns smiling, book in hand. "If that package of Cowie's had, indeed, been … er, uh, tampered with, then we'd have quite a little miracle on our hands, wouldn't we? I mean Gracie gagging up the host like that. Is that why you're angry, Gil? Because there was no miracle? Oh, I think so. For reviving a lagging faith, there ain't nothing like a little miracle, eh? Better than a kiss from the Pope. Oh, Gil, Gil. 'It's an evil generation that seeks a sign.' Isn't that how it goes?"

In late autumn, the old brown Manos looks quite different. The cottonwood leaves haven't changed much, but they do look tired—ready to drop, in fact. The three fishing buddies sit closer to the lamps now, for in autumn the flying insect population is greatly reduced. In fact, life along the Manos is generally a lot more comfortable as the year wears on. Except for *toxicodendron radicans*, that is. The leaves have fallen in the poison ivy forest, but the bare stalks and twigs are still dangerous. Whipping across bare skin they leave great blistery streaks as bad as the rash produced by those green leaves with their evil reddish tinge. But of course, nobody but a tourist would be caught bare-legged down here.

In the quiet of the fading (actually pretty well-faded) autumn light, the three friends discuss, albeit desultorily, a rather peculiar topic: poison—a subject none of them knows very much about.

"Poison," says Billy Gates. "Arsenic, cyanide … oh, yeah, deadly nightshade, whatever that is."

"Curare," adds DJ, "but I guess the native herbalists know a lot more. Oh, hemlock."

"That's right, DJ," says the priest, "there are many more."

"And this Jack Brown guy from somewhere in Africa—"

"That's right, DJ. Brown is the world's leading expert on Nahuatl language and ancient Mexican history."

"And he believes Montezuma got hold of some poisoned host, or altar bread or whatever you call it that was meant for the Spaniards?"

"Yes, but they're not sure what the poison was, or if it was in the wine or in the bread. The best guess is *atlepatli*, a little herb growing in the mud close to water. But … who knows?"

"Atlepatli." In wonderment DJ mouths the word. "This is really weird. Oh, man, this is strange." Billy Gates and the father raise their eyes from the darkening river and eye DJ quizzically.

"Well, something like that happened in my family," he says. "Anyway, there's this family story."

"What story?" the other two sound off like a Greek chorus.

"Oh, forget it. I don't believe it myself."

"What's the story? What's the story?" the chorus sounds off again.

"Well, you know, I'm related to Diego Rivera, the artist, and that's a fact, no story." Father Gil and Billy Gates nod their heads. This much they know about Diego James.

"Well, the story goes like this: Frida and Diego had Leon Trotsky over for dinner one night, and the cook put a big bowl of kasha on the table. Father, you know what kasha is?"

"Do I know what kasha is? DJ, I was raised in the Ukraine. Of course, I know what kasha is

"I don't know what kasha is," says Billy Gates. "What's kasha?"

"Buckwheat. Groats. They boil it up with spices and serve it like rice, or it's used in stuffings. In this country it's considered pretty much a Jewish dish, but in east Europe everybody eats it. And, of course, Frida was half Jewish."

"Right, right," says DJ in a thoughtful tone. "So, anyway, Diego, Frida, and Trotsky are sitting there, and they get into this big argument.

The Riveras are dedicated Stalinists, of course, and Trotsky hates the guy's guts. 'Your revolutionary pacifism does not differ by a hair's breadth from the pacifism of your stock exchange,' Trotsky yells at Frida, and while she doesn't have a clue what he's talking about, it drives her wild."

DJ looks up at the stars, but it's a cloudy night, and they are not around. "You know, my grandmother told this story so often, I know it word for word," he says, and flips his cigarette into the river, where it can be clearly heard hissing itself to death.

"So anyway, Trotsky happens to glance into the kasha bowl, and what does he see in there? Chili. Pieces of chili floating around in the kasha. 'Kasha with chili? Well, that's not right,' says Trotsky to himself, and then he gets back into the argument. Now Diego, who doesn't get mad too often, starts banging his fist on the table. 'But the proletariat's inferior status was based solely on financial hardship, rather than on their deprivation of information in general. That's something everyone knows.'"

"Well," DJ continues, "with each knock on the table the kasha bowl slides closer to the edge. Finally it crashes to the floor, but nobody pays the slightest attention. Frida, or somebody, yells for Matilda to come clean up the mess, but Matilda appears to have split. At last they all calm down and notice the pile of kasha on the floor. Well, lying next to it is the cat and also Frida's parrot—both dead as doornails."

The bishop seems to be fidgeting around on his little stool. "I hope the turtles aren't feeding on our bait," he says, and DJ and Billy Gates look at him questioningly. The father knows turtles don't feed at night, and that's why they are always down here in the dark. Total night has now descended on the Manos, and the fishermen can see only as far as the lamplight's edge, where their lines enter the water.

"So there you have it," says DJ with a sigh. "That's the family miracle. You know, I forgot all about it, but with everything that's happened lately ..."

At this point Billy Gates' natural mode of expression would include a "my God" or "good Lord," but association with Father Gil has long since conditioned an automatic censorship of third commandment violations. "You mean the cook was trying to poison them all?" he says.

"Nah, they were only after Trotsky. And they got him, all right. Got him in his office with an ice pick."

Father Gil sits all bent over so that his back almost forms a half circle, and when he speaks, his voice seems to emerge from the black water. "It was an ice ax," he says. "One of those short-handled ice axes like the mountaineers use, and Lev Bronstein bled to death. Well, they got him to the hospital, and that's where he died."

Billy Gates and DJ again sound off together, only this time the chorus is slightly contrapuntal and a little off-key.

"Is that right, Father?"

"Father, is that right?"

"Oh, yes. The killer was a Spaniard. Ramon Mercader del Rio Hernandez, the heartthrob of Barcelona. That's why they picked him, you know. He had such a way with the women. I met him when I was in seminary, and in those days I was thinking a lot about St. Francis and Marx, and oh, all that sort of thing. Ramon's mother was a friend of Stalin, so they got him a scholarship to go to spy school in Moscow. When he graduated, they sent him to Mexico to get Bronstein, Trotsky, whatever you want to call ..." Father waves a hand in the air. "Ramon took his time. They taught him a lot, the NKVD. Now he was Frank Jacson, a Frenchman, and the first thing he did was put the make on Sylvia Ageloff because Sylvia's sister Ruth was Leon's typist."

DJ and Billy Gates are stunned. "Put the make on?" Such language from the bishop's mouth seems inconceivable. Relating these events, however, seems to have perked him up a bit.

"He got an introduction to Leon and played him for quite a while. Well, why not? They were all good Communists together. That's all he was, Ramon. Just an ordinary good Communist 'til the NKVD got hold of him. They turned him into something ... unspeakable."

"So one day Ramon called him up and said, 'Hey, Leon, I've got an article here you've got to read. It's about your idea for a Fourth International.'"

"'Come on over,' said Leon. 'I was about to leave for Chez Rivera, but I'll wait for you.' Ramon walks in, takes off his raincoat and lays it on the table so he can easily get at the ax. Then while Lev is reading, he takes it out and whacks him on the back of the head, but not hard enough. Trotsky was no wimp, you know, and he fights back. Finally, he collapses, and Ruth calls the cops."

"Holy cow." "Holy mackerel," breathe DJ and Billy Gates, again in unison and somewhat contrapuntally.

"The Feds gave him twenty years. How much time he actually did, I don't know. I think it was Castro got him out. Made a big hero out of him in Cuba."

The Father stands and stretches a couple of times. "Ay!" he exclaims, echoing his creaking muscles.

"So the miracle at Coyoacan was strictly for Frida and Diego, I guess," says DJ in tones of wonderment. "It sure didn't do Trotsky any good."

Bishop Guillermo Trachtenburg has had enough of the supernatural for one evening. "If there's a catfish anywhere around here, now that would be a miracle," he says mildly. "Come on, fellows. Let's pull them up for the night."

"Yeah. Anyway it should be warmer next week."

"So they say," adds Billy Gates.

The group crunches along the gravel path heading toward the little urban strip above the bank. At the top, they walk across the dying grass behind Our Lady of the Pillar of the Village of New Prague, past the picnic tables under their rusty metal-roofed shelter, and onto the concrete sidewalk. This time of year very few insects flutter around the lone street lamp, and absolutely no crickets are in sight. Who knows where they go in autumn? The group reaches a point no more than ten yards beyond the lamppost, when the evening breeze switches gently around and into their faces. A north wind from across the river, it's the first real sign of winter.

"You know," says DJ, breaking the rather profound silence. "That would've been quite a miracle. I mean if that communion bread'd really had poison in it—and Gracie throwing it up like that? Man, that would've been some miracle."

The End